CRESTED BUTTE

A NOVEL

MARILYN BROWN ODEN

WESTERN REFLECTIONS
PUBLISHING COMPANY®

Lake City, Colorado

2002, 2019
Revised Edition
Printed in the United States of America
Library of Congress Catalog Card Number 2002100372

ISBN 978-1-937851-34-7
Cover and book design by Laurie Goralka Design

Western Reflections Publishing Company®
P.O. Box 1149
951 N. Highway 149
Lake City, Colorado 81235
www.westernreflectionspublishing.com
(970) 944-0110

In memory of

The Miners

killed in the Jokerville Disaster

Crested Butte, Colorado

January 24, 1884

and

The Little Ones

killed in the Ludlow Massacre

Ludlow, Colorado

April 20, 1914

ACKNOWLEDGMENTS

First, with deep gratitude and respect, I want to acknowledge the man who taught me about mining: Tim Morgan, a Crested Butte coal miner. Like so many others, Tim died of black lung disease.

Many additional people helped with this book, and I want also to express appreciation to them: Terry and Sally Kelley, Sandra Estess and Judy Gibbs for their encouragement; authors Boyce Bowdon, Marilyn Bailey Ogilvie, James C. Taylor and Marshall Terry for their suggestions; Gayle Maddin, Dirk Oden, Valerie Oden, Dale Prothro, Carl Rhoads, P. David Smith and Joe Yeakel for specialized help with history and foreign language; David Shawver for his interest; and especially Bryant Oden for his compelling motivation. Two people of primary importance in this writing journey are my beloved husband Bill, and my supportive mother, Maxine Miller Edens. I also want to acknowledge Doug and Mary MacPherson and Dan Batchelor, with whom Bill and I first skied Crested Butte Mountain; Barbara Batchelor, who read the first draft of this novel; MacKenzie and Edith Thompson, with whom we share fond Crested Butte memories; Clifton Warren in the Creative Studies Department of Central Oklahoma University. Others who contribute to my joy in life and, therefore, add joy to my work are Danna Lee and Nathan Bowen; Angela, Chelsea, Sarah, and Graham Oden; and Harold Brown.

"Courage consists not in hazarding without fear,
But being resolutely minded in a just cause."

—Plutarch, Greek philosopher
First Century

"They always told you to 'Stay low' in the mine and you'd be safe.
But man was not meant to stoop!"

—Tim Morgan, Crested Butte coal miner
Twentieth Century

CONTENTS

PROLOGUE

I'm old, but death won't kill me. I died long ago. Secrets make us sick.

It's time to tell the President the truth. Past time. I spin the dials of my black leather attaché and hand it to my bodyguard, a Croat by ancestry and the one man in the world I trust. "If anything happens to me before the meeting, get this to the White House. Directly to the President." Our eyes lock. "I need your word, Joseph."

"You have it, Mr. Heffron. But nothing will happen."

The key clicks in the door of the old yellow house. I step off the porch, and the ornate silver handle of my ebony cane glints in the morning sun. As always, I glance toward the cemetery on the hill beyond, a cemetery that houses the victims of Heffron greed.

Joseph opens the door of the forest-green Land Rover for me and sets the oversized briefcase behind the tan leather seats. Stiffly, I climb in.

He pushes a memory button on the cell phone. "We're on our way." . . . "Good." He nods to me. "The plane's ready, Sir." A horn honks as he forces his way into the traffic on Elk Avenue, narrow and snow-banked.

I yearn for that earlier day when Crested Butte was hidden away, before condominiums crowded the valley floor and bumper-to-bumper Jeeps inched along Elk. Everything has changed. Even Crested Butte Mountain. I gaze up at the snow-capped peak rising above the cemetery, an ancient sentinel now scarred by ski trails—Jokerville, Ruby Road, International, Twister, Resurrection. I look away, reminded of my own scars, my own changes.

Joseph checks his watch. "You'll be at the White House by three, Mr. Heffron."

I sigh, dreading this ordeal too long postponed.

In the right rear-view mirror I can still see the old yellow house. What a story its walls could tell! How simply it all began! Howard F. Smith developed his town. General William Jackson Palmer expanded his railroad. And financier M. Morgan Heffron Sr. called the shots. But the story really began when Marie-Vincente Prejean stepped off the first train into Crested Butte, Colorado.

ONE

JOKERVILLE

1881

The shrill whistle of the iron horse resounded through our streets and avenues and was echoed back by the belting cliffs, and crags, and mountain peaks at 11:59 3/4 a.m. last Monday, and now Crested Butte is a railroad terminus.

Crested Butte Republican
Nov. 23, 1881

CHAPTER 1

*M*arie-Vincent Prejean squinted into the sun raining light on the snow-covered peaks. Their treacherous splendor lured her, repelled her. Love fought fear. A secret fear.

Red hot cinders flew through the air, and her anxiety grew with each click of the wheels on their narrow gauge track. The scent of coal mingled with the perfumed and pungent odors of passengers. She lifted her eyes to the ceiling and watched the kerosene lamp dance to and fro with the sway of the train, wondering if she would ever dance again.

From the moment Marcel's letter arrived asking her to come, she'd known she shouldn't. But she couldn't tell Papa. She'd missed her last chance when they waited together for the paddleboat that would take her up the Mississippi River away from New Orleans. His words echoed in her mind: *The Blessed Virgin watch over you.* His voice cracked, and tenderness filled the blue-green eyes she'd inherited. Ashamed of his tears, he turned quickly away and commanded gruffly, *Be off with you, Vini!* Her own tears pooled at the memory, and she clasped his small leather money purse, empty now, but still charged with his love.

The conductor smiled at her and took center stage at the front of the passenger car. "Ladies and gentlemen, your attention please." He pointed dramatically. "That magnificent monolith is Crested Butte Mountain. Hayden's Rover Boys surveyed the area and gave it that name because it looks like the crest of a helmet. They even wrote a poem:

> In granite armor, strong and gray,
> A sentinel it guards the way."

He paused for effect. "It stands over 12,000 feet!"

She wondered what future it guarded for her. *L'inconnu.* The unknown.

They rounded a bend, the whistle shrieked, and the steam engine hissed to a stop. The conductor drew his watch from his vest pocket. "Ladies and gentlemen, let history record that fifteen seconds before noon on this great day, Monday, November 21, 1881, the Denver and Rio Grande Railroad reached Crested Butte, Colorado! The end of the line."

The end, thought Vini. Or the beginning? She tightened her grip on the money purse, like clutching a crucifix before leaping a chasm, and reached deep inside herself for courage. *If I could handle the journey here, I can handle anything! Even Marcel!* She tucked back a dark lock of hair and lifted her chin, pretending she believed it.

Joel McGragor trotted around the arena of his life like a Roman rider on two horses—one foot seeking his identity, the other seeking his dream. Both had brought him West. But today he dismounted and enjoyed the scene.

The crowd surged toward the train as it stopped in front of the new depot. A hundred excited voices buzzed—nearly all of them male. They stamped and whistled as the passengers disboarded—nearly all of them female. Long colorful skirts swished down the train steps and across the boardwalk. Thin black shoes peeked under muslin petticoats. Bits of gold glittered in ear lobes, and over-stuffed tapestry bags tilted small shoulders to one side. Lavender scented the cold mountain air. Eager eyes searched the crowd. Delighted shrieks followed discovery. Rushing boots clicked against the boardwalk. Arms entwined. Sniffles, giggles and greetings of joy jumbled forth in a human symphony.

Joel watched the women step off the train, one after another. Wives, sisters, nieces, daughters. Brides-to-be by correspondence. And six painted ladies for the Forest Queen. "It's like a rainbow after a long drought!"

"Ladies bring change like clouds bring rain," warned Nick Laffey.

Joel glanced at the old freighter. Deep lines etched his leathery face, mapping a journey of decades and difficulties. Nick was as different from himself as night from day. But underneath all that hot air was one of the best men Joel knew, the reverse of most people. Instead of hiding hollowness beneath a fine smooth surface, he was like the good Earth—a solid core wrapped in colorful exhibition.

Nick aimed and spat in the snow, leaving a brown circle that matched his boots. "Ain't nothing going to be the same around here now."

Joel watched the last young woman take the conductor's hand and step down gracefully from the train, careful not to show her ankles. She did nothing to attract attention, yet drew it like a magnet. He judged her to be about seventeen.

Nick exhaled through his frizzy gray beard. "*She* is a huckleberry above a persimmon!"

Joel nodded, mesmerized. Large blue-green eyes, wide-set above a delicate nose, matched the color of her scarf. The sun highlighted her dark curly hair, as shiny as a new-minted coin. Cheeks rosy from the cold brightened her fair complexion.

She stood on tiptoe and peered through the chaos, her hand shading her eyes. She caught Joel's gaze and held it for an instant. He bowed his head to her and tipped his Stetson hat.

She smiled, then blushed and looked away.

"I knew it!" said Joel. "I knew she'd have dimples if she smiled." He watched her maneuver through the crowd toward the platform. Broad shouldered men smiled down at her and made way like a parting of the waters. Instead of flirting back, she moved on with an air of shyness, unaware of her charm. Joel marveled at the way she walked, like gliding on ice. When she reached the front, she turned back toward the crowd to search through the faces. Her lovely brow puckered into a frown. Again her eyes met Joel's. He wondered how anyone could keep a woman like her waiting.

Mayor Howard F. Smith stood on the rough-hewn platform, straining his voice to bring order to bedlam. Red and blue swags hung bright against the snow. Finally hushing the crowd, he lifted both arms, encompassing all the people, all the mountains, all creation. "For centuries the Utes claimed this lush valley. Then came the mountainmen, miners, and entrepreneurs. And on July 3, 1880, the town of Crested Butte, Colorado, was born!" The mob roared. "Last year scattered tents dotted our town. And now we've got a newspaper, a bank—"

"And nineteen saloons!" came a shout from the back. The crowd clapped and hooted.

"And no churches," muttered Nick. "But with the ladies here, we'll probably end up with nineteen churches and no saloons!"

Joel kept his eyes on the dark-haired beauty scanning the crowd. He felt sorry for her, the only new arrival still alone. But she didn't look alone. She stood obliviously in the midst of the painted ladies.

"Hey, Mayor!" hollered a man in a muskrat hat. "Don't forget the Forest Queen!"

The painted ladies smiled and dipped in a curtsy. The madam put her arm around the newcomer. Catcalls welcomed them all—including a crimson-faced Catholic from New Orleans.

Sainte Marie, Mère de Dieu! Vini looked into the painted faces of the six women around her, and felt her cheeks burn as red as Lake Ponchartrain at sunset. "Excuse me, Ma'am." She stepped back.

"I like to call people by their name. I'm Tillie."

"I am Marie-Vincente Prejean. I'm called Vini." Immediately she wished she hadn't introduced herself. What would Mama think! Wanting so much for me to be a lady. Whispering to me about a certain district in the French Quarter where ladies must never go—whispering about *always* staying away from that kind of woman under *any* circumstance. And the first person I meet in Crested Butte is a whisper woman!

"Vini, I suspicion some no-account got you here," said Tillie with disgust in her voice and pity in her eyes. "Then he left you at the little end of the horn."

The first part was true. Surely not the last part too.

"Why don't you just get right back on that train and pull foot for home, honey?"

Papa's empty money purse reminded her that she'd been sent on a one-way passage. "I can't, Ma'am. I'm needed here."

"You sure are a polite little thing. If you're still stranded by dark, you come to the Forest Queen and ask for me."

Vini gasped.

"I didn't mean like that. You don't have to . . . You know." She patted Vini's arm. "It's just that you wouldn't be safe alone. Especially with all the rabble in a mining town."

Mama hadn't told her that a whisper woman could be nice. "Thank you, Ma'am, but I'll be fine."

Vini scanned the crowd once more. Again she saw the handsome young man who'd been eying her since she stepped off the train. His thin lips drew a stubborn line between high cheekbones and dimpled chin, and he stood out from the others like the tallest cypress in a bayou. His eyes held hers, and he raised one eyebrow and touched the brim of his hat. Papa would not approve of the smile on her face.

But she didn't see Marcel. What if he didn't come? As the mayor droned on, even the sun grew bored and ducked behind a cloud, stealing warmth and color. The valley turned gray, matching her mood. She drew her thin cloak closer, shut her eyes, and wrapped herself in the comforting memory of Jackson Park in the French Quarter, its azalea bushes aburst with winter blossoms.

A man brushed against her. "Permit me. I'm Mr. King." He wore his face like a *Mardi Gras* mask, eyes of fire-ice dominating it. "Mr. Frederick Rodewald King—to be exact," he added pompously.

Tetu. He's full of himself.

"And your name, Miss?"

She decided to handle him like all the others since leaving New Orleans. *"Parlez-vous français, monsieur?"*

He frowned.

"She's French," said Tillie, joining the conspiracy. "And she's not one of us." With a provocative smile she added, "But my girls would love to see you at the Forest Queen *any* time, Mr. Frederick Rodewald King."

He nodded as the mayor motioned him toward the platform.

"Well now, honey," said Tillie, glancing up over Vini's shoulder. "This one looks like he could whip his weight in wild cats. I'd say he's a man worth waiting for."

"Definitely," said the young man in the Stetson hat. He wore scuffed boots, faded Levi's, and a sheepskin coat. Up close he seemed even taller than Vini had thought. "My name is Joel McGragor, Ma'am." He took her arm and ushered her away from the painted ladies. "May I help you find someone?"

She hesitated. Papa had sternly forbidden her to talk with any man during her journey. But she liked Joel McGragor's looks. His voice. His name. *The journey is over, Papa.*

"I know about everybody around these parts," Joel added.

"I'm not surprised, *monsieur.*" She gave him a dimpled smile. "You are very friendly."

He raised an eyebrow and looked down at her with honest eyes. "Well now, I can't tell whether you mean that as a compliment or a criticism of my forwardness."

She liked his directness, rare in her part of the country. But she didn't like being in a situation where she appeared to need help. She sighed and watched her breath form a thin spiral and float away like her choices. "Marcel Joubert is to meet me here."

"Joubert?"

"He owns a ranch near Crested Butte."

Joel frowned. "I don't recollect anyone by that name."

"His letter said it's as large as a Louisiana plantation."

"I can't place him, Ma'am," was all that he said. But his eyes told her he didn't believe it. Confused, she turned away and again listened to the mayor.

"Last year," he bellowed, "we had no industry. But now, thanks to Heffron Enterprises, we can boast of a 40-ton smelter, 150 coke ovens and the Jokerville Mine. I'm proud to call on Mr. Fred King."

King stepped forward and tried without success to silence the crowd. "It is my honor," he shouted, "to bring you greetings from the great coal baron and humanitarian—"

"A contradiction of terms," mumbled Joel.

"—Mr. *M. Morgan Heffron.*"

Vini noted the respect in King's voice as he said the name, like the tone Papa used when he spoke of the Holy Mother. *M. Morgan Heffron.* She etched the name in her memory.

"Please don't worry, Ma'am," said Joel. "I'll find out about Marcel Joubert."

She heard her name in the distance and recognized Marcel staggering toward the crowd. "VINNNI!" he shouted like calling a dog. "VINNNI!"

Embarrassed, she pretended not to hear and pled silently, *Holy Mother, please take him away!*

Marcel spotted her. "Vini! Vini! You made it!" Everyone watched him grab her around the waist, pick her up, and swing her around.

He stumbled. They sprawled into a snowdrift at the edge of the board-walk, their legs entangled together like Spanish moss after a hurricane. Vini's dress and petticoats twisted above her ankles—right in front of all these people. What would Mama think! Mortified, she wanted to disappear. To wake up and find herself back in New Orleans after a bad dream. To lie across the tracks and let the train back over her.

Marcel's weight pressed her into the snow. She forgot about the people. She felt his breath on her cheek. It reeked with whiskey. She fought to free herself. The more she struggled, the deeper she sank. Yellow-flecked eyes stared down at her. She remembered that look. Fear shot through her. "Get off me, Marcel Joubert!"

Joel didn't bother with words. He grabbed Marcel's shoulders, jerked him up, and threw him into another drift.

Tenderness replaced anger as he reached down for Vini. She grasped his hand and he put his other arm around her waist, lifting her chastely from the snow. For a moment she rested in his arms and he could hear her lungs suck the thin air. "I can't believe you belong to him!"

"No, *monsieur*! I don't!" She noted the staring crowd and abruptly stepped back.

He could tell she was humiliated beyond bounds and near tears. But she didn't cry.

She straightened her twisted snow-covered clothes and lifted her chin. "*Merci, Monsieur* McGragor."

In that instant he knew he was lost. He was charmed by her accent and admired the way she mustered her dignity. He didn't even know her full name. But he knew he would love her forever. He picked up her scarf from the snow, tempted to hold it close.

"He is the husband of *ma sœur*—my sister," she mumbled.

"Your *brother-in-law*!" Joel glanced at Marcel prone in the snow and shook his head.

"Francine is ill. Papa sent me here to help her."

"Begging your pardon, Ma'am, but 'Papa' made a mistake."

CHAPTER 2

S tunned, Vini stood on the porch of one of the small log cabins lined up in a straight row like toy blocks. Marcel's letter had been filled with lies. He had no land. No ranch. No cattle. No way to buy her the promised return ticket. Instead he had a job at the Jokerville Coal Mine and a one-room cabin in Company housing. She tried to take a deep breath but the thin air cheated her.

Joel looked down at her, his dark eyes thoughtful. "Are you all right, Ma'am?"

She nodded, aware that this man stood tall in more ways than one. He hadn't mentioned the ranch she was expecting. Nor her humiliation at the depot. He'd simply found out where Marcel really lived and borrowed his friend's freight wagon with sleigh runners to bring her here. "You have been very kind."

He set her trunk inside the cabin door and turned back to her. "If you need me, I stay at Rozick's on Elk. By the Livery Stable." He hesitated, then pointed back up Second Street. "Marshal Hays is only a couple of blocks away near Coal Creek."

"*Merci.*"

He stepped down from the porch, and bowed his head as he had at the depot, reminding her of a lord greeting his lady. He turned and began walking away, his boots crunching on the deep snow.

She called to him. "*Monsieur* McGragor."

He looked back at her, his straight nose and strong chin cutting a handsome profile. "I didn't introduce myself. I am Marie-Vincente Prejean." She curtsied. "You may call me Vini." The moment froze in her memory. She'd seen appreciation in the eyes of the boys back home, but never in her whole life had anyone looked at her the way he did now. She held on to it, fueled with the courage to walk through the door to her new life.

Inside, the cabin was as still as a windmill at dawn. Vini reeled from the stench. Gradually her eyes adjusted to the darkness. Days of unwashed food crusted the plates. Molded scraps littered the hand-hewn table. The cast iron pot sat empty and foul on the coal stove. The slop jar brimmed to the top.

Trying to hide her shock, she wove her way through the clutter toward her sister's bed in the back corner of the room. It stood at an angle away from the wall. The high oak headboard provided the only privacy in the cabin. She sat down on the edge of the soiled sheet and stifled a gasp.

"*Petite sœur,*" murmured Francine weakly.

Vini looked into blue-green eyes, wide-set in a face framed by black hair—traits that told the world they were sisters. But now those eyes sank into a skeletal face, and limp hair splayed across the dirty pillowslip. Vini's heart overflowed with love and pity. Tenderly she lifted Francine's cold bony hand to her own cheek.

Her sister's cracked lips stretched into a shallow smile. "Thank you for coming."

"I want to take care of you, *chère.*" She meant it, whatever the consequences.

Her sister's eyes filled. Slowly she lifted her index finger. "One thing." She paused for a wheezing breath. "Mama must not know how we live." A tear spilled over and rolled down her cheek.

Dear Mama. Vini thought of her across the miles. Sitting up late at night in the rocker, her fingers nimbly tatting white lace. Worrying about Francine when Marcel's letter arrived. Selling all of her beautiful handwork to help Papa get the money for the ticket. Vini knew it would break her heart to see her first daughter this ill and living in filth.

Leaning down, Vini kissed the tear on Francine's cheek. "I will make it better," she whispered. "I promise you that." She put her arms around her sister's emaciated frame and held her like fragile crystal until her tears stopped.

Vini reached into her pocket. "*Chère,* do you remember how we used to play with cotton bolls?"

Francine nodded, the memory turning up her lips at the corners.

"I brought you one." Vini laughed. "It's silly I know. But I wanted to." She removed the hanky wrapped around the cotton boll and laid its softness in her sister's hand.

Francine wrapped her fingers around it as though she held a crown jewel. "It seems like a very long time ago," she wheezed. "Oh, *petite sœur,* I'm so glad you got here before I di—"

"*No!* Don't say that word!" Vini willed her own young strength into Francine's frail body. "I'm going to fix everything!" she vowed. "With the Holy Mother as my witness!"

Vini attacked the squalor as fiercely as the Rebs attacked the Yanks. After five days that seemed like five weeks the cabin sparkled. Her nails were broken and her hands as red as boiled crawfish, but it was worth it. She glanced toward the bed where Francine lay propped against fresh pillowslips, perhaps a bit stronger, definitely lifted in spirit.

"Tomorrow is the first Sunday in Advent," said Vini, determined to bring some joy inside these walls. "I'll gather evergreen and pine cones on my way back from the Company Store and decorate for the season."

Francine smiled, a hint of life in her eyes. "Maybe get a bit of red ribbon?"

Vini nodded as she put on her cloak and gloves and picked up the woven basket. "I'll hurry."

"Don't worry, *petite sœur*," she wheezed. "I'm used to being alone."

No more! Vini stopped next door at the Donegans and knocked.

"Come in, baby," said Martha, the doorway framing her kind weathered face and boxlike figure that had borne eight children.

"I can't, Miss Martha, but thank you. How is your family?"

"Little Davey has a cold. But other than that we're all fine."

"I hope he gets well soon. I'm going to the Company Store and—"

"Not that it's any of my business, but listen to me, baby. You stay on this side of Second. You want to keep clear of the Bucket of Blood. It's the worst place in town."

"Yes, Ma'am. I wondered if you would mind checking on Francine in a little while."

"That poor child. I can't tell you how bad I feel that I didn't know about her being so sick. Marcel didn't say a word to Iber. I would've been glad to help."

Vini doubted that Marcel had done a single thing for Francine.

"Sometimes I popped over, but she never answered my knock. I figured she just didn't want to be bothered."

"I think she was embarrassed to see anyone. Things had gotten so—" Vini searched for a word besides filthy "—so far behind."

"I'm ashamed I was a bad neighbor. I should've just barged right on in."

"I'll hurry back, Miss Martha."

"No need to, baby. I'll pop in on Francine."

While seeking his dream and also his identity, Joel worked for McAllister and Craig as foreman of the Elk Mountain House building crew. Descending the stairs, he rubbed his hand along the walnut banister. The hotel deserved its billing: "The Pride of the West." But finishing it before the grand opening would be nip and tuck. Only ten days left.

His thoughts swirled. I don't have time to talk to King. What does he want? It'll end badly. It always does with him.

He crossed Elk in a hurry. The smell of manure mingled with the odor of the coke ovens. Wagons rumbled down the snow-packed road. Wheels creaked. Horses neighed. Mules brayed. Whips cracked. Freighters shouted words forbidden in books.

Joel glanced up at the Red Lady glistening in the sun. Beneath the snow her ruby lips smiled down at him with the promise of treasure. Come summer he'd find gold and be a rich man. Unconsciously he began whistling a lively old tune from his childhood. He dodged a twenty-four-horse team pulling a freight load and opened the door to the Company Store.

Vini waited in line for the cashier, trying not to compare the Company Store to the French Market in New Orleans. Her fingers were still numb from carrying the basket, her thin gloves useless here. A nameplate on the office door at the back caught her eye: FREDERICK RODEWALD KING. Fred King and Joel McGragor, two men as different as a peacock and an eagle.

"Next!" called the cashier, a balding man with a high-pitched voice and thick spectacles that drooped on his nose.

She smiled at him. "How are you, *monsieur*?"

He frowned, strictly business. No friendly greeting. No cordial preliminaries about family and health like in Louisiana. "Charge to . . .?"

"Marcel Joubert, *s'il vous plaît*."

He flipped through the ledger and found the page, ran his finger down a long column and shook his head. "The Company is generous with credit," he said loudly, "but Marcel Joubert is over the limit."

People turned to stare. Vini felt her cheeks turn crimson.

"Next!" he called.

She rose to her full five feet and refused to budge. "*Monsieur*, I must have the cough syrup for my sister."

The cashier wagged his finger at her. "I don't have time to argue!"

A loud clomp of boots rushed forward, silencing the people in line. "Greetings, Henry. Would you like to point that finger at me?"

Surprised, Vini felt both glad and embarrassed to see Joel. *Again* he was present in a humiliating situation.

"You need to improve your manners, Henry. That isn't the way we treat ladies around here."

Fear flickered behind the cashier's glasses. "I didn't mean—"

"If there's a problem, fix it."

"But Company policy—"

"You can make an exception."

Henry hesitated.

"You've done it before."

He picked up his pen and with trembling fingers began to record Vini's items on the ledger sheet: "Cough syrup, one bottle. Rice and beans, one pound each. Flour, two pounds."

Vini set aside everything else except the red ribbon, even the pair of warm deerskin gloves. "This will do."

Henry peered at her over the rims of his spectacles. "Tell Joubert that from now on the Company will apply all his salary to this account until his debt is paid in full." After a quick glance up at Joel, he added, "If you would, please, Ma'am."

Joel picked up her basket, and she felt his hand on her elbow as he escorted her out. She knew that no one would dare snigger at her with Joel McGragor by her side.

As they came out of the Company Store, Joel squinted into the glare of the snowdrifts in the noontime sun. He was late for his appointment with King but didn't care. "I'm sorry about the way Henry Coughlin treated you."

Vini's eyes sparked. "I'm as mad as a mama gator!"

"Gator? *Alligator?*" She was full of surprises.

"Papa and I got too close to a mama gator once when we rowed down the bayou. She snapped her jaws and splashed her tail so hard I thought our *pirogue* was going to tip." She paused. "I'd like to tip that cashier's *pirogue* in a gator swamp!"

He couldn't help laughing. Then she did too, a gentle bubbling sound like a clear mountain stream dancing over rocks.

"Don't be too hard on Henry," he said. "He's been mad at the world since his wife died last year giving birth to their fifth child."

"Oh, *monsieur.* His poor family."

"The mining system traps people."

"I won't let mining trap Francine!"

"How is she?"

"Perhaps a little better. The cabin is clean now."

He remembered the stench when he set her trunk inside. Not a shirker, this one. "And your brother-in-law?"

She shrugged silently and her eyes clouded before she lowered them, hiding a secret beneath long curling lashes.

Joel's muscles tightened with a desire to protect her.

"*Merci, monsieur.*" She reached for the basket handle, and her small hand touched his. He noticed her flimsy gloves and remembered the deerskin ones she had set aside. When he owned a mine, he would treat the workers and their families right.

"Again you have been very kind to me."

As he looked into the blue-green sea of her eyes, he knew he would never see a more beautiful woman. He couldn't lose her! He pointed to the Elk

Mountain House. "That's going to be the biggest hotel in the Gunnison Country. I'm the building foreman," he added with pride.

"It looks like a fine hotel."

"The grand opening is December 7. I'd be honored to take you."

Her dimpled smile lit her face, and she curtsied. "*Oui. Avec grand plaisir, monsieur.*"

"Forgive my boldness, Ma'am, but your smile could melt the snow on Breasted Butte Mountain. *Crested* Butte Mountain," he corrected. The Lord help me!

A blush rose up her cheeks, but her eyes twinkled. "I'll remember December 7, Joel McGragor. Good day."

As she walked up Elk Avenue, he watched with pleasure the swing of her hips. He had observed several differences between unmarried girls and wives. Girls looked fresh; wives looked worn from the worries and responsibilities of caring for a family. Girls acted eager for life; wives acted as though they'd seen too much of it. Girls spoke with sweet enthusiasm; wives sounded tired. He wouldn't marry until he was rich enough to make life comfortable for Mrs. Joel McGragor. For the first time in his life, a specific face came to mind.

"I do believe my young friend is smitten." A hearty laugh spread contagiously, a deep rolling sound that seemed to ripple up from the toes.

With effort Joel pulled his eyes away from Vini's disappearing figure and smiled at his good friend Will Chaney, a reporter for the *Rocky Mountain News*. "Greetings, Will."

The reporter shook Joel's hand with both of his. Glasses framed his ink-black eyes that pierced facades, and his slightly rotund body hid itself in a dark, disheveled suit. "I saw you at the depot, but your gaze was pasted on that pretty little package that just swished away."

"I'm surprised you stayed in town."

Will's face turned as somber as a judge. "I've been doing some investigating. Do you still eat at the Star Restaurant on Saturday evenings?"

"Join me tonight?"

Will nodded. "I know I can trust you to keep something confidential."

"Always."

"How it's handled is important." Will waited for a couple of people to pass by on the boardwalk and lowered his voice. "The Jokerville Mine leaks methane."

"Methane!"

"It's a suicide trap!"

As Joel re-entered the Company Store for his appointment with King, he thought about the coal miners. Working in the black bowels of the earth. Unaware that death seeped in around them. The flames on their hats like a myriad of candles on a dark night. Twelve-hour shifts. Paid in scrip. Trapped by debts. No way out. He wondered if the new Federation of Organized Trades and Labor Unions would ever find its way to Crested Butte. Not if M. Morgan Heffron had his way.

"McGragor! You're late! Seven and a half minutes—to be exact."

"You are a stickler for details."

King's blade-gray eyes narrowed. "Remembering details can mean the difference between life and death." He claimed authority behind his large desk, the top cleared except for a single letter, a dirty metal ashtray, and the *Crested Butte Republican.*

Joel sat in an oak armchair and scanned the headlines upside down. One noted the Austro-Serbian Treaty of Alliance. "I hope Austria honors its treaty with the Serbs better than our government honored treaties with the Utes."

"You never change!"

"Not about injustice." Joel's outrage surged. "Like Mears—who paid Utes to sign the last treaty! Like Interior Secretary Kirkwood—who overruled Indian Commissioner Manypenny when he charged Mears with bribery and refused to endorse the treaty! And again—when Kirkwood had the audacity both to clear Mears of bribery *and* reimburse his expenses!"

King took a long draw on his cigar, and exhaled slowly. "Otto Mears is a hero. People wanted this land."

"*People* had this land." Joel thought of his father's most frequent advice: *The measure of a man is honor, Son, and sometimes it calls for the courage to break ranks.* Honor was not a word in King's vocabulary. "You wanted to see me. The point?"

King snuffed his cigar stub in the metal ashtray. Its stale smoke rose like a wall between the two men. "I have a letter from Mr. Heffron." He picked it up and read: " 'If we want a winning team in lawn tennis, we get R. D. Sears on our side. If we want to build a self-sufficient steel industry in Colorado, we get Joel McGragor on our team.' "

The compliment surprised and flattered Joel. Then he remembered the methane.

"You start Monday—to be exact."

"Not so fast!"

"You'll make good money."

The money tempted him like a cup of cool water in the desert. He could save enough to go prospecting by summer for sure. But in the meantime he wouldn't be able to look himself in the eye when he shaved each morning. He couldn't be like Heffron and King, filling their coffers on the coffins of others.

"A little money wouldn't hurt with that beautiful French girl you were ogling at the depot. She's quite a coquette!"

"Back off on that one, King!"

"Touched a nerve, did I? It's too bad she doesn't speak English."

Puzzled, Joel suddenly realized what must have happened. *Good for you, Vini.*

"Besides money, this job also puts the power of Heffron Enterprises in your hands."

"The power to play chess with human pawns?"

King's eyes flashed. "I warned Mr. Heffron against you. But what he wants, I deliver."

"Not this time." Joel stood and looked down at the man sitting across the desk, twisting his gold ring, afraid of failure. "I feel sorry for you."

King leaped up like a stallion wanting to fight. But he feared his master. "I jumped the track, Joel. Let's get back to Mr. Heffron's offer. Name your price."

"You think that's all it takes."

"We can buy anything. Or anyone."

Joel shook his head and opened the door.

"Two items for you to consider, McGragor," said King ominously. "One, no one crosses M. Morgan Heffron. You work for him or you don't work. And two, no one gets in my way."

"Three, you don't scare me. And you can't buy me."

"We'll see," said King with eyes of ice. "We'll see."

CHAPTER 3

*V*ini arranged evergreens in a circle on the table and scattered a few pinecones on top. Thinking about Joel and the Grand Opening, she began to hum.

"I remember our whole family joining in *Il Est Né*," said Francine. "It's lovely to hear you sing."

"I'm glad to be here with you."

Francine laughed weakly, a thin echo of the soul-deep laughter that Vini remembered. "It has nothing to do with Joel McGragor?"

Vini dropped a pinecone. "How did you—"

"This morning Martha told me about him bringing you home from the depot. And how you curtsied when he left. She said she'd never seen such a look on any man's face."

"She sees everything."

Francine took a wheezing breath. "But she's a good neighbor."

"Yes," agreed Vini, weaving the red ribbon through the circle of spruce.

"She said he's known as a man of his word. And he's handsome."

Vini nodded, basking in a warm glow like the Mississippi River aflame at sunrise. She stepped back to look at the table, then placed a candle in the center.

"*Parfait*. You remind me of Mama—always making things pretty."

"Dear Mama." Vini sat down on the clean bed. "Are you homesick, *chère*?"

"I dream of going back."

Struck by the fragility of human life, she tenderly pushed Francine's hair back from her gaunt face, once so beautiful. "First we'll get you well enough to travel. Then we'll figure out how to get you home."

"I don't think Marcel would go. He's afraid of Papa." Tears filled Francine's eyes. "I'm sorry he drinks so much."

"He won't when you get back to New Orleans. Papa will see to it." Back in those earlier days Marcel was a dandy with dreams. Now he was a drunk without any. Vini wondered what had changed him. Or whether this was who he was all along.

"He'll be home late. He always goes to the Bucket of Blood on Saturday night."

"Talking wears you out. Rest now, *chère*."

Francine closed her eyes and Vini moved quietly to the coal stove and picked up the wooden spoon to stir the red beans. She felt ashamed as she recalled being flattered by the flirtations of her big sister's beau. But that had changed on her thirteenth birthday. She remembered the three-layer coconut cake Mama had baked. And everyone gathered around the table singing "Happy Birthday," watching her make a wish and blow out the candles. And Marcel's eyes looking at her as though seeing her for the first time. Staring in a strange, frightening way.

"*Petite sœur*, do you think you love Joel McGragor?" asked Francine, too weary to open her eyes.

"I just met him."

Francine's lips curved into a smile from the past. "I remember when I met Marcel." Her voice cracked from the effort to talk, and she cleared her throat. "That very moment I knew I wanted to marry him."

A vivid memory of their wedding day tumbled through Vini's mind. A Cajun band played at the reception, and Marcel approached her, bowing. As the accordion wailed, they danced "The Window"—their arms forming a square between them that framed each other's face. Marcel's eyes locked upon her. Like at her thirteenth birthday party. Like at the depot. Ever since that dance she'd known never to risk being alone with him. But she hadn't told anyone. How could she?

Now, here she stood, stirring red beans in his one-room cabin in the light of day, and feeling his eyes in the darkness each night as she lay on her pallet not five feet away. A shiver crawled down her spine as she walked over to her sister's side once more and kissed her forehead. "Please get some sleep."

Francine looked into Vini's face and then focused on a knothole in the ceiling. "I've become an awful disappointment to him since my illness," she said with a raspy sigh.

Tenderly, Vini tucked the quilt around her. "He's just worried about you, *chère*."

Francine closed her eyes. *"L'innocente!"*

The sun had made its early winter descent, and Joel stopped work. He strode west down Elk, greeting people by name. Fresh snow carpeted the earth, seducing the unwary man with its illusion of innocence—like women, he thought, enjoying the swish and color they brought to the winter scene. Especially Vini, that queen in masquerade whose curtsy could transform the porch of a miner's shack into a royal balcony and a common builder into a king. He began whistling the lively old tune that rose unconsciously from the recesses of his mind.

He stopped in at James Groenendyke's news and confectionery next door to the bank. The bells on the door jingled as he entered. Heat from the coal stove warmed the room. "Greetings, Jim."

"Good evening. I'd be whistling too since the train brought all those ladies to town," he said with a chuckle. "That is, if I weren't already a family man. The Missus predicts a lot of quick marriages."

"I'll leave that to the other men. Do you have the *Rocky Mountain News*?"

Jim handed him a copy and frowned. "I've been hearing all afternoon about an argument between you and Mr. King today."

"News spreads fast in Crested Butte."

"You're one of the best men around, Joel McGragor. But you hurt yourself making an enemy like him."

"I'm not running for mayor." He plunked a coin on the counter and tucked the newspaper under his arm. "Thanks, Jim."

"Watch your back with King. Even when you're face to face."

Snowflakes swirled into Joel's face as he hurried the half-block to Pat Daly's Saloon. He glanced up at the snow-covered peaks, barely visible but magnificent in the moonlight. Their grandeur always amazed him.

"You're grinning like a boy that just stole his first kiss."

"Greetings, Nick. I was admiring the mountains."

"The mountains is the enemy," warned the freighter. "They promise a man treasure—and then freeze him with sleet in the heat of a summer day. They beckon him to their cool meadows—and fry him with a lightning bolt. They bid him climb higher—and bury him in an avalanche. They swallow him up in their bowels—and then belch him out." His voice fell to a hush. "The mountains is the enemy Joel McGragor. And don't you never forget it."

"You sure do get carried away." Joel opened the door to Pat Daly's Saloon.

"When you borrowed my wagon at the depot, you was a might carried away yourself." He raised a bushy eyebrow and shaped an hour-glass in the air. "She's certain-sure something pretty to look at."

"Certain-sure," mocked Joel with a smile. They stepped up to the bar that was two feet across and twenty feet long, made from a single spruce tree split lengthwise through the middle.

"I warn you, friend, women bring a man nothing but trouble—even blue-eyed brunettes from New Orleans."

"This one may be worth the trouble."

Nick put one foot on the rail. "I'll have a beer."

"Greetings, Pat. Make it two."

"Two wee beers now, that's you," said the stocky man with the Dublin brogue.

Nick aimed for the spittoon seven feet away and hit it with a ping. He pulled out his Burley and cut a new chew with his knife. "Pat, I'm mighty glad to see the ladies haven't shut you down yet. I figgered we'd open the door and find ourselves in church."

Pat chuckled. "'Tis a Catholic Church me mother would want. God rest her soul." He set heavy glass mugs before them and wiped his hands on his mottled apron stained by the most popular drinks in Crested Butte.

Nick took a long gulp from his glass. Eying Joel, he wiped the foam from his mouth with the back of his hand. "I heard about your little tea party with King. It's all over town that you 'geed' when he said 'haw.' "

Joel grinned, feeling he'd won a sparring match. Victory tasted sweet.

"You might ought to wipe that grin off your face. You just as well fight a griz without a gun!"

"Me thinks that in a fight with Joel McGragor 'tis the griz t'would need the gun." Pat winked at him and moved on down to tend the other end of the bar.

"Heffron's as greedy as a tough old bison grazing new spring grass," said Nick, aiming again for the spittoon. "But the way I figger it, his money will take a man prospecting just as good as anybody else's. What got into you?"

"If you work for Heffron, you sell your soul."

"Well, you might ought to worry more about your body right now. People get ascared. And they're ascared of King. He's going to get you back just as sure as a hungry mule heads for home."

Joel shrugged.

"Don't never say that Old Nick didn't warn you."

"Not a chance." Joel raised his glass to the weather-beaten freighter. "Here's to the man who's been warning me since '75."

"I remember that day like it was six hours ago instead of six years ago. I looked down from my wagon seat and there you was. A scrawny kid walking along. You might have died by the wayside, Joel McGragor, if I hadn't give you a ride to Saguache and talked Otto Mears into giving you a job!"

"You just wanted the Lake Fork and Ouray Toll Road finished. Scrawny or not, I was another pair of hands."

"Well, I certain-sure didn't know I was going to have to babysit you the rest of my life!" Nick looked at Joel and his eyes softened. All the buffoonery evaporated. "You never did tell me how old you were then."

"I'm not exactly sure. Around thirteen I suppose."

"And you'd already made it clear across the country from Washington City! By yourself." Nick lifted his own mug. "Here's to the man who's been a man well-nigh since he was born."

"Excuse me." The Company Store cashier tapped Joel on the shoulder and looked up at him over the rims of his glasses.

"Greetings, Henry. I appreciated your taking care of that little matter this morning."

"Mr. King sent me. He said on Saturday nights you always stop at Pat's and then go to the Star." He hunkered down nervously. "He's making me do this."

"Do what?"

"Give you this letter from McAllister and Craig."

"What does King have to do with a letter from them?"

"He wrote it and they signed it." He handed Joel the envelope and left as fast as a runaway skier down the Red Lady.

Joel opened the letter and read silently. He stood very still, staring at it as King's words came back to him: *No one crosses M. Morgan Heffron. You work for him or you don't work.* "I've been fired."

Dusk darkened the cabin, and Vini's mood darkened with it. She felt weary to the bone, homesick for crawfish *etoufee*, banana trees and azaleas at Christmas, and as embarrassed as a weed in a convent garden by her public humiliation at the depot and the Company Store. She heard her sister wheezing in her sleep and wondered about getting the doctor. How much would he charge? How could she pay him? She closed the curtain that separated the bed from the rest of the room, feeling she was running her own private chapter of the new Red Cross.

She cut a piece of cornbread, then remembered the debt at the Company Store and sliced it in half. She used a napkin and kept one hand properly in her lap as Mama had taught her—though sitting on a spruce stump, the bark unstripped, all alone at a rough-hewn table in a drafty log cabin nearly buried by snow.

At first she was glad Marcel would be late. The later, the better. But the later, also the drunker. And the drunker, the scarier. She chased away her fear with thoughts of Joel. Watching the candle flame dance, she fantasized conversations with him and thought of clever things to say when he took her to the Elk Mountain House. She chuckled at her own silliness but continued the game. Francine was right. She was a bit smitten—more than a bit—with Joel McGragor.

The door jerked open, and she shielded the candle from the cold wind. "Marcel! You're not late."

"I came straight home."

"Please wipe your feet."

He grinned. "You nag me like a wife." He poured water into the wash basin and scrubbed his hands in a fierce attack on the coal dust clinging to his fingernails and filling the cracks in his skin. "You're going out for dinner," he announced.

She spooned red beans and rice into a tin plate. "I don't understand."

Marcel sat down on the other log stool. "One of the big bugs called me up from my shift this afternoon to talk about my debt to the Company Store. He wants you to meet him at the Star Restaurant tonight."

"And you agreed? Without asking me?" She set the plate down in front of him so hard the beans bounced.

"Sh-h-h. You'll wake Francine."

"You will not make arrangements for me, Marcel! You are not Papa!"

He grabbed her wrist. "This is my house, and you will do what I say!"

Instinct told her not to show fear. She jerked free and turned away from him to the coal stove.

The log stool scratched against the floor behind her. "I'm sorry, Vini." He spoke softly, donning the remaining scraps of the southern gentleman. "You only have to go to dinner. Nothing more. I would allow nothing more." He stepped close behind her.

She felt his breath on the nape of her neck. *I shouldn't be here. I need to be here.*

His finger curled a lock of her hair. "You are near me all the time. But I can't touch you." He placed his hands on her shoulders. "Surely you know how I feel about you."

The words pounded through her mind like nails hammered into her sister's heart.

He tightened his grip on her shoulders and turned her around.

She grabbed the teakettle. He jumped back. "Stay away from me, Marcel Joubert!" His eyes burned into her. Silently she glared back, holding the teakettle, its steam rising between them.

Finally, he drew a deep breath and sat back down. "You are right, Vini. I give you my word as a southern gentleman. I'll stay away from you." His yellow-flecked eyes narrowed and his lips drew into a malevolent smile. "For now."

Her hand shook as she set the kettle back on the coal stove.

"But you *will* go to dinner tonight. I could lose my job. If you don't care about helping me, you must do it for your sister."

With that statement he turned the key to her will. She would do anything possible to help Francine.

"You need to hurry, Vini. He's sending Henry Coughlin here to take you in a sleigh."

Humiliating Henry!

"Wear your best dress. None other than Mr. Fred King himself will be waiting for you at the Star."

Bending against the howling wind, his soul as numb from the firing as his feet from the cold, Joel opened the door to the Star Restaurant and stamped the snow off his boots. "Greetings, Rose."

"It's good to see you, Joel." Her voice was low for a woman, the kind that carries across the room. Tall and big-boned, she had kind eyes that matched her cinnamon colored hair.

Joel hung his sheepskin coat on the antler rack. "This is the coldest night I can remember."

She motioned him to an empty table and brought a mug of steaming coffee. "I'm glad you came."

"I thought it was a law on Saturday night."

She softened her voice. "I know about your job."

"How?" Had he been the last to find out?

"King was in here this afternoon for pie and coffee. He had your bosses in tow—'to be exact,'" she mocked.

"Ex-bosses."

"Don't be too hard on them. I picked up bits of the conversation. He told them he'd make sure they didn't get any more construction jobs unless they fired you."

"And they were worried about their families and the other men who work for them." Angry as he was, he understood. "McAllister and Craig are good men," he said, meaning it. But they scare too easily, he thought.

"I hear a lot of talk around these tables, Joel. People look up to you because you aren't afraid of Heffron and his lackeys. Crested Butte needs someone who shows courage for the rest of us."

He studied the worn face of this widow who'd made a respectable life for herself in a rough mountain town. "I'm looking at courage."

"What King did wasn't fair. Like a lot of life. But don't let it keep you down." She patted his shoulder. "I baked your favorite dessert."

"Chocolate cake?"

She nodded.

"When a man is wounded, you treat his stomach."

"It's the best I can do."

"You're a kind woman, Rose."

"Are you by yourself?"

"I'm waiting for Will Chaney."

"The *Rocky Mountain News* reporter?"

Will stepped up behind her. "The man with the power of the pen himself." He laughed. A deep rumble filled the room.

"Greetings, Will."

"It's cold out there!" He hung his plaid wool coat on the back of his chair.

"I'll bring some coffee to warm you up, Mr. Chaney."

Will pulled a white handkerchief from his pocket and began wiping the snow off his glasses. "King had a busy afternoon."

"You know about my job?"

"He didn't exactly try to keep it a secret."

"I feel like I smoked a victory cigar after beating him—and ended up with the fire end in my mouth."

"Isn't the banker's house one of McAllister and Craig's projects?"

Joel nodded.

"If Richard Sterling is the man I think he is, I'd be willing to wager that he'll get you un-fired."

The clock chimed half past seven, and King entered the cafe. Joel clutched his coffee mug so tight his knuckles turned white.

"Settle down, Joel! You look like you could start a fire without a match."

King pulled out his gold watch and clicked it open, pacing impatiently in front of the door.

"Here's a table, Mr. King," gestured Rose.

"I'm waiting for someone." The door opened, and he looked up expectantly.

Marshal Hays entered. Snow covered his brown overcoat. "Evening, Fred." He saw Joel and waved.

"Greetings, Marshal."

"Joel McGragor," he grinned, "you tell that big-city reporter to write only the good news about this town."

"I'll write good things about its marshal," said Will with admiration in his voice.

"Thank you, Mr. Chaney." He took a seat at the next table. "What's for dessert, Rose?"

The door opened again, this time framing Vini. Surprised, Joel started to rise.

"Here she is!" said King, projecting his voice like the star of a melodrama.

Joel caught Vini's eye. She winced and looked away.

King helped her remove her cloak and ushered her toward a table near Joel's. "Good evening, Mr. Chaney. I'd introduce you to this lovely creature, but she doesn't speak English."

Vini glanced at Joel, her eyes suddenly full of mischief and her lips fighting a smile.

"McGragor, I understand you're jobless—to be exact. Too bad."

Joel met King's eyes evenly, refusing to be hooked in front of Vini.

King turned again to Will. "Earlier today, I was telling your friend here what a coquette this little thing is. Money speaks to a girl like her. This is going to be a memorable Saturday night!"

Joel jumped up so fast his chair fell over.

The marshal leaped to the table.

Vini's eyes blazed. She held up her small hand, palm facing Joel as though holding him back. She stepped apart from King and looked at Will. "*Monsieur* Chaney, I am Marie-Vincente Prejean. Any friend of Joel McGragor may call me Vini."

Will grinned. "You speak English. And what a delightful accent."

King stood silent, his mouth agape.

She turned to the marshal. "*Monsieur*, my brother-in-law made a commitment for me tonight that I can no longer honor. If Mr. King is gentleman enough to lend his sleigh, would you be so kind as to see me home?"

"My pleasure, Ma'am. As I recall, you're the young lady from New Orleans."

"I'm flattered that you know of me, Marshal Hays."

"I can assure you, Miss Prejean, that Fred will loan me his sleigh."

Vini peered at King like a queen at a court jester. "I speak English—but only to those whom I wish to know better." As she walked away, she looked back over her shoulder. "Monsieur King, I hope I have made this 'a memorable Saturday night!' "

"If you don't marry that woman, Joel, I'm going to!" said Will, still clapping. King had charged from the cafe and slammed the door right after Vini left with the marshal. An excited buzz followed his exit, like at the intermission of a suspenseful play. Rose led the applause for Vini, who would never again be a stranger in Crested Butte.

Joel grinned, marveling. "She whipped King without even raising her voice!"

Rose brought them plates heaped with fried chicken, corn, mashed potatoes, cream gravy and oversized biscuits. "That woman fancies you, Joel McGragor. You let her go and you're hiding a fool beneath your skin."

"Do you bake chocolate cake for fools?"

"Never!"

"You're putting me in a tight spot, Rose."

Will leaned across the table, closer to Joel, his voice hushed. "King also had a busy afternoon with Heffron and the *Rocky Mountain News*. I received a telegram directing me to drop the Jokerville story and return to Denver."

"Come on, Will. Even France established freedom of the press this year."

"A story wouldn't make any difference. Heffron would don his humanitarian costume and deny the danger."

"The methane is a fact."

"One of the first things a reporter learns is that perception is what counts with people. Not facts."

"But perception can be manipulated."

"That's the second thing a reporter learns." He was thoughtful for a moment. "The truth is the miners wouldn't quit anyway. They need jobs."

His words settled over Joel like a pall. "They can't quit! They're in debt to the Company Store."

As the two men left the Star, the snow fell in a white sheet. Will stopped suddenly.

"With the methane and your job, I almost forgot. I have something for you. From Chipeta."

His words brought new hope. Chipeta was his last chance. "Some information?"

"A present. It's in my room at the hotel."

Will's room was much like his own at Rozick's—a bed, chair, and table. What more did a man need? Joel thought of Vini. And then come the trappings. First—strike it rich.

"It's good to get out of the storm," said Will, offering Joel the chair and plopping himself on the edge of the bed. "I interviewed Chipeta in September when I covered the Ute removal."

"I haven't seen her in over a year—just before Chief Ouray died."

"Without signing the new treaty."

Joel nodded. "Over the decades he dealt with Lincoln, Johnson, Grant, and Hayes. New Presidents. New treaties. If you ask me, he gave up and died of broken-treaty disease."

"Don't you speak Ute?"

"Chief Ouray taught me."

"I wish you could have been my interpreter."

"Chipeta understands English better than people realize."

"How did you get to know them?"

"That's a long story. We'll save it for another night."

"I'll never forget my interview with her." Will stared into memory, telling the story:

I knock on the door of her adobe house. She greets me in a white buckskin dress fringed around the bottom and trimmed with colorful beads. It looks as soft and fine as silk. Her dark hair is parted in the middle, long and shiny. Her posture is as straight as a plumb line. She wears a white cross around her neck and she tells me she is a Methodist and so was the chief.

I dust off my pants before I sit on her fine furniture. Fancy curtains hang at the parlor windows and carpets brighten the floor. She shows me pictures of their trips to Washington, a stack of newspaper articles, and the gifts from Presidents. She answers all my questions with keen insight. I ask her about the new treaty.

She reminds me that it had to be signed by three-fourths of the adult Ute males to be legal, but was ratified with only 110 signatures. Numberwise that implies that there were only 147 Ute men. She looks at me with those dark eyes and asks why the United States chiefs aren't smart enough to know that a tribe of over 3000 will have more than 147 grown men.

I squirm, embarrassed.

Toward the end of the interview, we take a walk and stop beside a beautiful stream. Chipeta reaches out and tenderly pats the shoulders of two children playing cat and the cradle with string. For a second her mask falls. I have never seen such pain on anyone's face.

Will came back from memory and looked at Joel. "I try to be objective as a reporter, but I ache for her. One morning she pours me tea from a gold-trimmed china pot; the next morning the military herds her away to the alkaline sands of Utah."

Joel swallowed the knot in his throat.

"I'm proud of our country, Joel. I love it enough to die for it. But that wasn't our finest hour."

"My father used to say that when we create instability, we become unstable ourselves. Look at this year, Will. We've had three presidents. Hayes finished his term. Garfield was inaugurated—and assassinated. And now we have Arthur."

"I hadn't thought about that."

"During the past sixteen years, six different presidents have served our country. Two of them assassinated."

"Maybe that theory of instability has some merit."

"Perhaps it fits people as well as countries."

Will handed him a slender object wrapped in brown paper. "Chipeta asked me to bring you this gift to remember them by."

"As if I could ever forget!" The paper crackled as Joel unwrapped it and removed a white bone-handled knife. He ran his fingers across the bone and the blade, drawn to the knife as though it held a power of its own.

"She also asked me to tell you she found out what you need to know."

Joel tensed, every nerve alert. "Say more."

Will shrugged. "That's it."

"Did she say a name?"

He shook his head. "She wants you to come to the Uintah Reservation to tell you personally."

"I can't get there in the dead of winter!"

"Don't even think about it!" Will grinned. "I don't want to have to write a story about Joel McGragor waking up one morning in a snow cave on some isolated peak—face-to-face with the Colorado Cannibal. Alferd Packer has proved a tough one to find, but they'll do it. People get resolve when somebody eats five men!"

Joel stared through the dark window, jobless and free, weighing the odds of making it through the mountains.

"Listen to me, Joel." Will's eyes grew grave behind his glasses, his tone somber once more. "Whatever message Chipeta has will keep till summer. The mountains can kill you."

"You sound like Nick Laffey." Joel put on his coat.

"My friend, stay out of the mountains in the winter. And out of the Jokerville year-round."

"Don't worry about that. I'm going to be a mine owner. Not a miner."

CHAPTER 4

*S*ainte Marie, Mère de Dieu! What have I done! The window framed the eerie glow of the snow, and Vini's mind played out ways King could take revenge. The one relief was Marcel's absence when she arrived home early from the restaurant. She lay on her pallet drifting in and out of nightmares, longing for morning to come.

"Vini."

She heard Francine's voice and bolted up. "Are you all right?"

"But are you, *petite sœur*? You are groaning with nightmares."

"Oh, *chère*, I've done a terrible thing. I am so scared. Not just for me. But for you and Marcel."

Francine patted the bed. "Come here and tell me about it."

"Marcel told King I'd dine with him tonight."

"He shouldn't have done that."

"He thought it would help. So I rode with that horrible Henry to the Star where pompous Frederick Rodewald King waited."

"Don't let Marcel get you to do things by using me. Next time don't go."

"There won't be any next time. I was angry. Angry at Marcel. Angry at Henry. Angry at King. And he didn't know I could speak English and—"

"Why not?"

"I didn't really lie." Vini hesitated. "But I may have left that impression with him at the depot."

"Like my letters home. There's not a single lie." Francine gazed toward the knothole, adding softly, "But the truth shocked you when you arrived."

Vini raced on. "King said some horrible things about me. He made me sound like a whisper woman!"

Francine giggled. "I'm sorry. I can't help it." She broke into a full laugh. "It's terrible what he did. But I hadn't thought about our 'whisper women' conversations in years."

Delighted to hear Francine laugh again, Vini joined her.

"Tell me, *petite sœur*." For an instant a twinkle chased the pain from her eyes. "Did you use the 'whisper weapon' on him?"

"Francine!" Trying to talk through her laughter, Vini said, "The only two things Mama ever whispered about: The women to stay away from in the French Quarter—"

"And what to do with your knee if you just had to!" Francine tried to whisper like Mama: "I don't like to talk to you young ladies about this, but you just can't be sure about those Yankees infiltrating New Orleans."

They laughed till the tears ran, sharing a feast after a famine. Francine began to cough, and Vini got her some water. After she drank, she said wheezily, "Tell me what happened next with Mr. King."

Vini recalled the rage she had felt. "A tidal wave of fury rolled over me. And I humiliated that man. Intentionally. In front of all those people." She sighed. "I did it the way we learn somehow in the South—so-o-o ladylike."

"I just wish I'd been there to see it!"

"Who do you think you are!"

Vini woke with a start.

Marcel grabbed her shoulders and jerked her up from the pallet. She held the cover over her chest. His breath reported the night's drinking. *Holy Mother, please don't let him know about tonight.*

"The Star story made its way to the Bucket of Blood."

Her heartbeat doubled. Her senses heightened. She smelled the coke ovens. Saw the moonglow through the window. Heard the spruce whisper. Tasted the danger of Marcel. Remembered not to act afraid.

"I get you a chance to be with an important man. The man who represents the richest financier in our country! And what do you do!" He gripped her arms and shook her. "You disgraced Frederick Rodewald King!"

Vini's neck jerked back and forth. The braid of her hair jostled loose.

"He won't just get revenge against you. He'll get back at me too!" He stopped shaking her and stood very still. His yellow-flecked eyes stared at her.

His silent gaze terrified her more than his violence. I shouldn't be here. I need to be here.

He jerked her closer, spitting staccato words in her face. "I asked one simple thing. But you are too high and mighty to do it. Even for your sister!"

He was right. "I'm sorry."

"When she dies in this cabin, it's on your head!" He drew back his hand and hit Vini hard across the face. It knocked her back on the pallet. She tasted blood on her lip.

"*Marcel!*" Francine tried to get out of bed to help her.

"It's all right, *chère.*"

He looked at Francine. Then at Vini. Turning his back to them, he sat down on the log stool and slumped over the kitchen table. "My God." He covered his face with his hands. "What have I come to?" His wracking sobs filled the cabin.

Joel trekked along the snow-packed path to Company Housing. There was freedom in being jobless, but he was deeply hurt. He'd planned to quit and go prospecting with Nick when Mr. Sterling's house was done, so he'd saved some money—but not enough. He glanced up at the Red Lady. Now what? He felt sure her ruby lips smiled down at him. He knocked on Vini's door softly, not wanting to wake Francine if she were sleeping.

"Joel McGragor!" Her voice sang with joy.

He stood still for a moment, letting his eyes adjust from the glare of the snow. The doorway framed a woman whose beauty contrasted to the rough-hewn cabin like the *Mona Lisa* on a sod-hut wall. Then he noticed the dark bruise on her face.

Following his eyes, she self-consciously put her hand up to cover her cheek and the edge of her mouth.

"What happened to you?"

"It was an acci—"

"Don't, Vini. Don't put any lies between us."

She lowered her eyes.

"Marcel!" He said it like pronouncing a death sentence.

"Try to understand, Joel. He is a weak man, but not a bad man."

Bending down, he gently moved her hand. "*That* is weak turned bad."

"Let it be. Please. For Francine's sake."

He studied the ugly bruise and her pleading eyes. The latter won. But he would have a little talk with Marcel and make very clear what to expect if anything like this ever happened again. But Joel didn't share those thoughts. Some things were best left unspoken.

"Please come in and meet my sister."

"Thank you." He stamped the snow off his boots and removed his hat. Vini offered to take his sheepskin coat, but he shook his head.

Francine smiled at him. "I have heard many good things about you."

"Thank you, Ma'am." She looked dangerously frail. He stood beside the bed holding his hat in both hands and noting the newspapers that covered the wall to block out drafts. "Vini, I came to ask if you would like to learn how to ski. I could teach you today."

"Isn't it hard?"

"Is it dangerous?" asked Francine.

"Not if people are careful. And we will be."

Vini looked at Joel, and rolled her eyes toward her sister. "I can't go."

"Of course you can, *petite sœur.* I would learn to ski if I could."

"I don't want to leave you."

"Ask Martha to check on me if you must. But please go," said Francine, excitement in her weak voice. "And come back and tell me the story—what it's like to ski down the mountains with the snow flying. I want to know how it feels."

"You may be frail in body, Ma'am," said Joel with admiration, "but not in spirit! I'll teach Vini now, and when you get well, Mrs. Joubert, I'd be honored to teach you too."

"When I get well . . ." Francine closed her eyes, almost like a prayer. "Thank you, Joel McGragor."

Vini looked at him with bright eyes and a brighter smile. "You're sure I can learn?"

"Positive. Do you have a warm pair of boots?"

"I do," said Francine. "My boots get to go skiing!"

He gestured toward Vini's long skirt. "Ladies ski like that. But I don't see how." There's a time for proper and a time for practical, he thought. "I wish I had some Levi's that would fit you."

Vini almost gasped. What would Mama think! But Mama had never skied.

"I'll get what we need and be back in about an hour."

Vini stepped out on the porch with him. "It is a beautiful day."

"Has your sister seen Doc?" he whispered.

Vini bit her lip, silent for a moment, the sparkle fading from her eyes. "Marcel said Doc Williams came before I arrived and said that there is nothing else to do but try to take good care of her."

Her melodic accent was like a sad song, and Joel saw a tear roll down over the bruise on her fine-boned cheek. He pulled his clean bandanna from his hip pocket and tenderly daubed the tear. Others welled in her beautiful eyes, reminding him of heaven holding back a gentle rain. Resisting the urge to take her in his arms, he tipped his hat and hurried away through the snow.

While waiting for Martha to answer the door, Vini tugged forward the wool scarf she'd put over her head and crisscrossed around her neck, trying to cover the bruise.

"Come in, baby." The Donegan cabin had two rooms. A large table that seated ten took up most of the front room. Davey slept in the cradle near the stove. Little Joan held on to her mother's apron, sucking her thumb, and Jamie played marshal and robber with two sock puppets. The cabin was as clean and neat as St. Louis Cathedral during Lent. "I saw Joel McGragor on your porch. Iber says they don't come any finer than Joel, that he has more courage than Daniel in the lions' den. Let me take your cloak."

"I can't stay."

Martha peered at her cheek. "What happened to your face! Did you bump into a door?"

Vini pulled at her scarf. "Something like that." She hurried on to change the subject. "I have a favor to ask, Miss Martha. Joel offered to teach me how to ski today."

"I wondered what was up. Not that it's any of my business, but I hear tell there only two bachelors in Crested Butte who are gentlemen. One is Joel McGragor. Most men can't even take a woman around the block and keep their hands to themselves. But not Joel. He's known as a man who respects a lady. You could go all the way to Denver with him, baby, and he'd still be a gentleman. The second is Mr. Sterling, the banker—and he's about not to be a bachelor. He's marrying that haughty Alisa Allen—the kind of woman who's nice to look at but gropes for the money purse. Now if it was Mr. King asking you, I'd watch out. He thinks he just smiles at a woman and her heart goes to fluttering." She grinned. "I heard about what happened at the Star Restaurant. He's been due for a comeuppance for a long time!"

When Martha paused for breath, Vini asked, "Does Iber Jr. have any outgrown overalls?"

"He sure does. He's growing so fast that he puts them on in the morning and by evening they come to his knees. There's a pair right here in the trunk. I'm saving them for Peter when he gets a little bigger."

"I know it doesn't sound proper, but I was wondering if I could borrow them today."

"To wear skiing! It sounds proper to me—a whole lot more so than for a lady to go toppling in the snow with her skirts all tangled up above her bloomers." Martha opened the trunk and took out a pair of neatly folded overalls and a red and black buffalo plaid wool shirt. She held them up and eyed Vini. "You're no bigger than a hummingbird, but these ought to fit you about right."

"Thank you, Ma'am."

"Now don't you worry about Francine. I've got some soup in the pot and some bread baking. I'll take dinner to her at noon and see if she needs anything."

"She always enjoys talking to you, Miss Martha. I wish I could do something back for you."

"You can, baby. When you return those clothes, you sit yourself down right here at my table and tell me all about going skiing with Joel McGragor."

Vini smiled.

"One more thing." Martha's chatty voice turned serious. "Not that it's any of my business, but a man hits a woman once, he'll hit her again. You can count on it as sure as changing a diaper and having to change it again." She pointed to Vini's cheek and lip. "If it ever looks like you might be about to bump into Marcel's fist again, you hie yourself over here as fast as you can." She hugged her broad arm around Vini's shoulders. "Iber knows how to take care of folks we like."

Vini stood beside Joel in homemade skis at the edge of a steep slope on the Red Lady. She gripped a long aspen ski pole and listened to him talk. The red ribbon from the centerpiece tied back her dark hair, and Iber Jr.'s overalls bagged over the buffalo plaid shirt. Marcel's brimmed hat shaded her face, its band lined with newspaper to fit her head, and Francine's boots warmed her feet. Her hands hid in the new deerskin gloves Joel had brought back with the skis and given to her with a shrug—*a Christmas present, early.* She sensed a completeness in him out here that was different from in town.

He leaned against a camel-shaped boulder. "I'd put this scenery against any in the whole country, Vini. In the summertime you can sit away from the world in the shade of that circle of spruce trees over there and hear the waterfall sing to the sun."

She soaked in his words as well as the panoramic view of the snowy valley below, surrounded by peaks that split the sky.

"I wasn't sure you could make it up here. You're doing very well."

"That's because all we've done is go uphill, slow and steady."

"I thought it was because of the overalls." He laughed.

She smiled at him. "It's downhill fast that would scare me."

"We'll go back home a gentle way, and save our downhill race for another day."

"You're a poet," she teased. "But a bad one." As she laughed, her skis slipped forward. They slid over the edge of the steep slope. Surprised and terrified, she headed straight down. Faster and faster. *Holy Mother, please stop them!*

The skis zipped on down the slope. But they stayed parallel. And she stayed vertical. She rode them! Suddenly it was fun! The wind in her face. The joy of speed. The skis shot down faster and faster. Faster and faster! And still she rode them! More and more excited! More and more sure that whatever the end, it was worth it!

And end it did. The slope shifted and rose sharply. Vini's skis jolted, lost their momentum, and she fell.

Joel skidded to a stop only moments behind. Fright paled his face. "Are you all right?"

"I just rode them down! It was even more fun than *Mardi Gras.*"

His face changed from fright to relief, then from relief to exasperation. "You scared me nearly to death, Vini Prejean!"

"I didn't mean to. But I can't be sorry. I'm glad I didn't miss that ride!"

He shook his head, then laughed. "You are something else!" He reached down to help her up. He took hold of one hand and put his other arm around her waist, lifting her from the snow like at the depot. But this time, not so chastely.

She felt small beside him, felt the nearness of his body to hers, felt the power of his presence. His face was close. Too close. "Joel—" What she wanted was for him to move in closer. But what she made herself say was, "Would you mind getting my pole?"

"I discovered this cave last summer, Vini." Joel set their skis inside and removed the saddlebag he'd carried down on his shoulder.

"I thought we were coming to a dead end. Those rocks hide the entrance like a secret."

"The mountains are full of secrets." The temperature dropped immediately without the sun. He saw her shiver from the cold dampness. "I'll make a fire and fix us some coffee."

"I've never been in a cave before. Even the cemeteries are above ground in New Orleans."

"That's hard to picture."

"People call them cities of the dead. It looks like narrow one-story houses are lined up in rows. Some even have fancy facades at the roof line."

"Unlike cemeteries, caves are for the living." He decided not to mention that among the living could be a hibernating bear. Some things were best left unspoken. Unbuckling his saddlebag, he took out a coffeepot and some coffee.

"I like the fancy *M* tooled on the flap."

Joel traced the letter with his finger. "This was my father's." He felt her eyes upon him as he knelt over a hollow in the stone floor encircled by rocks, and lit kindling he'd stored last summer. "I wouldn't have risked bringing you down that slope today. But since you came on your own, so to speak, this is a good place for lunch." He dipped the coffeepot into the underground stream that ran beside the cave wall.

"I should have fixed us something."

"Rose did. From the Star. You didn't have time to meet her Saturday night." He grinned as he added some logs and set the coffeepot on a rock at the edge of the fire. "You got a round of applause after King stormed out."

Vini's eyes sparkled with mischief. "I haven't been so mad at anyone since I was seven years old and got kicked out of the Christmas pageant."

"You'd be a perfect Madonna."

"The Sister didn't think so after I tackled Robert E. Lee Thibodaux during rehearsal."

"*Tackled* him?" He couldn't get his mind around petite Vini leaping in a tackle.

"He grabbed the Baby Jesus, and I was sure the Holy Mother would have tackled anyone who snatched up her son from the manger."

Joel wasn't much of a churchgoer any more, but he disagreed with Vini about the serene Madonna tackling someone.

"Robert E. Lee Thibodaux crashed into the magi's wooden camel and got a bloody nose. So I didn't get to be in the pageant."

"I guess I better behave," he said.

Vini's rich laughter rippled through the cave.

He loved hearing her laugh. It would take some doing to keep up with this woman.

She sobered. "I was not wise Saturday night."

"You were amazing!"

She moved closer to the fire and held her hands over it, palms down. "I may have hurt Francine. Indirectly."

"That sounds like something Marcel would say to make you feel guilty so you'll do what he wants."

Dread filled her voice. "Somehow King will get revenge against me." She glanced up at him, the flames bringing a glow to her face. "Just as he did with you."

Joel figured King had set up dinner with Vini at the Star to bait him. But some things were best left unspoken. He tried to ease her anxiety. "Not even King would stoop to taking revenge against a woman."

Her blue-green eyes looked into his. "I'm afraid you are wrong, Joel McGragor, but I hope you're right."

He heard that trusted voice within him whisper: *You've overestimated King's character before.* He questioned his decision to go to the Uintah Reservation. But he must.

As the flames grew, light played tag with the shadows on the wall. They could see where water dripped like an artist's brush, painting colorful streaks along the rock. "There's something I'd like to show you in the next chamber, Vini."

She hesitated.

"It isn't far. Besides, it's like the ski slope. It's worth it." Lighting one end of some dried branches to make a torch, he took her hand and led her over the rough cave floor into a narrow passage. Even she had to duck. It widened into another chamber. Silence reigned except for the stream. Only the torch defended them against total darkness. He felt Vini's hand tighten against his.

"About ten more feet," he said. He raised the torch close to the wall. "Look." A large painting in muted shades of blue and yellow, green and brown depicted a beautiful Indian woman and child. They danced on the cave wall in the torch light.

"*Magie!* It's like magic!" She stepped close to the wall admiring the painting. "A mother and baby in a cave."

"I wish I knew the story."

"We could make one up."

He took her hand in his, deciding to tell her the story of another mother and baby. "We'd better go back before we lose our light."

They sat close to the fire on a small blanket eating Rose's ham sandwiches, the oatmeal-raisin cookies still in the tin beside them. Joel withdrew a leather pouch from his saddlebag and pulled out an old picture, pointing to the most prominent person. "That's Ouray, Head Chief of the Utes." The ebony eyes portrayed power and strength, misplaced in a face depicting pain and suffering. He was strong and stocky, with a furrowed brow and black braids that reached almost to his waist.

"This picture says so much."

"He was willing for men to come in and get the gold, but he didn't want them to settle and build houses."

She looked up at Joel, her eyes as clear as Emerald Lake. "Do you think the miners and settlers were wrong?"

"We wanted their land, and we stole their soul in the process."

"You feel sorry for Chief Ouray." Her voice was soothing, gently enfolding his heart.

He felt vulnerable. He could handle King better than kindness. Without looking at her, he moved his finger over the picture to the man sitting beside the chief. "That's my father. He and Chief Ouray became friends in '68 during the first Ute trip to Washington. When the Utes returned in '72, he arranged for this picture."

Vini pointed to the boy sitting on the other side of the Chief. "You?"

He nodded. "I was about ten."

She took hold of the picture and peered closely at the boy. "I like what I see."

"My father died soon afterward."

"Oh, Joel! I can't imagine what it would be like to lose Papa. And you were so young."

Her tone caressed an empty place in his soul. He looked into the fire. "The day before my father died, he asked me to sit beside him on his bed. He said he had something important to tell me. I remember how he took my hand. But his eyes stared beyond me as though seeing the past, reliving it as he talked:

The day is hot and cloudless. We are mounted and mighty, riding along in our military uniforms like waves of blue under a clear blue sky. I sit tall in the saddle as always, proud to serve my country.

Until this day.

From the time the sun rises I have a bad feeling. Our new commander has fought at Fort Sumter and is angry to be called away from the War between the States. He transfers his hate for the Rebs to hate for the Redskins. His goal here isn't to win a battle but to exterminate a people.

Our scouts discover an Apache rancheria. We look down on it with our binoculars. Children are laughing and splashing in the stream. Women are cooking and going about their work, watching the little ones play. We can tell that all the men are away. Except for a very old man sitting in the shade of a tree.

Yet the commander orders our battalion to charge. Not against armed warriors. But against these helpless, innocent women and children. And blood rains on this cloudless day.

I stand at the edge of the rancheria. I am trained to protect the helpless, not slaughter them. I can't follow that order.

But I can't stop the massacre! Rifles fire. Women scream. Children wail. Horses ride them down. Swords flash blood red. The women try to run. Carrying their babies. Dragging their children. Trying to place their own bodies between the bullets and their little ones.

I stand at the edge, sickened. In all the battles I've fought, I've never before seen such evil unleashed. The men mutilate bodies. Dismember limbs. Some take scalps, scalps dripping with the blood of women and babies. Then they ride away in a blood-spattered sea of blue.

Still I stand at the edge. Ashamed of my uniform. Ashamed of my country. Ashamed of my race. The horse hooves grow silent in the distance. And before me death screams at the sky, and the rocks in the stream mourn, and the trees begin to weep.

Then in the silence comes the whimper of a child. I dismount and walk through the carnage toward the sound. A little one lies under his mother, his tiny arms clinging to her. Blood soaks her clothes. Gently, I roll her over.

Her head covering falls loose, and strands of blond hair show beneath the smears of blood.

She opens her eyes, eyes as blue as the sky. Terrified, she grasps the little one. I smile at her and tenderly run my hands over the baby, checking for injuries. She has protected him well.

When she sees that I care about her baby, the terror leaves her face. I stand to get my canteen. By sheer will, she tries to lift the toddler toward me. Her pain-filled blue eyes beg me to save her baby. She grasps something around her neck. And she dies. I open her clutched fingers and see a gold cross outlined in silver.

And that day, Joel, was the first time I picked you up.

I rode out of there with you in my arms and the cross in my pocket. And I kept on riding. And I got rid of that uniform. And I started over.

I do not know who your father is, Joel. But I do know this. You are my son."

Vini sat still beside Joel, too moved to speak. He stared at the leaping flames. She gathered all her internal power and wrapped it silently around him like a quilt of healing comfort.

Finally, he spoke. "It was the first time I was aware that the father who reared me, the only father I ever knew, wasn't my birth father."

She longed to touch him, to place her hand over his.

"As I think back, he didn't ever lie to me about this. But he left a lot of things unspoken."

Her hand, seemingly of its own accord, reached out and tenderly enfolded his. Even that small gesture sent fire through her veins. Startled, she almost withdrew it.

He turned to her. There was no courtly nod now. No raised eyebrow. No taking charge. This was the Joel stripped of surface habits, raw from telling his story. It was this man that she fell wholly in love with. There would be no one else. No turning back. No future unlinked to his.

"He gave me my mother's gold and silver cross that day. He'd saved it all those years. And I've kept it ever since."

"I can't even begin to imagine what it would be like not to know Mama."

"I came West to find out who she was. And how she came to be with the Apaches. And who my birth father was."

"Yes." She understood about family roots. "That would be necessary."

"Chief Ouray and Chipeta tried to get information. I had almost given up, but I've learned that she has some news for me."

"And your search can end."

"I hope so. But now that I may find out, I almost feel scared to know." He put his arm around her, drawing her closer.

She didn't resist. How natural and good his nearness felt. There was no place she'd rather be.

"Chipeta has been removed to the Uintah Reservation, and I need to go there to talk with her."

Vini caught her breath but managed a smile. The weather would keep him here until winter ended. *Holy Mother, I love, adore, cherish this man. Please don't let him leave before summer.*

"So . . ." He put his finger under her chin and lifted her face toward his. "I'll be heading out the day after the grand opening of the Elk Mountain House."

CHAPTER 5

*V*ini felt self-conscious as she walked ahead of Joel on the slippery snow-banked boardwalk to the Elk Mountain House. It was not easy to balance that imaginary book on her head while walking on ice. Mama had never had to contend with snow. She tasted her breath in the cold and tried not to shiver in her thin cloak.

Joel removed his hat and nodded to her in his courtly way as he opened the door. "Welcome to 'The Pride of the West,' Ma'am."

The smell of new paint cut into the odor of the coke ovens as they stepped into a large wainscoted room with a linoleum floor and an immense stove in the center. On the right-hand side stood an elegant counter with a large Detroit safe behind it and a Bell telephone on the wall. Plush chairs and settees lined the walls, and two chandeliers hung from the ceiling. Joel put their wraps in the cloak alcove off to the side. He took her arm and ushered her through the packed room, greeting everyone by name.

Vini's self-consciousness returned as the men took note of her. She felt sized up, like when the shrimp boats come in and the catch is sorted. They winked at Joel or made low-voiced comments or raised their eyebrows in a knowing way, as though she was a trophy instead of a person.

He bent down and whispered, "Don't let them get to you. They don't mean any harm—it's just their way of saying you're a beautiful woman and I'm a lucky man."

She smiled at him, appreciating his knack for sensing her feelings. In New Orleans she'd always looked forward to parties and *Mardi Gras* parades and crowds of people. But not today. Tomorrow Joel would go away. She felt furious with King. If Joel still had his job, he couldn't leave in deep winter. She didn't believe in voodoo like some of her French Quarter friends, but if she did she would put a hex on Frederick Rodewald King—to be exact. Mama would tell her not to judge. But Mama wasn't here.

The ceremony was in process, and the mayor was holding forth before a more attentive audience than at the depot. Vini glanced around the parlor. It was beautiful. Her feet sank into the thick blue-bordered Brussels carpet. The windows reached nearly floor to ceiling, reminding her of the French Quarter. Through them she could see the roof of the portico catching the snow. The wooden balustrade around it looked rough and unfinished compared to the fancy wrought-iron work of the Pontalba galleries lining Jackson Square. She knew it wasn't fair to compare anything in this new town with an old city like New Orleans—civilized by the French and Spanish long before the rowdy Americans came. She knew also that she should be ashamed for feeling sorry for herself that Joel was going away. The first deadly sin in her family was self-pity. The second was ruining today by sulking over something that would happen tomorrow. By the time she saw a priest again—if one ever came—she'd have to spend a whole day in confession.

Yes, she had much to confess. Especially about Marcel's growing attraction to her. And ironically, also his growing anger. She shuddered.

"Are you cold, Vini?" asked Joel.

"No." Startled back to the present moment, she shoved from her mind thoughts about Marcel's cabin and Joel's leaving, and focused instead on this place, this moment, this remarkable man by her side. There would be no more sadness today!

"And now," said the mayor, "may I introduce a man who needs no introduction? The esteemed president of The Bank of Crested Butte—Mr. Richard Sterling."

The people clapped as the banker stepped forward, his black boots polished. A gray three-button jacket topped his black vest. A gold watch chain draped across his vest at the waist, and a gold pin glinted in the knot of his tie.

A gentleman even by New Orleans standards, noted Vini. His bearing reminded her of the bishop at St. Louis Cathedral, a family friend whose confidence and humility blended together like *café au lait*. Instantly she felt she could trust him.

A woman in green velvet attached herself to his arm, tilting her head coyly as though posing for a portrait. Vini had noticed her on the train. Mayor Smith gestured toward her. "I have saved until last the most pleasant introduction of the day. This lovely lady is Alisa Allen, the future Mrs. Sterling." He grinned. "The good banker is building her that big house on Elk for a wedding present."

She received the applause like an encore on the stage of the Orleans Theatre.

The mayor nodded as she whispered something to him. "The bride-to-be tells me their house is to be painted yellow and will be the finest one in Crested Butte."

Her mama forgot to teach her about humility, thought Vini.

"Let's get some coffee," said Joel, ushering her through the crowd. He reached for a cup on the white damask cloth.

"Let me, *monsieur*." She drew his coffee from the silver samovar and handed it to him with a smile. Choosing tea for herself, she unconsciously poured it as Mama had taught her.

"You are amazing! You seem to feel at home whether you're standing on the porch of Company housing or surrounded by all this elegance."

As she sipped from the china cup, she raised her eyes to his. "I feel at home when I'm with you." She wanted to add *cher*. Too shy to use the word, she hoped her eyes said it for her.

"You make it hard for a man to leave, Marie-Vincente Prejean."

She glimpsed Fred King approaching them with hate-filled eyes. She stiffened like a soldier at the Battle of Vicksburg.

Marshal Hays intersected him. The two men spoke with a quiet intensity more deadly than a shouting match. "I've been looking for you this week."

"I had to go to Denver."

"For a memorable Saturday night?" It was obvious that the marshal was enjoying grandstanding. The story had spread, and swallowed titters echoed around them.

King's eyes glinted steel.

"Let's get something straight. That little shenanigan you pulled may work in the big city. But nobody in my town tells people who to hire and fire. It creates a gust of bad feelings that turns into a cyclone."

"You—"

"I'm not finished." Marshal Hays rubbed his hand across his star. "My great-grandfather fought in the Revolution to free this land from royalty, and my grandfather fought in the War of 1812 to ensure that same freedom, and my father fought in the Civil War to make our country free for all people. And I'll be damned—pardon me, Ma'am—if anybody is going to turn my town into a monarchy! Not even Mr. Heffron. And certainly not you!"

"You are forgetting one important detail, Marshal," countered King with his cocky smirk. "Before long Heffron Enterprises will own most of the town, a lot of the state, and a chunk of the country. There will come a day when you need someone of influence to help you keep your office."

The marshal's face turned red with rage and his hand flew automatically to his holster. The gasp of the crowd stopped him just short of drawing. "I don't know whether that was a bribe or a threat. But any more hints at either, and you'll need 'someone of influence' to get you out of my jail!"

King's smirk faded. Silently he twisted the gold ring on his little finger.

As the marshal passed Vini, he smiled. "You be sure to call on me if anyone bothers you, Miss Prejean."

"Thank you, Marshal Hays."

"And I'll feel free to do the same, Ma'am. I learned at the Star that you've got grit!" He grinned and winked at Joel.

"I'll put our cups back and then let me show you the next floor, Vini." On his way the banker called to him, and Joel smiled. "Greetings, Mr. Sterling."

"Could you visit with me for a minute?" He came straight to the point. "I had a discussion with McAllister and Craig about a rumor I'd heard."

Joel shrugged. "I was fired. I know they didn't want to do it."

"Exactly. King threatened to ruin their business." He sighed heavily. "People have a hard time understanding that a man like him has no power unless they give it to him."

"But it happens time and time again."

"He's a master of intimidation. I made it clear to McAllister and Craig that Joel McGragor continues as building foreman for my house, or I hire a different company to finish it."

"Thank you, Mr. Sterling. But I don't want a job that's going to cause folk problems."

"King won't make trouble for them. I've taken full responsibility."

"I have other plans now. But I should be back in about six weeks."

"Six weeks it is then."

"Aren't you afraid of the bank's losing Heffron Enterprise business?"

"The money in my bank comes from the locals and other investors who want to shape this new state in a great way. I refuse be controlled by an outside entrepreneur. Besides," he smiled, "it's the only bank in town."

Raw silk trimmed the windows of the third-story parlor, and a grate stove gave the room a warm glow. Best of all it was empty and quiet. Joel realized that Vini, too, was quiet. "Is something wrong?"

"If this were Louisiana, Fred King would challenge you to a duel."

"Because we disagree?"

"Because he hates you. Have you ever noticed his eyes when he looks at you?"

Joel shrugged. "He thrives on being a puppeteer, and I don't hook up to strings."

Vini frowned. "You bristle like a Doberman Pinscher when he's around. Does he pull that string?"

"Whoa!" His anger flared. A man would have flinched, but Vini's eyes caressed him. He wondered if he had heard the truth. Was he not as free of King as he thought? Joel heaved a deep sigh. "He represents everything I dislike in a man."

"For me too. Enough of King." She took his arm and pointed to the settee. "I want to show you something. Francine saved a stack of old newspapers for the cabin walls. I've been reading while I papered. Guess what I found!" Opening her handbag, she withdrew a clipping and unfolded it. "Chief Ouray's obituary!" She leaned beside him, sharing the clipping while reading it aloud:

"Born in Colorado c. 1833.

Married Chipeta, 1859.

Became chief of the Uncompahgre Utes, 1860.

Became a Methodist, 1878.

Died at Los Pinos Agency, August 24, 1880."

He listened to her musical accent chanting the lines in a beautiful eulogy for his friend.

"Chief Ouray's whole life in only five lines," she said sadly.

"So far, my life is only one line: Born about 1862."

"Mine, too. Born St. Valentine's Day, 1864."

"I'm almost ready for the second line. As soon as I strike it rich." He yearned to enfold her in his arms, but instead he rose from the settee. "There's an adjoining room I want you to see." He took her hand and led her to the door. Holding the brass pull, he opened it. "The bridal chamber."

The lace curtains glistened as white as the peaks, forming beautiful patterns of light on the crimson carpet. Lace pillow shams and a coverlet lined in blue satin topped the Eastlake maple bed. Matching satin pleats edged in lace adorned the canopy above.

"This is where I'm spending my honeymoon." He stepped closer to Vini. His chin brushed her hair. She looked up at him, and their eyes held. The sun danced through the lace curtains, and the shadows played on her face. Desire for her broiled within him like a volcano on the verge of eruption. "Dearest Vini. I love you."

Her eyes looked into his soul. "*Cher monsieur.*"

Through the window he saw the Red Lady shimmering in the sun, reminding him of treasure. But in that moment he discovered he'd already found it.

CHAPTER 6

ini measured time from Saturday to Saturday when she went to the Company Store. She longed for Joel's return, missing him more than she'd thought possible. He'd been gone a long time. Nearly a month and a half. What if he didn't come back? She shoved away the thought. *Holy Mother, please keep him safe.* But she drew little confidence from the prayer, beginning to wonder if the Holy Mother's interest in folk stopped on the east bank of the Mississippi.

She had finished papering the whole cabin, but it was still too cold. And Francine seemed to be getting worse. Care of her filled the bleak winter days and fear of Marcel lengthened the cold dark nights. How she wanted to get away from this one-room cabin! From undressing each night in the corner behind the tall oak headboard and walking to the pallet in her gown and lying there feeling Marcel's haunting eyes in the night after the candle was blown out. She shouldn't be here. She needed to be here.

She opened her old brown trunk and took from the *fleur-de-lis* patterned tray the pair of deerskin gloves Joel had given her for Christmas, feeling his presence.

"Your . . . young man," wheezed Francine, "is . . . thoughtful."

Vini smiled at her. "I love being with him, *chère*. Looking up at him and seeing his honest eyes. Feeling his big hand enfold mine. Talking together about things important to us both." She didn't add how much she longed to be held securely in his strong arms. And, yes, to hold him also. Just thinking of him brought a song to her soul.

But thoughts were not enough. What emptiness she felt. Lonely for Joel. Lonely for family and friends. Lonely for New Orleans. Christmas had brought little joy and lots of homesickness. Part of the problem was the short days. The high peaks surrounding the small valley hoarded the light till long after dawn and stole it away early at dusk. A wave of homesickness splashed over her.

She thought about three-spired Saint Louis Cathedral dominating Jackson Square. And the magnificent paintings on its ceiling. And the way the windows caught the light. And sitting with Mama and Papa at mass. And the bells tolling on special occasions. There had been no bells this Christmas. And Joel had been away.

Even the waters here flowed the wrong direction—toward the Pacific Ocean instead of the Atlantic. And the Slate was a mere ribbon of a river compared to the mighty Mississippi. And Coal Creek rushed through Crested Butte, so different from the slow-moving bayous of Louisiana. She missed chicory coffee. And Café du Monde where Papa would take her for *café au lait* and *beignets* on Saturday mornings, and they would clap to the beat of the street musicians. There would be no music today. And Joel was still away.

She glanced up at the peaks he enjoyed so much, wishing she could share with him her own favorite view—a silent bayou ambling along and filled with tall cypress trees, their limbs dripping Spanish moss and filtering the sunlight as it danced on the water. The view before her was rugged; memory's view was refined. Like the rugged West, and the refined South. Perhaps like Joel, and herself.

Martha opened the door following her soft knock. "You take your time at the Company Store, child. I'm going to tell Francine all about the banker's big wedding. I heard about it from someone who heard about it from someone who'd actually been there." She hung her coat on the wooden peg by the door. "Is that handsome Joel McGragor back yet?"

"No, Ma'am."

"I heard Mr. Sterling took care of his job," said Martha.

Vini nodded. "McAllister and Craig are saving it for him."

Martha scooted one of the stump stools beside the bed, sat down, and began darning the socks she'd brought. "Not that it's any of my business, but I feel sorry for Mr. Sterling with that new wife. They say she shows up at the house when the workers come and bosses everybody around. She's in such a hurry for it to get done that she expects them to work in thunderstorm and blizzard."

"She won't be able to boss Joel around," Vini commented.

"Anyway, the wedding was some pumpkins! A big affair at the Elk Mountain House. That is no picayune place! They say it has water closets at the back and three bath tubs with hot and cold running water. And would you believe a three-story outhouse—inside!" Martha shook her head. "But I always suspicion a wedding that isn't held in a church. A justice of the peace performed the ceremony instead of a priest. That's just next to living in sin!"

"Thank you for staying, Martha." Vini took down her cloak, got her basket, and blew her sister a kiss. Weakly, Francine raised her fingers in a silent goodbye.

The January snow danced around Vini, and the smell of the coke ovens permeated the thin air. Henry had continued to give her credit at the Company

Store, and he'd been nice to her today—as always now. She wondered if he'd heard about what happened after delivering her to the Star. Perhaps Henry disliked King too but was afraid to show it. No one wanted to be treated like a lackey, and his boss excelled at that.

As she crossed to the south side of Elk, meager groceries in hand, she saw Doc Williams opening the door to his office. Maybe he wouldn't charge just for talking with her about Francine. "Good morning, Doc Williams. I hope you and your family are well."

His glasses hung on his nose, and his brows arched in a question beneath his receding red hair.

"I am Vini Prejean. I'm worried about my sister."

"Come on in." A strong odor of disinfectant permeated the room. Everything was black or white or silver. Unconsciously Vini put her hands behind her back as she'd done as a child when she wasn't supposed to touch anything. Doc Williams took off his coat and hung it on the rack. "Have I seen her?"

Vini nodded. "Francine Joubert."

He looked puzzled.

"Her husband is Marcel. He works for the Jokerville, and they live in Company housing.

"She isn't still here!" he shouted.

Vini jumped. She pulled her cape close around her like armor against impending doom. "I don't understand."

He gestured her to the black leather settee. "Marcel was to make arrangements."

"Arrangements? He told me you said that nothing else could be done."

He stared at her silently, a fierce frown on his face.

"I try to take good care of her, *monsieur*."

Kindness softened his worn face and he sank down beside her. "I'm sure you do. But no one can make her well here."

"Not even you?"

"It's too cold, and the altitude is too high. I made it absolutely clear to Marcel some months ago that she needed to get out of Crested Butte immediately."

The edges of Vini's mind groped for the full meaning of his words.

"Otherwise she won't make it till spring."

Icy claws knotted her stomach and traveled to her throat.

"I told him to get her back to . . . Was it New Orleans? Is that where your family is?"

She nodded, sickened by the realization that the money to get her here should have been used to get Francine home. She bit her lip and stared at her white knuckles gripping the arm rest.

"Vini, are you all right?"

No! She nodded yes.

Doc Williams got up and paced angrily. "Why didn't Marcel do something about it! Doesn't that man love his own wife?"

"He loves her very much, *monsieur.*" An unthinkable alternative pounded at her conscience. Numbly she rose. "Thank you for your time."

"You're pale. Sit back down."

She obeyed, and the tears came. "Marcel is afraid of Papa."

Doc Williams put his hand gently on her shoulder. "Like so many here, he hungers for the dreams that brought him West and turns to drinking to fill the emptiness."

Something in Doc Williams' tone made her wonder if he had experienced the same thing.

He sat down beside her again, quietly reflective. "Marcel is too prideful to go back home a failure with his tail between his legs. Especially if he's afraid to face your father." He looked at the floor, elbow on knee, forehead in hand. "Oh, Vini. I've seen it time and time again."

"Well right now he can't afford the luxury of self-pity!" With a sigh of resignation she added almost in a whisper, "But neither can he afford the tickets."

"And he's trapped by his debt to the Company Store."

"I'll fix it! Somehow."

"Oh, little one." Doc Williams' voice reminded her of Papa's gentleness. "It isn't your responsibility. It is Marcel's. By now it's probably too late for her to make the trip anyway."

Sainte Marie, Mère de Dieu!

"You just do your best to make each day she has left a beautiful gift. That's the only way you can help her now. But it's an important one."

Vini stood, tucking back a lock of hair. She set her jaw and lifted her chin. "She will get back home, Doc Williams! I will see to it!"

Vini stumbled from his office and crisscrossed Elk and Third toward Groenendyke's window where the job notices were posted. She read every single one but found no night job for a woman. She felt like she'd slammed into a stone levee. She trudged on unseeing. People and buildings blurred around her. As she passed the Star Restaurant, the door opened and she heard her name.

"Vini! You're as white as a clean apron. Come in here."

As though in a sleepwalk she felt Rose's hand on her arm and found herself seated at the far corner table. She tried to stop shivering but couldn't. She wrapped her cloak tighter, drawing a wall around herself.

"Are you sick? Let me get you some tea." Rose brought it immediately and added two spoons of sugar.

"Thank you." Vini's hand trembled as she lifted the blue and white stoneware cup from the saucer.

Rose sat down with her and asked kindly, "What happened, hon?"

Vini didn't know how to begin.

"It isn't Joel?" Fear filled Rose's face.

She shook her head, realizing that would be worse. Guilt for the thought struck her heart.

"I'm glad he's all right. Fred King hasn't done something to you?"

"No. Yes—the way he traps miners."

"Is it your sister? I heard she's ill."

"She won't live till spring unless I earn the money to get her home. And I have to hurry before it's too late." She heard her own words as though from a distance.

"I wish I could offer you a job. But I barely make enough to live on."

Rose's kindness and the strong sweet tea brought Vini to herself. She held back tears. She always had trouble with tears when people were kind to her. "I couldn't work days anyway. I need to stay with her while Marcel is at the mine."

"I'm afraid there is only one kind of night work for women in this town."

Vini felt that awful blush, and awareness of it caused the flush to deepen.

"We'll have to figure something out. But it may take some time."

"There isn't any time." Vini finished her tea. "I'm better now. Thank you. You're as kind as Joel said, Rose."

"He told you that I'm kind?" The joy in her face revealed that even though she was at least fifteen years older than Joel, she was in love with him—a long distance kind of love that knew its passion would never be returned, and also, suspected Vini, would never die.

Vini walked on along the boardwalk feeling utterly powerless and desperate. When she reached Second, instead of turning toward Company housing her feet crossed the Coal Creek bridge and made their way to the Forest Queen. She mustered her courage. *I have to do this, Mama. For Francine.*

As she opened the door, Tillie saw her and smiled, then looked horrified. "What are you doing here!"

"At the depot, Ma'am, you said if I needed help to come to the Forest Queen and ask for you."

"Come up to my room quick before anyone sees you."

Vini sat down in a red velvet chair against a wall papered in scarlet. She told Tillie about Francine and what Doc Williams had said. Tillie listened quietly with full attention. How easy it was to talk to her. "So . . . I don't know what to do."

"Vini, getting Francine to New Orleans is Marcel's responsibility."

"Yes, Ma'am. But he has known for a long time and hasn't done anything." Guilt tugged her heart.

Tillie was silent for a few moments, her blue eyes moving back and forth as thoughts connected. "I think I see it all, Vini. That man isn't worth shucks. You do need to get out of that cabin at night—job or no job. If you don't, you're going to wind up the victim of his rage or his passion. Or both."

Tillie had spoken aloud what Vini feared silently. "Is there a . . . a job here?"

"No! I'm sorry, but if you work here—even doing something . . . else— your reputation would be ruined forever. People see it as all on one stick."

"I care about my sister, not my reputation."

Tillie put her arm around Vini's shoulders. "There is something about you that stands out from other people. Something special, something so rare I can't even describe it. I can only recognize it."

"I don't know what you're talking about."

"Of course not. And not knowing it is part of what makes you so special." Tillie stared at the bed with its red coverlet. "I'm not going to be part of wrecking your life. It's too late for me. No one turned me away."

"But Francine—"

"If she's anything like you, she'd be here too if the tables were turned. And if you found out, you'd be horrified."

Vini knew that was true.

"And if she knew you were here right now, she would be just as horrified."

That too was true.

"Stick to your destiny, Vini."

"What good is destiny if my sister dies?"

"I have some money saved. You can borrow it."

The offer tempted her, but she couldn't take money she didn't know how she would repay. She sighed, close to tears at this kindness. "No, but thank you, Ma'am." *Holy Mother, please show me a way.*

"Don't hang up your fiddle, Vini. It will work out. Just don't do anything you know is wrong." Tillie smiled at her. "Now, let's get you out of here without anyone seeing you."

They started down the back stairs just as Fred King started up them.

Vini rushed out the door of the Forest Queen and almost collided with Joel.

"Whoa, there!"

"*Joel*!" She fell against him, overwhelmed with gratitude.

He wrapped her in his arms. "Dearest Vini. I've missed you so!" He bent and kissed her right there on Elk Avenue. He kissed her again. And again. Kissed her until they heard the applause. They opened their eyes to a circle of folk on the boardwalk.

She felt herself blush, but she didn't step back.

"Greetings, friends," said Joel, keeping his arm around her waist like he was afraid she'd get away.

Not a chance, she thought.

The people moved jovially on down the boardwalk with their grins and whistles and "Way to go, Joel."

He tucked his finger under her chin. "Let me just look at you again. I thought you couldn't be as pretty as my memory of you, Marie-Vincente Prejean. But you're even more beautiful."

"Did Chipeta know about your father?"

"Yes." He hesitated. "I have a lot to tell you. Would you have dinner with me tonight?"

"I'm fixing red beans and rice if you would like to come."

"Let me take you to the Star."

She nodded. "I can't believe you're back!"

"I just got here. I checked with McAllister and Craig first thing, then planned to clean up and drop by your cabin before going to work." He raised one eyebrow. "I didn't expect to find you coming out of the Forest Queen."

The Forest Queen. "I'm looking for a night job." The shock on his face sent her reeling. "Surely you don't think . . ."

"Of course not." He frowned. "But what's this about a job?"

Her words tumbled forth. "I need to get the money for Francine and Marcel to go back to New Orleans. Doc Williams told Marcel a long time ago that Francine must leave. Or she'll—" She couldn't say it.

Joel's jaw tightened. "How could a woman like your sister marry him!"

"He should have taken her home instead of sending for me."

"I can't be sorry that he sent for you." He held her tenderly.

She lost the battle for control and began to weep.

Lifting her chin again, he studied her face. "I'll take care of it. You will always be able to count on me, dearest Vini."

Yes, she thought. Always and forever.

"We need to settle one thing. A job at the Forest Queen is out of the question."

"Tillie wouldn't hire me."

"Especially for the lady who is my future wife." He tipped his hat and gave her his courtly nod. "If you'll have me, Ma'am."

He'd turned away before she could answer, leaving her standing there dumbfounded in front of the Forest Queen. She stared after him, waving her gloved hand. A warm hand. A claimed hand!

Then she remembered Fred King watching her coming down the stairs of the Forest Queen, that smirk on his face. What kind of story would he tell? And tell it, he would. A sordid one for revenge, she was sure. One contrived to hurt her. And to hurt Joel. And folk love a whisper story.

As she walked back to Company housing, she thought again of Joel. His tipped hat and courtly nod. His words, *my future wife.* And she thought again of Francine. She felt severed in two by ecstasy and agony. Hope and helplessness. The offering of new life and the threat of death. The joy of a beginning and the fear of an ending. Her soul seemed to split. She could hardly endure the wrenching pain.

CHAPTER 7

*V*ini and Joel climbed the attic steps in the banker's unfinished house. A candle flickered in the darkness, and a moonglow lit the white earth, casting soft light through the attic windows. Dinner at the Star had been a series of interruptions by people welcoming him back to town. Afterward he'd offered to show her this house. It felt good to be alone with him.

His eyes grew intense. "Finally I know who I am." They sat on a saw-horse hand-in-hand as he shared the story Chipeta had told him:

There was a little girl four years old whose family headed west. Their covered wagon was last. The wagon train had been delayed many times, and now they were moving fast, afraid of winter. She fell out of the back of the covered wagon and hit her head on a rock. When she came to, she couldn't see any sign of the wagon train. She ran as fast as she could following the ruts until she became hot and thirsty. She saw some willows and thought there might be a stream. She wandered toward them. The willows were over her head, but she kept going until she found a creek. She cupped the water in her hand to drink and splashed it on her face to cool off. She felt tired and weak from hunger, and she rested beside the creek. She probably fell asleep.

Later she saw a horseman topping the hill on the horizon, headed away. She thought he might be from the wagon train and looking for her. She ran through the willows, shouting at him. But she was too small to be seen, and he was too far away to hear. By the time she reached the edge of the willows, he was gone.

Thunder and rain came that night and she burrowed in the willows near the creek.

A few days later a band of Apaches found her. Blond hair, blue eyes, alone, dirty and hungry, and a bump on her head where she had hit the rock. But she wasn't crying. The chief respected that. When she saw him, she didn't scream or try to run away. She didn't even seem to notice he was different. She ran toward him in total trust and threw her arms around his neck. That hug gave her a special place in his heart.

The chief could speak some English, and she told him what had happened. Still she didn't cry. He set her on his pony and took her to his sister whose little girl about the same age had recently died.

When she was grown, the chief's son married her and became chief himself. In time they had a little boy. And two years afterwards while the men were away hunting, the blue coats came and massacred all the women and children in the camp. They never found the chief's son.

"So, that's it, Vini. I'm the son of a Chiricahua Apache chief and a woman whose family headed west. And I was reared by a gentleman with more integrity than anyone I've ever known. And all three are dead."

Vini put her arms around him and held him. Held him for the mother who'd been so brave. Held him for the chief who'd never found him. Held him for the father who'd reared him so well. She had no words. She gave of her presence and the tears that rose from her soul.

Vini checked on Francine and drew the curtain around her bed. She changed quickly into her gown for she'd learned the wisdom of pretending to be asleep by the arrival of the Saturday night drunk from the Bucket of Blood. She would deal with Marcel about Doc Williams tomorrow when he was sober enough to think like a gentleman—if he could still remember how. She poured hot water from the kettle to wash her face, listening with pleasure to the sound as it trickled into the tin basin. She put the kettle back on the stove and heard heavy footsteps on the porch. Trapped!

The door creaked open and closed. Marcel swaggered toward her.

She sensed a difference in his attitude. Unabashedly brazen. No barriers. Like the wall of respect had tumbled.

"Too good for me, huh? That game is over." His yellow-flecked eyes took in her face. They moved downward inch by inch. Feasting on her. Then back up again, once more. Slowly.

Her heart raced in terror. Don't show fear! She continued washing her face.

"You and me, Vini." His lips curled into a half-smile. With one hand he yanked the washrag from her and dropped it. With the other he took hold of her wrist and pinned one arm behind her back.

She tried to jerk away and winced from pain.

He pinned the other arm and grasped them both with one hand. He gripped her tight.

She felt his body against hers. Nausea rose to her throat. "Don't, Marcel," she whispered. "Francine . . . "

"You act like Miss Prim and Proper in this cabin. Then you prance down to the Forest Queen."

"But—"

"Don't deny it!" He started to strike her.

She turned her face sideways and closed her eyes, steeled for the blow.

He stopped himself. "It's all over town that Mr. King saw you coming down the stairs."

Holy Mother, please let me wake up and find this a nightmare.

His free hand clutched the neck of her gown.

She silenced a scream. Don't wake Francine! Don't let her see this.

"You and me. That's how it's going to be." His face came closer. His breath quickened. His tongue slid between his lips like a snake.

NO! Rage surged. Strength doubled. She broke his grip on her arms. Jumped back from him.

His grasp on her gown held. It ripped. His eyes hungered. He grabbed her. *The whisper weapon!* She focused all her force. Rammed her knee.

He groaned and doubled over.

She sprang to the door and leaped off the porch, running barefoot through the snow. She banged on the Donegans' door, shivering. Nausea made her dizzy. She gagged and vomited over the porch rail, her torn white gown shimmering in the silver moonlight.

Iber opened the door, shotgun in hand. "Vini! Come in here before you freeze to death!"

Safely inside, she leaned back against the log wall, breathing heavily. Her knees buckled. She willed them to stand.

He struck a match and lit a candle. For a moment he stared at her, his eyes shocked and angry. "Marcel?"

She nodded, holding her torn gown together.

"Do you need Doc?"

Vini closed her eyes and shook her head.

Iber led her around the pallets of his children to a chair. Martha removed the quilt from their bed and put it around her. For once, she gave no advice. Instead, she said, "I'm sorry, child."

Child. The word took Vini back to New Orleans and a happy childhood world, untainted. Farewell innocence.

The sun painted the sky with shades of blue and pink before it rose over the mountains on this quiet Sunday morning. Joel opened the door to Mr. Sterling's house and climbed the stairs to the northeast bedroom. He began to check the quality of the work, partly because McAllister and Craig had requested it, but mostly because after he struck it rich he might buy this house from the banker. This room of morning sun would be his and Vini's bedroom. It was an amazing thing to be loved by the prettiest girl in Colorado. He fantasized placing a big diamond ring on her fourth finger.

His joy faded as he remembered her fear for Francine. The best present he could give Vini wasn't a diamond ring in the future but fare to New Orleans for her sister now. He thought about the money in his savings account. It should be just about enough to get two people to New Orleans.

A miner couldn't quit the Jokerville if he owed any money to the Company Store. Every fiber in Joel resisted the idea of taking on Marcel Joubert's debt, but he could see no other way. He felt sure Mr. Sterling would lend him the money. This encumbrance would slow down his plans. But it seemed necessary. For the sake of Francine. For Vini.

Maybe Marcel would take a turn for the better back in New Orleans. Maybe he would get a good job and do the honorable thing and repay him. As likely as manmade snow!

Joel glanced out the upstairs window and saw Nick coming down the boardwalk. His pace showed purpose. Joel noted his bowed head and sagging shoulders. Bad news. He heard the front door open and leaned over the banister. "Greetings, Nick."

"It's cold enough out there to freeze a mule whip midair."

"You sound testy this morning."

"Joel McGragor, you're certain-sure as hard to find as an empty bar stool on pay day. You get back yesterday and you don't tell the man whose been worrying about you like a freighter hauling nitro. Old Nick has to learn about it at Pat Daly's. And you don't even show up there."

"I'm sorry," said Joel as he reached the bottom step.

"So I'm the one who hears the bad rumor. I'm the one who has to go to the Bucket of Blood to check it out."

"Nice place," said Joel sarcastically. "What's eating at you?" He'd long ago learned Nick's tendency to rant like this when something was wrong—as though shooting off enough words could dispel the demon in the air.

"Where do you spit in this house?"

"Off the boardwalk."

"You don't make nothing easy for a man." Nick returned and closed the door behind him. He took a deep breath and began talking fast. "Last night King sent Henry from saloon to saloon to invite the men to the Bucket of Blood for the best entertainment in town. He said a miner was telling stories they wouldn't want to miss."

No one could tell windier tales than Nick. "Did you have a contest? You're not all testy this morning because someone topped you?"

Nick raised his bushy brows. "King is at the Bucket of Blood. He corners a particular miner and tells him about seeing a girl at the Forest Queen. It seems that miner knows her pretty well and gets as mad as a prospector whose claim is jumped. King offers him drinks to goad him into telling stories about her."

Joel only half-listened, wondering how many colorful and off-color stories he'd heard Nick tell.

"He tells about this pretty little thing. 'Just dropped on my doorstep,'" Nick mimicked, "'like a present from Santa Claus. What's a man to do?'" Nick looked at the floor, the ceiling, out the parlor window—everywhere but at Joel. "He begins to describe his nightly capers with her. One tale after another for one drink after another." The old freighter whistled softly. "He sure don't leave nothing out. And some of the men are fool enough to believe him."

"So?" Joel sat down on the bottom step, waiting for Nick to repeat one of the stories.

But instead, Nick concentrated on tracing the windowsill with his finger. "I'll give it to you straight, but you aren't going to like it." He turned from the window, the mask of buffoonery set aside. "The girl that miner told those imaginary filthy stories about lives with him. She is seventeen. Came in on the first train. From New Orleans."

"*Joubert!*" Red washed the room. Joel knocked a sawhorse out of the way and slammed out the door. Fists clenching. Blood sizzling. He rammed two men aside on Elk. Others stepped out of his way.

Nick followed. People joined in line behind, sure to see a fight.

Joel's long legs raced to Second Street. He turned and collided with Iber Donegan. "Out of my way, Iber!" Joel picked him up by his coat collar and lifted him off the snow-packed path.

Iber grabbed his arm. "I was coming to find you. Joubert attacked Vini last night. She's at my cabin."

Rage! Red rage! Rage of hot molten lava ran through his blood, muscles, mind. He charged ahead to tear Joubert apart.

The crowd followed, deadly silent now.

He saw Marcel pounding on the Donegans' door. "Joubert!" Joel closed the gap. Leaped over the porch rail. Grabbed him and spun him around. The first blow rammed Joubert against the log wall of the cabin. The second pitched him off the porch. Joel dived after him in the snow. Blindly he hit him. Again and again. He saw nothing but red. Red everywhere. The red of Joubert's bandanna. The red of blood. The red glow of the coke ovens. The red of the Lady's ruby lips. The red sky of the sunrise. And then a red ribbon and a desperate voice cried through the spinning red of rage.

"Joel! No! Stop! You'll kill him!" Tears fell from red eyes down red cheeks.

Vini's voice called him back to sanity. He wiped the back of his hand across his mouth and glanced down at Joubert. He left him there like a heap of garbage in the snow. He put his hands gently on Vini's slight shoulders. "Are you all right?"

She nodded.

But as he looked at her, small and scared, he knew that she was not. He realized that she would carry the scar of Marcel with her all the rest of her life.

He took her in his arms and held her, hating himself for not being there to protect her when she needed him.

"I forgot to tell you about my temper," he said finally. "Will you marry me anyway?" The magic question. Without moonlight and music and a diamond ring.

Her loving eyes said yes. But her voice said, "Francine—" The word came in deep, torn agony.

"Don't worry, Vini. I told you I'll take care of everything."

The next morning Joel set out determined to do what he had to do. First he went to the bank, drew out all his money, and walked briskly to the railroad station. The ticket agent exchanged his cash for two train tickets and paddleboat vouchers to New Orleans. Joel counted his change. Ten silver dollars. All that was left of his savings for prospecting.

He tightened his jaw and went straight to the Jokerville Mine to see Jim Robbins, superintendent. He explained the situation and answered a few questions.

"That sounds reasonable to me," said Jim. "I have to telephone Mr. King for approval."

Joel watched him crank the telephone. "You don't see any problem?"

Jim smiled, reassuring him. "It's fair and no risk to the company. Mr. King knows that we can trust you to pay off Joubert's debt."

Still, Joel had a sense of foreboding. He began to pace the floor.

"Mr. King, Jim Robbins here," he said into the mouthpiece in the box on the wall. . . . "Mrs. Joubert is quite ill and must leave Crested Butte." . . . "Yes, I know that rule, but a man is willing to sign an IOU for Marcel's debts. Or get a loan and pay them off now." . . . "Yes. It seems like a fair request to me too." . . . "No need to worry about the debt. Joel McGragor is a man of his word."

Joel saw Jim's smile disappear. A deep frown creased his forehead.

"But, Mr. King—" . . . Robbins listened in silence, slowly shaking his head. "But—" . . . "I understand." He placed the ear piece back on its hook and stared at the telephone box for a long moment.

Joel waited while doom reverberated silently through the room.

Finally Jim turned to him, his face grave. "King will release Joubert from the Jokerville. But he has three restrictions. He said they're nonnegotiable." When he spoke again, his voice was barely audible and filled with shame. "One, the debt must be transferred in full to you instead of paid in cash. Two, you must repay it through labor for Heffron Enterprises. Three, you must take Marcel Joubert's shift in the Jokerville Mine."

In the darkest reaches of Joel's mind, he'd known this was possible. But he hadn't believed even King would stoop so low. "That's the deal?"

"That's King's deal—not mine. But he has the final word."

"Right." But it was terribly wrong. Don't feel. Don't think. Just get it done. Jim Robbins sighed and shook his head. "I'm sorry, Joel. If I could afford to quit in protest, I would. But my family . . ."

"The Jokerville." The blow to his dream left a hollow cavity. Despair hovered to fill the void. "Life is a Jokerville."

In his mind he could see King gloating, caressing his gold ring. But there is all the difference, he realized, between *giving* myself and *selling* myself—a difference men of expediency like King can't even begin to understand. *I'll take care of everything.* Steadfast, he lifted the yoke and put it on.

Robbins went with him to speak to the cashier at the Company Store. Henry Coughlin eyed Joel nervously and fumbled through the ledger. He found Joubert's sheet, marked through the name, transferred the account to Joel McGragor, and handed it to him to sign.

For a moment Joel faltered. Once done there would be no way out of this sentence to the methane-leaking dungeon. He knew that King would do everything possible to thwart the repayment of Joubert's debt and keep him there permanently.

Fully aware of the system of entrapment and of his own vulnerability to that entrapment, he picked up the pen, dipped it into the inkwell, and signed his name. The pen scratched across the paper like a death rattle.

Done! One more day of freedom, of sunshine, of the fresh smell of the spruce trees before Joel descended into hell. He attached his handmade eleven-foot wooden skis to his boots. He held the single aspen pole in his right hand and tossed his saddlebag over his left shoulder. Gliding across the snow, he followed the old Kebler Indian Trail for a ways and then headed upward toward the Red Lady and the camel-shaped boulder he called his own. He'd always felt in control of his destiny when he raced through space on his skis with the wind rushing into his face. But not today. His life had come to its Continental Divide, with the waters of yesterday flowing one way and the waters of tomorrow another way.

Breathing heavily, he reached the boulder and scanned the panoramic view of the Elk Mountains stretching into the cloudy sky. He thought about all his hopes and dreams the first time he'd stood here mesmerized by the beauty around him: *No man could ask for more!* To the west rose Kebler Pass that the Utes would trod no more. Northward, the Oh-Be-Joyful Mountains loomed above him, leaving him joyless. Crested Butte Mountain stood guard to the east, a monolith once calling to him in a special way. His eyes slid down its jagged peak to the cemetery just below. He knew the cold gray tombstones stared back. His skin tingled.

He turned to face the basin of the Red Lady, whose lips had always smiled down at him. "You whore!" he yelled. "You tempt a man with hidden treasure and tease him with false promises! You give him the pleasure of a moment's dream. Then leave him empty and unfulfilled!"

The Lady continued to smile.

He laid his bandanna on the snow-covered boulder, unbuckled his saddlebag and pulled out his meager collection of valued possessions. First he opened the small box which held his mother's distinctive cross of gold outlined in silver—the only gold and silver he might ever have. The feel of the cross seared him with the power of her love and the image of her death. The cacophony of soldiers, the screams of women and children, the stench of blood, the massacred bodies scattered among the tepees.

He leaned against the boulder and stared at the second object, the picture of his father, Chief Ouray, and himself. A vivid memory stung him anew—his father lying on his death bed, sharing the story of his mother, while Joel watched the transformation of his loved face into a hollow ghostlike mask. Again the self-obliterating pain of his father's death filled his senses, his mind, his soul.

He looked at the third item, Chief Ouray's white bone-handled knife. It had been a gift to Ouray, who was half-Apache, from a Chiricahua Apache chief. Now he knew from Chipeta why she had passed it on to him, and he understood why it had drawn him so powerfully. He lifted the knife with reverence, tingling with awareness of the lingering touch of his birth father's hand.

Joel looked again at the view. *No man could ask for more.* There would be no view in the dungeon. Primeval despair filled his soul. Rising to his full height, he shouted into the universe: "None but the rich can afford to dream!" His own words echoed back to him, and he lifted high his arms, bearing the knife and shaking his fist at the Giver and the Taker of Dreams.

That evening Joel tramped through the snow to Company Housing. Vini ran down the snowy path to meet him and threw her arms around his neck, burying her head in his chest. "I've been worried about you," she said breathlessly.

"I had a lot to think about."

She looked up at him in the moonlight, and her smile faded. "You look terrible."

He pulled the tickets from his pocket. "These will get Francine and Marcel back to New Orleans. They leave tomorrow."

She stared at the tickets as though the miracle might disappear if she took her eyes away. "How did you get them?"

"I told you I'd take care of everything."

"But how?"

"I had some money saved."

She groaned. "That was for prospecting."

"Marcel's debt at the Company Store has been transferred to me." He said the words staccato-like, distancing them, pronouncing his own sentence. "I'll be working in the Jokerville."

"Sainte Marie, Mère de Dieu!"

"I start Wednesday."

"I can't let you do that!"

"It's already done. And it can't be undone." Strangely, the finality brought him comfort. This was the hand he'd accepted. Now the task was to play it as well as he could.

"No, Joel!" She began to sob. "I thought I wanted Francine to get to New Orleans more than anything," she said brokenly. "But I don't want you to pay that price."

"Don't look at this as permanent, Vini. I don't intend to get trapped in the mining system. This may take a couple of years. But Francine's life is well worth the delay of a dream."

"Cher monsieur. I love you with all my heart."

"You and I are getting married tomorrow afternoon." As he kissed her, he felt the ache in his soul begin to ebb and new life begin to stir. Whatever the future held, the one thing he knew for sure was that he wanted Vini to share it with him.

For a long time he held her close. "I came to Colorado to find treasure. I used to think it was buried in the mountains, but now I know that it's a five-foot package of jewels. Hair of darkest onyx, eyes of opal, cheeks of ruby, complexion of pearl. And a sparkling spirit like diamonds." He lifted her chin. "For me, wherever is Vini, *there* is treasure."

On Tuesday morning Vini fluffed Francine's pillow so she could lie propped up and give packing orders as needed. Vini wondered if her sister knew of Marcel's attack. If so, she pretended otherwise. As much as Vini wanted healing for Francine, she could hardly endure the agony of Joel's decision. She'd never known anyone like him. But there were lots of folk like Marcel, walking heavy on the earth, flailing about, knocking other people's lives out of kilter.

Martha came over to help. Organizing everything, her hands constantly busy. And all the time, talking about the wedding. "Of course it's none of my business, but Father Michael Barrett in Gunnison could tie the knot. It's important for a wedding to be performed by a priest." She eyed Vini. "It would please your mama and papa."

The idea also pleased Vini. "Come with us, Martha. Be my matron of honor." Martha beamed. Vini glanced toward Francine, wishing she could be there, knowing she wished so too. They finished the packing well before noon, and Martha went home "to get all dolled up." Vini began to dress for the wedding. The wedding. She smiled. Mama would want her to wear white. But Mama wasn't here and there wasn't time nor money to make a dress. She donned the special one her mother had made as a present for her when she left New Orleans. She straightened the front and looked over each shoulder to check the back. She glanced into the mirror above the wash basin and noted that the deep blue-green of the dress matched her eyes. Mama was good at choosing colors.

"You look lovely, *petite sœur*," said Francine.

"*Merci.*" Tenderly she smoothed the elegant white collar, feeling the presence of love in Mama's beautiful tatting. What would she think about all that had happened? "Do you remember how strict Mama was about the social graces?"

Francine nodded.

"How we would watch out the window for her to come trudging home from her hard day's work at the mansion and she would teach us everything the young heiress had learned that day." Vini's mind went back in time to their small cottage where they would spread the table with a white cloth and napkins for their simple dinner and set it "*parfait.*" And Mama would light the candle before the blessing, and insist on good manners. The social graces were not foreign to that little cottage, nor were they something Mama put on for special occasions. Vini had grown up with them. Suddenly, her heart ached. "I wish Mama could be here, and Papa could give me away." She took a deep breath to gain control.

"He'd be proud to give your hand in marriage to Joel McGragor."

The comparison with Marcel floated silently in the air like a feather, and Vini wondered if Papa had been concerned about Francine's marriage.

"I know Joel dreamed of being a mine owner, not a miner," said Francine.

"There is time. We'll be frugal and get this behind us. Joel says that being together is what counts and that will help the time go fast."

"I'm so sorry." Tears pooled in Francine's eyes. "And so grateful." She began one of her coughing spells. "One more thing," she gasped.

"Don't talk, Francine. Please. You'll choke."

Weakly she raised her hand, silencing Vini and patting the bed for her to come sit.

Vini sat down, held her sister's hand, and caressed her forehead.

"Let Joel know," she paused for breath, "that what's he's doing . . . is not in vain." She lifted her head from the pillow, and fought to get the coughing under control. "I will make it to New Orleans. . . . And I will live. . . . I promise you that." Poignantly she added, "And one day . . . Marcel will love me again."

They hugged each other, their tears mingling. At noon the train would come and take a grateful Francine and a meek Marcel away. There were no more words to say.

❈

By two-thirty that afternoon, Tuesday, January 24, 1882, Joel stood with Vini before young Father Barrett at the altar of the Roman Catholic Church in Gunnison. Nick grinned as a best man should, and Martha Donegan beamed happily beside Vini, having successfully loaded them all into Nick's wagon for the trip to Gunnison and a proper wedding.

The gentle blue eyes of the newly ordained priest contrasted markedly to his strong jaw, and his six-foot frame embodied humility of spirit. "For better, for worse; for richer, for poorer; in sickness and in health," he chanted. "Till death us do part."

Joel and Vini faced each other and repeated the words.

"Is there a ring?" asked Father Barrett.

Joel winced, recalling the big diamond ring of his fantasy. "I offer my mother's cross." He handed it to the priest who smiled and blessed it, then returned it to Joel. He fastened it around Vini's neck, looking into her eyes and floating through their sea of love.

As she touched the cross, her eyes danced with pleasure. He realized a big diamond ring wouldn't have meant as much.

"I now pronounce you husband and wife," said Father Barrett, their lives united by the timeless ritual tolling like a bell.

Joel kissed his bride. Martha dried a tear. Vini hugged her, then stood on tiptoe and kissed Nick on the cheek. The old freighter turned his other cheek. "Do it again, Mrs. McGragor. I ain't been kissed by a lady in many a year!"

As they left, Vini paused at the door to speak to Father Barrett. Then with a sudden blush she smiled shyly at Joel. Slowly, she turned and came toward him, a creature of beauty and grace—her curly hair glinting in the sun, her blue-green eyes sparkling with love, her joyful smile promising a rainbow after every storm. Suddenly she laughed and flew into his arms, a butterfly freed at last from her cocoon.

TWO

RUBY ROAD

1883

About nine o'clock this morning telegrams were received in this city stating that a fearful explosion . . . had taken place in the coal mine belonging to the Colorado Coal and Iron Company at Crested Butte . . . . [The miners] were in a second of time ushered into eternity. It is the most fearful disaster entailing a greater loss of life than any accident that has ever occurred in Colorado, or for that matter in the western states.

. . . The shed to the entrance of the mine was badly torn for fully one hundred feet . . . . The whole number killed is fifty-nine or sixty.

Gunnison Review-Press
Jan. 24, 1884

CHAPTER 8

As dawn lit the sky, Vini lay on her side in the four-poster spruce bed Joel had made, feeling him snug against her back and his arm wrapped over her waist. A kind of rare ecstasy arose within her, gratitude for life and joy in being his wife, a joy beyond any she had imagined possible, far greater than she had expected or could ever deserve. Silently she echoed Mama's daily ritual:

This is the day the Lord has made;
Let us rejoice and be glad in it.

But on the heels of this wondrous swelling of ecstasy followed a terrible dread that the trap door would open and she would free fall through the darkness of loss. "Are you awake?" she whispered.

"I thought you were still asleep."

She rolled over to face him. "I've been your wife for one year, two months, and a day. I'm so fearfully happy, *cher monsieur.*"

"*Fearfully* happy?" His eyes clouded for an instant. "You don't need to be afraid, Vini. You're my wife. No one is going to hurt you ever again."

"I didn't know it was possible to love someone so much." His eyes told her he felt the same way.

The beautiful morning reflected their joy. A false spring had rushed in, clearing the snow and fooling the earth that warm weather was here to stay. "Let's do something outside today, Vini. Are you up to a hike?"

She bounced out of bed. "I just hope you can keep up with me." She knew he loved to be outdoors on Sundays, especially during these winter months. The other six days of the week he trudged to the mine before sunrise and back again after sunset, working in darkness all day long and seeing no daylight at all.

"Let's go to the boulder."

"The place we went when you taught me to ski?"

He nodded.

"I'll fix a picnic lunch." She listened as he whistled his rhythmical tune while he dressed, common on Sundays but buried by coal dust the rest of the week. "What is that tune, Joel?"

"I didn't even realize I was whistling." He paused for a minute. "I don't know. My father whistled it when I was a boy. I suppose his father whistled it before him."

"I'll just call it 'Joel's Tune.'" She began humming along with him as she packed a lunch of homemade bread, a chunk of cheese, and summer sausage. He put their lunch in his saddlebag and flipped it over his shoulder.

They crossed Coal Creek where it curved into town, and began hiking beside it up the old Ute trail that led to Kebler Pass. A deer skirted in front of them, and chipmunks scurried passed, squeaking disapproval of their intrusion. Joel led the way, offering Vini his hand up the rough parts of the terrain.

As they climbed, Coal Creek became a chain of beaver ponds. The water separated a thick spruce forest to the left from the barren land to the right that offered only a few ponderosa pines and some scattered aspens. The separation reminded Vini of how Marcel's debt separated Joel from his dream and left him in the barren reality of the Jokerville. That debt was taking its toll on Joel. But they were on track. Ten more months to go. They left the trail and climbed up toward the Red Lady. "Isn't this the same way we came on skis, Joel?"

"Generally."

"Skiing was easier!" she said, lifting her skirt.

He laughed. "It was the overalls that made the difference."

"Let's go back to the cave."

"I'd like that too. We'll save it for another Sunday."

They ascended the ridge and stopped at the top, leaning against the camel-shaped boulder to catch their breath, silently admiring the view. Ruby Peak rose beyond Mt. Emmons. A waterfall cascaded down the rocky cliff, splashing into the stream. A miniature rainbow arched above it along the cliff wall. Rugged peaks stood like ancient sculptures against the skyline, and ageless spruce trees flowed down the mountains like green rivers. "Since the first time I came up here, I've dreamed of buying this land," said Joel softly, as though hesitant to break the spell of silence.

"And maybe build us a cabin?"

"I've thought a lot about that."

"Would it have a window overlooking the waterfall and an east bedroom for the morning sun?"

"I'll show you." He took her hand and led her to a circle of spruce trees.

"Let's pretend that your dream has come true, Joel," she said, not wanting it to fade. "Let's pretend this land is already ours."

Suddenly he lifted her. "I'll carry you over the threshold, Mrs. Joel McGragor."

She clung to him. He dropped to his knees and laid her on the bed of pine needles. She lay on her back, looking into the face she loved and beyond it to the circle of blue sky above. Thin clouds drew white feathers. As he began to undo her buttons, she felt uneasy at first about their privacy. But the spruce trees gifted them with shelter and the wilderness hid them from the world.

Tenderly his eyes took in her bare body. She felt a shyness in the sunlight, different from the shadows of night. "You are beautiful," he said. "A soft mystery." He covered her with light kisses like autumn leaves fluttering gently down to caress the earth. His close body warmed hers like the mountain sun on a cloudless day. His aroma intermingled with the scent of the pine needles as though the two belonged together. They joined in the high pleasure that is not a taking, but a giving, knowing oneness in body and spirit. Their song of love harmonizing with nature's symphony. Their dance of union synchronizing with the primordial rhythm of the universe. Their pleasure rose. Fast, faster their dance. *Fortissimo* their song. Until they touched the blue sky of ecstasy. A billowy cloud carried them aloft. They floated in each other's arms. The moment passed all too swiftly. Their ecstasy languished, but its symbolic renewal of their covenant lingered as they lay on the bed of pine needles wrapped in each other's arms. Adam and Eve in the garden.

Winter returned in a few days, seeking the last laugh by burying the earth in snow once again. Joel stepped off the dark porch of Company housing and joined the other miners for the single-file march to the Jokerville a mile west of town. They followed the time-worn custom of each man's taking a turn at being first, the most difficult position in the new fallen snow. Joel stood at the head of the line, taking the first turn as trail breaker. He sank into the fresh deep powder, exerting every leg muscle as he lifted his boots heavy with snow, one step after another, plowing a path for those behind.

Second in line was Iber Donegan Jr., his first day on the job. He had his father's high cheek bones and ruddy complexion, and his jaw jutted out with that same no-nonsense final decision. Twelve years old and already trapped in the Jokerville—spending his days in darkness and breathing coal dust into his young lungs. How could he ever get free? Joel's resentment broiled toward the mining system of entrapment.

As he trudged heavily through the snow, his thoughts chased each other in a circle. He needed money to buy that piece of land he wanted. He couldn't get the money until he freed himself from the Jokerville. When he freed himself, he and Vini wouldn't have a good place to live until he built the cabin. He couldn't build the cabin until he bought the land. Damn Marcel Joubert! Damn Fred King! Damn Heffron Enterprises!

Iber Jr. interrupted his thoughts. "Do you like being married to Vini?"

"As my friend Nick would say, 'certain-sure'!"

"Someday I'm going to marry Susie Robbins."

"The super's daughter?"

"But she doesn't know it yet."

Ah, a youth with dreams. How long would it be before the Company snuffed them out? Joel's toes froze, and the snow seeped through his pants, but he tramped on enduring the cold as long as he could to spare the boy.

"Drop back, Joel!" shouted Iber Donegan, third in line.

Finally exhausted, Joel stepped aside, and Iber Jr. plowed into the snow without flinching. Joel waited for the line of men to pass him by as he had many times before. But this morning the hint of dawn cast a soft light, and he peered at each face. He saw not a spark of a dream in a single eye.

He fell in at the rear of the line on a path now packed by the others. A path that led to the possibility of death by methane. In the beginning he had thought about that every morning, but less and less so as time went by. Today, however, the dreaded thought revisited him in full intensity. Heffron greed harmed a lot of people, and the only thing ultimately it could do for the man was buy him a fancy coffin.

Coffin. Joel shook loose from despair. He'd agreed to this hand, and he would play it out with confidence and courage. He straightened his back bowed against the cold and lifted his down-turned face, letting the beloved image of Vini warm him.

The Jokerville's long wooden tipple came into view, projecting out for over a hundred feet. The long line of men met the night shift miners who finished their work at 7:00 A.M. as the day shift began. The two groups nodded and spoke to each other just as they would again at seven o'clock tonight when the directions were reversed and the day shift trudged back home. Joel greeted them by name as they passed.

Carl Roach was first. His narrow eyes squinted between thin brows and a broken nose, and coal bits hid haphazardly in his unkempt beard. Most notable was a two-inch scar on his cheek shaped like a Z. His mouth was full of lecherous stories, and he'd been a drinking buddy of Marcel. Proud of his reputation as the meanest man in the mine, he bullied most of the other men but cut a wide berth around Joel. Still, there were times when Joel had an itch to resection that broken nose.

Joel and his co-workers went to their stations, looking at the chalk marks the fire boss had made in rooms and entries. "Always check these marks everyday," Iber told his son, just as he had told Joel on his own first day, which seemed so long ago. "The fire boss checks the mine for fire-damp and these marks warn us if one of the chambers is too dangerous to work."

"All four are clear today," announced Joel, and the miners moved on. They descended from the earth's spacious white surface into the narrow blackness of its bowels. Musty dampness enveloped them. The familiar ticking sound warned of the methane leaking in through cracks around the tunnel and reminded Joel that his life hung by two threads: the accuracy of the fire boss and the operation of the ventilating fans that forced the gas to the surface.

Beneath him lumps of coal littered the floor. Above him pillars of timber supported the overburden of the tunnel. In places the tunnel twisted around faults, and the passageways narrowed, barely wide enough to swing a pick. He had worked in all the chambers. Three of them were like manmade caverns being hollowed out by miners' picks. The miners' open lamps burned like stars in the eternal darkness. The flame from his lamp flashed on the rough wall, making fool's gold sparkle as he moved his head. The sound of picks echoed in his ears.

Chamber two was different from the others. It held an aura all its own, a vague eerie quiescence. Since he couldn't explain it, he'd never mentioned it to Iber. Some would say it was due to the presence of the ghosts of the miners killed by cave-ins or falling rock, but he wasn't superstitious. Yet, the aura lingered, something he couldn't see, yet was ever present.

Finally he reached chamber four, 1800 feet inside the mine, his chamber for the day. He began to chisel the wall, and coal dust filled his lungs. On his first day Iber had said nonchalantly: *You'll just throw it up.* Joel had found those words to be true.

He made it through each day by staying in his mind, separating himself mentally from the man with the flame on his lamp who held the pick in his hand. He rewrote his present by planning his future. Howard Smith had real estate sewed up in town, Otto Mears had most of the road building business, Dave Wood the freighting business, and Heffron Enterprises the railroads, coal, iron and steel. His hope rested on going prospecting, opening his own mine, and treating the miners like persons instead of pawns. Like dripped wax on a candle, his memories from yesterday helped shape who he was today, and his vision of tomorrow influenced how he lived through the day, his past and present rising like smoke into the future.

The miners chiseled and loaded and hauled until the whistle shrieked the end of the twelve-hour shift—a single blast, which meant work tomorrow. Mentally, Joel marked an X on the dungeon wall, one day closer to being a free man again.

With the dark day in the mine behind him, the bright night holding Vini in his arms awaited him. Of one thing he was sure, whatever the outcome, he had never known greater joy than being married to her. She was the treasure of his life.

After burial under twenty-five feet of winter snowfall, the land had resurrected into full bloom with the return of summer. Colorful wildflowers sprang up, scattered like rainbow confetti across the green valley. Blue harebells and purple fringe, scarlet gilia and orange poppies, and Joel's favorite—yellow columbines. As Vini washed the breakfast dishes, she basked in the warm June sun shining through the window.

This is the day the Lord has made;
let us rejoice and be glad in it.

She stirred the red beans, pleased that Will Chaney was coming to dinner tonight. The reporter was good for Joel, bringing laughter and interest in the outside world and keeping Joel focused beyond the Jokerville.

She heard footsteps on the porch, softer ones than Martha's. She peeked out the front window. A woman she didn't recognize knocked lightly. She wore a high-necked tailored gray dress and a black cabriolet bonnet, its flaring brim low on her forehead hiding her face. Vini opened the door. "Tillie!"

"Sh-h-h!" White gloves covered her painted nails. There was no make up on her face. No jewelry adorned her ears and neck. Not a strand of red hair showed beneath her bonnet. "Let me in quickly before someone recognizes me. The last thing I want to do is disgrace you."

"I'm happy to see you. Please sit down."

Tillie took off the bonnet, revealing her red hair done up in a bun. She looked around the room at the red and white checked curtains Vini had made, the matching tablecloth and cushions for the stumps, and the two pictures of flower gardens cut from an old magazine to brighten the walls. "What a good job you have done with this room. It is homey and inviting."

"Thank you. Would you like coffee?" What would Mama think about her sitting across the table from a whisper woman guest! There's a lot here in the West that Mama wouldn't understand.

Tillie shook her head. "I need to get this done quickly and be on my way." She sat down and fidgeted with the bonnet on her lap. "I don't cotton to what I'm about to do. But I've been in a fine pucker over something and feel it's only right to share it with you." Her blue eyes met Vini's. "Sometimes our Forest Queen visitors just have to tell somebody what's shouting inside of them, and they know they can trust me. You have to promise me that you won't use my name."

Puzzled, Vini nodded.

"Last night a man who works for the Company was in a talkative mood. He said that King kept Marcel Joubert's name on the miners' payroll list but pays Joel that salary. It seemed weird to him, but there are lots of strange goings-on at the Company."

"Joel thinks so too."

"He didn't get worried about it until yesterday. Fred King was out of town, and while Henry—" Tillie covered her mouth. "I've used his name! He would have a conniption fit if he knew. You've got to protect him, Vini, just like you've promised to protect me."

Again Vini nodded.

"Henry handles the Jokerville Mine payroll, and while he was putting some information on King's desk, he happened to see a ledger sheet under the ashtray. Thinking it was for him, he picked it up. He'd never seen it before. Now he wishes he hadn't seen it at all."

"What was it?"

"It had to do with salaries Heffron Enterprises pays direct. The sheet listed a position called "Trouble Shooter" with Joel McGragor's name."

"Joel turned that job down."

"Evidently King didn't relay that information and pockets the money." She paused. "Of course it's a lot higher than a miner's wages."

"Isn't he afraid to deceive M. Morgan Heffron?"

"It's Henry who is scared. He feels that because he knows about it, he's a party to cheating Mr. Heffron, and that terrifies him. But he's even more scared of King since he is right here in Crested Butte."

"Why doesn't he notify Mr. Heffron?"

"He knows that King would give himself a whitewash and accuse Henry of embezzlement. He's afraid he's the one who will get catawamptiously chawed up."

Vini could hardly bear the thought of Joel being a pawn in a scheme for King to get richer. Her thoughts whirled. "What can Joel do?"

"I don't know if he can do anything. What I do know is that the way King has treated Joel sickens me. It's wrong and King needs to be found out."

"Papa always said it's shameful how careless some people are about the wake they make in the river."

"Remember, Vini, however you handle this, you can't tell where you found out. And you mustn't do anything that risks hurting Henry."

"I'll remember, Tillie. Thank you for being my friend."

Tillie was silent for a moment, and blinked quickly as though a tear had come. "'Friend.' You are indeed special." She stuffed her hair back under her bonnet. "I'll help if I can, but tricking King is like catching a weasel asleep."

How do you catch a weasel asleep? How do you talk with Joel but keep Tillie and Henry out of it? Vini always looked forward to her and Joel's good times with Will. But right now she couldn't look forward at all.

How do you catch a weasel asleep? She pondered it as she prepared dinner. The aroma of baking bread mingled with the smell of red beans and rice. Unable to afford eggs and sugar to make bread pudding for dessert, she'd picked tiny wild strawberries. She whipped some of the cream that had risen to the top of the milk and mixed it with them. Perhaps someday she would be able to splurge on food for special occasions. But until they were free of Marcel's debt, keeping down expenses was essential.

On impulse she opened the trunk where she hid her surprise for Joel. Every day that he spent in the mine, she spent doing needlework like Mama's. She would show it all to him the night of their second anniversary, come January. Unless they were derailed, the labor debt would be paid by then and it would be his last day in the Jokerville. Then they would sell her needlework so he could go prospecting. She couldn't give him back his days in the mine, but she could help provide money to give him a chance at his dream.

It hadn't been easy to figure out how to help. As different as the South and the West were, they were not different in their customs regarding work. Whereas job and wealth defined a man's position, a woman's was defined by her relation to a man, and a wife who worked outside the home could disgrace her husband by leaving the impression that he wasn't a good provider. For tonight she chose a white tablecloth intricately embroidered with wildflowers, mostly yellow columbines. She also removed three matching napkins from the trunk. Afterward she would wash them very carefully. Surely they could still be sold as new if they were used only once. I'll tell Joel I made them for special occasions, she thought, stepping back and admiring the table. *Parfait!* She set it with their tin plates and unmatched flatware, using jars for glasses. The table didn't look so pretty now. She thought of Mama. *Don't ever worry about what you don't have, girls. Just be sure you make the most of what you do have.* She needed flowers for a centerpiece.

How do you catch a weasel asleep? She thought about that as she ambled down Second Street to pick a bouquet of wildflowers to go well with the tablecloth. She picked some yellow and purple columbines and arranged them. As she studied the bouquet, she felt someone watching her. Wariness crept through her veins—a *déjà vu* of those terrifying nights when she was aware of Marcel's staring at her in the darkness. She had not had this feeling since her marriage to Joel. But it was real and she trusted it. Carefully nonchalant, she turned back toward the cabin with her eyes on the bouquet, avoiding the risk of meeting a pair of staring eyes.

When she reached the safety of the porch, she glanced over her shoulder and saw a man across the street. A two-inch scar that formed a Z on his cheek dominated his face. His beard was unkempt, and his narrow close-set eyes shouted meanness. She felt herself shudder.

As she locked the cabin door, she remembered that dreadful evening Joel had insisted on teaching her how to use the white bone-handled knife to protect herself. How he had guided her hand time and again as though thrusting it into a man's jugular vein. Each time reminding her that she would have to depend on surprise and move quickly because of her small size.

She put the bouquet in the small aspen vase Joel had carved for her, and tried to convince herself that she was being silly and merely reliving her old fear of Marcel. Despite her bravado, her hands still trembled. She could never kill anyone. But as she recalled those cruel eyes, she considered, for the first time, withdrawing the knife from the saddlebag.

CHAPTER 9

"*A* delicious dinner!" Will lifted a spoonful of strawberries and whipped cream to his mouth. "Thank you, Vini."

Joel saw the pleasure on her face that he'd noticed when Will complimented the table earlier. She was an amazing woman. A miner's cabin wasn't the kind of house he'd intended for his wife, but she had made it their home, and tonight she'd provided a meal as fine as a banquet for his friend. "It takes a dozen of these tiny berries to fill a spoon!" he said with a smile.

"I took a walk around town this morning. Crested Butte has changed a lot since I was here last."

"It's a real town now," said Joel. "You can even telephone long distance to Gunnison."

"I heard the *Crested Butte Republican* is going to be sold to a couple of Democrats. I wish I could buy a newspaper and settle down instead of running all over the state as a reporter." He looked at Vini. "The only good home cooking I get is yours."

She smiled and offered him more coffee. "Did you walk by the new schoolhouse being built at Fifth and Maroon?"

He nodded. "Two-story rock. Good and sturdy."

"Constructed none too soon." Joel grinned and reached beneath the table and patted Vini's stomach, glad she didn't blush.

Will raised his water jar in a toast. "To a son like Joel or a daughter like Vini!"

As Joel lifted his own jar, he felt nearly perfect contentment. A good dinner. Enjoyable conversation. A baby coming. Only seven months left in the Jokerville. "Life is good," he said, "in spite of Heffron Enterprises."

Vini cleared her throat. "Speaking of Heffron Enterprises, I was thinking today about your turning down the trouble shooter job, Joel."

"That was a long time back. In another world."

"What if King made it look like you accepted the job? And has been pocketing the salary himself."

Joel laughed and shook his head. "Have you been reading those Dime Novels?"

Will studied her. "King is devious enough to think of that, all right, and he's greedy enough to do it. But he wouldn't dare risk cheating M. Morgan Heffron."

"If the salary is high enough, he might think it's worth the risk," she persisted. "He knows Mr. Heffron isn't going to come out here to check things in person."

"But he has to send in records, and my name would appear twice on the payroll."

"Not necessarily, Joel. Your wages as a miner could still be under Marcel's name."

He put down his spoon. "This doesn't sound like you, Vini. Plotting suspicious fantasies." He heard the edge in his own voice, unable to face the idea of King's profiting from his decisions.

Will stirred his coffee thoughtfully. "The theory has merit. King takes great pride in handling details—'to be exact.' I think he considers himself invincible."

The table grew silent all around.

"I don't want to sound offensive, Vini," said Will, "but you don't have any connection with Tillie Taylor do you?"

"Tillie Taylor?"

"At the Forest Queen. Because of the varied backgrounds of her . . . contacts, she has her pulse on Crested Butte better than anyone I know. Men trust her and let their mouths run."

"I've met her. I've never heard her last name." She looked down at her plate and scooted the strawberries around with her spoon.

Joel eyed her. He found himself in a quandary, not approving of mistreating anyone including Tillie, but simultaneously not wanting Vini to be hurt by the townsfolk because of her association with someone not respected. Marriage makes philosophical ideals so much more difficult! "Did you go to the Forest Queen, Vini?"

Innocent blue-green eyes met his. "No, I didn't." Her voice caught as she added, "I'm feeling attacked, Joel."

Will apologized. "I'm sorry, Vini. Tillie has to keep her mouth shut or she'd lose business. If she did ever feel compelled to tell something, she'd first get the person's word not to use her name."

Joel spoke gently. "The source doesn't matter anyway. But King . . . I should have thought of that possibility myself."

"Me, too," agreed Will. "I must be slipping. I want to check this out. I can say I'm doing an article on the success of Heffron Enterprises in Colorado." He sighed with distaste. "Which means I actually have to do one! But it would give me a reason to request the records."

"King won't let you have anything suspicious."

"Maybe I could 'stumble' onto something and appear to put two and two together. Threatening King with exposure might give us some leverage to get you out of the Jokerville sooner."

The words brought a hairline crack to Joel's inner defenses against despair. Chiseling away two years of his life was almost more than he could handle.

"I'm not sure when I can begin. I have two assignments already lined up that are important to the *News*."

Joel nodded. "I understand." Despair, heretofore deeply buried, began to seep into his soul through the hairline crack. "Even getting out of the Jokerville a single day early would be a great gift, Will." His words dragged heavily across the table.

That night Vini couldn't sleep. She hadn't lied, but she'd rowed down the river of deceit, and she wasn't proud of that. She'd kept her promise to Tillie, but she had the feeling that Joel and Will had figured it out. Before tonight Joel had hidden his despair so well that she hadn't fully realized how costly these Jokerville months were for him. She felt him rise from the bed, assuming she was asleep and careful not to wake her. She listened to him pace around the cabin like a powerful steed on a longeline. And Heffron held the rope. She longed with all her heart to free him.

Vini caught Martha's eye across the crowd at the Fourth of July celebration. She waved, mouthing congratulations as Iber Jr. won the pie eating contest.

"Way to go!" shouted Joel.

He took Vini's hand, his eyes filled with love, and they strolled down Elk. She always felt proud to be by his side. They greeted everyone by name—people from all walks of life—and their greetings were warmly returned. She thought she felt the baby move. "Only five and a half more months until the baby comes."

He gave her the wonderful smile that lit his face when they talked about the baby. His eyes dipped to her waist. "You sure can't tell it. I'll be glad when the whole town knows just by looking."

She laughed, feeling pride in her pregnancy instead of the shyness custom dictated. "It's going to be a little boy just like you."

"A little girl just like you would be fine too."

There were many contests during this double celebration of Independence Day and Crested Butte's third anniversary. They didn't want to miss a single one. A man who'd worked with Joel on the building crew won the sawing contest. Next they saw the spike hammering contest which a miner won, and then a shooting match which a cowboy won.

Nick joined them as the street cleared for the burro race. "Did I ever tell you about the burro on snowshoes?"

"I heard there was one in Crested Butte once," said Joel with that little grin on his face that forewarned Vini of being teased.

"But did you see him? I tell you certain-sure I saw a burro on snowshoes."

Vini looked up at Nick, knowing he was itching to share his story. "Tell us about it."

"I was taking my wagon over East Maroon Pass and got caught in a late spring snowstorm. The way was buried in snow belly-deep on my mule team and as soft as talcum powder. While I was waiting it out, an old prospector passed me by on his snowshoes. He was in a mighty hurry to get to the assay office, but his pack burro kept sinking into the snow. He howdied me. Then he sighed and shook his head and pulled four snowshoes out of that pack. They was for the burro. It certain-sure took a lot of patience and a lot more swearing to get the beast to agree to wear them. But once that burro figgered out they made things easier, he settled down. Off they went leaving a trail of six snowshoe tracks."

Vini laughed, trying to picture a burro on snowshoes.

Nick looked at them with a twinkle in his eye and shifted the wad of tobacco in his mouth. "Alferd Packer sure would have been disappointed to find that trail led only to one scrawny old man and a burro!"

Joel grinned and then looked serious. "I'll remember that burro. When we feel like we're sinking, it's time to come up with a new approach."

Nick nodded. "You know the old miner's saying. It's better not to wait for something to turn up, but to go to work at once and turn something up."

The volunteer firemen's race followed the burro race. Nick moved on, and Joel found a spot for Vini in front of the Star Restaurant. "This will be a good place to watch. I'll meet you here afterwards." He bent down and tapped his cheek. "How about a kiss for luck?"

She complied gladly and watched him head west toward the new City Hall on the corner of Elk and Second, a large two-story white frame building with the fire house downstairs and a small room off to the side for the town council chambers. The community used the large room upstairs for meetings, parties, and dancing.

Dancing. It had been a long time. Not since leaving New Orleans. She wished Mama and Papa could see the baby when he was born. Maybe someday. She would write them often and tell about all the new things he was doing as he grew. Francine's last letter had brought the good news that she had kept her promise. She was well and Marcel was working hard and they were happy together once more. She had also said that Marcel would be sending money soon to repay Joel. But Vini was sure he never would. The memory here was too shameful for him.

The three teams of volunteer firemen, eighteen members each, had a hard time clearing the people off Elk Avenue to make room for their man-drawn carts. As Vini waited, she suddenly felt someone's eyes on her. That old wariness rose. She tried to stuff it back down. Of course people looked at each other in crowds like this. She was being silly. Then, across Elk in front of Groenendyke's, her eyes met the cruel ones she'd seen before. They stared at her until she looked away. She recognized not only the eyes but also the large scar like a Z on the man's cheek.

Rose came out of the Star and stood beside Vini. "Rose, don't look now, but I'd like to know who that man is in front of Groenendyke's who looks like his cheek was branded with a Z."

"I don't have to see him to know who you're talking about. It's Carl Roach, the meanest man in town. If he ever gets on the day shift, Crested Butte won't be safe for man or woman at night." Her eyes side-glanced toward him. "Right now I bet his temper is as hot as the coke ovens. None of the volunteer firemen teams would have him."

Finally the carts were lined up and waiting for the mayor to start the race. Vini pointed to the slogan on the side of a cart and laughed: WE'VE NEVER SAVED A BUILDING, BUT WE ALWAYS SAVE THE LOT.

But Rose didn't laugh. Tears filled her eyes.

Vini patted her arm. "What is it, Rose?"

"I was thinking about my husband. Paul was a volunteer fireman in Saguache." She closed her eyes, and Vini couldn't tell whether she was trying to remember or to shut out the memory. "One night a log cabin caught fire. He was trying to save a little girl trapped in the loft when the roof caved in." She took a deep breath and opened her eyes. "That was five years ago."

Not knowing what to say, Vini put her arm around Rose. Does everyone in the world have to deal with pain, she wondered. If so, where is the God of love in the midst of all the pain? She knew immediately what the good bishop in New Orleans would say: *Right there, Vini, in the midst of all the pain. God is with the suffering.*

The gun fired, and the race began. Joel's team inched ahead as they reached the Star Restaurant. Their lead grew as they passed the bank and the Elk Mountain House and the banker's big yellow house. They won by half a cart length. The crowd cheered wildly.

"Take care of that man, Vini," said Rose. "There isn't another one like him still walking the earth."

By mid-afternoon thin white clouds scribbled across the blue sky. The crowd gathered for the final contest, billed as the main event—the tug-of-war between the miners and the cowboys on opposite sides of Coal Creek.

Vini watched as Joel took the lead position for the miners. Iber Donegan took hold next. Young Iber Jr. fell in behind him. Each of the miners found his place and put his hands on the rope like a ritual.

The cowboys lined up on the other side of Coal Creek, matching the miners' intensity. A man nearly as tall as Joel stood opposite him for the cowboys. This tug-of-war was not just a game, but a symbol. More than pride was at stake. Two styles of life competed. Each man concentrated totally on the rope.

"Ready!" shouted the mayor. "Begin!"

One-two-*heave*!

One-two-*heave*! Men who fueled the country against men who fed the country.

One-two-*heave*! Those paled by the darkness against those tanned by the sun.

Rocks flew. Boots skidded. Each team linked themselves as brothers. Legs strained at 45 degree angles. People yelled and clapped for the long centipede divided against itself. Some cheered when it went one way. Others cheered as it reversed.

The crowd chanted with the men. One-two-*heave*! The onlookers' bodies swayed, pulling with the team of choice. Vini felt mesmerized, part of the battle.

"Mrs. McGragor." Fred King startled her. His steel eyes contradicted his smiling lips.

She turned back to the contest without speaking to this man she loathed.

"It isn't smart for a woman to ignore her husband's boss." He flaunted his power, yet spoke in a soft tone so that others couldn't hear. "How does it feel to be a Jokerville wife?"

Fury mounted. *Holy Mother, please don't let me make things worse.* "I love being Joel's wife. Now if you will excuse me." She stepped away.

He followed her. "You are far too beautiful to waste yourself on a miner. You deserve someone who could give you so much more."

She watched Joel's muscles heave against the rope, and tightened her own lips against surging words. She could not endure another sentence from this man who wanted anything Joel had, including her.

"McGragor need never know. You deserve a gentleman like me—to be exact."

"You exaggerate your social standing. To be a *gentleman*—to be exact— one must first be a *man*."

He twisted his gold ring rapidly back and forth. "To recognize a gentleman, a woman must first be a lady! I recall brushing passed you on the Forest Queen stairs. I remember the stories Marcel told at the Bucket of Blood about your escapades with him."

She fought back nausea.

King shifted like a boxer ready for the knock-out punch. Power exuded from his stance, from his eyes, from the hard lines of his face. "I didn't cause your husband's plight. You did. I'm not the one who involved him in Joubert's affairs. You are. I wasn't the one who manipulated him into taking over your brother-in-law's debts to get your sister back to New Orleans. You were. You are the one responsible for McGragor being a miner. Not me."

Sainte Marie, Mère de Dieu! The cymbals of awareness crashed together. Illusion collapsed. Nothing had really changed—yet everything changed. She had trapped Joel in the Jokerville.

King started to walk away but turned back to her. "Joel McGragor is indeed a rare man, but he's a fool."

She couldn't breathe. She was afraid she would faint.

"Rare because he won't compromise his principles. And a fool because principles are a luxury only a man born rich can afford."

King's words beat like a drum in Vini's head as he walked away.

One-two-*heave*! A-rare-man!

One-two-*heave*! But-a-fool!

The sudden splash of the cowboys brought victory to the miners and chaos to Coal Creek. The crowd converged. Cheers for the miners. Curses from the cowboys.

Joel joined Vini, his eyes bright with triumph. "A kiss for the winner?"

He had won, but as Vini kissed him, the truth rang in her conscience. He had lost the day she came in on the train, November 21, 1881—to be exact.

"What a holiday!" said Joel. He hadn't felt so alive in a long, long time. "A whole day in the sunshine, and not even Sunday. A win for my volunteer firemen team. And a tug-of-war victory. This has been a fine day off!" He watched her clear the supper dishes. "Come on, Vini. Cheer up!" Polka music drifted in through the open window. "Let's go to the City Hall and dance away the night on this Fourth of July."

Her eyes lit up. "We've never danced together."

"No, but I've seen you do that Cajun two-step around this room."

"I don't know how to polka, Joel."

He smiled at her and danced a few quick steps around the table. "Tonight the master will teach you."

They walked up Second Street holding hands and laughing at nothing, filled with the joy of being together. They argued teasingly over whether the baby was going to be a boy or a girl, and by the time they reached the City Hall they had decided on a name for each.

The upstairs floor vibrated as the people of Crested Butte danced to the lively beat of the fiddle, accordion, and tamburitza. Joel bowed to Vini and waited for her delightful curtsy. Then he took her right hand and put his other arm around her waist. "Tonight, my lady, you learn to polka. All you have to do is follow my lead."

"I always will, *cher monsieur*."

He grinned. "At least in the major things—like dancing."

As they started to dance, her bright smile doubled the light in the room. How quickly she learned the steps. How light she was in his arms. How agile her feet. How radiant her face. How could he ever despair when he was blessed with Marie-Vincente for a wife!

Fiddle Jack called a break, and they sat down to rest. Will Chaney joined them. "Greetings, Will. It's good to see you back in town."

"I haven't seen you dancing," said Vini.

"I thought maybe I could get a story or two," he said, always the reporter.

Joel had noticed Will talking to people throughout the evening, primarily to the Company clerks who might know something about the financial records. The investigation has begun, he thought. "Were you in town today? We didn't see you."

"I was working on that matter we discussed." With a slight nod of his head, he motioned Joel toward the stairs.

"Excuse me, Vini. I'll be right back."

Once downstairs, Will spoke softly. "I'm afraid it's going to be impossible to get any information. As usual, King has covered his tracks well."

"That's all right. Six more months. Three quarters down and one quarter to go. I can handle it."

"I tried chatting with Henry. He may be Tillie's source. He was unduly nervous and kept watching to see if King knew he was talking to me."

"No one is more afraid of King than Henry."

"This task would be easy if we didn't care whether we put Tillie and him at risk."

"But we do care, Will. Otherwise we're no better than King or Heffron."

Will sighed. "I wish I could help with this."

"I'll send a letter to Heffron about my experiences as a miner. Partly so he'll know I didn't accept the trouble shooter job, but also because I want him to know the injustices against the miners."

"You never give up on anyone, do you? Not even Heffron."

Joel shrugged.

"You'd be wise to wait until you get out of the Jokerville to write that letter. Apparently there are no bounds to King's deceit."

"I'll wait." He shook hands with Will. "Thanks for trying."

Joel rejoined Vini as the music began again. He bowed to her and took her in his arms. They stepped and bounced and whirled. She followed with ease wherever he led. On that July Fourth night Joel taught Vini to polka. And they danced and danced together.

Danced for miners, freighters, ranchers. Danced for lively Crested Butte. Danced for loved ones dead and living. Danced for hope and faith and truth. Danced their magic joy of oneness. Danced their present, future, past. Danced for unborn sons and daughters. Danced the gift of love and life.

CHAPTER 10

*D*eftly Vini's fingers kneaded the bread dough as she thought about King's words. For once he had spoken the truth. She had trapped Joel in the Jokerville. She flopped the dough over and began to knead faster. She had to get him out. But how? She poked and kneaded the bread as though it hid a solution.

Suddenly the mine whistle shrieked. An accident! Vini's terror exploded. Embers scorched her heart. She dropped the dough and bolted out the door. She ran toward the Jokerville with other miners' wives and their children and most of the townspeople.

Doc Williams called to her from his buggy. "Go back, Vini!" She rushed on. "Well then, get in! You know a pregnant woman shouldn't run like that!" He offered his hand and pulled her in beside him. "It may not be too bad," he comforted. "I didn't hear a blast. There's no smoke."

Her senses tingled, raw and alert. Dread weighed heavy on her shoulders. The strong sweet odor of the coke ovens brought a wave of nausea.

They rounded the curve. Smokestacks rose skyward, undisturbed. The frame tipple came into view. "It's intact. That's a good sign too," said Doc. "Whoa!" He jumped out of the buggy.

"It's the tram!" shouted Superintendent Robbins. "The coal cars broke loose. They're piled up at the bottom."

"How many injured?" asked Doc.

"We don't know yet."

The tragedy hid beneath the ground. Unseen. Unheard. Irreversible. Vini watched the miners begin to file out of the Jokerville—Heffron's coal-blackened slaves, unfreed by the War between the States. She looked carefully as each man stepped out into the sunlight. Hoping each time to recognize Joel's face behind the coal dust. Each time her heart sank.

Iber Jr. appeared, and she gave a prayer of thanks, realizing how much she cared for the boy. Martha daubed her eyes with her flour-sack apron, one hand grasping Iber Jr. as though he might yet be snatched away.

Vini lost count after thirty miners. Anxiety mounted. Nausea rose to her throat. Her hand protected her womb.

As suddenly as it had begun, the steady stream of miners stopped. She waited. And waited.

She watched the last man check off his name and say something to the super. Robbins nodded and studied the list of men. Vini waited.

"All but five of the miners are out," said Robbins, looking at Doc. "Four are trying to move the debris. One man is buried."

"He's probably d—" Doc Williams glanced toward Vini and stopped the word.

Robbins nodded. "Just one. That's good."

Just one, echoed Vini's mind. But one is One. Joel? She trembled and shoved the thought from her mind. She stared at the entrance as though sheer will could make Joel materialize. She felt the baby move.

Martha Donegan put her arm around Vini. "They're helping, child. That's what Iber and Joel would do." Her words were hushed, a dull monotone that lacked persuasion.

Vini and Martha stood together, each withdrawn into an inner world of fear.

The people of Crested Butte, relieved earlier by the appearance of each miner, now waited in silent dread. Who? Which of the remaining families would mourn?

"They're coming!" shouted Robbins. The crowd moved in.

Vini and Martha made the sign of the cross. A coal-dusty miner came out into the sun. Both women stepped forward arm-in-arm. Then they stopped. Once more they waited. The next man surfaced with his back to them, too short to be Joel, too thin to be Iber. Again, they waited.

Finally a man with Iber's build backed out of the shaft. His hands gripped the legs of a miner. Two strong bare arms of another man lifted the victim's shoulders clear of the shaft. The crowd moaned as they saw a shirt draped over his face, announcing his death.

Joel's shirt. A cold chill spread through Vini. She closed her eyes and swayed toward Martha.

"Look, child!"

Joel's coal-stained face and shirtless chest followed his raised arms out of the shaft. Vini lifted her eyes to the heavens. *"Merci, Holy Mother,"* she whispered. *"Merci."* She ran to Joel as he and Iber laid the miner down, and Doc Williams moved in to take over. She held him sobbing, her head against his bare chest where coal dust intermingled with blood from the dead man's injuries.

"Sh-h-h." He kissed the tears on her cheeks and stroked her hair.

She clung to him. "I'm the reason you are in the Jokerville," she sobbed.

"No, Vini, no! There may have been a better way than I could see at the time. But I'm the one who made the decision."

"You wouldn't be working down there if you hadn't met me."

"Listen to me, dearest Vini. My life with you as my wife, even working in the mine, is filled with more light than I could experience without you even at the top of the sunniest peak." He lifted her chin. "If all the rest of my days were spent in the Jokerville, it would be worth it for you to be by my side. Don't ever forget that."

But she knew it was her fault, and if anything happened to him she would never forgive herself.

The aspen trees turned gold, then dropped their leaves altogether, then snow clothed their branches. Joel noticed the passage of time in Vini's changing form. As for himself, he felt like a racehorse at the starting gate—only one more month in the Jokerville! He still dreamed of buying that land by the camel-shaped boulder and building a cabin with a window overlooking the waterfall like Vini wanted. Maybe someday he could even buy the banker's big yellow house on Elk and give it to her for Christmas. But on this cold Christmas Eve he would surprise her with a rocking chair.

After work he walked to Glick Brothers where they waited for him to pick up the chair before closing. "Greetings, Adam."

"Merry Christmas, Joel."

"Thanks for staying until I could get here."

"No trouble." Adam had tied a red bow on the rocker, and the oak wood smelled of furniture oil. He gave it a little nudge, and it began to rock. Joel smiled, picturing Vini sitting in it, singing a lullaby, and rocking his son to sleep. Or his daughter. The chair would go well with the cradle he'd built. He was proud of that cradle, he admitted to himself, especially since Vini's eyes sparkled every time she glanced at it. He didn't want his baby to have to sleep in a bureau drawer or his wife to have to sit on an old log stump to feed their baby.

"When is the baby due?"

"Anytime now." Joel plunked ten silver dollars on the counter, the same ones left from buying the tickets to New Orleans. As long as they were in his saddlebag, he hadn't felt totally dependent on Heffron Enterprises scrip. Being without U.S. dollars stole away some of his freedom and dignity. Of all the injustices to miners, scrip rankled him most.

"How are you getting the rocker home?"

"Nick's freight wagon. Happy holidays to you and your family, Adam."

"And a happy new year to yours."

"I'm certain-sure looking forward to Christmas Eve supper with you and Vini," said Nick, snapping the reins across the backs of his mule team. "Get up, you lucky old fools!"

Joel looked over at his friend, aged yet ageless. "Something has been weighing on my mind ever since the mine accident. I have a favor to ask, Nick." He hesitated, finding it difficult to say the words. "If something happens to me, would you drop in on Vini and the baby from time to time? Sort of see after them?"

A long pause followed.

Joel felt he'd made a mistake. Nick wouldn't want to be saddled with that kind of responsibility. He shouldn't have asked.

The old freighter brought his gloved hand to his cheeks, like flicking off dust under each eye. "You—" His voice cracked. "You honor me, friend." He snapped the reins again. "Get along there, you sentimental old fools!"

"Thank you, Nick," said Joel, once again realizing what a soft heart lodged inside the tough old freighter.

Nick turned to him, his voice under control again. "But nothing is going to happen. You don't want to be aborrowin' trouble like that."

"There's something else I've been wanting to discuss with you."

"For a quiet man you sure are talkative tonight."

"From the beginning my goal was to have Marcel's debt paid off in two years. That's next month, and we're going to make it."

"You'll be able to get out of that suicide trap in one piece! Does that mean we're going prospecting come summer?"

"'Certain-sure!' Remember the burro on snowshoes? Well, it's time for a new approach."

"There's another Golden Fleece just waiting for us. These old bones can feel it."

"Let's hope that your old friend Al Packer doesn't escape from jail," joked Joel. "I wouldn't want to meet up with the Colorado Cannibal at timberline."

"He ain't my friend. He ate my friend. Rumor has it that he fattened hisself up on five of the seven Democrats in Hinsdale County!"

Joel laughed. "Maybe the Republicans hired him." He began whistling his old tune.

Nick popped the reins. "Get up there, you happy old fools!"

As Joel set the rocker on the porch, eager to surprise Vini, he noticed silhouettes flickering through the closed curtains. The locked door refused to budge. He knocked impatiently. "Vini!"

The skeleton key squeaked against the lock, and Martha Donegan cracked open the door. "The midwife is here, Joel. You can wait at our cabin." She started to close the door, but he shoved it open and entered.

Vini lay on the four-poster bed, the empty cradle beside her. She looked pale and exhausted. Her dark hair waved in ringlets across the white pillowcase. Her eyes followed his face as he approached, a smile on her lips. "I'm giving you a son for Christmas," she said weakly.

He bent and kissed her forehead. "I love you, dearest Vini."

She reached for his hand and for a moment touched it against her cheek. His other hand caressed a damp ringlet that strayed down her temple.

Suddenly pain filled her eyes. "Go on now," she whispered. She turned her face away from him, biting her lip.

Gently, he placed his big calloused hand on her forehead, powerless to protect her from this suffering, longing to bear it in her stead. He saw her tiny form strain under the quilt. A moan escaped her tight lips. She clutched the cross around her neck, the same cross his mother had clutched.

Finally, her face relaxed. "Please, Joel. Wait at Iber's." Her voice was barely audible, pleading. Again, pain dulled her eyes.

No more children, decided Joel. He turned from her bed and went outside. No more children!

"How is she?" asked Nick.

"I feel helpless."

Nick shrugged. "There's nothing we can do. But a new father and godfather certain-sure need some cigars to pass out. I'll get us some." He jumped on the freight wagon and clucked his mules. "Get up, you proud old fools!"

Joel couldn't go next door to Iber's. He felt compelled to stand guard near the door, as though he could somehow wrap the cloak of his protective love around the cabin. For a while he paced back and forth, packing the snow with his boots. For a while he stood still and watched the ruddy glare from the long banks of coke ovens. The sickening sweet smell of baking coke settled heavily over the winter night. Each minute passed like an hour. He began to pace again.

At long last the door opened. "She's too tiny," called Martha. "Hurry, Joel! Get Doc!"

Joel raced up Second Street passed White Rock and Sopris, Elk and Maroon, Gothic and Teocali. He bounded up Doc Williams' steps and rapped on the door. His heart pounded. Through the windows he saw a large Christmas tree glowing with candles and tinsel. Brightly wrapped presents crowded beneath it. Children laughed and someone played "Silent Night" on the piano. No one answered the door.

"Doc Williams!" he yelled into the night. This time he banged so loud the door shook. Finally Doc opened it. "My wife!" Joel shouted. "Hurry! The baby—"

"I'll get my bag." Doc rushed away leaving the door open.

Joel heard a woman's voice and recognized the banker's wife. "Do you have to go out even on Christmas Eve?"

Doc chuckled. "Babies are born on this night just like any other, Alisa."

"I'm used to it," said his wife pleasantly.

Doc smiled at her. "I'm not sure how long it will take, Maggie. This is a firstborn."

"How lovely!" she said. "A Christmas Eve baby!"

"Take my sleigh," offered Richard Sterling. "It's already rigged and will be faster."

"Don't wait to open the presents. I'll be at Company housing if someone else needs me."

"But you might miss the party," said Alisa. "And it's just a miner's baby."

Joel drove the banker's sleigh back to the cabin, Alisa's words echoing in his ears—*just a miner's baby.*

※

"Stay out here, Joel," ordered Doc, jumping from the sleigh. "A mother needs all my attention, and a father might pass out."

Joel paced the snow-packed path in a daze. He saw the image of Vini's suffering face. Then her image became distorted, and he saw in its place the face of his mother with all her features appearing clearly to him for the first time, somehow summoned from the depths of his subconscious memory—her blond hair and blue eyes, her dimpled chin and fair skin, and the nose that he wore. The images of those two beloved faces filled his mind. First one and then the other. They blurred together. He sat down on the porch in the new chair and began to rock. Back and forth. Vini's face. His mother's face. He rocked the seconds away while time stood still.

Just before midnight on Christmas Eve, 1883, Joel heard a smack and a cry. He opened the door and walked quietly to the bed, his love overflowing. "Will she be all right, Doc?" he whispered.

"I think so, Joel." Doc sighed wearily. "But we almost lost her."

Vini's dim eyes opened a slit and she smiled. "Merry Christmas." Her words came heavily, pulled from the well of exhaustion. "You have a son."

Joel leaned down and kissed her gently. He looked at the tiny baby and tenderly picked him up. No man could ask for more! Primeval joy filled his soul. Rising to his full height, he lifted his firstborn son toward the heavens and proclaimed to the universe: "Benjamin Joel McGragor." He hurled the name into the future, bowing his head in gratitude before the Giver and the Taker of life.

CHAPTER 11

*O*n this beautiful January Sunday, Vini dressed in her best. Ben was nearly three weeks old and she, though still weak, was growing stronger each day. As she brushed her hair, she glanced at her tall husband bent low toward the cradle, gently rocking it and whistling his old tune as his son drifted off to sleep.

To her, today was one of the most important days in Ben's life—perhaps the most important—even though he wouldn't remember it. Today he would be baptized, a defining moment, a moment that expressed his identity and direction. Like his marriage would later and also the day he became a father.

Vini heard the tolling of the Union Congregational Church bell. "Listen to that, Joel. Every time I hear it I think of St. Louis Cathedral in the French Quarter."

"Nick was right about the ladies coming," he grinned. "We've lost seven saloons and built a church."

"I wish it were Catholic."

He raised one eyebrow. "If so, I suppose you would hie me to mass."

"Nonnegotiable!"

He saluted her. "Even President Arthur would bow to such a voice of authority."

"Did your papa take you to church very often when you were growing up in Washington City?"

Joel nodded. "He thought it would be important to my mother since she wanted to pass on her cross. He felt he should honor that. A Methodist church happened to be the nearest to us. Foundry Methodist Church. So that's where we went every Sunday morning."

"I went to mass each week at St. Louis Cathedral."

"Foundry Church is where we first met Chief Ouray and Chipeta. He wanted to visit it, and the government officials allowed them to worship there."

"What about after your papa died? Did you still go?"

He shrugged. "I came out west. Once I heard Father Dyer preach, but I found myself thinking more about how much I missed my father than about the sermon. It was different without him. Lonely."

"You won't ever again have to be alone in church."

"Marriage to you took care of my loneliness, dearest Vini."

She had Martha to thank for today. *Now it's none of my business, child, but Father Barrett is coming from Gunnison on Sunday, January 13. I saw a notice posted at the Company Store. All the Catholics in Crested Butte are invited to meet with him. He wants to talk to us about organizing a church here. I wrote him a letter telling him about Ben's birth. After all, he married you and Joel. It asks him if he could baptize the baby while he's here. Thank the good Lord the train takes the mail back and forth to Gunnison. I won't send it if you don't want me to, of course. But since he's coming . . . I just thought it might be good to get that done.*

And so did Vini and Joel.

They were expecting the priest at their cabin right after the meeting. Vini had planned a party. There were always parties in her family back in New Orleans to celebrate weddings and baptisms and other major events. For that matter, anything could be an excuse. She had missed having parties.

Martha had helped her prepare, asking all the good Catholic women to make a double batch of cookies, one for the meeting and one for the baptism. Nick had lent his freight wagon tarps to spread out on the snow in front of their cabin if the sun cooperated—just as carpets were pulled outside for lawn parties in the South. Fiddle Jack worked in the Jokerville and Joel had invited him to play. Ben was being baptized! It was a time to dance!

Vini could visualize Mama and Papa in the midst of the guests, proud grandparents showing Ben off. And his Aunt Francine and his uncles. They would all be here with her in her heart. As would Joel's father and mother and birth father. It brought her joy to think that all the family—both far away and gone before—would be present in spirit.

Father Michael Barrett arrived first and questioned her and especially Joel. "So you are a Methodist, Joel. Then the Anglican Church is your denomination's mother and the Catholic Church your grandmother. I personally believe all churches can express God's love. However, I ask you always to honor your grandmother."

Joel nodded assent and then surprised the priest by asking some questions of his own in his amiable and sincere way. Afterwards he said with a warm smile, "You know, Father Barrett, I think you are a Methodist Catholic!"

The priest chuckled, his blue eyes reflecting his fondness for Joel.

As their friends gathered inside and spilled over outside, Father Barrett took tiny Ben in his long arms. The baby nestled comfortably against his shoulder. "What name shall be given this child?" he asked, dipping his long fingers in water. He laid his wet hand on Ben's little head and proclaimed to the cosmos, "Benjamin Joel, I baptize you in the name of the Father, the Son, and the Holy Ghost."

Tears rolled down Vini's cheeks, moved by the awareness that this holy sacrament was done exactly the same, wherever the place and whoever the priest. Whether the good bishop in St. Louis Cathedral in New Orleans or young Father Barrett in a miner's cabin in the small mountain town of Crested Butte.

After the baptism the party began. The sun played its part and warmed the earth. Fiddle Jack played. People danced the polka on the tarps. Vini passed out cookies. Joel passed out kind words to each person. And Nick passed out cigars. Perhaps, thought Vini, even the Holy Mother has finally crossed the Mississippi River and is present among us today.

Joel awoke in the cold darkness of the January 24 morning and put his arms around Vini. "Happy second anniversary."

She snuggled against him. "I am so happy!"

"It'll be even better when we buy that land up by the Red Lady and build our own cabin."

Ben made a little sucking smack, dreaming in his cradle, and they both beamed down at him in pride and gratitude.

"A month old today!" she said.

He recalled his fear for her during the birth. "Life would lose its meaning without you, dearest Vini." He held her tenderly.

She ran her hand through his hair in a gentle caress. "*Cher, cher monsieur.* I have a big surprise for you when you get home tonight."

"My last day in the Jokerville." Unless King pulls something unforeseen, he thought. But some things were best left unspoken. He hurried to dress and sat down at the table as she dished up their oatmeal.

"I don't even know how to begin to thank you for saving Francine's life."

He grinned. "I can think of some ways."

"You are a wonderful man, Joel McGragor."

"A lucky one to have you for my wife." Not for a moment did he ever doubt that.

"And now we have baby Ben."

Joel stirred milk into his oatmeal. "My only regret is that I couldn't organize the miners. I thought the accident might make a difference, but it didn't."

"They're afraid. Look at Iber. He has eight children to feed, and mining is all he knows."

"Young Iber Jr. will never have a chance to know anything besides mining either."

Vini sighed. "He's a fine boy and proud to be a miner like his father."

"Mining is honorable work. What is dishonorable is the coal barons' lack of regard for miners and their working conditions."

"Like M. Morgan Heffron?"

"Exactly." She poured him a second cup of coffee, a rare extravagance in their frugal lifestyle. He glanced around the cabin, knowing he couldn't have been happier in a castle. His eyes fell on the dried wildflowers in the vase on the table, and he used them to change the subject. "Even in winter you capture the rainbow." Her loving smile assured him he'd found the pot of gold.

When he rose from the table, he stopped beside his son's cradle, picked him up, and hugged him for a moment. "Goodbye, wee Ben." He kissed Vini soundly. "You are a beautiful lady, Mrs. Joel McGragor."

She handed him his dented lunch pail. "Your final day in the Jokerville!"

As he put on his coat, he brushed his hand across the *M* on the flap of the saddlebag hanging on the wooden peg and went out the door whistling his lively old tune.

Vini waved to him from the porch as he trudged through the snow to join the other miners. "I'm making your favorite dessert for dinner tonight," she called. "And remember, I'll have a grand surprise."

As the miners marched toward the Jokerville in their single-file line, Joel remembered his joy the first time he reached these rugged mountains, where peaks rose 14,000 feet into the sky and canyons broke deep into the earth and streams rushed by—sure where they were going, as clear as the sky. So different from cities, where buildings butted together and hid the sun and houses divided the earth with white picket fences and people rushed by—unsure where they were going, unclear about why.

At the first light of dawn, Joel could see the belfries of the church, the school, and the City Hall outlined against the pastel streaks of the sky. Spirit, mind, and community, he thought. These are the values honored by the spires of Crested Butte—its *raison d'être,* as Vini would say. Sadly he realized that the town's major means of existence contradicted its reason for being, for its economy was primarily controlled outside its boundaries and turned many of its citizens into marionettes. Chief Ouray would have enjoyed this irony, so typical of the *Maricat'z*—the white men—who came naming the land and claiming the land, with their chain of treaties and broken promises, with their gold pans and their greed.

Joel wondered again if King had lied to Heffron about the trouble shooter job and was pocketing the salary. Will had been unable to find out for sure without implicating innocent people. Joel planned to write a letter to Heffron tomorrow stating that even though he had not accepted the position offered to him, he wanted to make some suggestions on behalf of the miners. For once, King would not get off unscathed.

Joel pondered the way things had turned out: refusing that job and ending up on Heffron's payroll anyway. But that all important difference still remained—the difference between selling yourself and choosing to give yourself, a difference which some people could never understand, yet the difference between losing or keeping your honor and integrity. "I'd do it again," he muttered aloud. "No matter the cost." With the rare joy of a pure heart, he resumed whistling his father's old tune, his breath blowing white in the cold morning air.

The chalk marks of the fire boss warned the miners not to enter chamber two, that chamber whose strange aura still disturbed Joel. As he began to chisel coal in chamber one, he thought of Vini's radiant face, his light in the darkness. He remembered his observation of the difference between girls and wives, glad that she'd kept her fresh eagerness toward life. He remembered taking her home the day she arrived in Crested Butte and her curtsy to him from the porch of Company housing, a queen in disguise. He remembered her flying into his arms after their wedding, and teaching her how to polka on the Fourth of July. He thought of his son who carried him forward beyond mortality. Vini and wee Ben—they were the treasures of his life. No man could ask for more.

Suddenly, a sense of foreboding tumbled into his reverie. Looking around, he could see an open lamp moving in the direction of chamber two. Hadn't the miner seen the warning? Had he looked? The flame bobbed up and down in the darkness heading toward the methane-ridden chamber. Fear gripped Joel.

He crawled down from his space and moved as fast as he could through the rough-floored mine trying to catch up with the miner. Stop!" he yelled. "STOP!"

The noise of the picks resounded. The open lamp bobbed on, unhearing. The man turned in at chamber two.

"NO!" shouted Joel desperately. He ran stumbling to the chamber entrance. He cupped his hands around his mouth. "STOP!"

The miner walked on.

Joel hesitated. An inner warning beat with his heart. Leave NOW! Leave NOW! But he blew out the flame of his lamp and entered the passage. All was darkness except for the single flame that bobbed along ahead of him. Joel felt the tentacles of the chamber's aura reach for him.

Once more he shouted, the force of his whole being in his voice.

The lamp halted and turned toward him. "WHAT?" The question echoed through the passage.

And the chamber itself answered. Its tentacles clutched Joel. Ripped him like claws. Seared him like fire. Joel stretched his arms high above his head, lifting Vini and wee Ben beyond its grasp.

CHAPTER 12

A thunderous blast resounded through the mountains. The frame tipple blew into bits. Debris fell all around. Gas and fire belched from the mine entrance. Smoke surged into the sky. Workers outside the mine were slammed to the ground. They put their hands over their heads and scattered for cover. Some dazed. Some screaming. Flames leaped to nearby buildings. Superintendent Robbins ran to the mine whistle.

The town shook. Buildings jarred. Windows shattered. Heads jerked toward the Jokerville. Horses spooked. People scurried like scared ants through the streets.

The mine whistle shrieked. Silence descended. Movement ceased. The anthill of humanity froze for an instant, captured on the still life canvas of doom.

Doc Williams looked at his watch—7:30 A.M. He grabbed his bag and raced to the mine.

The miners were trapped inside. Word spread that the air fan stopped, that essential link to life. Superintendent Robbins immediately sent three telegrams: the first to the State Inspector, the second to the General Superintendent, and the third to M. Morgan Heffron in Washington City.

Late that afternoon Nick pulled his mules up at Jack's Cabin to water them. Ahead of schedule for a change, he looked forward to warming himself by the wood stove and drinking a leisurely cup of strong black coffee. "Br-r-r!" He shivered and closed the door.

"Did you come from Crested Butte?" Jack asked.

"No. From Tincup. Why?"

"The Jokerville exploded this morning. Killed 59 or, 60 miners."

Nick's blood iced in his veins.

"It's all here in the *Gunnison Review Press*. The stage brought it just before you got here." He handed it to Nick.

> It is the most fearful disaster entailing a greater
> loss of life than any accident that has ever occurred in
> Colorado, or for that matter in the western states.
> . . . Eleven men were working in chamber
> number four, the farthest away, a distance of eighteen
> hundred feet, all of whom groped their way out in the

> darkness. The time required was about twenty min-
> utes, and their escape was really miraculous. . . .
> Seventeen persons found in one heap were trying to
> make their way out, and would have been successful
> had not the air fan stopped. They were within two-
> hundred feet of the furnace. These men were employed
> in chamber number one.

Hurriedly Nick scanned the list of men killed. Henry Anderson, John Williams, J. J. Stewart. With each unknown name, Nick feared the next one. John Martin, James O'Neil, Thomas Rogers. His palms grew moist against the newspaper. Jacob Laux, Thomas Roberts, James McCourt . . . He went through the list to the last name. Thomas Stewart. "Joel's name isn't here!" He sighed with relief and then felt guilty about his lack of concern for the others.

"Terrible tragedy!" said Jack.

Nick returned the newspaper to him. "Have you heard anything else? Anything about the injured?"

"Not a thing. No one from Crested Butte has passed through."

Nick jumped back on his freight wagon, whipped his mules, and raced toward Crested Butte. He loved Joel like the son he'd never had. He could see his smile and hear him whistle that old tune. He pictured Vini and the baby. He prayed to the Jewish God he'd left behind: "Let Joel be all right." Then he punctuated the prayer by crossing himself like Vini. For good measure he stuck his hand in his pocket and rubbed his thumb across his lucky silver dollar. Again he whipped his mules. "Faster, you scared old fools! Faster!"

He reached Company housing after dark, left his tired mules untethered and leaped from the wagon. "Joel!" he called. He flung the door open to silent darkness.

Nick dug through his pockets for a match and struck it, moving to the table to light the candle. It flickered on such disarray he wondered if he had the wrong cabin. The breakfast dishes cluttered the table, along with oatmeal left in a pot and chocolate cake batter in a pan, unbaked. The cold air blew in through the shattered window. He turned, and the vision before him wrenched his heart from his soul.

Vini sat in the corner of the room, rocking her baby. He stepped to her and bent forward. The stench of the baby's urine filled his nostrils. He saw her paleness in the dim candlelight. "Vini," he said gently.

She lifted her face. Empty eyes stared through him. She cuddled her baby close to her heart, rocking slowly back and forth.

"The mine—" Nick began. "Is Joel—" He struggled to form the words. The question refused to come.

"This is his last day in the Jokerville," she said in a flat monotone voice. "I'll have a grand surprise when he comes home." She touched the cross around her neck and with lifeless eyes looked at the tiny infant and began to hum a slow, broken version of Joel's tune.

Nick stared at the silhouette of mother and babe in the shadows, truth stabbing his heart. He was a shadow without the sun. He was a gray cloud floating in a world gone skyless. He was Abraham without Isaac. Nick knew the answer to his unasked question. He knew that rocking before him was a widow in shock. He knew that the *Gunnison Review Press* had omitted a name from its listing of the dead.

CHAPTER 13

ini held five-week-old Ben in her arms and knelt numbly in the snow
beside Joel's grave in the northwest corner of the cemetery at the foot
of Crested Butte Mountain. Silent snowflakes swept away the footsteps of
that other day—the burial day. The gray bleak days of sunless sadness had
spun a web around a week since Joel's death. Seven days of timeless movement
since the mine cars brought out the first mangled men—identified and
unidentifiable. "It's a nameless grave, wee Ben," she mumbled. Battered bodies
buried together. One mass grave marked with a single stone. "Listen. I'll read
you what it says:

Their lives were gentle,
And the elements so mixed in them,
that nature might stand up and
say to all the world:
'They were men.'

Your papa was a special kind of man." The words choked in her throat,
stifled by the irreversible silence of separation. She clung to her son and stared
at the tombstone, dazed by death's unchangeable cruelty. A thick fog of
despair enveloped her.

As she knelt before the stone, snow deepened around her. The soft
white blanket invited her to sleep. To escape from the struggle. Just sleep on
the puffy pillow of snow. Eternal sleep. She lay down on her back in the snow
to rest a minute and closed her eyes, wrapping herself in the warm memory of
Joel's arms and hearing his old tune like a lullaby.

Ben whimpered. "Sh-h-h," she whispered without opening her eyes.
"We'll sleep now." He began to cry. Softly at first. Then louder, until his shrill
howling penetrated her illusion of tranquility.

Something deep within her awakened, called her to rise and protect her
child. She felt the cold snow mattress beneath her and opened her eyes to a
duvet of white flakes covering her and baby Ben.

The inner call came again, louder. Save the baby! Get him home! She
shook off her semiconscious numbness and struggled to rise with her baby in
her arms. The snow fell hard, burying the tombstone of the mass grave.

Joel would have me stand. She felt his strong arm around her, offering his
hand as at the depot. She willed herself to stand. To begin the long walk back to

Company housing. To take a step. To pull free from the heavy knee-deep powder. To take another step. And again pull free. And another. Stumbling. Falling. Rising again. Her knees buckling. Willing them to carry her forward. Protect the baby. Step after sinking step. On and on through the heavy blinding snow.

Finally, Company housing blurred into view behind the blinding snowflakes that covered the cabins like a white shroud. Grief twisted her heart, wracking her with pain as she approached the cabins. They were lined up like prison cells. A few prisoners still awaited the death penalty. Most had been executed the week before.

Beyond endurance, she focused on the cabin porch, and forced herself to reach it. She tried to step up. The porch whirled. She leaned against the log post. Once more the contentment of painless nothingness called to her. And once more Ben whimpered. She willed herself to stop spinning. To step up. To reach the door.

A piece of white paper tacked to the wall blurred before her eyes. She nestled her baby closer and made her eyes focus:

NOTICE OF EVICTION
THESE PREMISES ARE TO BE VACATED
BY FEBRUARY 1

Tomorrow! *Sainte Marie, Mère de Dieu!*

Vini awoke to silent warmth and realized she was lying on Joel's and her bed. Now only hers. She glanced at Ben sleeping soundly in the nearby cradle. A bed for her. A bed for the baby. Both made by Joel's hands. Joel's hands.

Her eyes moved to the oak rocker, and she was surprised to see Father Barrett sitting in it, praying. His presence brought her a sense of peace, a feeling foreign to her since the disaster. She noticed the white piece of paper in his hand, the paper that left her and her baby homeless. She sank back into the abyss of hopeless despair.

As though feeling her pain, the young priest instantly opened his blue eyes. "I'm sorry I wasn't here sooner, Vini. Joel's name wasn't in the newspaper. I would have come here first if I'd known."

She felt the gentle caress of his eyes. "I have sinned, Father," she said. "I caused Joel to—" She forced the words. "To die. I trapped him in the Jokerville."

The priest shook his head.

"If he hadn't met me, he wouldn't have worked in the mine."

"We both know that if he hadn't met you—no matter how long he lived—he would have been cheated out of the greatest joys he knew. You and

Ben." He took her hand. "Let me pray for you, Vini. God will hear the silent words of our hearts."

She felt his tender strength flowing into her like healing oil poured upon her soul.

When he finished praying, he spoke to her in a soft but firm tone that wrapped her in the comfort of his own assuredness. "You did not cause Joel's death."

"But why, Father Barrett? Why did Joel die? Why on his last day in the Jokerville?"

"I don't know. But I do know that death comes for the best and the worst of people, and it comes at the best and worst of times."

"Aren't you going to tell me it was God's will?"

"I'm not one who says that. The demonic forces caused Joel's death, the shadow sides of human beings."

She didn't understand what he was talking about and was too weary to put forth the effort to try. She yearned to sink back into sleep and wake up from a week-long nightmare.

He spoke urgently, his extraordinary eyes focused on hers, drawing her into his presence as a magnet draws metal. "Greed comes from the shadow side, and because of his greed M. Morgan Heffron opened a mine with too dangerous a level of methane. Despair also comes from the shadow side, and despair blinded Marcel Joubert to hope for his wife and his life, and in that hopelessness he did shameful things. Revenge, too, comes from the shadow side, and in order to get revenge King required Marcel's debt to be repaid with labor, an act of gross injustice—another demonic force." His hand held hers firmly. "Marie-Vincente, you are free of all responsibility for Joel's death."

The tears of loss and confusion and grief dampened her pillow as she felt his words wash her guilt away. But a lethal force rose within her to take its place. Something she knew was wrong. Something she was sure would never go away. Something she must not confess to this kind priest. It was her own deep desire for revenge.

"You were a source of love. You were facing toward God."

She started to interrupt, but he continued.

"And so was Joel."

The teachings of her faith crashed in upon her. "He wasn't a Catholic! And he—none of them—received the last rites!"

"Please hear me, Vini. There is a scripture in James that says religion that is pure and undefiled before God is this: 'to care for orphans and widows in their distress, and to keep oneself unstained by the world.' Not only was he willing to risk his life so that one in distress might live, but I've never known anyone who did a better job of keeping himself unstained by the world than Joel McGragor."

As she thought about his words, he took her other hand also. His countenance changed, and he spoke softly to her. "Please hear me. We mourn the loss of Joel. We always will—you and Ben and Martha and Nick and I, and all the people in Crested Butte who looked up to him. But in the light of God's love, we can also celebrate his life—that we had the privilege of knowing him and walking with him and sharing in his life." He looked tenderly toward the cradle. "We can also celebrate that among us remains the precious son of Joel. That part of Joel that you can still care for."

A sliver of hope glimmered in the distance that—not now—but someday she would be able to endure life again.

"Please hear me, Vini. Joel is present with you now and always will be, but in a different way."

Maybe even . . . Could it be possible? . . . Maybe even she would one day know joy once more through Joel's presence in memory and spirit. "Thank you, Father." But she realized she wasn't the least bit thankful. Her hope turned to anger. Not only at Heffron and Marcel and King. But at God. "What good is a god who won't even save a man of integrity? What good is a god who won't let a baby know his wonderful father? What good is a god who lets people suffer?"

"God is not a good luck charm. God is a powerful presence from whom we can draw strength in our times of suffering."

Realizing her blasphemy, she felt scared. "I shouldn't have said those things!"

He smiled at her, and his face and voice were filled with compassion. "God loves you, Vini. God suffers with you. Let me read you a scripture." He pulled a small Bible from his coat pocket:

> "*Yet, even now, says the Lord, return to me with all your heart,
> . . . with weeping, with mourning. . . . Return to the Lord, your God,
> for he is gracious and merciful, slow to anger, and abounding in stead-
> fast love, and relents from punishing.*

Do you know where that's from?"

She shook her head.

"The Book of Joel. That is the message of Joel for you."

Martha entered without knocking, carrying a steaming pot. "Thank you, Father, for staying until I could get back." She sat down on the bed, bowl and spoon in hand. "Here, child. Taste this chicken soup. It'll be good for you."

"What are you going to do?" asked the priest.

"I haven't thought about any of that. I don't know what is best."

"Maybe you should go back to New Orleans, baby," Martha said tenderly.

"I can't afford a ticket."

"Perhaps I could help," offered Father Barrett.

Her thoughts tumbled together. Longing to be in Papa's and Mama's arms and not feeling so alone. Being with all her family again. Marcel! She glanced out the window at the mountains and knew the answer. "All my time with Joel was here. To leave would separate me from him even more—from the places he walked and the things he touched. I want Ben to know the mountains his papa loved."

The priest folded up the eviction notice. "I'll try to get this extended."

Nick arrived as Father Barrett left. They talked for a few minutes at the door. The young priest showed the old man the notice. Nick shook his head.

"Vini, I should've built me a cabin years ago," Nick said, sitting down in the rocker. "I just never counted on a woman and a young'un."

Tears came to Martha's eyes. "Vini never counted on being a widow, especially with a baby. I wish with all my heart that Joel could have been assigned that day to chamber four with my two Ibers."

"It's my fault he was there at all."

"Joel did what he had to do," said Nick. "What he wanted to do. Having something worth dying for is what makes a man's life worth living. It's better to swim in that deep sea for a short time than wade through the shallows three score and ten."

Ben squeaked in his cradle. Martha put the empty soup bowl on the table and handed him to Vini.

"I don't know what to do, wee Ben," Vini mumbled.

"We'll figger it out. I ain't much. But I'm a man of my word. Besides," the old man's eyes grew moist, "Joel was like a son to me." He looked at Vini, shyness replacing his facade of buffoonery. "Maybe you can try to see me as your pa-in-law. And maybe Ben can call me Grandpa."

She smiled at him, suddenly not feeling so totally alone. "Thank you, Nick. We'd both be obliged."

"Maybe Marcel will help. He owes Joel a big one." Then he shook his head. "We'll never hear from him again, will we, Vini?"

"It is just as well," said Martha coldly.

Nick glanced at the baby. "Don't you worry none, Vini. We'll think of something."

Yes. Think. Think.

"I heard a Widows and Orphans Fund has been collected," said Martha.

Widow. Orphan. "Maybe I can find a job."

"What kind? A lady can't freight for Dave Wood."

"Something with room and board."

"And you're certain-sure a lady." Admiration filled Nick's voice.

Perhaps Mama's careful teachings could somehow help. She remembered all the needlework she'd done to surprise Joel by selling it to help him go prospecting. Her grand surprise for him that he would never receive. She couldn't bear even to think about that now.

"You got looks going for you, too. And you're the best cook I ever knew."

"There may be some job notices in the *Crested Butte Gazette*. Could you get me a copy, Nick?"

"I'd be pleased to."

Vini could tell he was glad to have a purpose, to do something—anything—to feel helpful. "Tomorrow I must look for work." One small decision, the first step on a long lonely climb. "I feel like I'm starting up Uncompahgre Peak."

"I'll help you on that climb, Vini, like I promised Joel. I won't let you slip on the boulders and fall to purgatory. Or skid down through the loose shale."

Shale composed of young men's dreams, she thought, dreams crumbled by Heffron.

The next morning Vini waited in line at the Company Store cashier's window to check on the Widows and Orphans Fund. The *Gazette* listed only two jobs with room and board for women. The Forest Queen had openings. And the Sterlings needed a housekeeper. It would have to be the latter. Vini remembered seeing Alisa on the train and at the Elk Mountain House. Martha Donegan had shared stories about how difficult she was to get along with. But a widow with a baby was not in a position to be choosey. Besides, Joel had always spoken highly of the banker, and she remembered her own first impression of him— how he had reminded her of the good bishop in New Orleans.

"Good morning, Mrs. McGragor," said Henry when it was her turn. He looked kindly at her over the rims of his glasses. "I'm very sorry about your husband's death."

"I was told to come here for the . . . the fund."

"The Widows and Orphans Fund."

Finality stabbed her once more.

"Mr. Heffron made the first contribution. Twelve hundred dollars! A generous man."

Other words chased through her mind to describe him.

"Mr. King is handling that fund. You need to go back to his office."

"Thank you." How she dreaded talking to King again. Desperation alone took her feet to the somber line outside his door. Again she waited, dread growing with each passing minute.

"Mrs. McGragor," said King. "Please have a chair."

"I'll stand, thank you."

He took his time sorting through the stack of envelopes, that disgusting smirk on his face all the while. "Here it is. This is your share."

She reached for the envelope.

"Just a moment." He opened it and pulled out the accompanying ledger sheet. "Let's see. Groceries. Baby things." He glanced across his desk, his smirk disappearing for an instant. "I didn't know about your baby."

"He was born Christmas Eve."

For a moment he seemed to waiver. But just for a moment. Again his eyes hardened. She knew she would continue to pay for humiliating him.

"You also owe the final payment on Joubert's debt." He totaled the bill, checked his figures, and deducted the total from her share of the fund. "Thanks to Mr. Heffron and other people who gave to the fund, your share is large enough to pay back every penny you owe the Company. In fact, Mrs. McGragor," he said patronizingly, "you have a balance coming. Seventeen cents—to be exact."

"Seventeen cents!" Panic surged. She repressed it. Mama's daily ritual came back to her:

> *This is the day the Lord has made;*
> *Let us rejoice and be glad in it.*

Relinquishing that ritual forever, she replaced it with a new one:

> This is the day that Heffron made;
> Let me survive and be strong in it.

"Ten, fifteen, sixteen, seventeen," King counted, plunking the four coins on his desk.

"Heffron gives, and Heffron takes away." Vini picked up the coins, cold to the touch. That same coldness entered her heart, and tenderness hardened into steel determination. She raised her chin, tucked back a dark lock of hair, and walked out of the Company Store for the last time in her life. Never again would she pass through those doors. Never!

CHAPTER 14

*S*till clutching the seventeen cents, Vini crossed the street to the bank. She noticed that the flags were no longer at half mast for the victims. Life goes on, she thought, feeling dead. Inside the bank, voices all around her buzzed about the Jokerville Disaster. Fighting the urge to hold her ears, she asked to see Mr. Sterling.

Again impeccably dressed, he moved from behind his desk to greet her. "Mrs. McGragor, I'm Richard Sterling." He smiled at her, and the beginnings of smile wrinkles etched around his kind brown eyes. "Please sit down."

Feeling small in the oversized chair, she noted the marked contrast between King's demeaning manner a few minutes before and the graciousness of the wealthiest man in town.

"Are you Joel McGragor's . . ."

His recognition brought comfort. But pain chased it away. "I'm his . . ." she forced out the hateful terminal truth. "His widow. His name wasn't in the newspaper."

"But word has spread. Everyone liked Joel." He turned from her and stared out the window, the shoveled snow blocking his view beyond the boardwalk. "He was a rare man, one of integrity. Crested Butte is a lesser place without him."

"Thank you, *monsieur.* Afraid she would cry, she quickly stated the point of her visit. "You have a notice in the newspaper for a housekeeper. I would like to apply for the job. I am trained in the domestic arts."

He smiled appreciatively. "'Trained in the domestic arts'? The last applicant said she was 'good at cook'n 'n clean'n'."

She smiled, feeling more at ease.

"Can you tell me about yourself?"

"I'm from New Orleans. Mama excels in the domestic arts and taught me all that she knows." Homesickness welled up inside her, and she longed to be with Mama and Papa, to feel their arms around her. She fought back tears.

"I imagine you feel very much alone." His voice was deep and soothing, a bass song of sympathy.

She felt her spirit touched by one who understood without being told. Cruelty she could handle; gentleness summoned those dreaded tears. She blinked them back and hurried on. "There's something you should know."

He waited, not pressing her to speak.

She swallowed. "I have a baby."

"A baby!"

Holy Mother, please don't let him say no because of my baby.

Again he stared out the snow-blocked window. "How old?"

"A month, a week, and a day. My neighbor is keeping him this morning."

"Mrs. McGragor!" He rose and stepped toward her. "You can't be strong enough yet to go to work."

"Oh, but I am," she pleaded. "I would do everything that needed to be done. I'm sure you would be pleased."

"I don't doubt that."

"And I wouldn't let Ben be a bother to you."

"Indeed he would not." He hesitated and then smiled. "The job is yours. When would you like to begin?"

"Today."

He frowned, his face falling with equal ease into a frown or smile. "I'll hold the job for you. Give yourself more time."

"I need to move today."

His eyes flashed. "You're being evicted from Company housing!"

She nodded.

"You are welcome to move into my house today, Mrs. McGragor, but please take time to get settled before you begin working. The northeast bedroom will be yours."

The northeast bedroom. She well remembered being there with Joel before the house was finished.

"I'll telephone Mrs. Sterling and make arrangements."

Alisa Sterling opened the door of the big yellow house on Elk.

"I am Vini McGragor."

"I am Mrs. Richard Sterling," she said haughtily. Her hand remained on the brass doorknob, and she stood in silence, frowning.

"Mr. Sterling called about me?"

"You are younger than I expected."

Again there was an awkward silence. Wanting to break it, Vini smiled and said, "We were on the first train into Crested Butte together."

"We may have been on the same train. But we were not *together*."

Confused by how badly things had begun and trying to improve the situation, she said politely, "Your husband was very kind to me."

Alisa's eyes moved slowly, deliberately, from tip to toe over Vini. "I bet he was."

Shocked by the innuendo, Vini put up an internal shield to protect herself from this woman who held the key to a roof over baby Ben's head.

"Mr. Sterling told me you are trained in the domestic arts. If that is so, it seems you would know that maids use the back door."

The fire within Vini smoldered from humiliation, but she reminded herself to hold her tongue. This job was essential, and she would bear whatever was necessary to get it and to keep it. If Joel could endure the Jokerville for Francine, surely she could bear Alisa Sterling for Ben.

"Under the circumstances, however . . . Your being a widow and all . . . This time you may enter here." She spoke not another word as she led the way upstairs and through the door to the northeast bedroom.

Vini went to the window that overlooked the rugged peaks that Joel loved. "What a beautiful view!" For a moment her hand touched the lace curtain. "I've always admired this house. My husband helped build it."

"You should admire it. It's the finest one in Crested Butte." She opened the door on the west wall that led to the attic.

The attic. Vini recalled sitting on the sawhorse with Joel that night long ago.

"You can stay up there."

"In the attic?" she asked surprised.

"Mr. Sterling may have mentioned this bedroom. But I don't want a little brat disturbing him. Or me."

Holding her tongue with difficulty, Vini went to the door and looked up into the attic, dark except for a window at each end.

Alisa motioned toward the attic steps. "Go on up. You can just set aside the things I've stored."

Vini felt Alisa watching her climb the narrow steep steps. She stifled a gasp. Boxes and junk cluttered the space. Cobwebs hung from the rafters. Dim light filtered through the dust-covered windows at each end of the attic. Her shoes made prints in the dirt on the floor.

"What's the matter? It's better than Company housing, isn't it?"

She would have so much work to do to get this clean! But she had no option. The steps creaked as she descended them, brushing a cobweb from her forehead.

"The entire house needs a thorough cleaning. I expect you to get started first thing in the morning."

"I understood Mr. Sterling to say—"

"If you want to go by what Mr. Sterling says, you'll need to apply for a job at the bank. In this house, you will work for me." Her smile reminded Vini of Fred King. "If you don't like my terms, maybe you'd better look elsewhere."

Vini realized that Alisa wanted to drive her away. Well, she couldn't! Ben needed a place to live. "My friend will help me move in this afternoon,

Madame," she replied, stepping onto the battlefield in a war with Alisa. One she didn't understand, but Ben's survival was at stake. She would never choose to start a war. However, finding herself in one, she did not intend to lose it!

Vini owned little so it did not take long to pack for the move. While Nick loaded the wagon, Martha Donegan organized a cleaning party of every good Catholic she could find. They filed upstairs through the northeast bedroom into the attic of the big yellow house on Elk. By sundown the attic sparkled, and they all hugged Vini goodbye. Fresh curtains hung over clean windows, and a cloth partition separated Vini's living area from Alisa's junk which they had pushed back under the rafters. The first victory was Vini's. But she wondered what battles would ensue in this war with Alisa. She knew she couldn't win them all.

She fed Ben and rocked him to sleep, then put him in his cradle. Exhausted herself, she picked up the candle and moved to the window to close the curtains. As she unhooked the first sash, she noticed a man staring up at her through the window. In the light of the snowglow she saw a large *Z* on his cheek. Roach!

Grateful that she was not alone but tucked safely in Mr. Sterling's house, she unhooked the other sash and set the candle on the stand beside her bed. She pulled Joel's saddlebag from the hook above her bed and rubbed her hand tenderly across the fancy *M* on the flap. She opened it, empty except for Joel's two valued possessions: the old picture of himself as a little boy sitting with his father and Chief Ouray, and the white bone-handled knife that had belonged to Joel's birth father, that unknown Chiricahua Apache chief. She touched her neck and felt his mother's cross of gold outlined in silver. She too would treasure these things and someday give them to Ben.

On impulse she tossed in the seventeen cents, one coin at a time. She unfolded the *Gunnison Review Press,* picked up her pen and painfully added Joel McGragor to the listing of the dead. She stared at the name of the one she had known so briefly and loved so deeply. Then she put the clipping into the saddlebag. *C'est dans le passé.* It is in the past. All is over.

CHAPTER 15

*T*wo days after Valentine's Day, her uncelebrated twentieth birthday, Vini found herself in serious trouble with Alisa. Asked to prepare dinner for a guest, she had done her best to make it perfect so Mr. Sterling would be pleased. The trouble started when the doorbell rang at seven o'clock.

Will Chaney's ink-black eyes lit up with pleasure. "Vini! What a good surprise!" He glanced around. "Where's Joel?"

The question racked her.

Mr. Sterling stepped forward and took her elbow. "He was killed in the disaster, Will."

"Not Joel!" He slowly shook his head, pain and shock in his eyes.

"His name was somehow omitted from the list Fred King gave the newspaper," added Mr. Sterling.

Will took Vini's hand. "I am so sorry."

"He admired you, Will." Her mouth spoke the words, but she felt removed from them, numb and invisible, as though she was not even here.

"If I'd been sent to cover the story, I would have known. I would have come to see you and the baby. Perhaps I could have been helpful in some way."

Alisa came down the stairs. "Good evening, Mr. Chaney. I see you are being properly welcomed."

He nodded. "Good evening, Mrs. Sterling." He turned again to Vini. "I'm so glad you're here tonight. We can talk over dinner."

She felt her face flush. "Oh, no. You misunderstand. I work here."

Mr. Sterling smiled at her. "I didn't know you and Will are friends. Please join us for dinner."

Alisa glared at her across the enemy line.

"I insist," he said firmly. "Alisa, please entertain Will while I help Mrs. McGragor set another place."

By dessert the Coroners jury dominated the men's conversation. Vini began to feel sick.

"You probably know, Will, that the Coroners jury cleared the Company."

"Isn't that a surprise," he said sarcastically. "Especially when an investigation lasts only seven days and an employee of Heffron Enterprises is the coroner and chooses the jurors. Jurors who just happen to be, to quote the *Gunnison Review-Press*, 'three warm political friends' of the superintendent."

"M. Morgan Heffron knows how to protect his investments."

"Isn't he one of our great humanitarians?" asked Alisa.

"He also knows how to protect his image," said Will. "What's the feeling here, Richard?"

"Sentiment leans toward seeing the inquest as a whitewash. The Company relied heavily on Luke Richardson, the fire boss. The investigation found that he had followed the rules—he had checked all the chambers and made the required chalk marks warning that chamber number two was too dangerous to work. They found that the explosion occurred in that chamber, and that some miner, or miners, entered it contrary to the fire boss's instructions."

"I read the verdict. They ignored the entrance law requiring a 300 foot separation, Richard. The Jokerville's are only 60 feet apart."

Alisa finished her *éclair* and yawned her boredom.

Will seemed not to notice. "Are you aware that the Company knew from the beginning that methane generated under the coal and poured out from the cracks around the tunnel?"

"At the inquest they didn't deny the danger, but they claimed they protected miners by using a fan that forced air into the mine."

"Protected them? The Jokerville is the biggest mining disaster in the history of the West!"

"At least they recommended one change. The managers are to require the use of safety lamps because open lamps are too dangerous."

"Give little Ben a couple more years, and he'll know that much!" Will pulled a magazine article from his vest pocket and unfolded it. "Listen to what *Harper's Weekly* concluded after they interviewed several miners:

> The mine is said to have always been dangerous.
> Experienced men declared it to be the worst they ever saw, the
> amount of gas generated being unusually large and very deadly.

Are you aware that the foreman rarely goes through the mine?"

The banker frowned and leaned forward.

"He knows it's extremely dangerous. When the mine first opened, I did a story and he refused to take me inside. He told me he could hear the ticking sound of gas leaking through the coal."

The ticking grandfather clock in the hall resounded in Vini's ears. Was this the sound that Joel heard as the gas filled the black pit? *Tick-tock. Tick-tock.*

Will took off his glasses, his sharp eyes deadly. "I'll tell you something, Richard. Joel McGragor was a very fine man and a good friend of mine, and I intend to do one major thing in his honor."

Tick-tock. Tick-tock.

The only power I have is the power of the pen. But I've learned to wield it effectively. So help me, God," he swore, looking at Vini, "the Jokerville will be closed!"

Tick-tock. Tick-tock. Too-late. Too-late.

The aftermath of the disaster loomed in Vini's mind—the coal cars loaded with mangled miners, some dismembered, others with gaping holes through their flesh. And then the third coal car rolling passed her, with the battered body of Joel. She stifled a scream and ran from the room.

Late that night Vini lay awake in the attic, longing to run into Joel's arms. Arms? She drifted into a fitful sleep. The dreaded dream returned. She was kneeling at a mass grave in the snow beside a wooden coffin. Inside were severed arms and legs entangled with hands and feet. She had to find all the pieces of Joel. He was in agony like this, and he needed her to put him together again so he could get out of the box and come home. Desperately she searched through the disconnected limbs, but she couldn't find the right ones. She awoke, sweating and trembling in the dark silence of the attic.

As the snow cleared and the days lengthened, it was not uncommon for Vini to see Roach staring up through the window when she closed the curtains at night. She considered mentioning it to Mr. Sterling. But when she thought about what to say, it sounded foolish.

Vini spent her nights trying to put Joel back together and her days trying to get along with Alisa. She reminded Vini of Parry's primrose, one of the loveliest wildflowers in the mountains, eye-catching and inviting—but it smelled like a carcass as one drew close. A daily barrage of orders followed Mr. Sterling's departure for the bank, and critical eyes watched for a mistake. But Vini learned not to worry about that. Mr. Sterling was kind, a sturdy spruce in her shaken world. She respected him and ran his house as well as she could. The special light in his eyes when she held Ben told her that he adored the baby. He even bought a pram so she could push Ben from room to room while she worked. She grew confident that as long as he was satisfied, she would keep her job.

Whereas her goal was to please Mr. Sterling, Alisa seemed uninterested in him. Martha had heard scandalous rumors about Alisa, but Vini refused to believe them. She didn't want Mr. Sterling to be hurt.

She worried even more about him when she found out the rumors were true. The first time he went away on business after her arrival, she heard a man's husky voice rise to the attic through the ceiling of Alisa's bedroom. Vini assumed Mr. Sterling had changed his plans.

The next morning when she began her work in the early dawn, the man she saw straightening his tie as he descended the stairs was Fred King—to be exact. Instead of looking embarrassed, that familiar smirk appeared on his face. "Good morning, Mrs. McGragor. Once again we meet on a staircase."

From that day forward Vini remained in the attic when Mr. Sterling was away until she was sure King had gone for the day. Alisa, King, and she—three parties in the deceit of poor Mr. Sterling. Parry's primrose. Unable to wash the smell from her own hands, Vini tried even harder to bring him happiness in his home.

Will Chaney had kept his word. Polka music filtered through the attic window from the City Hall on this beautiful May evening as Crested Butte celebrated the closing of the old Jokerville Mine and its new opening on the mesa near Company housing. Little good it did her. But perhaps it saved Iber Donegan and Iber Jr., and Vini was grateful for that.

The Sterlings were in Gunnison for the weekend where he was the speaker for the regional bankers' meeting. Alone for the first time in the big house, she felt somewhat uneasy. Refusing to give in to such silliness, she celebrated Ben's five-month birthday by carrying him in her arms and dancing with him like mamas and daddies danced with their babies back in New Orleans. Except instead of the Cajun two-step, she and Ben danced around the attic to the polka beat. He laughed. When the tune ended, he wanted to dance again.

"Your papa is with us tonight," she told him. "He's the one who taught me to polka."

Ben laughed and bounced up and down, wanting her to dance him around again. It grew late, and she hugged him. "We'd better settle you down for the night." She sat in the rocker and softly hummed Joel's tune until Ben fell asleep.

After she crawled into bed, it began to drizzle. The wind blew the rain through the window. The starless, moonless night placed her in total darkness except for the fragile little flame of her candle. As she carried it across the room to close the window, her shadow flickered eerily. Suddenly, a gust of wind blew it out. A bolt of lightning zigzagged and a loud BOOM shook the house.

She closed the window. Lightning streaked again. Thunder clapped. She thought she saw the shadow of a man in the yard below. She shuddered. "Don't be silly," she scolded herself. "It's probably just a tree limb bending in the wind." But she decided not to relight the candle and risk a silhouette. She felt her way back to the bed Joel had made and shared. She supposed she would never get used to sleeping alone, especially during storms. They terrified her.

She lay awake in the darkness, counting flashes of lightning and crashes of thunder instead of sheep. Then she was at the mass grave again, looking through the pieces of flesh that filled the wooden box, trying once more to put Joel back together. Suddenly, the coffin lid slammed shut. She awoke, startled. Was it the thunder? A new twist in her old nightmare? Or had something banged in the house? She lay totally still, listening intently. Beads of perspiration gathered on her forehead.

The stairs creaked once. She strained to hear, every nerve alert. Silence. Was it my imagination? Am I letting the storm get the best of me?

Again the stairs creaked. She held her breath. A long silence followed. It has to be my imagination. She exhaled softly. Lightning flashed. Thunder crashed.

She heard the stairs creak again. Yes. She was sure this time. Someone is coming! The danger is real!

She reached into Joel's saddlebag and pulled out the bone-handled knife. Her hand shook as she held it.

Silently, she moved down the five steps that led from the attic and peeked around the open door into the northeast bedroom. The stairs creaked louder now. One by one. Clearer. Closer. Rising toward her. She crept across the room and stood next to the wall behind the closed door that led to the hall. She held the knife handle tightly in her right hand as Joel had taught her. She wondered whether she could use it.

The stairs were silent now. She could hear her own heart beating. The quiet was worse than the creaking. She could feel the presence of someone in the hall, someone on the other side of the wall, someone at the door.

She heard the porcelain knob move. Lightning streaked in the darkness. She saw the knob slowly turn. The door began to open.

She hid behind it and raised her right arm, the knife blade poised to strike.

She heard the two steps through the doorway. She saw the figure of a large man. Lightning flashed. In the split-second of light, she recognized the scar shaped like a *Z* on his cheek. A gasp escaped her throat.

Roach turned. Thunder boomed.

She stood half behind the door, the knife in her right hand, not visible.

"Mrs. McGragor," he slurred. "I've wanted you since Joubert told his stories that night at the Bucket of Blood. I've been watching you and waiting. Biding my time."

Lightning flashed, and his eyes stared at her, the meanest eyes she had ever seen.

"You were generous to him with your favors. But you won't even so much as give me a smile from the window. You turn away, scorning me. But tonight you will do everything I want." His huge right hand grabbed the back of her neck, pressing her forward.

In that instant Joel stood with her as long before, guiding her arm and centering on the throat. Lightning flashed. With one swift blow, she thrust the knife into the jugular vein. Thunder crashed. She held onto the knife as Joel taught her until the thrashing arms that beat about her ceased to move, and the form shuddered into lifelessness. Lightning streaked across Roach's body sprawled on the floor, the knife sticking out of his throat.

The morning sun came up over the big yellow house on Elk, shrouded in the silence of death. Marshal Hays cranked up the telephone and asked the operator to call Mr. Sterling in Gunnison. It had taken him most of the night to settle down the town after the celebration, find out the details of the stabbing, take care of Roach's body, and get the mess cleaned up. Vini heard the marshal's voice through a fog.

"Mr. Sterling, last night a man broke into your home and attacked Mrs. McGragor." He paused. "No. She's all right. But he's dead."

He's dead. The words echoed a thousand times through her mind.

"No," the marshal said. "We're both at your house. It was pure and simple self-defense.

Pure and simple. Again, Vini saw the blood spurt out of Roach's throat. Again, the lightning flashed on the knife sticking out of the body on the floor. Again, she saw her own blood-spattered hand which would never wash clean.

The marshal hung up the telephone. "Mr. Sterling says they'll come home right away. He was real concerned about you."

"Thank you, Marshal Hays."

"I'll stay till they get here. Why don't you go rest, Mrs. McGragor?"

Unsure that she could walk through the northeast bedroom ever again, she sat on the sofa.

The marshal sat across from her, his hat on the table beside the chair. "Could I get you something to drink or eat?"

She shook her head and began humming Joel's tune to Ben in his pram, pushing it lightly back and forth.

The grandfather clock chimed ten o'clock as Mr. Sterling walked in the door. She rose from the sofa, and he took her hand in both of his. "Are you all right, Mrs. McGragor?

His concern made her think of Papa so far away. A lump rose in her throat. She'd learned how to handle hardship during these months, but gentleness still made her cry.

Mr. Sterling turned to the marshal. "Who was the man?"

"Roach. Carl Roach."

Alisa lowered her eyes, feigning shyness, and her lips curled into that familiar false smile that forewarned Vini of an attack. "Was Mr. Roach one of Vini's callers?"

The marshal's mouth fell open in disbelief. Mr. Sterling glared at Alisa.

She shot an icy glance toward Vini. "What else could you expect, Richard, after all those stories about her carrying on with her sick sister's husband?"

"That's not true!" cried Vini. She sank to the sofa defeated by the knowledge that she would never be free of Marcel's lies.

Mr. Sterling stood unmoving except for clenching and unclenching his fists.

"I told you to fire her," said Alisa. "Now she's committed murder in our beautiful house."

"Go to your room!" Mr. Sterling spoke in a cold harsh tone that Vini had never heard before.

Alisa didn't move.

"NOW!" he thundered.

Slowly, like a martyr, Alisa climbed the stairs.

Mr. Sterling turned to Vini. "I apologize for my wife."

"I'll be on my way now," said the marshal, picking up his hat.

Mr. Sterling stood silent for a moment, as though he'd forgotten the marshal's presence. "Thank you for staying with Mrs. McGragor."

"She's been through a lot."

As soon as the door closed, Mr. Sterling went upstairs. The next few minutes produced a scene that Vini couldn't see and wished she couldn't hear.

Mr. Sterling's rage-filled voice reverberated down the stairs and into the parlor. "ONE OF VINI'S CALLERS! Do you think I don't know what you do! The only difference between you and the women at the Forest Queen is that they are honest about it and at least they draw a fee. Why should Fred King go there if he can stop off here for free!"

"He comes to see her!" screamed Alisa.

"You are a common slut! You dishonor my name!"

Vini heard a crash—like a heavy ewer thrown against the wall.

"One of Vini's callers indeed! She is the only lady in this house!"

"LADY!" Alisa shouted. "I've seen the way you look at her! If she's too much of a goody-goody to be your mistress in reality, she's still your mistress in your mind!"

A sharp slap followed. Alisa began to cry hysterically.

Vini could endure no more. She ran up to the attic to pack. She would not spend another night in this unhappy house where she'd lived with ridicule, insults, and lies. And had killed a human being.

Vini's trunk was half-filled when she heard a knock on the attic door.

"Mrs. McGragor, may I come up?"

"Yes, Mr. Sterling," she said though she felt uncomfortable.

He climbed the attic steps and looked around. "I shouldn't have allowed Alisa to put you and Ben up here. I am ashamed of that."

She noticed that the formality of "Mrs. Sterling" was gone.

"But as with everything else, you've turned it into a homey place." He looked at the open trunk. "You're not leaving!"

"I can't stay here any longer, Mr. Sterling."

"Oh, Vini!"

He said those two words with a woeful sadness that she did not know the rich could experience. Then she realized that the formality of "Mrs. McGragor" was also gone.

"I suppose you could hear the argument."

"I tried not to listen."

"Alisa was not totally wrong." That special tenderness in his eyes she'd attributed to his love for Ben fell full force upon her now—and Ben was in his cradle. "You know that I would never touch you, Vini." He said her name with such tenderness. "I would not debase you in any way."

She felt uneasy. Knowing that he was going to say too much. Not knowing how to stop him. She realized that she had pleased him too well.

He sat down on the bed and took her hand. "I remember the day you came to my office and applied for this job. A beautiful young woman filled with love for your dead husband and loneliness for your family. I wanted to protect you then. And I want to protect you now."

"You've been very kind, Mr. Sterling."

"You looked so sweet and innocent, so frail and helpless sitting in that big chair talking about your new baby. And yet, in the face of a thousand odds against you, you spoke with determination and courage."

That day seemed like years ago to Vini. What a long journey life had become without Joel.

"You have brought into this house grace and charm and gentleness. The only joy I've known here is that given by you and Ben." His deep soothing voice caressed her. "I have come to . . . to love you." He allowed the word only once.

A part of her wanted to fall into his arms and feel their strength enfold her, ending this hard battle alone. She longed for the caring touch of someone she could depend on. That touch taken for granted in childhood and abounding in marriage. Now void in her life. Hold me, a part of her wanted to say to him. Put your arms around me and hold me. Like a daughter. Like a sister. Like a— She would not allow herself to think the word, even once. Other words took its place. "I appreciate you, Mr. Sterling, and I respect you. But I'll always love Joel. I'll love him until the day I die."

"I know. And that is part of why I love you." Once more he allowed the word.

They looked at each other in the rich kind of silence that speaks without words. Again, as that first day in his office, she felt her spirit touched by one who understood, who would always understand.

She forced herself to turn back to the open trunk. It blurred, transforming itself into the wooden coffin of the mass grave. No! She reached up with both hands and with a fierce bang of finality she slammed the lid on her nightmare.

Like the initial fluttering of baby Ben in her womb, an ember of life glowed in her soul. It was time to get off this ruby road spattered with the blood of the innocent and the guilty. It was time for a new dream.

THREE

INTERNATIONAL
1894

About 3 o'clock, fire was discovered issuing from Carlisle and Tetard's cellar. The alarm was given and the firemen responded promptly but upon making connection with the hose, it was found that the water was frozen up and nothing could be done to stop the destruction . . . . The fire burned both directions from Carlisle and Tetard's building, destroying the entire block . . . .

The origin of the fire is unknown, but it is probably the work of an incendiary, as Messers. Carlisle and Tetard say that there was no fire in their building that could have started it.

Gunnison Tribune
Jan. 14, 1893

CHAPTER 16

*U*ini McGragor lifted the lace curtain and watched ten-year-old Ben saunter down the boardwalk to school, his lunch pail and books in his hands. She liked the view from her second story home above Carlisle and Tetard's Market on Elk Avenue. Each morning she watched the sunrise over Crested Butte Mountain. Its reds and yellows reflected on the snowy peak above and the scraggly town below. In the late winter afternoons she paused to see the shadows of the setting sun gradually robe the Red Lady in a purple mantle of majesty. Now, the long-skirted ladies and dark-suited gentlemen nodded to one another as they met. A man tightened the cinch of his saddle, horses and sleighs waited in the cold, and great piles of snow stood as high as the buildings.

She told herself she was standing at the window to watch Ben and because she liked the view. She didn't admit the other reason, but automatically she looked down at the bank across the street on the corner and then her eyes followed Elk Avenue eastward until she spotted Richard crossing Third Street as he walked to work from the big yellow house. He glanced toward her window, a daily habit, and she smiled and waved. He tipped his hat slightly as he entered the bank.

Before beginning her day of needlework, she opened the newspaper, gasped at the headline, and grinned. She grabbed her old gray cloak that was worn beyond warmth and hurried to St. Patrick's Catholic Church. She rushed into the study to show Father Michael Barrett. Her trusted priest and revered friend had performed her wedding, baptized her son, and left Gunnison to serve Crested Butte. He had heard her confessions for a decade now. "It's a great day, Father Mike!"

She tossed the newspaper down and moved around to his side of the desk, looking over his shoulder and silently re-reading the article with him:

M. MORGAN HEFFRON DEAD

M. Morgan Heffron, coal baron and philanthropist, collapsed yesterday while delivering a speech at the Million Dollar Round Table Conference in Washington. His final words were an impassioned plea against recognizing organized labor.

He said: "Collective bargaining is a monster that will barge in and take whatever it wants. No business, industry, or institution will be spared. There will be strike after strike by group after group. Labor-management strife will grow and spread until we reach a point in our nation's future when our policemen go on strike, and our children's teachers, and even our baseball players!"

At that point Mr. Heffron grabbed his chest and fell dead to the floor.

"May God rest his soul in hell!" said Vini.

Father Mike frowned at her, the wrinkles set early in his brow from sharing the burdens of his people. "I know no better person than you, Vini. But hatred can take over a person's heart if we give vent to it."

She sat down in the pine chair in front of his desk. "Don't you rejoice that we're rid of him, Father Mike?" She measured an inch between her thumb and index finger. "Just a tiny bit?"

He walked to the window, his back to her. "Mrs. Heffron was in the large parish I served as a student in seminary. She is a kind and generous lady. At this very moment, she is feeling the pain of loss."

For an instant another widow's grief touched Vini. Quickly she shoved it from her mind and heart. No one named Heffron would ever have her sympathy. "Now that he's gone, maybe things will be better for the miners."

Father Mike turned back to Vini. "Mrs. Heffron's husband did not attend mass with her. Neither did their son."

She froze in the chair. "Son?"

"M. Morgan Heffron Jr."

"Sainte Marie, Mère de Dieu!"

"He's been involved in the business behind the scenes for at least a decade now."

"Then he must be as hard and greedy as his father."

"Unfortunately."

Change brought no change. "This isn't a great day after all."

Father Mike sat back down at his desk. "Please hear me, Vini." His extraordinary blue eyes drew hers and held them in his powerful magnetic gaze, looking straight into her damaged soul. "God loves all people—even those named Heffron."

She forced her eyes away from his. "Then God isn't very particular."

"Give thanks, Vini. We'd all be in trouble."

The odor of the coke ovens filled the air as she plodded back toward Elk. She knew she could recognize Crested Butte blindfolded by that smell. She wanted changes in mining conditions—to remove total dependence on scrip and the Company, to break the cycle of sons becoming miners at twelve because of their families' financial burdens, to provide more options for the young people of Crested Butte. With one Heffron gone and another come, she could no longer wait for changes from the top. She couldn't do much, but she felt a strong pull to do what little she could. In her secret heart she knew this was not a desire born of altruism but of revenge. So be it!

Her thoughts played tag, birthing a plan, as she marched straight from St. Patrick's to the Forest Queen and opened the forbidden door, uncomfortable but unashamed.

Tillie was seated nearby and came to her at once. "What are you doing here, Vini!"

"Could we talk?"

Tillie smiled. "The last time you came you wanted a job. What do you need to fix your flint this time?"

"Some advice."

"Let's go upstairs."

Tillie's room looked just as it had years ago, and Vini sat down in the same red velvet chair, newly reupholstered. After the cordial preliminaries, she came straight to the point. "I want to expand my business. Mining is important enough in Colorado to include a pick and hammer in the state seal—but not important enough to take care of the miners. I want to hire miners' wives. Even though we can vote now in this state, customs haven't changed."

Tillie poured a cup of coffee and handed it to her, looking puzzled. "I'd be glad to help, but I don't see how I can."

"You know a lot about men. To expand, I need to get them on my side."

"Well now," Tillie grinned, "I might know something about that."

"The husbands have to feel good about it. Not threatened and ashamed."

"You've got a considerable problem."

"Otherwise, the women won't hire on."

"And if they did, they'd pay for it in an almighty way. Believe me, Vini, social customs are powerful." Tillie's eyes grew sad. "You ask for lumps when you get on the wrong side of them."

Vini felt impatient with social mores that held people down. "It's the custom, not a wife's job in itself, that disgraces her husband."

Tillie sighed. "One thing for sure. You can't go full chisel. Husbands have been worried about their wives disgracing them since Adam lost his rib."

"I want to go about this in a way that helps men feel proud when their wives are selected. Like it's a feather in a man's cap to have his wife's needlework qualify for the Marie-Vincente label."

"And you need my help figuring out how to do that."

"Please, Tillie. You are a wise friend."

She glanced down, plainly struck by that word. They sat quietly together, sipping their coffee. Tillie thinking. Vini waiting.

Finally Tillie spoke. "I don't know about any of this from book learning. I can't even read."

It was always hard for Vini to remember that a lot of people in Crested Butte couldn't read. That was another thing she wanted to help change someday.

"But I can tell you what I've learned from experience—about men generally. We both know exceptions."

Vini leaned forward in her chair, eager to listen.

Tillie held up her index finger. "First, if you don't want to threaten them, just call it 'a lady thing.' Then they can look down on it, and shake their heads together about what the little ladies will think of next, and go on feeling superior."

"Like the way some men give their wives a little pat on the head for holding insignificant church bazaars—that raise significant amounts of money for missions."

"While the men are busy carrying on the important business of the world—like coming here."

They both laughed.

"Second," Tillie added her middle finger to her index one. "If you don't want to threaten men, don't call it 'work.'"

"So . . . needle arts might be better than needlework."

"There you go! The arts don't seem to threaten a pick-toting man. Or a gun-toting man. Or any of the beer-barreled men around here who hitch up their britches and get on with it."

Again they both laughed.

"Come to think of it, Vini, I don't know any man in Crested Butte who is going to pick up a needle and some pastel threads."

"So they won't feel we are competing with them or invading their world."

Tillie nodded. "Third, be sure you don't pay higher wages than the Company."

"I don't want to do anything that hurts a miner's pride, but I could give bonuses at the end of the year in an education fund for their children."

"Then we're down to the biggest problem—the wives working away from home."

"I used to do needlework at home while Joel was at the Jokerville." She thought for the thousandth time about her grand anniversary surprise that she'd not been able to give him. "I used those things to start my business."

"Maybe, at least in the beginning, the miners' wives could do that, Vini. Men assume that anything done at home can't be important. What man stays home to work? If they don't actually leave, they go downstairs. Even if they're just in the next room, they call it an office and 'go' to work. Men like to be the ones who do the 'going' and like for their wives to do the 'staying.'"

"It's understandable, I suppose," said Vini, not wanting to be too hard on men. "They're the ones who used to face the bears and bring home the meat and claws and fur."

"While the little woman stayed safely close to the fire in the cave." Tillie smiled. "They still protect us. I'll give them that."

"I always felt so safe when Joel was alive."

"Let's face it. It's nice to have a strong man nearby," admitted Tillie. "I like that feeling."

Vini set her cup and saucer on the table, aware of the void in her own life. "Thank you," she said, embracing Tillie. She thought of her deceased mama who might be looking down from heaven at her hugging a whisper woman. But now, she realized, Mama would be able to see Tillie's good heart. "Stop in for tea sometime." Remembering the incognito visit to Company housing long ago, Vini added with a chuckle, "And there's no need for a disguise."

The next morning Benjamin Joel McGragor, aged ten, stood in his father's homemade skis with the long aspen pole in his hand. Saturday was his favorite day because he could ski with his friends. He and Dave Donegan and Martin Boyd scanned the panoramic view above the ancient Ute trail that had become Kebler Road. For as long as he could remember, he and his mother had hiked up here toward the Red Lady for a picnic in the circle of old spruce trees when the yellow columbines began to bloom each year. She'd often talked about how much his papa had loved this place. Ben took in the circle of spruce and the waterfall and the snow-covered peaks against the clear January sky, trying to look at them through his father's eyes. It brought him closer to the man he'd never known. "Someday," said Ben, "I'm going to own this land." He didn't tell his friends why he wanted it. Some things were best left unspoken.

"Where are you going to get the money?" asked Martin Boyd.

"He's going to rob Mr. Sterling's bank," Dave Donegan quipped.

"I'll have money when I'm the news editor for the *Rocky Mountain News*," Ben said proudly. "Like Uncle Will."

"I might be a barber like my granddaddy," said Martin.

"In just three more months I'll be twelve and a working man." Dave straightened his shoulders and stretched to his full height. "Big Mine, here I come!"

Ben had overheard enough of his mother's conversations to know that Heffron Enterprises owned Big Mine and that she held anyone named Heffron personally responsible for the Jokerville Disaster and his father's death. Ben knew he could not forgive M. Morgan Heffron. Not so much because of losing his father. How could you miss a man you'd never had a chance to know? But because of his mother's hardships. Things were all right now, but those painful early years were etched in his memory—when his mother would go all day without food and say she wasn't hungry, and stay up all night doing needlework so she could earn enough money to take care of them. Heffron was the enemy. But Ben didn't tell Dave and Martin all this. Some things were best left unspoken.

Martin pointed toward the waterfall. "A dipper!" The bird swooped into the mist and out again, defying winter rather than flying south. "Once I got beat up because some kids didn't want someone like me in their class. And I wanted to run away and never go back to school again. That night Granddaddy told me about dippers. And how they don't run away just because things get tough." His words came from deep within his own world, that familiar hurt look in his dark eyes.

Ben heard the echo of Grandpa Nick's words the last time he saw him: *Your pa certain-sure didn't run away from anything, Ben. He faced life straight on with honor and integrity. Joel McGragor would be ashamed to call you his son if you ever turn tail and run.* The next day an avalanche buried the old man he loved so much. Mama had wept, and so had he—but not in public.

"Let's ski to the cave," said Dave.

Ben eyed the steep grade of the drop to the cave far below. "Grandpa Nick always said that the snow is like a woman—'soft and smooth, but treacherous.'"

"But a woman is worth it!" said Dave smugly from the seniority of his age.

"I'll beat you both!" challenged Martin, bending low and heaving himself over the edge and down the harrowing descent.

Ben and Dave followed. The wind blew in the boys' faces, and the thrill of risk and boldness beat in their hearts. White powder rose and swirled around their skis. They twisted down the ravine with the snow clouds chasing them, small locomotives freed from the bondage of tracks.

Vini looked at the clock and paced to the window again. She knew that Ben, agile and well coordinated, could hold his own with the best of skiers in spite of his age. But she'd expected him to be home by now. She pulled back her lace curtain and scanned the peak—an empty gesture. She couldn't see the boys even if they were there. She felt torn as Ben grew older. She didn't want to be an over-protective mother, but she felt an overwhelming dread of accidents. Joel. Nick. If anything happened to Ben . . . She shuddered, refusing to complete the thought.

She had wanted him to go to the bank with her. But she couldn't wait any longer. She opened Joel's old saddlebag hanging on a peg by her bedroom door and pulled out the envelope marked "Mortgage—Final Payment." Richard had been patient with her over the years, especially in those difficult early days when she had missed so many payments. Not once had he mentioned how far behind she was, and he had never charged her interest.

She looked around at her home above the market—living room, kitchen, and two bedrooms. The aspen vase carved by Joel sat on the table, and the rocking chair was drawn close to the coal stove. A second chair with a floral needlepoint cushion in pastels stood by the blue settee, her basket of unfinished needlework nearby. She glanced into the bedrooms where a comforter she'd made of navy and gray wool scraps topped Ben's bed, and the colorful quilt she'd stitched still covered her spruce four-poster bed Joel had built. She smiled, feeling his presence on this special day.

She stretched her arms out, hugging the whole place. "Within the hour this cozy home will be truly mine!" Her excitement bubbled up in a warm, soft laugh.

Vini crossed Elk mid-block, deciding to stop at the barbershop where Martin lived in the back with his grandfather. Ben had spent a lot of time with them over the years. She stepped somewhat timidly into the barbershop's male domain. "Good afternoon, Mr. Boyd."

"Excuse me, Marshal." Mr. Boyd came to the door.

The marshal lay back in the black leather chair, his face lathered. "I'll wait for Vini McGragor any day."

She smiled at him and turned to Mr. Boyd. "I thought the boys would be home by now. Have you seen them?"

"They're all right, Mrs. McGragor."

"They're boys, Vini," added the marshal. "They're just out having a good time."

"I guess I just needed reassurance."

"Sometimes mothers do," said Mr. Boyd kindly. "I noticed Ben's eye was better this morning. I hear he got it helping Martin in a fight."

"That's right."

"I hear Sam Shun and his bully friends called Martin a name." He sighed and softened his voice. "Some white folks are going to do that. I suppose Martin needs to learn to ignore it, but that Shun boy has been feeling his oats ever since the Company promoted his daddy to assistant super."

"Sam Shun called you a name, Mr. Boyd. Not Martin. He isn't going to stand for that. Neither is Ben."

"He's his father's son," said the marshal. "You can be proud, Vini."

Mr. Boyd grinned, and his eyes twinkled. "I hear the Shun bunch got the worst end of the deal."

She nodded. She didn't like for Ben to fight. He had Joel's sense of justice, and she felt torn between wanting that characteristic in her son and at the same time knowing it could bring him harm. Why couldn't rearing a child be simple like it used to be in past generations?

"Ben told Martin you pay off your home today."

She wished Ben would keep their financial affairs to himself. "I'm on my way to the bank now."

"Congratulations!" said the marshal behind his lathered face. "This is one 'thirteenth' that's a lucky day."

Mr. Boyd smiled broadly. "I'm happy for you, Mrs. McGragor. I know it's been hard."

Hard was too soft a word to describe the struggle—those years of caring for Ben and trying to establish her needlework business. They were hungry years, but now business was growing so fast she couldn't keep up with it. Ben had everything he needed and some of what he wanted. But she still spent almost nothing on herself, saving frugally and giving generously. From the beginning, no matter how desperately she needed the money, the first ten percent earned went to the church. She told herself she gave in response to God's love. But in her secret heart she knew it was really in contrast to M. Morgan Heffron's greed. Senior or Junior, it didn't matter; the two had merged in her mind. "It's been worth it," she said. "No one can evict me now!"

"You're free." The intensity of Mr. Boyd's eyes reflected his own struggle as a former slave. "There's nothing like freedom!"

"Would you please send Ben to the bank if the boys come back soon?" She glanced outside toward the peak, her anxiety returning.

"Now don't you worry yourself about those boys."

"They know how to take care of themselves," added the marshal.

He was right. The boys had mountain sense. But they were also adventurous. Apprehension nipped at her heels as she walked to the bank.

Vini sat down in one of the bank chairs lined up against the wall for waiting customers. "Hello, Mr. Daly," she said to the saloonkeeper.

He nodded and went back to reading the newspaper while he waited.

She avoided worrying about Ben by forcing her thoughts into the past. She remembered that January long ago when she came for a job interview, and now felt sad amazement at the swift passage of time, with one day blending unnoticed into the next until suddenly a year of days had passed. And now a decade. Vanished.

Unlike that first day, the voices buzzing around her didn't mention the Jokerville Disaster. But they still spoke of mining. Change brought no change.

Today they talked about the opening of Big Mine, bragging that it was one of the largest coal mines in Colorado and would need 400 miners—more by far than currently lived in town. She wouldn't be surprised if the Company decreased the working age below twelve to meet the labor demand. She shuddered.

"A wee bit chilly now, that's you," sat Pat Daly, folding his newspaper front to back.

"January is a shivery month."

"Me thinks this will warm you up." He handed her the *Rocky Mountain News.* "'Tis a fiery editorial by Will Chaney."

"If he's written something fiery, it must be about Heffron Enterprises," she said with a smile.

The editorial featured the opening of Big Mine and mentioned Fred King, who lived in Denver and was in charge of the whole western region for Heffron Enterprises. Will wrote about M. Morgan Heffron Jr.'s latest merger and called attention to the fact that Colorado was not the only state in the grip of Heffron Enterprises. Under the names of various companies, Heffron had quietly and simultaneously developed his scheme all over the land. With control of the country's steel production, he could set the price without any serious threat of competition. He could also determine steel distribution, allowing him to dominate steel-dependent industries.

"'Tis scary, me thinks," said Pat.

Vini nodded and read on. Will accused Heffron Enterprises of trying to expand the Company Town concept to the Company State. He said the plans included Company communities run by Company rules. Children would be educated in Company schools until old enough to begin working in the mines, and that age would be subject to the Company's labor needs. Company roads and railroads, as well as canals where needed, would link every Company Town to a Company steel mill. In Colorado that would be Pueblo.

Will concluded with the warning that control of the steel industry was only the beginning for M. Morgan Heffron, that he planned eventually for every kind of product needed throughout the entire country to be produced by Company mines and mills and factories.

Vini shook her head. "From the Company Town to the Company State to the Company Country!" She caressed the envelope containing her final mortgage payment, grateful that she had been able to protect Ben from bondage to Heffron. She thought of Iber and Martha Donegan, their sons, one by one, going into the mine upon reaching age twelve. And someday their sons' sons would also work in the mine—infinite links in Heffron's chain. Reaffirming her decision to do her small part to break this entrapment, she exclaimed, "Something has to be done!"

"Watch out, Pat!" said Richard, stepping from his office with a grin. "The lady has a cause!"

Pat pointed to the editorial. "A good cause, me thinks. 'Tis the whole damned country Heffron wants to run! Excuse me, Ma'am."

"M. Morgan Heffron Jr. is the one who needs to apologize," she said.

"Pat is waiting for some papers to be prepared, Mrs. McGragor. Please come into my office."

Vini noted the look of tenderness that crossed Richard's face as he offered her a chair. "This is the big day."

She smiled at him. "I wanted Ben to come. He should have been back from skiing by now."

"Boys lose track of time when they're having fun," he assured her.

She sat down in the oversized chair as she had when she interviewed for a job after the Jokerville disaster. He was older now but still distinguished and impeccably dressed. His kind brown eyes stood out in a face that no longer fell as easily into a smile. What a strange relationship they'd developed over the years. A glance, a nod, a monthly visit to the bank—no more than that. And yet, to a large degree her feeling of security stemmed from her belief that if something terrible happened, she could count on him. And that if she should die, he would care for Ben like a son. No words had ever been spoken; it was something she knew in her heart.

"Vini, you put me in a miserable position when you refused to live in that building rent-free."

"It was better this way." She pulled the envelope with the final payment from her pocket and gave it to him. "Now, I own it." Four words so simple in the saying, so mighty in the meaning.

"Now, yes. But God knows how I've abhorred taking your money. Especially in those first years when the only thing keeping you going was steel determination."

His words brought back her old morning ritual:

> *This is the day that Heffron made;*
> *let me survive and be strong in it.*

She smiled, aware of a new confidence and sense of pride, for she had indeed survived and grown stronger. "I own it!" she repeated with her soft bubbly laugh.

"The whole building!" His smile showed his joy for her. "To be honest, I didn't think you had a chance of keeping up the payments. And yet, you've managed—even with a baby and nothing to begin with."

"Don't forget the seventeen cents."

He shook his head, marveling. "And you didn't even touch the money Nick left you."

"That's untouchable!" she said firmly. Nick had kept his word to Joel. The last few years of his life he'd worked hard and saved frugally in a fund for Ben and her. She'd kept every penny of that fund except the amount she'd paid for the marker in the cemetery:

> NICK LAFFEY
> BELOVED GRANDPA AND PA-IN-LAW.

"That money is for Ben's education."

"With no high school here, that's important."

"He may even want to go on to college."

"You've done remarkably well, Vini."

And become remarkably independent, she thought. "I plan to expand."

"Oh?"

"The demand for my work is greater than I can meet. I get new orders every day from Denver."

"You were right on target, Vini. High quality and a high price."

Stubbornly she'd followed her instinct to provide excellence and charge exorbitantly. It had paid off. "Quality isn't all they're buying. Elitism also."

"Elitism?"

"Only the rich can afford the Marie-Vincente label. It's the same principle as puddling drapes or setting out expensive lemons in a silver bowl. It's a way to flaunt wealth." She didn't say that observing Alisa had taught her a great deal about elitism. Some things were best left unspoken.

He frowned. "That sounds so pretentious."

"It's my version of Robin Hood." Though she smiled, she meant it.

He laughed and pulled a document from his desk drawer. "Here is the deed. It's all ready."

A brief exchange, money for a piece of paper. She found herself wishing for something more than a mere transaction.

As usual he seemed to read her thoughts. "We didn't have a written agreement, Vini, so we can't do anything dramatic like burn the mortgage."

"You've been very kind to me, Richard." She stood, conscious of the deed in her hand. Ten long years of payments for ten short minutes of business. Again she wished for more. Something special to commemorate this significant event. A celebration. A party. Like back in New Orleans with dinner and dancing and laughter.

"Something is wrong," he said, his sensitive brown eyes studying her.

She fingered the deed. "I've looked forward to this for a long time. Thank you."

Suddenly his eyes brightened and his face broke into that old easy smile. "Let's celebrate. Let me take you out for dinner tonight."

She hesitated.

"It's all right. I'm a long-time friend."

"What about Alisa?"

He laughed off the question. "Oh, Vini, you've become like a sister to me."

Part of her pretended to believe him. "You'll bring her, won't you?"

"Of course I would invite her."

Again she pretended to believe him.

"But," he added nonchalantly in his deep soothing voice, "if she can't come, I still want to celebrate this occasion." He came forward and took her hand in his. "Let me give you a grand evening."

"Like a brother for his sister?"

"Like a brother for his sister," he assured her. "Yes?"

"Yes," she smiled, totally aware that the tenderness in his eyes belied his words and the beating of her heart belied hers.

CHAPTER 17

*B*en, Dave Donegan, and Martin Boyd removed their skis and stood them against the cold damp wall of the cave. They had discovered it the previous summer and kept it a secret. Dave lit the candle they had left on a ledge and led the way beside the underground stream through a narrow passage. They ducked under the rough low ceiling. Soon the passage widened into the second chamber. Their boots echoed in the silence. When they stopped, the only sound was the soft ripple of the water.

Last summer's wood and kindling were still there, and they built a fire beneath the large painting of an Indian woman and her child. Its soft colors of blue, yellow, green, and brown danced with the light of the flames.

The boys sat cross-legged beside the stream, eating apple butter sandwiches and looking at the mysterious painting. "I wonder who painted it," said Martin. "What's the story? There is always a story."

Ben began to make one up, trying to use a deep voice like Grandpa Nick's when he told his tales. "Once upon a time, many years ago when the soldiers came to take the Utes away from this beloved land of their ancestors, a brave warrior refused to leave. He hid in these mountains."

Martin picked up the story. "The Ku Klux Klan came for him with their torches and their ropes. They scoured the high meadows and the rocky cliffs, but they couldn't find him."

"A chinook blew in," continued Dave, "chasing the soldiers and the Klan away. The brave warrior was nearly dead when he discovered this cave."

"He lived," added Martin, saving their hero. "But he was very lonely. So he painted this picture on the wall."

"It is a picture of his own wife and baby," concluded Ben, "left alone without him."

They decided the story was true—which made it so for them. They looked at the picture while they finished their sandwiches, and Ben silently added his own sequel:

Once upon a time, when my father worked in the Jokerville, an explosion in chamber two blew a hole in a fault in the mine floor. My father was knocked through it and tumbled through space. He landed in a deep underground pool and whirled helplessly around and around before floating down the winding waters that flowed through this cave. The brave Ute warrior found him and took care of him. But the blow caused permanent memory loss, and still, after all these years, he wanders through this cave wondering how to get back to wherever he belongs.

One day I come to explore, and I discover a narrow crevice. A gleam of light flickers. I squeeze through the crevice and find myself in a large chamber never before explored. The stony floor has a small hollow surrounded by a circle of rocks that enclose a fire. I smell a rabbit cooking. And there, on the other side of the underground stream, stands a man. Immediately I know it is my father. He is smiling at me. I take him by the hand, and lead him home.

What a great surprise for my mother!

"Ben!" said Dave, calling him back to the present. "Don't you want one?" A ginger cookie was in his extended hand. "Ma sent them for us."

Ben took it and ate in silence, not sharing his private sequel to the story. Some things were best left unspoken.

When Richard knocked on Vini's door that evening, he felt the nervous excitement of a boy calling on his girlfriend for the first time. The day she'd moved out of his house after that horrifying experience with Roach, he'd resisted the impulse to ask her to be his mistress, fearing she would not only refuse him but also never forgive him. Instead, he'd put her on a pedestal, committed himself to watching over her, and hushed the inner voice that asked for more.

Ben opened the door. "Hello, Mr. Sterling."

"Good evening, son. I hear about town that you're quite a skier."

"Thank you, Sir." He frowned and lowered his voice. "I got into trouble today for being gone too long. Do you think you could get Mother not to worry about me so much?"

"I'll talk to her."

"Maybe it will help." Ben smiled and put on his cap. "I'm going to spend the night at Martin's house. Good night, Sir."

Richard's eyes followed him out the door. The boy grew to look more like his father every year.

The bedroom door opened, and Vini's loveliness stunned him. He was accustomed to her tired eyes and drawn lips, scars from the struggle to survive. But tonight a warm dimpled smile reflected the happiness of youth. Normally she wore her shining hair pulled back, as if impatient to get it out of the way. But tonight dark curls softly framed her face. A radiant face. Her blue-green dress enhanced her eyes which were bright with pleasure. He realized that he'd never seen her in flattering clothes. All these years her wardrobe had been limited to a few baggy dresses which hid a figure full but not overstated and a tiny waist that could fit in the circle of his hands. That first day when she'd sat in his office in that gray cloak, he'd recognized the beauty of her spirit—so different from Alisa's. He'd felt her vulnerability as one who stood alone against the world. But the baggy aprons she'd worn in their house had not done her justice! He wasn't prepared for the physical attraction of the stranger who stood before him. He stared dumfounded, seeing her totally for the first time. "How lovely you are!"

She curtsied. "*Merci.*"

He took hold of her small hand and twirled her around. With considerable difficulty, he reminded himself to behave as her brother.

"I went to Glick Brothers this afternoon. Look at my new coat!" Proudly she held it up, and he assisted her in putting it on. "Where's Alisa?" she asked.

"She had a headache."

Vini hesitated.

Did he see a flicker of a smile on her lips? "It's all right. I'm like your big brother by now."

She nodded. "Let's celebrate!"

Richard had arranged for a special dinner at The Rose Petal, Rose's elegant new restaurant just west of the City Hall. He could tell that Vini was pleased. During the leisurely five-course meal, he talked about his childhood and the adventurous spirit of boys—keeping his word to Ben. He told her of his dreams for the future, and how Crested Butte would grow, and how important it was to him that it be more than just another Company Town. He found it easy to speak to her of things significant to him. She listened attentively, encouraged him, and asked a few appropriate questions. Her soft voice and lilting accent rose and fell like a symphony that captures the joy and pain of the universe.

Intense contradictory feelings swelled within him. At thirty when he met her, time was ahead of him. Over the years she'd delighted him with her grace and charm, her gentle sweetness. His love for her had grown as his affection for Alisa had waned. Now forty, he feared time was behind him. The candlelight flickered on the lovely face of the woman who was everything he desired. He was poignantly aware of wasting a decade. Tonight he wanted to drag her down from the pedestal and be her lover. Each flutter of the candle flame, each syllable spoken, each breath taken reminded him of a second gone, never to be lived again. Time was running out.

He reached for her hand across the table. Their eyes held. Their souls touched.

Suddenly she lowered her eyes and said, "Thank you, Richard." With an almost inaudible sigh she placed her napkin on the table, announcing the conclusion of dinner.

"Vini, I'd like to . . ." He searched for a word. "To lengthen this evening together."

She avoided looking at him.

He couldn't just take her back home and let it all end now. Robust music in the distance reminded him of the dance at the City Hall. He stood and held her chair as she rose. "Do you know how to polka?"

"I learned once. A long time ago. I've probably forgotten."

"You've lived in Crested Butte how many years?"

"Since the first train came in. Like Alisa," she added.

Alisa, he thought. Joel had been the lucky one that day. "It's practically treason to live in Crested Butte that long and go to only one polka party. Tonight I will reteach you!"

On that night the people of Crested Butte watched Vini McGragor polka for the second night in her life. She danced and danced, whirling in her blue-green dress, her whole body feeling the vigorous beat and making up for lost years. And Richard Sterling danced with her.

Some people raised an eyebrow or two as the beautiful young widow danced with the town banker—a married man. But most of them were exhilarated by the striking couple. The old-timers thought nostalgically that this was exactly how they had been when they were young. And the young people thought enthusiastically that this is exactly how they would become. Both the young and the old loved gentle Vini, and most didn't see how a man as kind as Mr. Sterling put up with a wife like Alisa.

The rumor spread that Vini was celebrating paying off her home. Fiddle Jack announced it, and the people shared in the celebration, laughing and clapping and dancing. These were people who dared to stand up to the mountains and the weather. People with the courage to build a town where snowdrifts reached ten feet high and skiing had occurred on the Fourth of July. People with the strength to struggle and the zest to play. And Vini stood with them, arm-in-arm. She had struggled, and now she played. On that night Vini McGragor danced the polka, and the people of Crested Butte danced with her.

As Vini walked with Richard down Elk Avenue in the moonlight under the bright twinkling stars, her happiness spilled over. "This has been a perfect evening, Richard. We made a memory."

He stopped, took her chin gently in his hand and raised her face toward his. "I don't know whether you are lovelier by candlelight or moonlight." His eyes were not the eyes of a brother.

Part of Vini was caught in the magic of the moment. She felt drawn to him like a drowning woman to the seashore. He offered a dimension of life absent for so long. And Ben was away for the night. But the other part of Vini forced her to step back from this married man.

They walked up the stairs to her door in silence. As he opened it, she said, "It's my door, Richard, and my home." She reached up and kissed him lightly on the cheek. "I know it couldn't have happened without you."

"Vini, I love—"

She put two fingers gently over his lips. "Sh-h-h. Good night."

"Good night, dearest Vini."

Dearest Vini. Joel's term of endearment rang in her ears as she closed the door. She began humming Joel's tune, knowing even now that she would never love another as she had loved him.

Undressing, she relived the special day. Paying off the mortgage. The delighted surprise in Richard's eyes tonight when he first saw her and twirled her around. His sharing deeply with her during dinner. And then dancing the polka. She stopped humming Joel's tune and whirled around in her night-gown, doing the polka across the room in her very own home.

As she drifted to sleep, she heard Joel's voice. *Dearest Vini.* And then somehow it changed, and something was suddenly subtly different. The words were the same, but the voice was Richard Sterling's. *Dearest Vini.* She smiled happily in her sleep.

Ben held Vini's chair as she sat down at the table. She looked toward Father Mike, a frequent Sunday dinner guest. No matter how busy he was, he almost always had time to come when invited. And there had been many invitations over the years. "Father Mike." They bowed as he blessed the food.

They crossed themselves, and Ben smiled at her. "You seem happy today, Mother."

"I feel more alive than I've felt since your papa died."

"Is it because of getting our home paid for?" Mischief twinkled in Ben's eyes. "Or because of dancing the polka with Mr. Sterling last night?"

Father Mike flashed his broad smile. "Ben and I are honored to dine with the Polka Queen of Crested Butte."

She laughed but felt uncomfortable.

The mischief disappeared from Ben's eyes. "At mass Dave Donegan said everyone is talking about you and Mr. Sterling."

Taken aback, she didn't know how to respond.

"I told him it better be everyone minus him or I'd beat him up."

"Fighting isn't necessary." She wished Ben had saved this conversation for a private time. If Father Mike was to be involved, she preferred the confessional booth to the dinner table. "Mr. Sterling is just an old friend. He's like a brother." Ben's sensitive eyes surveyed her, and she flushed. For the first time in her life she had lied to her son.

Ben glanced at the priest and then again at her. "It's wrong, Mother. Mr. Sterling is a married man."

She leaned back in her chair. "You have a way of saying exactly what you think, Ben." She wondered if part of his intensity was born of wanting their little family to remain just the two of them.

The priest concentrated on buttering a homemade roll, hiding his judgment behind gentle blue eyes and an expressionless mask.

Abruptly she changed the subject. "Father Mike, something has to be done about the Company Town concept. Since we're evidently never going to run out of Heffrons, I've decided to do my small part by expanding my business. I'm going to hire miners' wives so their families don't have to depend on scrip."

His perceptive eyes looked into her, seeing the motivation behind her words. "You want to wage a one-woman war against the Company—without stopping to consider the odds."

"There'll be two of us—one woman and one man!" said Ben protectively. "May I be excused?"

She noticed his empty plate. "You ate too fast. Don't you want to wait for dessert?"

"Martin and I are going skiing. We'll take some chocolate cake with us."

"Be careful," she called after him.

Father Mike set his coffee cup down and removed his mask. "You be careful, Vini. And I'm not talking about the Company."

The set of his strong jaw warned her that she didn't want to hear what he was about to say.

"The Church takes a firm stand on the sanctity and permanence of marriage."

Just as she'd expected. "I know."

He paused and added sadly, "The problem is that the Church can't ensure the right decision about marriage in the first place."

She looked up surprised. "Are you saying that a marriage can be a mistake? That there are times when . . . That maybe it's all right for Richard and me—"

He raised his palm to silence her. "It's not all right. It's all wrong. The whole situation. An unhappy marriage is wrong. Adultery is wrong. Divorce is wrong." The blue of his eyes deepened in intensity. "Don't you see, Vini? It can never be right. Not for you and Richard."

"But if he divorced? Without any encouragement from me? If I had nothing to do with it?"

The priest shook his head. "Oh, Vini. You would have everything to do with it."

Father Michael Barrett could not get to sleep that night. He had sinned in his heart. He rose from bed and knelt at the altar at St. Patrick's Catholic Church. Filled with despair, he began to pray:

Loving Holy One, you know that what I told Vini at dinner today is true by church law. At that level I was not wrong to hold it up before her. But you also know that I grievously sinned on this sabbath day.

You gave your son to teach us of you, and he healed on the sabbath. He broke church law because he was compelled to do so in order to keep the Spirit of the Law, the law of love which he proclaimed to be the Greatest Commandment. I confess that I threw the law of judgment at one of your children when the Spirit of the Law called for offering compassion and extending hope.

Knowing my heart, you know that there is still more to confess. You know that my motives were not pure. As a priest I cannot have her. I confess that, even so, I do not want another to have her. You know of my shame. There is no test to celibacy I encounter that calls for more strength than the sweet face of Vini McGragor. The test grows more difficult with the years! Not easier!

You know that she is totally innocent and would be confused and guilt-ridden if she were aware of my feelings. O God, help me! Don't let me do anything that makes her suspect!

Please cleanse me with your grace. May it abound in my life that I may reflect your holy love to all those whose lives I touch. I plead for forgiveness and that you will strengthen me in my weakness.

He made the sign of the cross. *In the name of the Father and the Son and the Holy Spirit.*

CHAPTER 18

*I*t can never be right for you and Richard. Father Mike's words catapulted against Vini's new found joy like a cannonball ripping through an oriental screen. They lingered in the forefront of her mind all week long as she laid the groundwork for hiring miners' wives.

First she visited with Martha Donegan, both to have a sounding board and to spread the word. She also put an ad in the *Elk Mountain Pilot*, inviting interested miners' wives to come to a sewing circle at her house the next week on Wednesday, January 24—a symbolic date for Vini, the anniversary of her marriage and of the Jokerville Disaster. Father Mike had said she was waging a one-woman war against the Company. She'd wage a full-scale war instead if she had the power, but she didn't. This venture was like the way the Quakers had helped the slaves find freedom, a few at a time.

It can never be right for you and Richard. The words ran over and over through Vini's mind as she turned and tossed on this exceptionally cold Friday night. She heard the clock strike three in the morning. Her mind wandered from paying off her mortgage to dancing the polka with Richard to the upcoming Wednesday and how many miners' wives would be here. Her ad had aroused a hubbub in town that surprised her. The Company, too, would be surprised if they knew the motivation behind her little sewing circle. She smiled at the absurdity of seeing it as a threat to Heffron Enterprises. But, she thought with glee, maybe someday.

Her smile left as quickly as it came. *It can never be right for you and Richard.*

Suddenly a blast like a thunder clap deafened her. An explosion! For an instant she flashed back to the Jokerville Disaster.

She smelled smoke and jumped up. Fear knotted her stomach.

She darted to the door. Flames snatched the lower steps. Smoke rolled upward. She ran to Ben. "FIRE!" She tried to lift him from his bed. He'd outgrown her. She shook him. "Hurry!" She wrapped the comforter around him. "Listen! The stairs are on fire. Try to make it. Keep this tight around you."

He rushed for the door.

"Take a deep breath. Hold it till you're safe! Don't stumble! Roll in the snow!" She ran to her bed. Grabbed the quilt.

He flung the door open. Flames reached through it. "We can't!" He closed it and raced across the room. A jagged piece of glass held in the shattered pane. He covered his fist with the comforter and knocked it out.

"*Jump!*" shouted Vini. "Land in the snow bank!"

"You first!"

"*Now*, Ben!"

He jumped into the snow bank and rolled down.

Vini glanced back over her shoulder. The saddlebag! It blurred on the wall through the heat waves. She shielded her face with the quilt and darted toward it.

The fury of flames leaped across the room. She touched the rocker Joel had given her. It flared in a crackling blaze. The heat caught her breath. The fire lapped at her legs and arms. Spreading! Snapping! Searing!

She grabbed the saddlebag. Smoke filled her lungs. The lace curtains burst into flames. She lunged for the window. Blinded. Breathless. She leaped and dived through it.

The fireball rang.

Ben pulled off her flaming quilt. Frantically with both hands he shoved snow over her.

Vini felt heat become cold.

Tears froze to Ben's cheeks. "What took you so long!" His voice choked.

Richard rushed to her. "Are you all right? Tell me you're all right!"

She nodded. He helped her up and put his coat around her. She collapsed against him.

"The saddlebag!" exclaimed Ben, picking it up. "You got it!"

She closed her eyes. "It's all I could save."

"That damned saddlebag!" shouted Richard. "It could have cost you your life."

"Don't you swear at my mother!" yelled Ben over the roar of the flames.

The second floor crashed to the first. The roof clattered into a burning heap.

Vini stared at the leaping flames as the blaze consumed everything she owned. Ten years in ten seconds.

Ben stood close to her. He held up the saddlebag. "We still have this, Mother."

Her courage trickled away like the fast-melting snow flowing down Elk. Numbness engulfed her, a welcome shield from the pain of defeat.

People from all over town stood on Elk and stared at the fire. Women shrieked. Children cried. Men ran about here and there without purpose.

Vini observed the chaos as though standing outside herself. She watched from afar the frenetic behavior of the mob. She lacked the strength to help them organize. She didn't even have the will to reattach herself to that dazed woman who clutched Ben's hand, afraid to let him go.

The volunteer firemen pulled the fire wagon, racing the half-block from City Hall. The warden shouted orders. They hooked up the hose and aimed their mighty weapon. An expectant hush fell over the crowd.

Nothing!

"The water's froze!" shouted the warden.

"*No!*" yelled the mayor. "We buried those pipes seven feet deep!"

The firemen stood powerless, their impotent weapon still aimed.

The wind fanned the flames. With a crackle of laughter, the blaze snatched the buildings next door, first to the east and then to the west. Chaos ensued. The firemen clutched the empty hose, helpless. The warden swore against the winter.

Richard took command. "The whole block is going to burn! Get things out!"

In a frenzy people ran into the various buildings. They grabbed things and threw them to safety. Indiscriminately. Trinkets. Trivia. Saving whatever was handy. Unable in their panic to think, to plan, to decide priorities. Glass dishes smashed as they hit the street. Furniture broke. Clothes tore.

Vini heard Richard's voice above the mob. "*The bank!*" She turned. The north side of the street glowed red in the black night, reflecting the blaze of the south side and absorbing its heat. The wind whipped the fire, and flaming arms arched over Elk. Its fingers reached for the two-story boarding house. The flames rose and fell. Brightened and dimmed. Scorched and seared. Closer, ever closer to the north side.

"Save the bank!" The cry rumbled through the hysterical mob. Quickly Richard organized a relay to get the money and records out. Marshal Hays guarded the growing mound of cash.

"Blankets!" shouted the warden. "Get blankets!"

Giving up on the south side of Elk, the people tried to protect the north. They covered the buildings with wet blankets and tossed snow on the roofs with scoop shovels.

Suddenly the boarding house windows shattered from the heat. The mob stilled like statues in the snow. The boarding house ignited. The people groaned.

The barbershop caught and blazed. The flames leaped toward the drug store, greedy for the bank. The relay team worked faster. The firemen fought valiantly with melted snow and wet blankets.

The bank burst into flames. Vini saw Richard standing alone in the background. For a moment she watched his flickering silhouette as he watched his bank burn down. Then she and Ben made their way through the crowd, wading in the river of melted snow that ran down Elk. Silently, she stood by Richard's side.

"It's going to cross Third!" shouted the warden. If it did cross eastward, those blocks would burn also. The people tossed buckets of slush on the Company Store on the north and Doc Williams' office on the south.

"It's about to cross Second Street!" shouted Adam Glick. Desperate to keep it from leaping across Second and spreading on westward, the warden decided to dynamite. He blew up the corner buildings on both the north and south sides of Elk in the burning block. The explosions blew a gaping hole in the City Hall and shattered the windows in the Forest Queen, but both buildings now stood safe from the fire.

There was nothing left to do but watch.

"Vini!" called Father Mike. "I've been looking for you! Thank God you and Ben got out!"

"My building is gone." Her hollow voice spoke from a bottomless pool of void.

"You cut your forehead." Gently he bent his six-foot frame and wiped it with his handkerchief. "Let's take Ben to the church." His voice offered strength and comfort. "I've sent Sister Margaret to set up some cots in the church for the homeless."

Homeless.

"You can stay there the rest of the night. And as long as you need."

She looked down at Richard's coat hanging open over her torn nightgown streaked with mud and ashes. "The new coat I bought is all burned up."

He took her hand and closed his eyes for an instant.

"Why did my home burn, Father Mike?"

"We'll talk tomorrow. Right now you need to get some rest." Putting one arm around her shoulders and holding Ben's hand, he led them to the church.

When Vini awoke mid-morning, everything crashed in on her again. She checked Ben who slept soundly in the cot next to hers, lined up beside those of all the other homeless families. She opened the saddlebag which held the sum total of their possessions—an old picture, a newspaper clipping that listed the Jokerville dead, four coins totaling seventeen cents, a white bone-handled knife, and Nick's lucky silver dollar. She recalled Ben's words: *We still have this.* She closed it and placed it under his cot.

In confusion and despair she rummaged through St. Patrick's charity barrel for some clothes to wear. Father Mike came toward her as she pulled out her old gray cloak and put it on. She looked up at him. "Vini giveth, and Vini taketh away."

Instead of scolding her for her blasphemy, his eyes filled with compassion.

"It's 'tomorrow,'" she said. "Why did my home burn? What did I do to deserve that?" Immediately the answer came. "God is punishing me for loving Richard Sterling!"

"Oh Vini, God doesn't punish us. We punish one another." He sighed wearily. "God created us free and gave us a Teacher. But most of us don't follow the teachings."

She thought about the smoldering ashes and debris that had been her home. "What is the point?"

"Sometimes I don't know."

"Then where is hope?"

He took both her hands in his. "Just as bad destroys, good enables. That's the hope."

"Hope is false. The fire speaks louder than you!"

His shoulders sagged.

She stared down at her old cloak, raw with awareness of the total loss it symbolized. She acknowledged the truth. "I'm defeated."

"*No!*" He took her firmly by the shoulders. His eyes held hers in that powerful way, transmitting his strength into her. "Think about the people of Crested Butte, Vini. They've watched your courage over the years. That courage has helped them face their own struggles. They need you! Ben needs you! Now more than ever!"

Vini walked south from the church, moving more and more slowly as she approached Elk Avenue, dreading what she would see but knowing that she must look. She forced herself to view the rubble where just yesterday so many buildings had stood on both sides of Elk in the Two Hundred block. How swiftly the fire had ravaged them! She took a deep breath and mustered the courage to glance at the blackened heap that had been her building. Her very own home. Final payment made.

Richard called to her from the charred remains of the bank. As he came to meet her, his haggard face and torn suit said that he had not been home since the fire. "I couldn't save all the money."

She remembered Father Mike's words and tried to comfort him. "We'll build the town back, Richard." But her words rang hollow. One week ago she had danced the polka. Now she wondered if anyone in Crested butte would ever dance again.

"It is so hard to accept. Twenty-two businesses are destroyed and ten families homeless. Just because an unknown fool throws dynamite into Carlisle and Tetard's Market for some ungodly reason. In your building, Vini, of all places!"

"Dynamite started the fire?"

He nodded. "The marshal and fire warden were up all night investigating. They're sure that's what happened."

"I heard a blast."

"It makes no sense. Carlisle and Tetard aren't a threat to anybody!"

"Threat?"

"The marshal questioned them, but they can't think of anyone who might have a grudge against them. And no one could wish you harm, Vini. The marshal knows there's no need even to question you."

She shrugged. "The only unusual thing I've done recently is put an ad in the newspaper about a sewing circle." There could be no jobs for miners' wives now. For an instant she wondered if the Company saw her little meeting as a threat. That sounded so preposterous she couldn't even share it with Richard, let alone the marshal.

"One thing is sure—the fire had to be deliberate."

Surely they were wrong. Vini couldn't believe that anyone would do all this on purpose.

"I must talk to you." Richard looked up and down the demolished block. "There's no place to go now."

"No place," she echoed, staring at the rubble where her home had stood.

"I'll hitch up my sleigh. We both need to get away from all this for a while."

They followed the Slate River northwestward toward the Oh-Be-Joyful Mountains, leaving behind them the ugly destruction of the fire and the confused hubbub of the people. Vini found the rhythm of the sleigh soothing. The white winter wilderness offered tranquility. Richard's presence brought comfort and strength as she sat close beside him under the fur lap robe.

Finally he stopped the horse. The frozen stream sparkled beside the road, and icicles hung from the spruce trees nearby. A sheepherder's cabin stood beyond nearly buried by snow. Richard put his arm around her and looked tenderly into her eyes.

She knew she should lower hers but didn't.

"Dearest Vini." He pulled her close to him. "I would give anything of mine—all that I own—if I could undo last night and keep your home from burning." He held her, rocking her back and forth as though comforting a child. "My bank was a terrible loss. But your building was everything."

His words lanced her wound like the blade of a surgeon's knife. She looked away from him. "Please, Richard. I don't want to talk about it."

"Last night when I heard that blast and saw your building on fire, I couldn't get there fast enough. If anything happened to you—" He broke off. Anguish filled his eyes. "You are the Life in my living." He pressed his cheek against hers. "There is something I must know, Vini. Do you love me?"

She felt the love between them, the joy they could share, the tenderness. She let her eyes speak for her.

"More than anything else in the world I want to protect you and care for you and provide you with comfort for the rest of your life." His eyes filled with passion. "And I want to hold you." He kissed her. Hungrily, as one who has waited too long.

The heat of his passion ignited her fiery desire for him. She returned his kiss. Completely, as one with much to give.

"I love you, dearest Vini."

The beautiful words swept away the gray ashes of nothingness and filled the void with hope and meaning, transporting her from winter ice to desert sun.

"Will you be my wife?"

A happy ending to the tragedy. For her. For Richard. For Ben. Ben! *It's wrong, Mother. Mr. Sterling is a married man.* With a shock she realized that she would be ashamed for Ben to see her now. Quickly she drew back. "You have a wife."

"I am willing to divorce Alisa."

His choice of words chilled her. "Willing?"

"Divorce isn't easy for me."

She thought of Alisa and wondered why. Vini steeled herself to ask the crucial question. "Was your marriage a mistake, Richard?"

"A mistake?"

"In itself. If it weren't for me, would you divorce her?"

He looked surprised. "No, Vini," he said with resignation. "I wouldn't."

"Then you're happy?"

He glanced toward the sheepherder's cabin. "No. You know my marriage to Alisa ranges from neutral to negative. It offers a kind of co-existence, a mutual indifference, a pretense until death." He turned back to her, and his voice tightened. "But divorce is a grave matter, and I told myself to continue loving you only from a distance."

Father Mike's words echoed in her mind: *You would have everything to do with it.*

"I intended to endure." That familiar tenderness filled his eyes. "Until our evening together. Dinner with you at The Rose Petal. Dancing the polka with you. Walking with you in the moonlight. I saw the possibility for so much more in life! Marriage to you . . . I cannot imagine such happiness!"

He kissed her again, and once more she felt the heat of the desert sun.

"I repeat myself. Will you marry me, my dearest Vini?"

Get out of your marriage, she begged silently. *Then ask me.*

"You love me. I can see it in your face."

I long to be your wife. But absolve me of responsibility.

"My greatest fear, dearest Vini, is that you wouldn't marry a divorced man because your church would not approve. And I would have humiliated Alisa and put her through a divorce for nothing."

I would marry you! But I can't be part of putting asunder what God has joined together. You must free yourself on your own.

"I must have your word before I act."

An impasse, she realized in silent desperation. He won't risk a divorce without a promise, and I won't risk a promise before a divorce. Like pulling the earth from the sun, she pulled away from him.

He looked at her, pleading.

Already she felt the stinging void of separation. She longed to move once again into his arms. But she didn't.

"Is that your answer then?"

For once, he could not see into her heart and read her thoughts. "Please, *cher* Richard." *Divorce Alisa,* she implored him. But she did so in silence. What she finally said aloud was, "Let's go back."

"I thought that knowing you love me would be the greatest joy I could have." The passion in his eyes changed to pain. "Now I know it. And I still must continue to live without you." He tried to say more, but couldn't.

He clutched her hand. His eyes held hers, entering her soul, merging with her, uniting the two of them for all time. The precious moment ended, but the indelible memory would forever remain in her soul.

They rode back to town in silence, disrupted only by the mare's squeaking harness taking them away from happiness. Our relationship ends, thought Vini, in an unfinished finish.

Richard helped Vini down from the sleigh, and she stood alone on Elk Avenue watching him depart, her heart breaking.

"Miss Vini!"

She turned and saw Martin Boyd calling to her from the heap of ashes where he and his granddaddy had lived and worked.

Drawing closer, he said, "Ben didn't want you to worry about him."

"Worry?" She felt weak from fear. What else could she bear?

"He asked me to tell you he got a job. And he won't be home till late."

"A job! Where?"

"Big Mine hired him."

"Sainte Marie, Mère de Dieu!

CHAPTER 19

*W*ill Chaney sank his stout frame into a chair at the back of the Big Mine office and began studying the statistical sheet. Though he'd come to Crested Butte to see the fire damage firsthand for a story, he also checked up on the Company. Keeping abreast of Heffron Enterprises was his continuing memorial to Joel McGragor. The report predicted production at 1,000 tons of coal a day and over 30,000 tons of coke a year.

Suddenly the door banged open, and Vini burst into the building. Wild-eyed and breathless, her face flushed, she accosted Ron Shun.

Will had looked for her as soon as he arrived but couldn't find her or Ben. He had seen the rubble, though, and grieved for her. He started toward the front of the office, then decided not to interrupt.

"Is Benjamin McGragor working here?" Rage shook her voice.

The question surprised Will.

Shun smiled. "Yes, Mrs. McGragor."

A Company-trained smile, observed Will from the background.

"You didn't know? I guess he wanted to surprise you." Like a rich man tossing a penny to the needy, he added, "Knowing how hard it is for a widow, and with the fire and all, we put him right on."

She caught her breath. Her eyes sparked rage. "You get my son out of that tomb!" Her small frame shook with fury. She advanced on Shun. Reached up. Gripped his arms. He took a step backward.

Will smiled to himself. Vini didn't need any help! She came only to Shun's shoulder but diminished her foe. The burly man was in retreat.

Shun recovered from his shock. He glanced around the room at the staring clerks. His face reddened. He looked down at the petite woman, then at the tiny hands holding his biceps. He flexed his powerful muscles, shook her grip with a single shrug, and took control of the situation. "Mrs. McGragor, we can't bring your boy out of the mine before the shift is over," he said condescendingly. "Besides, a twelve-year-old can handle the job."

"He's ten, and you know it!"

"The Company is not responsible if he lied about his age."

"*YOU—GET—HIM—OUT—OF—THERE!*" Each word blasted like a bullet from a six-shooter.

Again Shun stepped backward.

"Or I'll go in and get him myself!"

"You can't do that. Women aren't allowed in the mine."

"But *children* are! Company logic!"

Score one, thought Will, for gentle Vini who just cut clear through the crap.

"I'm sorry we can't help you. Talk it over with Ben tonight." Shun gave her shoulder a little chauvinistic pat.

"Don't touch me!" She turned and slammed the door as she left.

"Whew! I'm glad that's over," Shun confessed as Will came toward the front of the office. "I can't believe it! Vini McGragor is known for her gentleness." He shook his head. "That is a fiery little lady!"

Will opened the door to catch her and saw her marching straight toward the mine entrance. "Your 'fiery little lady' is going to be walking into Big Mine in about five seconds."

"That's impossible! It's against Company rules."

"Well, Shun, Company rules notwithstanding, Vini McGragor just did." He started after her.

Shun followed. "If she gets hurt, the Company is not responsible."

"It never is!" Will rushed toward the mine. "Vini! Wait!"

"Come back, Mrs. McGragor!" ordered Shun.

Will reached the mine and called to her again. She turned, surprised by his presence.

Shun ran to her. "Go back! The miners think a woman is bad luck!"

"I'm staying right here, Ron Shun, until you get Ben. If he's going to get blown up, this time I am too." She planted her feet on the floor of the mine tunnel. Nothing short of bodily removal would budge her.

Shun took a menacing step forward.

"Hold it!" Will ordered.

Shun stopped.

Vini turned and advanced into the mine. "I'm getting Ben out of here."

"No!" yelled Shun.

She kept going.

Shun blocked her. "The Company doesn't set work times based on the whims of women! You must accept that fact!"

"And you must accept the fact that if you refuse to get Ben, I will proceed through this tunnel and find him myself!" She started around him.

Shun held her back. "Ben needed a safety lamp and a pick. He got credit for them. He'll have to work out his debt to the Company Store."

A primeval growl erupted from deep within Vini. "You *bâtard*!" She lunged at Shun. Her closed hand stabbed into his jugular vein.

He gagged and held his throat with one hand. His other fist swung brutally toward her. She dodged, but the blow caught her shoulder and knocked her backwards. She fell on her back and hit her head on the cold rough floor of the mine.

Will shoved Shun against the wall.

Vini tried to get up and fell back. She rolled to her stomach and started to crawl farther into the tunnel.

Gently Will took hold of her shoulders.

"Don't!" she said sharply. "I intend . . . to get Ben . . . out of this mine."

Will lifted her from the floor. "I'm on your side, Vini." He glared at Shun. "If you don't want a story in the *Rocky Mountain News* that will make Heffron's skin crawl, I suggest that you get Ben McGragor. Immediately!"

"Are you threatening me?"

"I'm clarifying your options. Take your choice."

Shun hesitated.

"Try this headline: *Company Owned by M. Morgan Heffron Conscripts Ten-Year-Old Boy. Jokerville Widow Battered by Ron Shun While Trying to Save Her Son.*"

The assistant superintendent made up his mind. "I'll get him." He looked at Vini with the contempt of a man who has lost face.

"I'm all right now, Will. I just couldn't catch my breath and felt dizzy for a minute. Wearily she asked, "Would you really have written that story?"

"You bet!" His thumbs and index fingers drew a caption box in the air: *"Fiery Little Lady Takes On Heffron Enterprises."* He chuckled.

"I would have failed without you. I'm so tired of being powerless. Someday I intend to have enough power myself to change things."

He took her elbow and walked her out of the tunnel toward the sunlight. "My power is the power of the pen, Vini. I fight with words, and I've won a few victories. But you have a different kind of power."

She didn't understand.

"This is a town where the odds are stacked against the people—poverty, mining tragedies, avalanches, fires." His voice softened. "They've all touched you in one way or another."

She sighed, a deep heavy breath of weary emptiness. Her stubborn shoulders sagged.

"You don't realize the powerful influence of your gentle strength, your quiet courage. God help us all, Vini McGragor, if you ever do!"

Ben followed Shun out of the mine. Coal dust smeared his face and permeated his clothes. The enemy had captured her son. But only temporarily, and he'd been released in one piece. Thank the Holy Mother!

Ben stopped in front of her. He looked from Sam Shun's father to Uncle Will to her. Rage shot from his eyes. "You made a fool of me, Mother! And I hate you for it!"

The words stabbed her heart. The fire. The Company. The words. Waves of raw feeling swirled and swelled like an ocean breaker. She pulled back her hand and slapped her son on his coal-smudged cheek.

Ben sat in the deep snow at the cemetery, huddled against the marker of the mass grave. The dark of the night was like the dark of the chamber in the mine. The snowflakes fell from the black dome sky above him like coal dust fell from the black roof of the tunnel. The cold hardness of the stone against his cheek felt like the cold hardness of the coal against his hand. Suddenly the clouds rolled aside and formed a window around the moon. The moon shadows on the tombstones cast a black and gray checkerboard over the cemetery. Slowly Ben rose and brushed the white flakes from the miners' marker and read the words that he had long ago engraved on his heart. Respectfully he took off his hat, backed up a step, and addressed his father.

"Sir, we are really in a mess now. With the fire and all. I wish you were here. I tried to be a man and wondered what to do to help Mother. I don't want her ever to go hungry like she used to. I remembered what you did long ago. How you hired on at the mine to save Aunt Francine. So I went to the Company too, and they hired me.

"But Mother didn't understand. She had them bring me up early. Like a baby! Can you imagine! When Mr. Shun tells Sam about this, I'm going to be the joke of the school. And that wasn't all, Sir. Mother slapped my face! Right in public. Right in front of Sam Shun's father.

"So, Sir, that's what happened. And I stomped off. And I walked and walked and ended up here." He brushed his hair back from his forehead. "Part of me is still mad. Red-mad. I want to run away. That's what she deserves!"

He brushed his fingers across the words engraved in the cold tombstone. "But I remember what Uncle Nick said—that you'd be ashamed to call me Son if I ever ran away from anything.

"Mother thinks I'm still a child, Sir. Before the fire I was. But a boy can't see his home burn down. Watch his mother's face turn to stone. See her eyes just stare like lifeless glass. And be a child anymore.

"Now I'm a man, Sir, and I don't know what to do. I wish you were here. I'm all alone."

"No, Ben. You're not alone."

Ben jumped at the sound of the voice. Uncle Will stepped up behind him and put his hand on his shoulder. Ben threw his arms around him and sobbed the last tears of his childhood.

Having no place to go, Vini sat alone at a table in The Rose Petal, empty now between the lunch and dinner crowds. Everything that had happened in the last twenty-four hours seemed small when placed beside Ben's alienation from her. She stared at the hand that slapped him and winced at the memory of the sting against his cheek, his stunned face, his strain to hold back the tears. Again she saw him trudge away, his hurried long gait so much like Joel's. Again she heard herself start to call him back. Again she saw Will press his forefinger across his lips, silencing her. *Let him be, Vini. Let him be.*

Staring at her tea rather than drinking it, she muttered to herself, "I was only trying to save him." The words echoed back to her and held a false ring. "No," she admitted aloud, "I was saving myself from my own fear."

"It's a bad sign when you start talking to yourself." Rose smiled at her and sat down, sharing in common the tragic bond of widowhood. "What are you going to do now?"

Talking with Rose had brought Vini comfort ever since Joel's death. "I don't know. I keep wondering what Joel would do." Vini stared at her tea. "I still miss him, especially when things are hard."

Rose touched the wedding band she'd never removed, even after all these years. "We don't ever get over it. We just get through it."

"Time takes care of habits. But not the hurt of the heart."

Rose nodded. "As I watched my old restaurant building burn last night, I kept thinking about how fortunate I am that I sold the Star in '93 and bought this place."

"It looked like the fire would take this block too. I'm glad you were spared."

"You've been on my mind all day long, Vini. I have plenty of room upstairs—more than any one person needs. I'd be happy for you and Ben to stay with me until you can rebuild."

Her generous offer comforted Vini.

"If my place had burned and yours hadn't, you would take me in. I know you would."

"That's so kind. I don't know what to say."

The grandfather clock chimed, and Rose stood. "The kitchen's calling me." She patted Vini's shoulder. "Think it over."

Vini continued to stare at her tea, so deep in thought that she didn't hear footsteps. Suddenly Ben scooted out the chair beside her, and his coal-blackened hand enfolded hers.

"I'm so sorry, Ben." Tears made streams down her cheeks. "I didn't mean to hurt you."

No tears from him. "You were afraid for me."

She hugged him. "I love you." Tenderly she brushed his dark hair back from his coal-streaked forehead.

He took her hand from his head, too grown up now for that kind of thing. "Let me tell you about the mine, Mother. Men hide unseen behind their lamps, and the noise of the picks drowns out their words. I want to see and hear, to be seen and heard."

Ben looked toward the door where Will hung back, giving them time alone. He motioned and Will joined them. "I'm going to be a reporter. That's what I've always wanted to do."

Will smiled at him. "You'll be a good one."

Vini watched Ben leave, his gait slowed by weariness. Thanks to Rose, this would be his last night on a cot at St. Patrick's. "He's only ten, Will, and suddenly he seems all grown up."

"He is. His life experiences are beyond his years."

"He's been cheated in so many ways."

"He's strong, Vini. Strong of will. Strong of character."

"I'll have to use Nick's money now." The painful words tumbled into the air. "I have no choice."

"Ben and I thought he could come live with me when he graduates from eighth grade. He can go to high school in Denver and work part-time at the *News.*"

"He would like that."

"So would I."

"Are you sure, Will?"

He smiled. "Ben is a fine boy."

"But you're used to living alone."

"We'd just be a couple of old bachelors—unless you want to come along, too. Some people are moving, you know."

"It would be hard to leave Crested Butte."

"I'm surprised Richard is."

She felt the crash of thunder without a warning flash of lightning. "Richard?" For once Will must have his facts wrong.

"I stopped by late this afternoon. He and Alisa were packing. He was tossing things in boxes like a man haunted."

Steel knots cramped her stomach.

"He said he's given up. They're moving to Denver."

The next day Vini sifted through the debris on her lot. Her coat and shoes were ashen from sorting through the pile of rubble. Ben helped in this hopeless search for something salvageable. Anything.

Martin Boyd called from across the street. "Hey, Ben." He held up the remainder of a charred ski. "This is all I found. How about you?"

Ben shook his head. "Nothing."

"I guess the Red Lady's safe the rest of this winter." Martin tried to smile as he walked slowly toward Ben. "Let's go some place where we can talk." His voice cracked.

Vini watched the boys walk solemnly down Elk Avenue, the frivolity of childhood snatched by the flames. She sat down to rest on a rock and glanced at the ruins surrounding her, wondering what to do.

Henry came up the street and waved. "Hello, Mrs. McGragor."

She assumed he was on his way to the Company Store. But why on Sunday? "How are the boys, Mr. Coughlin?"

"Fine, thank you." He made his way through the ashes where she sat.

Vini was surprised by this forward gesture from a man who, in Joel's words long ago, had been mad at the world since his wife died.

"I'm really sorry about . . . all this." His eyes swept across her blackened lot. "What are you going to do?"

She sighed. "I don't know." Stay? Go? Rebuild? She must make a decision.

"Mrs. McGragor, could I talk with you about a matter?"

Surprised again, she pointed to a second rock nearby. "Have a chair."

He took off his glasses, started to say something, and then put them back on. "I've always been afraid of getting fired. If that happened, how would I support my children? I promised Matilda when she was dying that I would take good care of them."

"Being both father and mother isn't easy."

He sighed. "I'm tired of pretending not to know things about the Company. Things I've seen. Things I've surmised by putting two and two together."

Like when Fred King used to pocket a salary intended for Joel, she thought. But some things were best left unspoken.

He looked down at his feet. "I let my children become an excuse for a lack of courage. But this time I can't let it go." For the first time he looked at her straight on. "I must warn you."

"Warn me?" Another surprise.

"If I don't, and something happens to you . . . If Ben ended up an orphan . . . Well, I would always feel it was on my head."

A sudden fear sent shivers through her.

"Now understand, Mrs. McGragor, I don't know anything for sure. I'm just putting two and two together." He leaned forward, and his voice softened to a whisper. "Day before yesterday I saw one of King's henchmen, a man named Jake Neath. He walked passed the Company Store at dusk and didn't know I saw him. He doesn't show up without a reason. But I couldn't think of any Company trouble."

She wished he would hurry and get to the point.

"Your newspaper ad about the sewing circle crossed my mind. Word got around that you want to hire miners' wives in your business. The Company won't have the same hold over miners if their families have more money, especially if some of it is in U.S. dollars. But at the time I dismissed that idea, sure King wouldn't send Neath just to deal with a sewing circle!"

"A gathering of ladies to sew doesn't sound like something that would scare Heffron Enterprises." But someday, she hoped. Someday.

"The fire was that night, and I haven't seen Neath since. When I learned that someone threw dynamite into your building, I began to wonder again whether you were the target." Once more his eyes met hers. "There's no place now for you to meet this Wednesday."

Vini touched the cross around her neck, stunned by the implication. "Do you really believe—"

"Now I'm just surmising you understand. Just putting two and two together. But I . . . I'm afraid for you, Mrs. McGragor."

Could he be right? Had she been the intended victim? Had they wanted to burn her out in the hope that she would move away? What if Ben and she had died! How seriously would Joel take this if he were here?

"Strange as it may sound, I'm afraid for Jake Neath, too. King has a passion about paying attention to details. Whoever set that fire, didn't bother with two important details—the night being so cold the water froze and the wind blowing the fire out of control." Henry shook his head. "If King did set it up, he would be furious about the whole Two Hundred block burning instead of one building! Neath would pay for that. Big time."

"Have you told the marshal all this?"

Henry looked horrified. "I'd lose my job! Not all my children are grown up yet, and I promised Matilda. Besides, he wouldn't believe it. And there's no way I can prove it."

She supposed he was right. Even she had a hard time believing the Company would see her as a threat.

Henry stared at his boots. "The real reason I haven't told the marshal is that I'm scared. If King knew I was talking to you about this, I'd pay too."

She realized King underestimated Henry, thinking him capable of nothing more important than trivia, like picking her up in a sleigh at Company housing and taking her to the Star Restaurant those many years ago. "I'm sure he would never suspect you, Mr. Coughlin."

"Regardless, I had to warn you, Mrs. McGragor." He stood taller and straighter than she had ever seen him. "Just in case."

She smiled at him. "Thank you."

"What are you going to do?"

That question again.

"Move away?"

For a moment Vini watched the gentle snowflakes bury the ashes of her home. Then from a deep place within, seldom reached but there waiting when she needed it, she felt new strength seep through her bones. She rose from the rock where she was sitting and stepped up on it. "I'm going to build back!" she proclaimed with calm defiance. "And I'm going to expand!"

CHAPTER 20

*S*pring hung back in silence as the melting snow brought the muddy season, and the Two Hundred block of Elk Avenue rose noisily from the ashes. Bow saws buzzed and log hammers banged, driving ten-inch nails into spruce logs.

Vini heard the commotion in the background as she sat at her cherry secretary downstairs in her new building, the first one finished. She and Ben lived on the second story, and instead of renting out the ground floor level as she had in the past, she used it for her own business. She took increasing numbers of orders and worked hard teaching and enhancing stitchery skills in her weekly sewing circles. She hired the miners' wives as they qualified. They worked at home and were well paid by the piece. Vini designed exquisite patterns for all the linens, did the most delicate stitches herself, and carefully inspected each article. Someday her employees would work here, and she would provide a nursery. In good time. She'd learned that the "when" was as important as the "what" in not failing, and even more important was the "how" to go about it.

With a satisfied smile she opened the *Elk Mountain Pilot*. The headline stole her joy. She stared at the article almost afraid to read on:

> A frozen body was discovered yesterday between Crested Butte and Gothic. The man was killed during the winter by a fall down a deep ravine. He lay buried in the snow until the melt. The body was battered and had a severe blow to the skull. There being no evidence of foul play, the coroner attributed the body's condition to the fall and certified the death as accidental.

The newspaper trembled in Vini's hands as she read the last sentence:

> The body was identified by Henry Coughlin as Jake Neath of Denver.

Vini's mind slowed like a turtle pulled back into its shell, hiding. As incredible as Henry's story had sounded, all the pieces fit together. That she had been the target. That King had set it up. That Neath had thrown the dynamite. And that he had paid "big time" for his carelessness regarding the details of freezing weather and strong wind. A question rolled over her like a twenty-four horse team: What would King's next step be?

Only half conscious of her actions, she unlocked her lower desk drawer, withdrew the paper signed by Richard, and ran her fingers over his signature. She found comfort from knowing that his hands had touched this same paper. She held it tenderly against her heart, like a child might clutch a blanket as a symbol of security.

The paper spelled out the terms of an education fund that he had created for Ben, naming Father Michael Barrett as trustee. After Richard moved away, Father Mike brought her the paper and explained that she had been bypassed in the process because Richard feared she would refuse his assistance. This fund had freed her to use her inheritance from Nick for rebuilding without worrying about Ben's future.

But in this moment it was Richard's touch, not the contents, which eased her sense of loneliness and fear. How she missed him! She still had a habit of looking toward the half-finished bank, and longed for the days of seeing him when he walked to work.

Father Mike entered, always knowing when to come. His eyes moved to the newspaper on her desk. "You've seen the article."

"It terrifies me," she said without explaining.

"I was afraid for you when I started over here, Vini. But as I walked, I realized that you are safe."

"How so?"

"Ironically, the spread of the fire ensures that you won't be harmed. King is too smart to risk that. If he tried anything again, it would become obvious that you were the target the night of the fire, not Carlisle and Tetard's Market."

"That makes sense."

"You have no enemies in Crested Butte except one—the Company, which you clearly and openly oppose. It would take the marshal no time at all to point there for motive if you personally were harmed. That would mean investigating King, which would lead back to the fire. King can't risk that."

"The wrath of the entire town would fall on him for all the fire damage." She saw it clearly now. "And that would bring upon King the wrath of M. Morgan Heffron." She felt relieved, but puzzled. "How did you know that King was connected to Neath and Neath to the fire?"

He didn't reply.

"You always know more about what's going on in our lives than you appear to know, Father Mike."

He smiled. "That's my job."

Above the clamor on Elk Avenue, Vini heard the D&RG blast its whistle. She started to the depot, pausing outside her new building to admire the sign in fancy yellow lettering: *MARIE-VINCENTE*. She felt proud of the place, tastefully decorated and smelling new. "Thank you, Nick" she muttered aloud. Then, catching her breath at the pain of a lost love, she whispered, "And thank you, *cher* Richard."

The triple-engine chugged to a halt. The passenger coach, freight cars, and a hundred coal cars jerked behind it in a rippled stop. She realized with a sigh that someday the train would carry Ben away to Denver. She waited for the freight to be unloaded and sorted, hoping her new fabric had arrived.

A boy about fourteen stood on the boardwalk in front of the depot. He wore threadbare clothes and had a sign around his neck that said *CRESTED BUTTE COLORADO*. She noticed that he was thin, his hair neatly combed, and he looked clean despite his travels. She had read about boys from foreign lands who came to America seeking jobs as miners, preceding their families to this new country. Unable to speak English, they wore signs stating their destinations. Word must have spread internationally about Big Mine.

She picked up her package and turned to go, then glanced once more at the boy, still waiting. Jerking off the sign, he squared his shoulders, raised his chin, and met her gaze straight on. His perceptive dark eyes probed her face, their alertness heightened because he had to rely on people's gestures and facial expressions in order to comprehend.

Remembering her own aloneness at the depot when she arrived in Crested Butte on the first train, she smiled. Hesitantly he returned her smile. She walked toward him. Pointing to herself, she said slowly and clearly, "Vini McGragor." Then she pointed to him, raising her eyebrows in an unspoken question.

He looked down at her and placed his thumb against his chest. "Stephen Machek."

"Stephen Machek," she repeated.

His eyes sparkled and he pointed to her. "Vin-ee—Ma—Grag—or." They both laughed, delighted to communicate.

She extended her arm and made a sweeping semi-circle of their surroundings. "Crested Butte. Colorado. America."

He nodded.

Again she pointed to him and raised her eyebrows.

At first he didn't understand what she wanted. Then comprehending, he smiled. "Maklen. Brod Moravice. Croatia." They laughed again together, sharing joy in their precious bond of understanding.

"Come." She signaled to him.

His sensitive eyes were uncertain.

She patted his arm as a mother might. "Come, Stephen Machek."

A moment's pause preceded a relieved smile. His eyes grew transparent with his release from the anxiety of being alone against the world, an anxiety that Vini well understood. A flood of foreign sounds flowed from his mouth. He stopped the words and frowned in concentration. Slowly, deliberately, he spoke his first English sentence: "Stephen Machek . . . come . . . Vini McGragor."

Stephen was here to work in the mine, and Vini didn't interfere with that—but he was one immigrant the Company better not try to cheat! Vini and Ben helped him learn English, and he taught them Serbo-Croatian words. She learned that he missed the beautiful plum trees in Croatia, and she bought plums whenever she could as a special treat for him. He shared Ben's room, and as the months mounted into a year, he became like the brother Ben had never had.

On a crisp fall evening Stephen stamped up the stairs from his long day in the mine and slammed his lunch pail on the table. A fine mist of coal dust fell on the cloth.

Vini glanced at the tablecloth, then looked at his angry face. Saying nothing, she began to ladle the *ajmoht* into bowls, glad she'd decided to fix his favorite Croatian dish on a day that must have gone so badly.

"What happened?" asked Ben.

Stephen ignored him, moved the pail, and washed his hands. He added red wine vinegar to his soup and stirred his spoon through the veal, potatoes, and green beans. His eyes smoldered, intense and thoughtful, as he ate in a contagious silence.

His bowl empty, he shoved it back and squared his shoulders defiantly. "They cut *novac*—money," he growled.

Vini's spoon stopped in midair. "Your wages were cut?"

His eyes narrowed and his jaw tightened. "Seventy-five cents to sixty-five cents a ton! *Suviše malo*! Too small!"

"Sixty-five cents a ton!" exclaimed Ben in disbelief.

Stephen lowered his voice. "We talk strike."

"A strike is very serious." Vini wondered if the miners had been encouraged because of former Governor Davis Waite's intervention in the Cripple Creek strike. He had broken ranks and allied himself with the miners—not only using state troops as peacekeepers, but also representing the gold miners and negotiating satisfactory terms for them. She pondered whether any other governor again would have that much character. "Be careful, Stephen. Follow Iber Donegan."

The strike moved beyond talk. On its third day, as Vini took a telephone order she saw Iber walk past her window with a shotgun in his hand. Behind him marched a dozen angry miners—some with weapons, others empty-handed. She finished the order hurriedly and hung up.

Ben and Stephen came downstairs and darted out the door. "Wait!" she called. "What's happening?"

The boys looked at each other.

"Please tell me what's going on, Ben," she said firmly.

"Doc Shores is coming to break the strike."

"The Gunnison sheriff!"

"With posse," added Stephen.

Ben grinned in excitement. "Iber found out they're trying to sneak into town on a special train."

"He call meeting at Hardware Store."

Ben drew a rectangle for a headline caption, a habit now: "*Miners Greet Posse With Loud Welcome.*" Still grinning, he started out the door.

"Stay here, Ben!" said Vini. Fear shook her voice.

His exhilaration vanished, and he looked at her with Joel's intense dark eyes. "Cutting wages is an injustice. Besides, Stephen is like a brother."

"We'll help him and all the miners, Ben. But on our terms. Not Heffron's." She placed her hand urgently on Stephen's arm, wishing she could hold him back. "The miners cannot win against Doc Shores. You do not have a chance!"

He grinned mischievously. "You tell me: 'Follow Iber Donegan.'" He turned to Ben. "You stay here."

Stephen walked down the middle of Elk Avenue to the Hardware Store. He had no gun, but his fists always served him well. In Croatia. In America. He tried a left hook in the air and then a right.

Inside the Hardware Store, Iber tried to speak to the unruly miners. "We just want to scare the posse away." The men were too excited to listen. "Don't fire first!" he shouted above the din. "If we kill a lawman, they'll shoot us all!" He gave up and signaled them toward the depot. They shoved out the door, boisterous and poorly armed.

Stephen helped them throw a barricade together outside the depot. He didn't like this. The miners were an undisciplined mob without a plan, pretending to be unafraid. *Nevolja*—much trouble! But he couldn't desert them.

The special train came around the bend without a whistle blast. The engine, passenger coach, and caboose stopped in front of the depot. "Get ready!" called Iber.

Doc Shores took a step down. For a moment the presence of the mighty lawman intimidated the miners. "Men!" he called. "Let's settle this peaceably!"

A shot ended the negotiations. Shores jumped back into the passenger coach. The deputies smashed the windows. Gunfire split the air. Bullets spattered into the make-shift barricade. Miners fell around Stephen. He felt his arm burn. Blood spurted from the wound.

The battle lasted only five minutes. Over three dozen miners lay wounded. The rest surrendered. The smell of gun powder filled the air, now silent.

Doc Shores and his twenty-four man posse descended from the train. "You're all under arrest," he declared.

Stephen watched him walk slowly passed each of the wounded miners, totally assured of his power. How easily he controlled the situation. The miners were defeated, the strike settled, and the Company secure in its wage cut.

Doc Shores shouted to his deputies, commending them. "Good job, men. None of them are dead."

Stephen saw Vini and Ben, Father Mike and Doc Williams hurry across the plaza carrying bandages and blankets. In minutes they converted the plaza into an open-air hospital. Vini found him and bathed his arm. He flinched.

"Wow!" said Ben, looking at it with admiration.

"No plan. Big mistake." Stephen felt more pain from the humiliating defeat than from the shot. "You know right, Vini. No chance!"

"Remember this, Stephen Machek," she said, addressing him like a grown man, "You can never win on Heffron's terms!"

Accustomed to success, Doc Shores addressed the miners in the plaza. "No one was killed, and anybody ought to be excused for losing his head once in a while." He released all of the miners from arrest.

Vini tied Stephen's bandage. "It could have been worse. Two years ago the state militia was used to protect Carnegie property."

Stephen didn't understand.

"Soldiers . . . *vojnik*," explained Ben. "State *vojnik*."

"And this year," added Vini, "President Cleveland sent in federal troops—national *vojnik*—to break the railway strike."

Ben whistled. "That makes Doc Shores look like Santa Claus!"

Stephen listened undaunted. "We strike again!" he vowed. "Next time we have good plan!"

Because of the Doc Shores incident, Vini decided to help more miners like Stephen. Her decision resulted in an exhausting but rewarding routine for both her and Ben over the next couple of years until his eighth grade graduation. Whenever the train left behind a boy with a sign around his neck, she greeted him with a smile and brought him home—whether German, Greek, Italian, Croat, Serb, or Slovene. She and Ben taught the boys English and continued to learn the basic words in each one's native tongue. Her cuisine broadened to include international fare, and she delighted in greeting young arrivals in their native language and welcoming them with an evening meal common to their homeland.

In time she began to need both stories of her building for her expanding business and also both stories for her growing number of international boys. She bought a lot near Coal Creek and built a new log cabin with a large loft upstairs which served as a bunkroom that could sleep a dozen boys. They stayed with her for a few weeks or a few months or permanently like Stephen Machek. Conflicts between the youths were few, except for the Serbs and Croats. Their centuries of political-religious animosities had not been left at the shoreline of the Adriatic Sea. The inflaming historic cruelties could be re-ignited by a word or a look. Vini wished they could be like her beautiful Ficus plant that stood by the door, its separate trunk-like stalks braided together and growing into one united magnificent plant.

Vini had only two requirements of her boys. Nonnegotiable. One was that they show one another respect despite their differences, including the Croats and Serbs. The second was Sunday morning mass, which found her flanked by Ben and the international boys.

Father Mike made some concessions for this multi-faith group. The Serbs and Greeks, in respect for their Orthodox roots, were allowed to stand during worship, and he arranged for an icon and candle to be placed on a shelf on the east wall. He did not require the Protestants to cross themselves. The major risk to this independent priest was that he broke church law in order to keep the spirit of the law of love and allowed all who were baptized Christians to receive the Eucharist.

Vini talked to Father Mike about opening the church on Sunday afternoons to teach English to immigrants. He was easily persuaded. Vini posted the English class opportunities in five languages at the Company Store. In a few months they began also to teach immigrant and native alike how to read. Remembering Tillie's remark that she couldn't read, Vini sent a note to the Forest Queen. Father Mike agreed—all were welcome.

While much of Crested Butte napped on Sunday afternoons, Vini's boys and some other folk gathered to learn. Some were motivated less by the educational opportunity than by Vini's bribe of *baklava* and *éclairs*. Her stamina grew out of her silent determination to educate and motivate the young miners so that eventually they could either get out of the mine or have the skills necessary to improve their working conditions.

With proud eyes Vini watched Ben and Stephen mature. She foresaw Stephen as the miners' leader and vowed to do everything in her power to make him an able opponent to Heffron's system of entrapment. *Next time we have good plan!*

CHAPTER 21

*M*artin Boyd waved at Vini through her window and entered the shop. "Is Ben here?"

"He's running an errand."

Martin nodded shyly.

The shyness surprised her in this exuberant boy. He shuffled uncomfortably, neither leaving nor advancing.

She wanted to put him at ease. "I have some lemonade, Martin," she said, moving to a table with two chairs. "Come join me until Ben gets here."

Still shy, he clutched the glass.

"It's hard to believe that you and Ben are going to graduate from eighth grade soon. Have you thought about what you're going to do?"

He looked down at his glass. "Granddaddy assumes I'm going to be a barber." He said it with respect but without enthusiasm.

"You can't go wrong being like Mr. Boyd."

He nodded and looked up at her with eyes that held something unsaid.

She ventured a guess. "Sometimes, though, we have our own dreams. Like Ben isn't interested in my business. He dreams of being a newspaperman."

"I also have a dream." He looked down again and fell into silence.

She didn't rush him. When he was ready to talk, she would listen.

He finished his lemonade and began to speak. His words cascaded from his heart like a dammed up waterfall, freed at last. "If I could be anything I wanted to be, I'd be just like Father Mike. I remember the way he helped us after the fire. Whenever there's a need of some kind, people can go to him. And we know he'll treat us with respect. When people are hungry, he finds food. But he also gives us hope. When people are raggedy, he gets clothes. But he does more. It's like he wraps us in love. And when we're all dried up and feeling sad, he shows us where to find that 'cup of joy' he talks about, not by looking for it for ourselves but by helping others find it." Martin lowered his eyes and sank into silence.

Fun-loving Martin Boyd had hidden well this serious side that saw deeply into life. Vini felt his embarrassment about exposing his soul. She touched his hand, honored and grateful that he had shared his dream with her. "Have you ever talked with Father Mike about this?"

"I'm not good enough to be like him."

"Think about those beautiful words you just spoke."

"I'll never be a priest. It would take a lot of schooling."

"There are scholarships. Talk to him."

"It's easy for you to talk serious with Father Mike, Mrs. McGragor. But I usually just kid around." He stood but didn't move, caught in a chasm between a life dreamed of and a life settled for.

Vini stood also. "Let's go see him now." She linked her arm through his, lady to gentleman, and whisked him up the street to St. Patrick's Catholic Church.

On the eve of Ben's graduation, the sun dipped low and painted its pastel farewell to all that had gone before. Vini finished her work for the day and did a mental evaluation of her business. She had dreamed of adding three fulltime miners' wives each year, as well as continuing the opportunities for others to work at home. Ahead of schedule, nine women now worked in her building and a dozen others in their homes. In good time it had become a thing of pride in Crested Butte to have a wife whose beautiful needle arts qualified her to work for *Marie-Vincente.* The men chuckled among themselves about the little ladies pulling a needle through cloth and actually bringing in money. U.S. dollars! The women silently viewed it differently, knowing that the wages and education fund they earned gave their children a choice about continuing in the mining cycle, their sons directly and their daughters through marriage. Perhaps, in the deepest and unspoken part of themselves, the men knew this also.

The bell in the rock schoolhouse tolled into history the graduation of the eighth grade class of 1897. The mayor fired the cannon, and when the reverberation through the mountains finally silenced, he reminded the community to gather again in the evening for the dance at the City Hall.

Vini looked up at her thirteen-year-old son who was not thirteen at all, who'd been catapulted from boyhood to manhood the night of the fire. "Congratulations!" She hugged him and tasted the void she would feel in his absence. A knot grew in her stomach to take up the space. "Your papa would be so proud of you, Benjamin Joel McGragor."

"I always want to be the kind of man that would make him proud."

They walked home together to Joel's tune, Vini humming and Ben whistling—mother and son so sensitive to each other that their thoughts and feelings could be transmitted without words. She felt both his eagerness and his tremor of anxiety about leaving tomorrow to begin his new adventure in Denver. The umbilical cord could not stretch that far and the snipping pained her. It was hard to hide her sadness. But she must, or he might stay in Crested Butte. It was her love for him that strengthened her to send him away.

"It's a good day for a hike." Perhaps our last one together, she thought with a pang.

"I know where there's a secret cave. I could take you to it."

She grinned. "With a picture of a mother and a child?"

"You know it!"

"Your papa showed it to me. Sometimes I feel his presence, Ben, as though he is walking right along with us. Like on this special day." Unsure what prompted her, wondering deep within her heart if it could be Joel, she suggested spontaneously, "Tonight we'll go to the dance. It's time you learned to polka!"

The crowd made way for Vini and Ben when they entered the large room on the second story of the City Hall. Its tall green walls rose into an arched ceiling scarred by occasional bullet holes. Heavy green and gold brocade drapes covered the windows. The plank floor was nicked by the heels of dancing boots.

"Vini's here!" called Fiddle Jack. "The polka can begin now!" The people laughed and began to clap. They pushed Vini and Ben gently through the crowd until hand-in-hand they stood on the dance floor near the band.

"Are you ready?" she asked, looking up at her son. It seemed like only yesterday that she had carried wee Ben in her arms and danced the polka around Richard Sterling's attic.

He nodded.

"Let's make a memory, Ben!" Hesitant in the beginning but agile in his step, he caught on quickly. "You are so like your papa!" she said proudly.

Ben smiled, equally proud. The vigorous beat flowed through her body, vibrating into the depths of her spirit, and she knew what it was to be fully alive.

When the music stopped, Fiddle Jack stepped forward. "May I have your attention, please?" His voice grew louder. "Give me your attention!" Then he stomped his boot down hard on the stage. "*Shut up!*"

The people did.

"Some of you know that Ben McGragor is leaving us tomorrow," he announced. "He's heading for Denver to go to high school and become a big newspaperman."

Heads nodded around the room. "We're with you, Ben!" someone called.

"We'll take good care of your mother!"

"And she'll take care of the Company!"

The people laughed. Boots stamped. Someone called out: "Three cheers for the Polka Queen of Crested Butte!"

HOORAY! HOORAY! HOORAY!

People sitting in the chairs along the walls began to rise. The women who worked for Vini applauded her with eyes that glistened from tears of gratitude. Soon the room rocked with a standing ovation—except for Ron Shun. And finally, even he stood.

Vini knew she didn't actually dance any better than the others, that the only real difference was that the townspeople had decided she did. But in their eyes, that made it true. In their eyes, she caught the spirit of Crested Butte. She had danced her life through the Jokerville days, and on the ruby road that followed, and through the ashes of the fire and the aftermath of welcoming the international boys, dancing on toward her dream. In their eyes, she danced the soul of a people.

FOUR

TWISTER

1904

Denver, Col., March 30—John Mitchell, President of the United Mine Workers of America, will appeal to the United States Supreme Court for an order, restraining Gov. Peabody from enforcing and maintaining martial law . . . .

New York Times
Mar. 31, 1904

"*I*t takes a strike to change things!" Stephen Machek paced the floor of Vini's kitchen, his hands behind his back.

"Those are worrisome words." Unfortunately, they were probably true. She stirred her tea and watched him, aware of the click of his boots against the floorboards. She compared him to her son. Ben, gentle and sensitive, quick to perceive what lay beneath the surface and grasp the core of a situation, courageous, debonair, polished—*savoir vivre.* Willing to stand alone. Stephen, muscular and tough, but equally quick and almost as perceptive, also courageous and handsome. He, too, willing to stand alone. Ben, the fast-rising young reporter for the *Rocky Mountain News;* Stephen, the radical young leader of the miners. Both of them were leaving footprints wherever they walked. Perhaps, too early.

"We need a strong union. But the miners are afraid."

Déjà vu Joel McGragor, she thought. Change brings no change.

"They're not only worried about what the Company will do, but the state." He frowned. "Word has gotten around that Governor Peabody allows miners to be taken by force into the desert and left there."

"You may not get another ally like former Governor Waite."

"The Company still pays us in scrip—illegal in Colorado since 1899!" His jaw tightened. "We can't even vote the way we want. The super stands at the polls and watches us to make sure we support the Company slate." He stopped pacing and announced defiantly, "I'm calling a miners' meeting to talk about a strike."

"It wouldn't be the same as the national strike two years ago when John Mitchell and 150,000 miners joined together."

"We'd be like little David facing Goliath. First I'll have to talk to Iber."

"You make a good team," she said, glad the wisdom of her old friend would temper his judgment. "How would Veronika feel about a strike?"

"She's my wife—she trusts my decisions."

"With all this worry, don't forget your anniversary tomorrow." She recalled his nervousness the day his bride-to-be arrived from Croatia, known to him only through a year's correspondence and a picture, not uncommon in Crested Butte.

"Two years!" He sat down in the oak chair across the table from her. "I didn't know it was possible to love anyone as much as I love her and little

Joseph." He reached across the table and touched her hand. "How long were you married, Vini?"

"Two years. Exactly."

"Did you ever think about marrying again?"

She sighed as memory's door opened.

Stephen's serious eyes began to twinkle. "There was someone. I can see it in your face."

"Once," she admitted hesitantly. "He was a kind and gentle man. But I . . . I thought it would be wrong."

"If you could do it over, would you marry him?"

She slammed memory's door. "Why look in a mirror at the past and wish for missed sunsets? Better to look through a window and greet the sunrise."

"Someday soon the sun is going to rise on a strike in Crested Butte."

"Do you remember Doc Shores? Have a good plan."

Stephen rubbed his hand over his old bullet wound in his arm and slammed his fist into his palm.

Vini's spoon pinged as she dropped it, staggered by his forcefulness.

"Never again will anyone take us down in five minutes!"

She dreaded what lay ahead. "May I give you a word of advice?"

"Always."

"Wait until spring is more than a promise. Have the weather on your side instead of Heffron's."

He nodded and kissed her on the cheek. "Good night, *Mudre*. Wise, wise woman."

"Not always wise," she said, allowing herself one glimpse in the mirror at the missed sunsets with Richard Sterling. "Be careful, Stephen."

Vini walked to the window and watched Stephen in the moonlight, a man with a mission. A strike would bring retaliation, but he was right—there was no hope for change without one. She wished she could attend the miners' meeting. Unthinkable for a woman. Stephen would never agree, partly for her own sake. He would assume that the miners would laugh her right out of the room. And they probably would. But so much was at stake.

When he was out of sight, she sat down at her small cherry secretary. The only way she knew to help was to expand her business again so she could hire more miners' wives. It was time to cross back over the Mississippi River and market nationally. For a moment she rested her head wearily on her hand, then picked up a sheet of *Marie-Vincente* stationery and wrote the *New York Times* for advertising information.

Frederick Rodewald King slipped his report into his attaché. His butler assisted him with his overcoat and opened the double door of his Virginia mansion. If things went well today with Morgan Heffron Jr., he would be second in command of Heffron Enterprises. Temporarily. A single serious error would terminate the position. His attention to detail saved him from most mistakes and covered the few he made. But how long could that continue? If he received the promotion, he needed a way to guarantee it for the rest of his life. Pressure mounted as he buttoned his coat against the blustery March wind.

His daughter called to him from her upstairs window, framed like a beautiful picture. "Daddy! Don't forget my present."

"I won't, my baby."

"Maybe a ruby? I love red."

"I'll surprise you."

"A ruby, Daddy," she cajoled. "Please."

He waved goodbye and started to climb into his new 1904 red Winton.

"Wait!" she called and vanished.

King obeyed, smiling. In a moment she would burst through the door and run toward him. Most unladylike for seventeen. But how eager for life! "I adore you, Crystal!" he exclaimed, receiving her in his arms.

"Why do you have to go to Washington?"

"Don't trouble your pretty little head about it."

"It's for a promotion, isn't it? And to talk about mining unrest."

"Do you read my mail?"

Her lips puckered in a pout. "Daddy, do you think I'd do a thing like that?"

He smiled. "My baby, I think you do whatever you want!"

"Those silly miners should be glad to get to work for you. What's wrong with them anyway?"

"Roosevelt's Investigating Commission." For a moment he stepped mentally into the boardroom and rehearsed his speech. "That report gave the miners a taste of change, and they'll want more and more until they share the whole feast. There may be wildcat strikes, and it is imperative to make examples of them. We must keep a tight fist over the miners and teach them what they're up against when they face Heffron Enterprises!" Crystal's applause brought him back to the moment at hand.

"Is that your speech for the meeting, Daddy?" She reached up and straightened his tie. "To be number two in Heffron Enterprises will make you very important."

"I'd stand right behind one of the most powerful men in the country."

"But will we have to move to Washington?" Again her face drew into a pout. "I don't want to live there. Unless it's in the White House."

"Maybe someday you'll be First Lady." He kissed her on the cheek. "I can't be late."

"Don't forget my ruby!" she called over the roar of the motor.

As King drove, he turned his attention to his report. His heart lusted after one thing, second in command—to be exact.

Spring had winter in retreat as Stephen and Iber hurried to St. Patrick's for the miners' meeting. "Unity is our major problem," said Stephen.

Iber agreed. "We're from different countries. We have different customs. Even different languages."

"And European conflicts spill over among us."

"You don't have to get that far away for conflict, Stephen. Colorado is in a mess."

"Is it ever! Three state governors in one week!"

"I wish Joel McGragor could be here tonight," Iber said as they walked into St. Patrick's. "He wanted the miners to organize twenty years ago!"

They found the men already segregated into national groups. Members of the American Slovenian Catholic Union sat at the front on the right. A group of Germans sat across from them on the left. The members of *Hrvatska Bratska Zajednice*—the Croatian Fraternal Union—sat at the back with their leader, Vladko Radich.

Nervously, Stephen looked around the room. "How are we going to bring them together, Iber?"

"I don't know."

Stephen mingled with the miners, shaking hands and asking about their families. Then he walked toward the front and took his place beside Iber. "I suppose we'd better start."

Iber touched his shoulder. "Be sure they understand how serious this is. It could be a long struggle."

Hiding a sigh, Stephen rose. He wanted a calm atmosphere and hoped to get the miners quiet without shouting. But he didn't have to worry. Heads began to turn toward the rear, voices lowered to a buzz of whispers. A hush fell across the room. Stephen glanced at Iber and raised his brows in surprise. Iber shook his head.

Petite Vini McGragor walked down the aisle, head lowered, as though she thought herself invisible while crashing through the wall of tradition. Every mouth gaped and every eye watched her find a seat.

Recovering from his shock, Stephen took advantage of the silence. He paced across the front of the room. "What a time for us to strike!" He made his voice light, his face smile. "It's good fishing weather, and we can all use a vacation."

"*Riposare un pó!*" shouted an Italian. "Rest a little."

The miners clapped and stamped their feet in agreement.

Stephen knew that if he stopped now, they would vote overwhelmingly to strike. Yet, it would be a short-lived decision without results. "But . . ." He stopped pacing and stood square in the center, intently eyeing each miner right down the line.

No one smiled now. No one moved.

"Will it still be fun when summer ends and the streams freeze and snows come? How will we feel then?"

Voices mumbled. Vladko Radich shouted, "*Izvinite.* Excuse me. The strike won't last longer than a couple of weeks."

"The national one did," countered Stephen. "And we'll be alone on this one. It's to the Company's advantage to refuse to negotiate as long as possible."

The room hushed.

"How long can we live without wages? A few weeks, certainly. But a few months?"

Tension thickened the silence.

"If the Company Store cuts off our credit, how will we eat? How will we feed our families? And if we are forced to leave Company housing, where will we live?"

Around the room the miners muttered to each other.

Stephen raised his hands, commanding silence. "To win, we must hang on. To hang on, our unity must go beyond a decision to strike. We must unite as brothers! Willing to share everything we have for as long as we must. Otherwise, the Company will drag the strike out until we give in—and they give nothing!" Stephen waited for the miners' response.

Schwartz rose slowly to his feet from his front row seat. "*Bedaure.* I'm sorry. But what if the strike goes on and on, and we run out of food and scrip?" The big German turned and faced the miners. "*Es gefällt mir nicht.* I don't like it."

"Σωστός. Right!" growled a Greek. "Maybe a strike is a mistake."

A Welshman bolted from his chair. "A mistake! There is dumb, there is. Forty years ago women in the Queen's land were used as draft animals in the mines! Not now. But not because someone asked politely for change and it was granted! If we want things to get better, boyo, we have to take risks!" He shook his head disgustedly and sat back down.

"Aye!" agreed a husky highlander. "It's not the same as asking for a dram of scotch!"

"Wait a minute, Scotty!" an Irishman shouted.

"*Schiopero!*" called the Italian. "Strike!"

Irish yelled again. "'Tis a short vacation himself is ready for. Not retirement!"

Schwartz, still standing, shouted, "*Richtig*, Irish! Quite so! Fishing in the summer is one thing. Starving in the winter is something else again! We must think of our families!"

Stephen scanned the room. The boys who'd learned English from Vini sat in their various groups and translated for those who couldn't understand. Many heads nodded agreement with Schwartz, too many. Other heads shook angrily in dissent, too angrily. Voices rose in volume. Bedlam spread. Stephen felt he'd lost control.

Six men jumped to their feet, eager to argue. Or fight. It didn't matter which.

"Do something, Stephen!" called Iber. "A free-for-all is the worst thing that could happen!"

Quietly, Vini McGragor stood and began walking to the front of the room. Curiosity silenced the rumblings. The six men yielded to the lady.

She stood before the miners and faced the German. "*Guten Abend, Herr Schwartzenburg.*"

The miners hushed one another to listen to her soft voice.

"Yes. Do think of the family. Think about how it took the deaths of nearly 60 miners, including my Joel, to force the Company to close the old Jokerville vein." She touched the cross at her neck. "My baby boy was one month old."

Stephen saw that her gentle lilting voice was calming the miners.

"I believe with all my heart that a strong Union could have forced that change without the Disaster." Tears came to her eyes. "Then my husband would be here tonight, and my son would have known his father. Do think of the family!"

Schwartz looked down at his feet.

She raised her eyes to the roomful of miners and looked at each group. "Your wives know that in the long run a strong union will help their families. We get there not by anger and division among us, but by unity, by sharing what we have. By being one family. No matter how long the strike goes on, your wives will do what it takes to outlast it, fighting back in their own way. They are not the pampered, helpless wives of eastern coal barons. They are courageous mountain women. Don't sell them short!"

She faced Schwartz directly once more, and the warmth in her voice suddenly chilled. "*Herr* Schwartzenburg, if you are afraid of being hungry or of what the Company might do to you for striking, please say so. Do not try to hide your own fear behind your wife's apron or your baby's bib."

Silently the miners watched her walk back to her chair, head lowered, again as though invisible. No one spoke for a few minutes, not even Stephen.

Finally a Slovene broke the silence. "We have meat in our smokehouses. We can share it."

"*Da*," called a Croat. "And we have our gardens. We will can extra."

A Serb rose from his seat. "Some of us have cows. Enough to give all the children milk."

Stephen took advantage of this change in attitude and dealt with the most crucial question. "What about housing?"

The room fell silent.

"We can set up tents this summer," suggested a Greek.

"At the edge of town near Coal Creek," said an Italian, "so we can have water."

"And build outhouses," added the Welshman.

An Italian from Grimaldi shook his head and shivered. "But what if the strike isn't over before the snows come?"

"We can ask people with homes to take in families," suggested Vladko Radich. "Like Vini McGragor took in many of us." He glanced toward her and smiled.

"It would be too crowded," argued Schwartz.

Stephen remembered when young miners were jammed into Ben's small room.

"So—what's being crowded?" called Iber, standing and speaking for the first time. "We're one family!"

"One family!" repeated Stephen.

"One family!" chanted Vladko, standing and leading his brothers from the Croatian Fraternal Union. "One family!" they called, raising their arms rhythmically into the air. Miners around them joined in. The momentum built.

"ONE FAMILY! ONE FAMILY! ONE FAMILY!"

The chant resounded throughout the room, filling the space that had earlier divided them into factions.

In good time Stephen raised his arms, palms toward the men, to silence them. "Yes! We are one family." He smiled and again looked at each miner down the line. "Let's form a good plan. Together!"

Vladko took the floor. "We could use the Croatian Fraternal Union for housing if the strike lasts till winter. Our building is three times the size of the City Hotel," he added proudly.

"Good!" Stephen agreed. "Maybe it could serve as a central dining place, too. Eating together would cost less for everyone." He moved on. "We need three separate plans: One for summer. One for fall. And—let's pray we won't need it—one for winter."

They organized committees to work on each plan. Finally even Schwartz cooperated.

At the end of the meeting, Stephen spoke again. "We'll beat the Company! Just as we've beaten mining disasters, avalanches, and fires! We'll stay united as one family!"

"ONE FAMILY! ONE FAMILY! ONE FAMILY!"

Only Vini remained seated, head bowed.

Stephen walked down the aisle to a standing ovation. When he came to Vini's row, he stopped and proudly offered his arm.

Before she rose, she crossed herself. *Holy Mother, please be with us all.*

CHAPTER 23

✠

*B*en arrived first in the lobby of the Denver Hotel. Will Chaney had insisted that he come tonight to meet Fred King. Ben wanted the mining story assignment more than any he'd ever had. For one thing it would be his big career chance, and he'd be lucky to get it at twenty. But more important was his desire for justice. He felt the two newspaper articles from the *New York Times* that he'd stuck in his pocket. The first was about the special train on March 23 that took 380 members of the National Guard to Trinidad, Colorado, where Major Hill placed the entire county under martial law. The second was about what happened four days later. He read it again as he waited:

> At Trinidad to-day the office of the Anarchist weekly paper, *Il Trovotore Italiano*, was seized by a squad of soldiers and this week's issue, which was ready for distribution, was confiscated. It is charged that the paper had incited strikers to violence. Major Hill has established a press censorship.

How dare they censor the press!

The mining assignment would give him a firsthand view of King and the inner workings of the Company. He hoped it would result in an incriminating documentary about Heffron Enterprises—his personal vendetta for his father's death. But as much as he wanted this assignment, he recoiled at the idea of dining socially with the cunning and ruthless man who held the number two post in Heffron Enterprises.

A change in the lobby caught his attention. It was not the noise, but the unexpected hush. Eyes turned toward the curving stairway and followed the vivacious young beauty who rustled gracefully down the steps. She paused a moment midway amplifying her grand entry. She wore a gown of lilac satin with long sleeves. The yoke of sheer white lace dipped low into the well-filled satin bodice and said *yes*—you may look and desire. But its high-necked ruffle said *no*—you may not touch. A heart-shaped ruby sparkled at her throat. The elegant gown fit tightly around her waist and hips and then flared out. It was a gown that fully covered her, and at the same time left nothing to the imagination. She glanced around the lobby, noting her admirers, and then shunned them all with a haughty toss of her head. She took the final step down the stairs and floated to the center of the lobby.

Ben felt like applauding. *Coup de théâtre,* his mother would have said.

When the beautiful young woman caught his gaze, she tilted her head and looked at him from the corner of her blue eyes. Her lips parted slightly in a smile both innocent and provocative.

Certain that he'd received a "come-on," the beat of Ben's heart quickened. *Coup de foudre,* love at first sight.

Then she turned away, flipping her blond hair back from her face and brushing him off like all the others.

Now he'd received a "whoa." A *coquette,* warned his head. But his heart didn't listen.

She glanced toward him again and lowered her eyes. The haughtiness had disappeared, and in its stead came an air of helplessness. She seemed unsure about what to do next in the lobby. She lifted her long dark lashes and looked at Ben once again, this time appearing shy and somewhat fearful of all the strangers staring at her.

A need to protect her surged through Ben—though protect her from what, he didn't know. He rose from the chair and stepped toward her.

Her blue eyes abandoned him, but she stood unmoving.

He bowed. "I am Ben McGragor. May I help you?" he asked, half expecting to be snubbed.

Instead, she took his arm and looked up at him, all sweetness, an innocent child in a woman's body. "Please, Sir," she pleaded in a soft southern accent, "stay close to me until my daddy comes down. All those men are staring at me."

His heart raced at her touch. *Beware,* warned his trustworthy inner voice. He shushed it. He felt angry at the men in the room gaping at her. She had merely walked into the lobby, and every man here was mentally undressing her. He felt her lean against him slightly and gladly shared his strength. What a charmingly vulnerable woman!

When Will Chaney arrived at the Denver Hotel, he saw Ben approaching a beautiful young woman in the center of the lobby. He smiled with amusement as he watched Ben bow. Vini had insisted on social graces that made Ben different in Crested Butte but debonair in Denver. Though only twenty, this reporter and son of a coal miner was a distinguished looking gentleman with impeccable manners, handsome in his attire, and easily mistaken for an aristocrat. Will smiled again, this time with pride. He planned for Ben to be his successor as editor at the *Rocky Mountain News.* In good time he would share that dream with the boy he'd known since infancy and loved as his own son.

As Will approached the couple, he noted Ben's rapt attention to the young woman and her tempting smile and tantalizing gown. Once long ago he'd encountered that kind of woman. Once was enough. A package of contradictions, a tease, the kind of woman who could drive a man crazy. *Benjamin Joel McGragor, watch out for this one!* "Good evening, Ben."

Ben seemed startled by the sound of his name, like being called back from a trance. "Hello, Will." He turned to the lady. "May I present Mr. Will Chaney, editor of the *Rocky Mountain News?*"

She smiled. "How do you do, Mr. Chaney? Daddy has often spoken of your newspaper."

There was an awkward moment of silence as Will waited for Ben to introduce her. "And in whose presence am I honored to be?"

Ben looked blank. "I'm sorry. Uh— Miss?"

"Miss King. I am Crystal King. You may have heard of my daddy," she added with a ring of pride. "Frederick Rodewald King."

Fred King's daughter! Ben stiffened. Distaste collided with desire.

"I see that you have met my daughter."

Ben looked at the stranger whose cold voice matched his stone-gray eyes, as fierce and penetrating as a lance. They stared into Ben's face and then moved pointedly to Crystal's arm linked in his.

Crystal stepped to his side. "Daddy, what took you so long?" She gave his arm a loving pat. "Mr. McGragor here has been so kind to me."

"I noticed." His sharp-edged tone could have cut a diamond.

"And this is Mr. Chaney, from the *Rocky Mountain News.*"

"Of course, Will. It's been a long time."

Ben noted King's abrupt change in demeanor, and that even when his lips smiled, his hard eyes didn't soften. He'd written enough human interest stories to know that eyes reveal a man's character.

"Ben McGragor is my associate," Will explained.

King shook hands with each of them. "My apologies for my abrasiveness, Mr. McGragor. My lovely daughter is quite naive."

"She is lovely indeed," said Will.

King's eyes softened as he looked at Crystal. "I've asked you not to come to the lobby without me."

She patted his arm again. "I just don't know what I'd do without my daddy to take care of me."

Ben held the dining room door for her.

"Thank you, Mr. McGragor." She brushed against him lightly, tilting her head back and parting her lips in her innocent/provocative smile. "You know, Sir, I did not expect to find a gentleman in the West." She put her arm through his again.

Ben enjoyed having this ornament linked to him, the sound of her accent, the smell of her perfume, the feel of her beside him.

"You must be so *smart* to be a newspaperman. And so *brave* to actually live here." She looked up at him wide-eyed.

So blatantly coy he thought, but oh so charming.

"I was afraid to come to the West, you know."

"Afraid?"

"It's so wild here." She shuddered, and Ben fought the urge to put his arm around her. "I don't feel the least wee bit frightened, though, beside you."

What a tease! Mentally repelled but emotionally attracted, he smiled to himself, confident that he could handle her.

"In spite of my fear, I wanted to see the West. I simply insisted on coming. Daddy finally gave in."

Fred King controls Heffron Enterprises, and this little package controls him.

Crystal's lips puckered into a pout. "I won't be with him when he goes to those awful mining towns, and I worry about him. He's getting older now. He needs someone to protect him."

Like a goldfish needs a bicycle.

King seated Crystal and sat beside her. He began caressing the diamond in his gold ring on his little finger. "Mr. McGragor," he said as Ben took the chair on the other side of Crystal, "tell me about yourself."

Will responded before he could answer. "Ben's father was involved in a venture that closed down after he died. His mother is an artist."

Ben noted Will's evasiveness about the kind of job and the kind of art. He trusted his friend's strategic judgment, but the false impression left him uncomfortable.

"Do you live in Washington now?" asked Will, changing the subject.

"No," said King. "Virginia."

Will nodded toward Crystal. "If all of Virginia's young ladies are as attractive as your daughter, I should have visited your state long ago."

Crystal smiled demurely. "Why, Mr. Chaney, how you do go on."

"My! My! What I've missed!" Will's chuckle rang through the dining room.

During dinner, Ben found himself delightfully entertained by Crystal. She was gorgeous, fascinating, unpredictable. He felt a growing contentment with leaving King to Will. Each course passed too quickly, and he ate dessert with the sad realization that the evening was ending.

As they rose to leave, Crystal paused to loosen the drawstrings on her small lace purse. She found a mirror, patted a golden lock of hair, and smiled at Ben. Her lingering pause placed the pair some distance behind Will and her father.

"May I show you around Denver tomorrow, Miss King?" he asked.

"I would love that, Mr. McGragor— Ben." She caressed his name. "But I'm afraid it's impossible."

"Oh?"

"There has been no public announcement yet." Her thick long lashes shyly veiled her eyes. "Daddy thinks it's best for me. The man is older, but he is wealthy." Suddenly her lower lip began to quiver. "I'm engaged to be married."

I'll take you home, Ben," said Will. He didn't speak again until they were in the buggy. "What in hellfire and damnation were you doing tonight, Benjamin Joel McGragor?"

His anger startled Ben.

"You not only deserted me on the battlefield, but you let that little flirt—"

"Don't call her a flirt!" But even as he shouted the words, his inner voice sided with Will. He shushed it.

"She led you right into the enemy camp. Treason, I believe it's called."

The intensity of his own feelings surprised Ben. He was battling with the man he respected more than any other, his mentor, a person he'd known all his life—over a woman of one evening's acquaintance. But what a charmingly vulnerable woman!

"What if her role in King's strategy is to play up to the reporter in order to get a favorable slant for Heffron Enterprises?"

A tease, yes. A trap, no. "You're getting paranoid, Will. She's engaged to be married."

"God help that poor soul!"

They both rode in silence until Will pulled up in front of Ben's boarding house. "King has agreed for the *News* to accompany him to the mining towns. He probably thinks he can con or pressure or bribe the reporter into good publicity. I need someone who can see through him and can't be bought." He put his hand on Ben's shoulder. "That's you. The mining assignment is yours."

His dream assignment placed right in his hands. But at the moment, foremost in his mind was the fact that Crystal had said she would remain in Denver during King's tour. There would be other assignments, but this was his only opportunity to be with her. Her father would take her back to Virginia and force her into an unwanted marriage. Ben brushed aside both the importance of this assignment and Crystal's engagement to another man. "Thanks, Will. But I don't want it."

"What is the matter with you?" Will's voice strained for control. "You've worked night and day for this paper, hoping for an opportunity like this. Now you flick it away like cigar ashes!"

"Maybe I'm tired of working all the time."

"But it has been your choice."

The image of Crystal danced in his mind. "Maybe the wrong choice."

Will frowned. "None of this makes any sense. Your desertion this evening. Your refusal now."

"I know you're disappointed." Ben stepped from the buggy. "I'm sorry," he said, unconscious of the smile on his face.

Fred King began his six-week tour of the mining towns in southern Colorado, and Ben began his tour of Denver with Crystal on his arm. The latter tour climaxed a week later in Ben's bribing the chaperon to take the night off, ordering dinner for two in Crystal's suite, and a belated proposal of marriage as she lay in bed nestled in his arms, her wondrous soft warmth against his flesh.

"We'll have an intimate little wedding ceremony," she said. "Here in Denver."

"The sooner the better."

"Just the two of us."

"And Mother and Will."

"No. Just the two of us, Ben."

He loved the way she caressed his name. "You're used to getting what you want when you want it."

She kissed his ear.

"I would like to have some friends from the *News*, too."

She drew back. "Not the newspapers!"

"Why?"

"We can't tell anyone in advance." Her eyes widened in fear. "If Daddy finds out, he'll stop our marriage."

"Why?"

"You know. My engagement."

"I think you broke your engagement tonight!" Curiosity coaxing him, he asked, "Who were you going to marry?"

"It doesn't matter. I don't love him. I love you."

He pulled her close again and waited for her to say more.

"Does it trouble you, Ben?" Her finger twirled a lock of hair on his chest. "All right. I'll tell you all about it."

Suddenly he didn't want to hear about another man in her life. "There's no need."

She raised her head from the pillow, her lips near his. "I'll tell you. He—"

Ben's lips shut off her words.

She drew back slightly. "Please, sugar," she begged. "Just the two of us at the ceremony."

He conceded to desire. After all, a bride should have the kind of wedding she wanted.

❀

On Saturday, June 4, 1904, the wedding ceremony for Benjamin Joel McGragor and Crystal Tabor King was performed by Peter Aubrey, a justice of the peace who was a friend of Ben's and would keep it quiet.

Their first quarrel occurred the next week after Ben received news about the strike in Victor. He clipped the *New York Times* version:

SHOTS FIRED FROM WINDOWS

MINERS HOISTED WHITE FLAG
WHEN TROOPS STORMED BUILDING

> Victor, Col., June 6.—Armed conflict between the union miners and the State troops has come at last in Colorado. Bitter feeling growing out of the great mining strike resulted today in a fight in which a squad of militiamen stormed the Miners' Union Hall at this place and wounded at least 20 men.
>
> . . . Lieut. Gov. Haggott, who is Acting Governor of the State during the absence of Gov. Peabody at St. Louis, has ordered out two companies of militia. Miners, union and non-union, are arming, and the prospects for to-morrow presage bloodshed and violence on every hand.

"I should have been there!" Ben muttered aloud from his cubicle at the *News*.

After work he still felt miserable. His anger grew as he walked to Crystal's hotel. Partly because of the militia. Partly because of his guilt over refusing the mining assignment. And partly because his wife refused to go home with him.

He banged the hotel suite door when he entered. "This is absurd, Crystal!"

Her smile fell and she stopped midway in her rush to welcome him home. "That's no way to greet a new bride!"

She looked lovely in her lavender lace peignoir, but he refused to let loose of his anger. "Sneaking around after work to see my wife, bribing your chaperon." He stepped around her and moved to the telephone. "I'm telling your father."

She gasped. "We can't do that! I need to be with Daddy when I tell him."

"You don't intend to keep our marriage a secret until his tour is over!"

Her dark lashes lowered over her beautiful blue eyes. "Please don't shout at me." Her lower lip trembled.

I'm acting like a cad, he thought. *You've been had,* said his inner voice. This time he didn't shush it. He picked up the receiver.

She grasped his arm. "I just can't do it. Please understand."

"You don't have to. I will."

"Oh, no!" She clicked down the hook. "That's worse!"

He watched those dreadful tears well up in her eyes. He could handle a gun pointed at his head easier than her eyes filled with tears. Slowly he replaced the receiver.

"We won't have to keep our secret much longer, Ben."

It occurred to him for the first time that she might always do exactly as she wanted, regardless of how he felt. "I am telephoning my mother."

"But you can't!"

"Watch me." He picked up the receiver, silently daring her to interfere. He observed her as she chose a ploy.

She put her arms around him and snuggled close. "But Ben, what if she tells someone?"

"What if she does?"

"Think of poor Daddy."

He had trouble thinking about "poor" Fred King. "Long distance, please. . . . Crested Butte, Colorado. . . . Vini McGragor."

Crystal's mouth puckered in a pout.

"Hello, Mother."

"Ben!"

Casually he asked, "How are Stephen and Veronika?"

"It's been a tough six weeks with the strike. Stephen is worried after what happened at Victor."

And I'm doing nothing to help, he thought.

"I wish you could come home and write a story about the miners. It might influence public opinion."

What could he say? Yet, he felt sure that she would understand. "I have some news for you."

"You got the King assignment!" she said excitedly.

Taken aback, he said, "No. I changed my plans."

"Oh." In the brief pause he heard her effort to hide disappointment. "What is it then?"

"You have a daughter-in-law."

"What?"

"I'm married, Mother."

Another pause. "That's wonderful!"

"I knew you'd be happy." He also knew that she felt hurt that he'd not given her the opportunity to attend the wedding. And that she would never say so. And that he had been wrong to deprive her of that privilege.

"Who is she? Did you get married in the church? When?"

"Wait a minute."

"How long have you known her? What's she like? Where's she from?"

"One question at a time!"

She laughed. "I'm just so surprised. Tell me one thing, Ben. Was it *coup de foudre?*"

"Indeed." How did she always know his heart? "Love at first sight. And forever."

"Just like your papa and me."

"We'll come to Crested Butte as soon as we can. Then you can see her for yourself."

"When?"

They would have to wait until King returned. The news would spread like a forest fire when he took Crystal to Crested Butte. "About a month, I'm afraid. I wish it could be sooner. I haven't been out of the city since Easter."

"You haven't put her in your awful boarding house, have you?"

"I'm getting a different place soon."

"Would you send me a picture?"

"That's a promise."

"Father Mike is leaving for Denver tomorrow. I'll send a present with him."

"No, Mother! This news is mine to tell."

She laughed again. "So you want to surprise everyone here and show her off yourself!"

He laughed too, neither explaining nor lying.

"What's her name, Ben? At least tell me—"

Suddenly he couldn't bring himself to tell her he'd married Fred King's daughter—not on the telephone. He clicked down the receiver hook, hating his deceit. She would assume they were cut off. Life was simpler in his pre-Crystal days. Kinder. More honest. But much more dull! He smiled at his beautiful bride and pulled her to him.

CHAPTER 24

I mpatiently waiting as usual for Crystal to dress, Ben tore open the brown paper on his mother's package. A note to him was attached to a small beautifully wrapped present:

> *Congratulations!*
> *This tagless present is for your wife. You didn't tell me her name, and "Mrs. McGragor" sounds much too formal for my only daughter. I've always wanted the woman you chose for your wife to have the cross your papa gave me at our wedding.*
> *Love,*
> *Mama*
> *P.S. I am eager for a picture.*

He held the wrapped present tenderly and stared out the hotel window at the motor cars and buggies in the busy street below. He wished it weren't the cross that meant everything to his mother. But what would it mean to Crystal, who never removed her heart-shaped ruby necklace and wouldn't understand the sentiment? He almost felt embarrassed to give it to her—and was immediately disgusted with himself. His inner voice asked if this post-Crystal life was beginning to stain his character. He shushed it.

Worth the wait as usual, Crystal took the present with delight. "How sweet of your mama to send me a gift." She tore the pretty paper greedily. "It must be jewelry. It's the right size package. I love jewelry." She glanced at Ben beneath thick lashes. "As soon as Daddy knows about our marriage, you can give me a big ring." The card fell to the floor, and she didn't bother to pick it up. As she opened the box, her face stiffened. "A cross," she said in a subdued tone. "It doesn't even look new."

"Read the card." Ben picked it up.

She read the words aloud:

> *My dear daughter,*
> *This cross belonged to Ben's grandmother, who wore it every day of her life. My husband gave it to me on our wedding day. It comes to you with my love.*
> *Vini*

Crystal removed the sparkling ruby and replaced it with the simple cross. "Fasten it, Ben." His big hands fumbled with the small hook. Tenderly she placed her hand over the cross. "Your mama's cross! Your grandmama's cross!" Her face glowed.

What a bundle of contradictions he had married! "You are sweet, Crystal."

"The cross is part of you. The same way the ruby is part of Daddy." Carelessly she tucked the ruby in the box. "But I'm not his anymore. I'm yours." She sat down on the love seat and patted the space beside her. "Tell me about yourself. All I know is what Mr. Chaney said the night we met."

He had forgotten Will's misleading introduction. "We don't know much about each other, do we, Crystal?" He sat down and put his arm around her. She leaned her head on his shoulder. "Will left out a few details regarding my family. My father was Joel McGragor, a miner."

She laughed. "You're teasing me, Ben."

"No, Crystal. He knew your father. They both lived in Crested Butte."

Her eyes searched his face. Then she shook her head. "I can't believe you're a miner's son. You're a gentleman."

Ben suppressed his irritation. "He was killed in a mine explosion."

She shuddered and snuggled closer to him. "Oh, Ben. How awful for you!"

"I never knew him. I was a month old." He paused, remembering the story and the intensity in his mother's eyes each time she told it. "Mother was evicted from Company housing."

"They wouldn't do anything like that now! My father wouldn't let them."

Ben chose not to argue with her. Instead, he pressed on. "She had only seventeen cents."

"*Seventeen cents!*"

"You can't even imagine that, can you, Crystal? You think of money in terms of dollars, hundreds and thousands of them."

Her beautiful eyes looked intently into his, the way they did when she stopped playing her charming little game of southern belle. "I've never thought of money at all."

For the first time he wondered if she could handle his world.

"Seventeen cents!" She scooted away from his arm and sat up straight, putting her hands to her temples. "I'm trying as hard as I can, but I really can't imagine how that would feel." She stared at him bewildered. "I look at you and see a fine gentleman. And you had no father. No money." She touched the cross at her throat. "Your mother must be a very special lady."

"I'm eager for you to meet her."

"I just had nannies. Never a mama. Mine died when I was born."

"You have one now."

"You promised her a picture. Let's go do that. Right now, Ben," she said impatiently.

He rose, aware that Crystal's world had developed into one where people waited for her but she waited for nothing.

Ben and Crystal posed together at Dan's Picture Parlor. Dan had done some work for Ben for the *News* and promised to give them fast service.

When they received the picture, Crystal held it up, admiring it. "I want to inscribe it."

"Mother would like that."

She took a gold pen from her beaded purse, then hesitated a moment. "Shall I write 'Mrs. McGragor' or 'Vini'?" She smiled radiantly, deciding. "'Mama'!"

Ben watched her form large fancy letters across the lower corner. "Your script is beautiful."

"Daddy let me learn calligraphy. I add my own little flourishes," she said proudly. "He says it's distinctive."

Ben leaned over her shoulder and read her inscription:

TO MAMA WITH LOVE
June 18, 1904

"She'll treasure that."

Crystal frowned. "But I don't have room for our names."

He laughed. "She'll know who we are—Mr. and Mrs. Benjamin Joel McGragor." As they walked to the post office, he began to whistle.

"I've never heard that melody before. What is it?"

"Just an old family tune. Mother learned it from my father, who'd learned it from his father—and so on back. She always called it Joel's tune."

"Whistle it again. I want to learn it too." She began to hum along with him. Hand-in-hand they made a duet of Joel's tune, oblivious to everyone around them.

On July 4, Vini heard the cannon blast. Strike or no strike, this was a day to celebrate. She had something else to celebrate, too, and it was hard to keep secret. But she kept faith with Ben and did not tell even Father Mike.

The expected retaliations against the miners had occurred immediately. Credit was denied at the Company Store and eviction notices were posted on Company housing. But in a single day the miners, their families, and other supporters put up tents beside Coal Creek for the homeless, dug two outhouses, and planted huge vegetable gardens on the grounds of St. Patrick's and the Union Congregational Church. Now they were in the expected waiting game. With Stephen Machek at the helm, the Crested Butte miners sailed united on the turbulent sea of the strike. And so far there had been no violence.

The miners Vini hired to renovate her building had done a good job. She especially liked her office. She raised her eyes from her ledger and scanned the room. *Fleur-de-lis* wallpaper picked up the sea-blue in the carpet. Two scaled-down wingback chairs faced her mahogany desk. The table between them held recent copies of the *Ladies Home Journal* and two books, Louisa May Alcott's *Little Women* and James Barrie's *Peter Pan*. On another small table stood a Wedgewood tea set with delicate white leaves on blue. She turned, and a little girl with a watering can looked back at her, a painting by Pierre Renoir which hung on the wall behind her desk. Vini smiled, satisfied.

She heard the cannon fire again and decided to put up her ledger and join the fun. She was astounded by the success of *Marie-Vincente*. She received orders for linens countrywide, including several from the White House because Mrs. Roosevelt liked her work. In addition, two orders would be sent abroad. The first was a banquet sized tablecloth and napkins which had been ordered by the French ambassador as a gift for President Émile Loubet. The second was for Czar Nicholas. She had been able to hire a dozen more employees. She paid good wages, continued the education fund for the children, and offered a profit sharing bonus during the strike. She deposited the bonus in individual accounts she opened in their names at The Bank of Crested Butte, where Richard Sterling maintained his presidency though he had never returned to town. As she hurried toward the plaza, she passed by his big yellow house on Elk and noticed its deterioration. His departure had left an indelible mark on more than her heart.

Another blast filled the air. She reached the plaza as Stephen Machek reloaded the cannon. "Here's Vini McGragor," he called. "Her business will keep a lot of families going."

The crowd cheered.

Vini saw Father Mike and he made room for her beside him.

"Fire the cannon, Vini!" shouted Vladko Radich. "You deserve a turn."

She hesitated.

"Women don't fire cannons!" called Schwartz.

Father Mike looked at her with a twinkle in his eyes. "Maybe this one does," he whispered.

"Why not!" With each stride, the cannon grew bigger. She seldom thought about being small, but now she wondered whether she was strong enough to fire it. She stepped up to the huge brass cannon and stood behind it, dwarfed.

Stephen looked at the weapon and then at her. He asked softly, "Do you need some help?"

She lifted her chin, raised herself to her full five feet, and retorted with a confidence she didn't feel. "Do you need a CRESTED BUTTE destination sign around your neck?"

He grinned.

Praying that her will would compensate for her size, she touched the hard metal. Then she saw Schwartz offer a bet, against her no doubt. Defiant energy surged. She centered her will on the firing pin, then jerked. The recoil knocked her backward against Stephen. The barrel of the over-heated cannon exploded. A large chunk of brass sailed through the air with the cannonball and landed near the reservoir.

Stephen shook his head and shouted over the noise of the crowd. "When we get a bargaining table, let's hope Vini McGragor is never on the opposite side!"

The cheers were unanimous. Almost. Vini noticed one person who did not join in. He stood at the edge of the crowd making notes. When he glanced up, she recognized the hard eyes of Fred King.

Crystal tried to keep her hand from trembling as she showed Ben the telegram about her father's return to Denver. "I want to tell Daddy by myself at dinner tonight."

Ben frowned. "We'll do it together."

"Please, Ben. He's my father, and it's important to me."

"I'll be glad put an end to all this sneaking around. I'm ready to take you home."

She put her arms around his neck. "Now tell me, sugar. Why do you want to take me home with you?"

He caressed her, his lips close to hers, his eyes dancing. "Why, 'sugah,'" he said, imitating her southern accent, "to get some cooking and cleaning out of you. Why else?"

She stepped back. "You mock me. You're mean."

He laughed. "I'm eager for us to pick a place together."

"Well, I don't know how to cook or clean. Servants do that." She put the telegram on the table and lifted her manicured hands. "Work would spoil my nails."

His eyes clouded. "I suppose it would."

"You just go on home now. I don't want you here when Daddy comes."

But she did want him to stay with her. She was afraid to tell her father. But she was even more afraid for Ben. "I love you. So very much." She clung to him when he kissed her goodby. Then she shoved him out the door, keeping her smile until she closed it behind him.

Fred King walked into the lobby, exhausted from the strain of travel. He had learned as much as possible about each mining situation, developed an over-all strategy, and been absolutely intentional with every word he'd said to each person he'd met during his entire six-week journey. Crested Butte was on its way to taking Trinidad's and Victor's place as the major problem in Colorado. He recalled the face of Stephen Machek whose charisma controlled the mob in the plaza at Crested Butte. A dangerous man. The Company will "befriend" him, he decided, wondering what his price would be.

King's beautiful daughter ran to meet him in the lobby. "Daddy! Daddy! I've missed you so!" She wore his favorite dress, a bright green satin with tiny pearl buttons and Belgian lace around the neck and sleeves. The ruby was at her throat. She put her arms around his neck. "I love you, Daddy."

"I love you too, my baby." He swung her around, proud to be her father and noting the admiring glances of people in the lobby.

"I've arranged for dinner in our suite. Then I have something to tell you that makes me very happy." She hesitated, and added, "Since you love me so much, I hope you will be happy too."

"I'm sure I will, my baby." He bathed and dressed for dinner, washing off every trace of that world of the inferior. That world of dirty poverty-stricken mining camps teeming with ignorant crude miners and shabby unkempt wives with their lined faces and rough work-worn hands. But worse than those were the ones who dreamed of something better. And the worst of all were people who helped the miners keep those dreams alive, like that infernal Vini McGragor—to be exact.

How good it felt to be back in the world of the superior, a world controlled by men of intelligence and brightened by beautiful ladies elegantly dressed, a world of the powerful.

Crystal's happy news piqued his curiosity. She'd probably bought a whole new wardrobe. As he tied his tie, he smiled into the mirror. "How I've spoiled her!"

King found Crystal waiting when he opened the door to their joint suite. "We are having your favorite," she said as he seated her at the dinner cart. "Prime rib."

"You always know how to please me." He put his napkin on his lap. "Now, what is your news?"

"It'll keep until after dinner, Daddy. I want to hear all about your trip."

He noticed that she played with her food. "Aren't you hungry?"

"Not very."

"You seem nervous."

She smiled at him. "I'm just excited that my daddy is home."

When he finished his dinner, he realized that she'd just pushed little bits of food around on her plate and none of them had made it to her mouth. "All right, my baby." He scooted back his chair and patted his lap. "Come here and tell Daddy what's wrong."

She didn't move. "The best thing has happened." Her attempt at a smile failed. "But I'm afraid it's going to disappoint you, Daddy. And I don't want it to. Because it's the happiest thing ever in my whole life."

He thought he saw fear in her eyes. Surely not. He'd do anything for her; she knew that. "If it makes you so happy, how could I be disappointed?"

"It changes some of your plans for me."

She was afraid. He was sure of it. He'd seen that same fear many times before in the eyes of the men he'd dealt with. But never in her eyes! "What is it, Crystal?"

"I'm married, Daddy."

Disbelief. Hurt. Anger! "*Married!*" Gan must have stopped in Denver on his return from San Francisco. King stood up and shoved his chair back. "He could have at least waited until I was here to give you away!" he shouted.

Her eyes widened in panic.

He couldn't stand to see her afraid of him. He softened his voice. "You were right. I am disappointed." He placed his hand gently over hers and watched her fear gradually subside. "My baby, I know how persuasive he can be, but I'm surprised Gan would do this without letting me know."

"Not *Gan*, Daddy! *Ben*," she shrieked, terrified.

"Ben who?"

"Ben McGragor." Her voice shook. "We had dinner with him. You know. From the *Rocky Mountain News*."

He jumped up. "That arrogant reporter? You didn't marry him!"

She shrank in her chair.

Suspicion. Grief. Rage! His mind swirled. He drew back his arm to strike her. The fear in her eyes stopped him. He hurled his chair. It crashed against the wall. "That sneaking spurious brigand! I'll kill him!"

"Daddy, no! I love him!" Crying, she flung herself into his arms. "Please understand."

He felt her cheeks wet against his shirt. Her tears cleared his head. "Oh, Crystal. What have you done!" He held her as she cried. "I knew better than to allow you to come to Denver. I shouldn't have given in to you." Fury seethed against Ben McGragor. A gold-digger. A gutless coward without the courage to ask for her hand. Or even to be present now! "My innocent naive baby! What advantage he took of you!"

He continued to enfold her. "Sh-h-h. Now. Now." He rubbed her back gently as he had when she was a child. "We'll work this out." We'll have to, he thought. How can I handle things with Gan? An annulment would do it, a quiet annulment. If I can keep him from finding out about this, everything can proceed as planned. "My baby, when did you marry?" he asked softly.

"June fourth."

"How many people know?"

"No one. I wanted to keep it a secret until I could tell you."

He saw hope. "Who performed the ceremony?"

"A justice of the peace."

"What was his name?"

"Peter Aubrey. He's a friend of Ben's." She stepped back. "Why are you asking all these questions?"

King took her hands in his. "I know what happened. You're young and beautiful, and you think you're in love because you've been lonely here without your friends. And Mr. McGragor is an experienced ladies' man—"

"He is not!"

"It's just puppy love." He cupped her chin in his hand and looked into her beautiful face. "This is what we'll do. We must have the marriage annulled."

She jerked away from him. "No!"

"Yes, Crystal," he said firmly. "Gan need never know about this foolishness, and you can go ahead and marry him."

"How can you say that! I told you I love Ben!"

"I know what is best for you. Obviously, you don't."

She sank to the floor, her arms around his knees. "Please, Daddy," she begged. "With Gan, I would be a possession to show off. But with Ben, I'm a woman—a real person. I'm *alive*." She sobbed at his feet.

He raised her from the floor. For an instant he wavered. Only for an instant. He would do what he had to do. "Being *alive,* as you call it, would harden you, make you wrinkled and gray before your time." Far better for her to be the ornament he'd reared her to be, shielded and protected from life. "Hush now, Crystal. It's settled."

Her sobbing stopped. She moved away from him, her stance defiant.

He looked at Crystal and saw a stranger. Yet not a stranger at all. The southern belle he loved to spoil stood before him transformed into a replica of himself.

"I am Mrs. Benjamin McGragor," she said fiercely. "I intend to remain so forever."

He started to fold her in his arms.

She glared at him. No fear now. No tears. Her red and swollen eyes narrowed and hardened into absolute determination. "If you have our marriage annulled, I will tell Gan the whole story."

He stared at his beloved daughter. The replica of himself stared back. She was not bluffing.

"Well," he said finally, moving to the settee, "this is quite a homecoming." He caressed the gold ring on his little finger, his mind racing toward a solution. "Tell me about Ben McGragor, Crystal." He forced his lips to smile and his voice to be gentle.

"He grew up in Crested Butte. His father was a miner."

"How could you do this!" he thundered. "To yourself? To me?" Crested Butte. That infernal Crested Butte!

She ignored his outburst. "Ben was just a baby when his father was killed in a mine explosion, the Jokerville Disaster. Ben said you knew him— Joel McGragor."

Joel McGragor. His ghost rose into the air. King could almost feel his presence in the room.

The telephone rang, and Crystal ran to answer it. "Hello." . . . "No, not yet." . . . "Please, not now," she said softly.

Her "husband" obviously. The son of Joel and Vini McGragor! King raged at the thought. He needed a strategy. As Crystal talked on the telephone, his mind went back in time, calling forth details and building on them.

Vini: The beautiful French girl at the depot nearly a quarter of a century ago. The humiliating scene at the Star Cafe. The tug-of-war over Coal Creek. The Widows and Orphans Fund. The live-in maid of Alisa Sterling. The dynamite debacle and Jake Neath's negligence. The successful business woman. The thorn in the Company's system. The cannon blast at the plaza. The powerful force in Crested Butte. How often their paths had crossed!

Ben: King concentrated on remembering each detail of the dinner with Will Chaney when Crystal met Ben. Though Ben had been distracted by her most of that evening, some things were evident when he did enter into the men's conversation. Two characteristics stood out—prideful independence and hostility toward Heffron Enterprises. His inheritance explained the former—like father, like son. Joel's death in the Jokerville Disaster explained the latter. He had tried unsuccessfully to hide his loathing of Heffron Enterprises. King knew that the antagonism would extend to himself as the man in the number two position. And finally Ben liked working for a paper that no longer buckled easily under pressure, regardless of the financial clout of the subject.

Suddenly King smiled, confident that he recognized Ben's Achilles heel. Crystal's, of course, was her love of luxury. No two-bit-miner's-son-turned-reporter could outmaneuver Frederick Rodewald King! All he had to do was set the stage.

CHAPTER 25

*I*n control once again, King walked toward the telephone to implement the first step of his strategy. "Crystal, I assume that is Mr. McGragor. Let me speak to him, please."

She tried to hang the receiver back on its hook.

He grabbed it and held his other hand under the hook so she couldn't disconnect him. "Mr. McGragor, Frederick King here. Crystal is ready to go with you now." He kept his tone courteous, cool and emotionless. "Maybe we can have a drink when you come for her. There's a matter I'd like to discuss with you."

King hung up and put his arm around his daughter, ushering her to the settee. "My baby," he made his voice gentle and loving, "my tour was a terrible strain, and today's trip back to Denver was long and tiring. I think you can understand that your news was a considerable shock to me. I apologize for the way I behaved."

She looked at him suspiciously.

"I love you too much to do anything to hurt you. I won't force an annulment, but if you change your mind I'll see that it's done."

"I won't change my mind."

"That's all right."

"Why did you invite Ben for a drink?

King forced a warm smile. "I need to get acquainted with my son-in-law. I don't know him at all." He looked at her worried face. "Don't fret, my baby. I'll be nice to him."

"Thank you, Daddy."

"In fact, I want to offer him a job. He can work for me, and eventually become my partner."

"Your partner?"

"I want you to be able to live in the way you're accustomed." He patted her hand. "And you and I won't be halfway across the country from each other."

"Then it really is all right with you? Everything between us is back like it was?"

"Of course. I want you to be happy."

Her eyes brightened and she hugged him. The southern belle spoke. "I love you, Daddy."

"And I you. Nothing is more important to me than your happiness. That's why I must do one other thing."

"What?" she asked cautiously.

"It may be hard for you to accept, but it's necessary. You must trust me."

"Trust you?"

"I'll not stand for any man marrying you for money. That would mean nothing but unhappiness for you in the long run."

"That's a horrible thing to say. Ben didn't marry me for money!"

"Then we don't have anything to worry about. But I can't risk you being way out West where I can't protect you if you need me, where some man could mistreat you and spend your money, and I wouldn't even know it."

"Ben wouldn't do that! He loves me."

"I've got to be sure. It hurts me to say this, but it's for your own good. If he is foolish enough to turn down my offer, which I promise you will be more than fair, then I will have no choice but to withdraw completely all my financial support of you—your allowance, for example—and to revoke your trusts and cut off your inheritance."

She gasped.

"It would tear my heart out to have to do that. But Mr. McGragor simply must realize that marrying you does not give him access to your money." He smiled. "Of course, my baby, if he loves you, it won't make any difference to him that you don't have a dime."

She frowned.

"Listen to me, Crystal. You need to know that I'm serious about this. It isn't like getting me to change my mind about your coming to Denver. This has to do with money. You know I don't change my mind about money or business."

Her frown deepened.

"If he accepts my offer, however, he won't put us in that position."

"He'll accept."

King caressed his ring. "I can't think of any reason why he wouldn't."

She hugged him. "I can always count on my daddy to take care of me. You've never once let me down. Not in my whole life."

They heard a knock. "It's Ben," she said, rushing to the door.

King poured two glasses of dry sherry and held them up to the light, deep in thought. *Unless I've miscalculated, the whole thing will soon be over. They will perform like puppets.*

❖

As Crystal opened the door, Ben took her arm. Possessively, she noted. She liked the feeling. "It's all right," she whispered. "Daddy has been wonderful."

King approached him. "Hello, Mr. McGragor." He extended his hand cordially. "Would you like a glass of sherry?"

Crystal smiled. "I'll get it." She could trust her daddy. She handed the first glass to him. "One for my daddy. And one for my husband. The two men I love most in all the world."

King gestured to a chair. "Please sit down, Mr. McGragor. I have a proposition for you."

Ben frowned.

Nervously, Crystal patted Ben's arm and seated herself on the settee opposite him.

"To be honest with you," said King, still standing, "when Crystal first told me what you'd done, I wanted the marriage annulled. But she seems to love you very much." He smiled at her. "I absolutely adore this child."

"I adore you too, Daddy."

King sat down beside her. "I'm afraid I've spoiled her. She twists me right around her little finger."

"You mentioned a 'proposition,'" said Ben.

Crystal winced at the inflection. "Daddy is going to help us, Ben."

Slowly King turned his glass. "I want to offer you a position working for me."

Ben started to respond, then closed his mouth on the words. He seemed to struggle for control. When he spoke, his voice was crisp. "Thank you, Mr. King. But I like the job I have."

"I'm not sure you understand what I'm offering, Mr. McGragor. My proposition gives you an opportunity to provide for my daughter—"

Ben interrupted. "I'll take care of my wife."

"At the level she's accustomed to? I'm offering servants and clothes and jewels. Entertainment and travel."

"Isn't that wonderful for us, Ben?" said Crystal, grateful that her daddy was doing exactly what he'd said.

Ben didn't answer.

She reached across the cocktail table, and he enfolded her hand. His eyes told her he loved her. But he didn't smile.

"When you know how to handle things, Ben," said King, warmly using his first name, "you can become my partner—to be exact."

"Your *partner!*" He spat the word.

Startled, Crystal jerked her hand back. She saw her father's jaw tighten and heard his voice strain to be civil.

"Out of love for my daughter, I'm offering you all that money can buy."

"I'm not for sale."

Inwardly King smiled. Like father, like son. His words to Ben's father so many years before came back to him. He repeated them. "Besides money, this job also puts the power of Heffron Enterprises in your hands."

"Power dependent upon the exploitation of the weak, those too unskilled to defend themselves and too poor to buy their way out."

Crystal caught her breath and looked at her father. No one talked to him like that.

King patted her hand. "It's all right, my baby." Yes, indeed. Like father, like son.

"Think about it, *Ben!*" She caressed his name; he'd always liked that. "Daddy is making a very generous offer."

"I'm sorry, Crystal, but if I chose to associate myself with Heffron Enterprises, it would make my father turn over in his mass grave and put my mother in hers." He stood. "I want no part of it."

"Please, Ben!"

"If you'll excuse us now, my wife and I will go home."

"Just a minute, McGragor!"

Crystal cringed at the return of authority in her father's voice.

"Since you won't work for me, you leave me no choice." King looked at Crystal.

She dreaded what was coming.

"You'll have none of my money, McGragor."

"I don't want it."

King's voice turned steel. "You need to know that I am changing my will so that Crystal inherits nothing. I'm revoking her trusts and cutting off all of her financial support. When she walks out that door with you, she will be penniless."

Penniless.

"When she walks out that door with me, I will take care of her."

King touched Crystal's arm. "You must understand that the minute I leave Denver, you will be completely dependent upon your husband's income. You may not be aware, my baby, but a newspaper reporter earns less per year than your allowance per month."

It had never occurred to her that she might have to live differently just because she married Ben.

"Crystal doesn't care about that." Ben reached for her hand to raise her from the settee.

She ignored the gesture.

"I don't think you know my daughter very well. I'm afraid she is pampered and expensive. She takes for granted a mansion, a personal maid, access to a motor car. To her, extravagant luxuries are necessities. Surely you love her enough not to force her to sacrifice everything."

"You are twisting things," said Ben.

"No he isn't!" shouted Crystal, jumping up. "It's very clear that your silly stubborn refusal to work for Heffron Enterprises is more important to you than I am!"

Ben put his arm around her. "You don't believe that, Crystal, any more than I believe money is more important to you than I am."

"Perhaps you'd like to reconsider my offer," said King. "You have until my train leaves tomorrow."

"Let's go home, Crystal."

King looked at his daughter. "Well, then . . ." He shook his head. "Of the two of us, Ben McGragor, you are the hard one." He kissed Crystal on the cheek. "I'm sorry, my baby. I really tried." He moved toward the door. "I'm going down to the bar now. This has been quite an evening."

When the door closed, Ben sighed in relief and smiled at Crystal. "Finally, Mrs. McGragor, we get to go home."

She broke into sobs. "If you loved me . . . you . . . would work for . . . Daddy."

He held her close and kissed the tears on her cheeks, longing for her to understand. "I know this is hard for you."

She clung to him. "Can't you understand, Ben? I don't know how to be poor."

"We aren't poor. But even if we were, that wouldn't make any difference. Not when we love each other so much."

"It's because I love you that I don't want to work myself to the bone cooking and cleaning until I'm not pretty for you anymore. I don't want to worry about facing starvation. Or eviction. Or ending up with only seventeen cents."

He lifted her chin. "That's absurd."

"Your daddy didn't intend for your mama to be hungry or homeless either. But it happened."

"He couldn't help it."

She backed away from him. "But you can! Accept Daddy's offer. Please, Ben."

"Never!"

"Then . . ." She held her throat as though it hurt. ". . . I want our marriage annulled."

He flinched. "You don't know what you're saying." An annulment was exactly what King would have desired. Ben felt he'd gone up against the big man, held his ground, thought he'd won—but somehow, he'd evidently lost. Suddenly he grasped the truth. King had set Crystal up! Her own father! She dangled before Ben like a pampered puppet on her father's money strings.

"Don't look like that, Ben."

He took a firm hold on her wrists. "We are going home now, Crystal."

"I can't."

He picked her up and carried her from the room.

"You're a brute!" She beat her fists against his chest. "Put me down!"

He ignored her and nodded nonchalantly to a couple in the hall unlocking their door.

Ben carried her down the flight of back stairs to the main floor—those same stairs he had sneaked up and down since his marriage. When he reached the door marked LOBBY, he stopped. "Decide, Mrs. McGragor, whether you are going to walk with me through the lobby like a lady. Or be carried like a spoiled brat."

"My daddy would never treat me like this!"

"Maybe he should have." Ben reached for the door knob. "Decide."

"All right," she whimpered. "You always get your way!"

"One thing more," he said, before putting her down. "If you ever go back to your father, or even so much as mention the word 'annulment' again—even once—I will erase our marriage from my mind. Nonnegotiable! Do you understand?"

She nodded, her eyes wide.

"For me, Crystal, it will be as though the whole thing didn't even happen." He put her down.

She straightened her dress, mustered her dignity, and transformed herself into the ornament she'd been reared to be. "I know how to be a lady, Benjamin McGragor, but you are no gentleman!"

He bowed, opened the door, and offered her his arm.

The next morning Crystal awoke early to a nightmare of reality. The rainy grayness matched her gloom and the shadowy fear growing within her. Ben still slept, silent as death.

Last night when he stopped at the boarding house, she'd at first thought it was a cruel joke. The dark hall. The dreary stairs. The dusty landings. Her dismay mounted as they climbed to the fourth floor and Ben opened the door to his bachelor room. "My father's servants live better than—" The look on Ben's face had stopped her.

"I have enough money to buy a small place," he promised.

But his promise was lost in her shock.

Now, she lay like a prisoner in this horrible place. Specks of brown paint fell from the ceiling, faded hexagon-patterned paper peeled from the walls, and cracked checkerboard linoleum covered the floor. A desk and chair, chest and bed fought for the crowded space.

She felt the queasiness that gave rise to her shadowy fear. Careful not to creak the lumpy mattress, she rolled to the side of the bed and stood. She put on Ben's robe draped over the chair, padded softly to the door, opened and closed it without a sound, and rushed down the hall to the shared water closet. She saw three black cockroaches crawling across the floor and knew she would scream if one touched her bare toes. Long dark hairs from a head unknown curled in the basin and began to swirl. The stench of urine from the unflushed toilet sickened her. She gripped the wash stand and heaved.

The wave of nausea passed, leaving her trembling. Sure now of what she'd suspected and feared, she looked into the mirror and faced the truth. Morning sickness. Pregnancy. A baby. She saw the ruby sparkle at her throat. Beneath it hung the cross, and she touched it. Suddenly her reflection dimmed, transfigured, as the image burned in her mind of a young widow, penniless and homeless, carrying a month old baby in her arms. A spasm of fear shook Crystal.

In the eerie gray light of dawn, she floated through the nightmare back down the hall. She stopped at Ben's door and leaned against it. The wood felt cold and hard to her upstretched palms and her cheek. Her heart cried out to the one she loved, and she reached for the knob, surrendering to this strange new world. But her head argued, freezing her arm midway, warning her against risking the baby to poverty.

She felt a roach crawl across her toe. She stifled a scream and fled. Down the stairs to the landing, twisting around and running. Down to the next landing. The roach. The baby. Running and twisting. Running and twisting. Fleeing. Desperate.

She reached the door to the street. She remembered that she wore only Ben's robe. But she couldn't force herself to go back. Half-crazed and panting, she flung the door open and ran outside into the rain.

A carriage waited a half block away. A familiar figure stood beside it under an umbrella. She fled from the nightmare of reality into the shielding arms of her daddy.

"It's all right, my baby. I'm here," said King, relieved to see her at last.

"Oh, Daddy!" she cried.

He helped her into the carriage. "Union Station!" he ordered the driver, explaining to Crystal that he'd had their things packed and taken on to the station.

"But how did you know to come?"

He put his arm around her. "My little girl was meant to be rich."

"How long have you been here?"

"Most of the night. You'll always be able to count on me."

"I want to go home. If Ben really loved me, he wouldn't ask me to be poor."

"He should have accepted my generous offer."

"This is what we'll do." She echoed his words from the evening before. "We must get an annulment. I want it right now. I want to marry Gan as soon as we get back." She looked at him, her eyes intense. "Immediately. Can you fix it, Daddy?"

"Yes, my baby."

"Gan won't find out about this, will he?"

"I can fix that too. But it's risky."

"You've got to!"

"The justice of the peace. You're sure it was a man named Peter Aubrey?"

She nodded and began to sob. "I think my heart shall break."

"Now, now, my baby." He patted her gently, thinking. I pulled the strings successfully. But have I broken her heart? Nonsense! I only did what was necessary. She will get caught up in Gan's gifts and decorating their home and spending his money. I did the right thing. He handed her his silk handkerchief. "Dry your eyes and listen."

She dabbed at her tears.

"What about Ben? Will he cause any problems?"

She shook her head. "He said that if I came back to you, it would be like—" She caught a sobbing breath. "It will be as though the whole thing didn't even happen." Suddenly her eyes glinted with fear. "No harm must come to Ben. You must promise me."

He wavered.

"Say it!"

Once more, against his better judgment, he yielded to his daughter.

"Thank you, Daddy. I'll always love him."

"Crystal," he said gravely. "This is the most important thing I've ever said to you. If we hide this from Gan now, he must never find out. He would not forgive your deceit."

She took a deep breath. "I understand." The blue irises in her reddened eyes turned to ice. "My marriage to Ben is erased. It never happened. And anyone who says it did," King's replica stated, "is a liar."

Ben awoke to the empty bed and a moment's fear. He saw Crystal's green satin dress in a heap on the floor and relaxed. He waited impatiently, realizing he had never known anyone who could be so slow. After a while, however, he became concerned.

He threw on his clothes. Checked the hall. The water closet. He raced down the stairs. Opened the door. Raindrops spattered the empty street.

Panicked he raced back up the four flights of stairs. Maybe he'd missed her. He looked in the same places again. Surely she hadn't . . . She couldn't . . . But his hand reached out to the telephone on the wall, and his voice gave the number for the Denver Hotel. King had checked out.

Ben tried one more number with dread in his heart. His friend at the depot, often a news source, confirmed his greatest fear: "Mr. King purchased two tickets for the early train out of Denver. He and his daughter departed five minutes ago."

Numbly Ben slumped in the chair by his desk. He felt like a human jigsaw puzzle pitched into a dark trunk, the pieces scattered about inside. He longed to put himself back together but feared that he never could.

Anger hit him, a slow burn that rose up the back of his neck. He grabbed up Crystal's clothes from the floor and began to shout. "One contradiction after another! Yes/no! Come-on/whoa! I was stupid enough to sneak around to see my wife! Prey to her *charming vulnerability*!" He stamped to the window and pitched out her clothes.

The church across the street had a new quip on its sign: GOD USES LITTLE BOYS TO MAKE MEN. He sneered. "It takes a woman to make a man!"

A double rainbow arched over the city, the calm after the storm. He stared at it, sure that the rainbow would shine no more in his own life. Then he willed himself not to think about her ever again. *The whole thing didn't even happen!*

Ben telephoned the *News* to apologize to his mentor. "I don't want to go into it, Will, but I was a fool to refuse the King assignment."

"Yes you were. And you haven't had your mind on your work since."

"I'm sorry." A volcano of hatred for Fred King broiled within him. "Believe me, you are talking to one totally committed reporter."

"You sound lethal, Ben."

"I have an idea for an assignment."

"What do you have in mind?" Will asked cautiously.

"A series of stories about miners all over Colorado."

"Why this interest in mining now? Why not six weeks ago?"

Ben told a partial truth. "To make up for my stupidity."

"I won't argue with that word choice."

"Miners across the state are watching Crested Butte. They're champing at the bit to strike themselves, but what happened at Victor scared them."

"I agree, Ben."

"So, I'd like to start in Crested Butte."

"Your ties there would help build trust."

"I think so too."

"And your knowledge of languages would help wherever you go. This idea is worth considering."

"Will, it's really important to me."

"Excitement about an assignment is good, but zeal clouds the mind."

"If the stories are well done, they'll put faces on the miners. And if the reading audience is broad enough, perhaps they could even help end the strike. Or at least deter violence. I don't want the militia sent to my home town."

"Could we count on you to report the facts objectively?"

"You know me, Will."

"You won't go on a crusade?"

"I'll be fair," responded Ben, already halfway through the starting gate of a crusade to arouse public sentiment for the miners. And against Heffron Enterprises and Frederick Rodewald King!

CHAPTER 26

*B*en stepped from the D&RG passenger coach in Crested Butte and watched his mother run to him, her arms outstretched. He bent down and hugged her.

She held him a long time, making up for all the missed hugs since his last visit. She kissed him on the cheek before stepping back and looking around. "Well . . . Where is she?"

He brushed his hair back from his forehead, dreading having to explain about Crystal. "I'm not married anymore. As far as I'm concerned I never was."

Pain filled her face. "Oh, Ben."

He recognized that tender tone he'd heard so often while growing up. But she couldn't kiss this hurt and make it well. "I don't want to talk about it. So don't ask me any questions."

"I'm so sorry."

"I don't want your sympathy either."

She said no more, but tears filled her blue-green eyes. She didn't let them spill over.

"Did you tell anyone?" he demanded.

"Of course not. You said it was yours to tell."

He knew his attack had stung, and he felt ashamed. "I'm sorry. I love—" Pain swelled with the word. Forget her, he reminded himself. The marriage didn't happen.

Vini looked up at him and said softly, "I understand if that word is too hurtful right now."

He forced the phrase. "I love you." Words of joy and hope. Words of despair and death. Words for mothers. And lovers. Sisters and brothers. Children and a few others. But words that could evoke deep sorrow.

He took Vini's arm as they started down the boardwalk. "Will sends his regards."

"He's an old and good friend to us, Ben."

"Speaking of old friends, I saw Richard Sterling a couple of months ago. He's looking well."

"I'm glad. I will always be grateful to him for your education funds." She sighed, and under her breath came the words, *C'est dans le passé.* It is in the past.

All is over. Painfully his heart echoed those words.

Ben set his satchel down and paused for a moment in the doorway that led to shared memories with Stephen Machek and the other international boys.

"I'm so glad you came," said Vini. "I'll make us some tea."

He went immediately to Vini's bed/sitting room to use her telephone and check in with Will. He scanned the room as he cranked the telephone and lifted the receiver. The old colorful quilt still topped her bed. On the night-stand stood a frame facing toward the pillows in such a way that the picture could only be seen from the bed. The picture. He let the receiver dangle, moved through space and time and a thousand emotions, and reached for it. He drew back his hand, then forced himself to touch it. Slowly he turned the frame around. He felt its sting and blinked his eyes against the pain. A beau-tiful young woman stared out at him. Dan had captured for all time her radi-ance that day, her joyful love for the man by her side, his adoration for her. In the lower corner he read once more her beautiful script:

TO MAMA WITH LOVE
June 18, 1904

He turned the picture face down and stared at his empty, tingling hand. Then he remembered to forget her.

Immediately he went back to the telephone and picked up the dangling receiver.

"Vini!" shouted the operator. "Vini! Are you all right?"

"I'm sorry," he apologized into the mouth piece.

"Ben? Is that you?"

"Yes, Ma'am," he said, unable to remember who was the operator.

"Welcome home! How can I help you?"

"I need long distance. Denver, please." He knew she would stay on the line to see if anything exciting was going on in the capital city.

"Did you have a good trip?" asked Will perfunctorily.

"Fine."

"How is Vini?"

"She's glad I came. She asked about you." The line sounded different now, and Ben knew the operator had moved on to listen in on a more inter-esting conversation. "I hope to meet with Stephen Machek tonight."

"Good. By the way, Ben, wasn't Peter Aubrey a friend of yours?"

"Yes." The man who married us, he thought. And once more he remem-bered to forget.

"He was killed in an accident this morning."

For three weeks Ben lost himself in the Crested Butte miners' stories, trying to remember to forget his marriage and pondering the death of the man who'd married them. Every afternoon the miners gathered at the Hardware Store and told the tall tales they had shared many times before. He interviewed several miners and wrote their stories. Stephen, Iber, and Vladko, Scotty, Irish, and a Welshman, a Serb, Slovene, and the Italian from Grimaldi. He included their dreams, their struggles, their families, their children. Each miner rose from the page in a memorable way. Will told him the *News* circulation was increasing and attributed it partly to his series.

On Ben's last night in Crested Butte, before he moved on to other towns and other stories, he went to the dance at the City Hall. When Fiddle Jack called a break, he and Stephen walked along Coal Creek. "Thank you for your help."

"The thanks goes the other way, Ben. You are showing readers that we are real people. Maybe as they see us as fellow human beings, they will also have sympathy for our cause."

"That's my hope."

"But that isn't all you're doing for us. We are learning something about ourselves through your stories—all of us, not just the ones you've written about. They show that each of us has an interesting life story to tell, a unique life to live, and that no life is boring. Not even the life of a poor man on strike. Thanks to you, we hold our heads a little higher and continue to dance."

Ben knew that the people of Crested Butte would dance on through the summer and into the fall. They would dance when the land became a spectrum of scarlet and orange and gold. They would dance when the snowflakes fell and buried the earth in white. Unless mighty winter could bring the strikers down.

Schwartz stamped the snow off his boots and tried to get the attention of the miners gathered around the George Tritch coal stove at the Hardware Store. "*Es ist wichtig!*" he shouted. "It's important!" He raised his right hand to hush them. "The super told me himself."

Stephen's voice brought silence. "Let's hear him."

"If we end the strike by December 15, the Company won't penalize us by cutting our wages."

Silence.

"In addition they'll give us unlimited credit at the Company Store to buy Christmas presents for our children." Inviting mutiny, he added, "Let's think of our families."

Whispers.

Stephen watched foreheads frown in opposition and heads nod in agreement. Arguments rose. The Company's timing was perfect, as usual. Food would grow scarce before the season ended. Families evicted from Company housing had spent the summer in tents and now overflowed in the Croatian Fraternal Union, Vini's cabin, Iber's, and his own. If the miners lost their sense of unity, the Company would win. But they were ready for a fight just to have purpose again. Stephen rose to his full stature with the quiet composure of one assured of his power.

He spoke in a somber tone. "I say this one time only. We know there was no World Series this year. Do you remember why? Because the manager of the Giants wanted it called off; some say he considered the other league inferior. We miners of Crested Butte are like a baseball team in the World Series. We are in the game of our lives, up against a team of giants managed by Heffron, who sees us as inferior and wants it called off. The giants whisper to some of our players. They try to break up our team!" He paused and looked at Schwartz. "If we think of our families, our team will stay united! We will not call it off! And we will win this game.

Stephen had swayed them, but they were weary and resigned. He, too, dreaded what lay ahead. Agitated, he stormed up Elk a block to Vini's and opened the door to a gentle hum of feminine chatter as circles of women kept their fingers busy. Vini rose and led him to her office.

The painting behind her desk caught his eye. "That child will have something for Christmas."

"Is that what's troubling you, Stephen? Christmas?"

"It's troubling all of us."

She poured him coffee.

"Last summer the Company offered me certain benefits if I would get the miners to end the strike."

"Without recognition of the union and no increase in benefits, I suppose."

He nodded. "Of course I didn't accept. But with each refusal, an employee higher in rank followed with a bigger offer. Recently King himself contacted me and hinted at a superintendency if I cooperated."

"And you still refused."

"But now the Company has turned to someone else."

"Schwartz?"

"He's the one who brought the news of their offer and tried to get us to accept it."

"Without meeting any of your demands?"

"Scrip, wages, hours—no change. It's not an offer. It's an insult!" He stood and began to pace. "But the strike has gone on too long. The men are restless. Too much time on our hands. No money in our pockets."

Vini sipped her tea thoughtfully. "Do you still believe the strike is your only hope?"

"Absolutely."

"Then don't worry about Christmas." She smiled. "Santa Claus is coming to Crested Butte."

He struggled for patience. "This is no time for children's myths."

"Don't underestimate the power of myths, Stephen."

"Myths are simple. Our problems are complex."

She sighed her own impatience. "We have an abundance of wood. The miners need something to do, a sense of purpose. What if they make wooden toys for the children?"

"I suppose they could," he replied more out of courtesy than conviction.

"The women can sew rag dolls."

"We have an abundance of rags." He grinned, his tension easing.

"The children can write letters to Santa Claus."

"But only ask for wooden toys and rag dolls."

"Have faith, Stephen." Her face glowed with excitement. "Don't forget the widow's mite."

He caught her vision and heard himself laugh with pleasure for the first time in weeks. "You mean, the widow's might."

At noon on Christmas Eve, Vini and Father Mike met Ben at the depot. She greeted him with a hug and "Happy birthday!"

"Thank you. It's good to be here."

Father Mike shook his hand. "I still miss you at the Sunday dinner table. You always livened things up!"

Ben laughed. "I did my best."

"Did you get everything?" asked Vini.

"We need Grandpa Nick's freight wagon to haul it all!"

"That 'certain-sure' would be more proper than what we have!" Father Mike grinned and pointed to a wagon with FOREST QUEEN painted in gaudy red and gold letters on the sides. "Tillie lent it to us. I caused quite a stir driving it down Elk to the depot!"

"I wish I had a picture of that to put on the front page of the *News*." They laughed and bantered together as they loaded the packages.

"Where did you get such a long list?" Ben asked.

"The postmaster let Reverend Lord and me borrow the letters the miners' children sent to Santa Claus," said Father Mike. "We loaned them to your mother."

"Did you say Reverend *Lord*?"

"That's truly his name," said Vini. "He's a retired Methodist minister."

"The Union Congregational Church asked him to serve while they look for a new pastor," explained Father Mike.

"Your papa would have felt right at home."

The priest climbed back into the Forest Queen wagon. Ben mimed taking his picture.

"Remember," said Vini, "I don't want anyone to know where the presents came from."

Ben watched Father Mike start toward the City Hall where he would enter through the big firehouse door and be joined by Reverend Lord and some volunteers to tag the gifts before the party. Vini linked her arm in Ben's for the walk home, and he felt a sense of peace—even joy—as they made their way up Elk Avenue, greeting people in this small valley town where he had grown up, the place he still called home.

After greeting the miners and their families that lived with Vini, she and Ben escaped to her bed/sitting room. She asked him to help her wrap presents for their friends. They talked together while he cut the paper and she wrapped. She glanced up from snipping some red ribbon and saw his eyes wander toward her bedside table. They reflected the hurt she had seen in July when he forgot to forget his marriage. "Are you looking for the picture?"

He feigned a casual air. "What picture?"

"I packed it away after you left. You never did tell me who she was."

"No matter. *C'est dans le passé.*"

She let it be. "I hope you know how proud I am of you and your series."

"I enjoy getting acquainted with miners across the state. They have amazing stories, and they trust me. It helps that I speak their languages."

"You have a fine reputation, Ben." She tied a bow. "Martha Donegan keeps wondering when you're going to write about Dave."

"I haven't been to Ludlow yet. I'll go next spring. Will needs me on some other assignments. We're interrupting the series until then."

"What are the other mining towns like?"

"About the same as here, except not so well organized. There's only one Stephen Machek!"

Vini smiled, proud of Stephen also and loving him and his family like her own.

"Your business helps, too—providing education funds and bank accounts. What a difference that makes in independence and pride!"

"Really?" She had often wondered.

He stopped cutting and looked at her. "Have you ever thought about expanding to other towns?"

"No."

"Ludlow would be a good place to begin. You already know Dave and Mary."

"Maybe I will." In good time, she thought.

When they finished wrapping, she opened a small drawer in her cherry secretary and gave him an envelope. "Happy birthday." She didn't tell him she had bought it as a wedding gift. Some things were best left unspoken.

"Thank you." He pulled out a deed. "What is this?"

"It's 160 acres up near the Red Lady. You know—with the camel-shaped boulder and the waterfall and the circle of spruce."

His eyes lit up. "And the cave! How did you know I wanted that land?"

She laughed. "When you've talked about it over the years, you always had the same look in your eyes as your papa. He dreamed of building a cabin there."

Ben spoke softly from time's distance. "I've never shared this with you. But when I was little, I pretended that he hadn't really been killed in the Jokerville explosion, but was wandering through the cave with amnesia. I fantasized that one day I would find him."

Moved beyond words, she reached up and tenderly brushed his hair back from his forehead as she had when he was a boy. This time he didn't flinch and draw away.

"Let's ski out there while I'm here."

"Yes, Ben!" How good life is!

That night at the City Hall the children strung popcorn and paper chains around the Christmas tree, a gigantic blue spruce cut from the forest. The younger children worked on the lower limbs, the older ones on the upper branches. Vini cut a tinsel star, and everyone watched as tall Father Mike stood on a chair on his tiptoes and reached as high as he could to top the tree with the star.

On a small table nearby stood the *bozinik* Veronika Machek had made, the Christmas Eve ritual bread, placed appropriately on a white cloth. The round loaf was decorated with dough figures of the Christ child surrounded by stable animals. A knife, coins, and a watch lay beside it, insuring that there would always be bread to cut, money to spend, and a long life. A key touched the bread, symbolizing the gates to heaven.

Ben squeezed Vini's hand. "Merry Christmas."

She bubbled over with happiness. Christmas Eve and Christmas with loved ones gathered near were her favorite days of the year.

The people picked up their plates and passed beside buffet tables crowded with food brought by everyone. Ample ingredients had magically appeared. Father Mike had simply told them, "The Lord provides." Vini's hams and turkeys were surrounded by venison, potatoes, dressing, steamed plum pudding, and cakes of all kinds. The Slovenes brought a kettle of *kokos i govedina župa iz rezance*. The Croats made *štruklji, kobase*, and *kiselo repa*. The Germans offered *kartoffel kloese* with *sauer fleisch*. The Greeks baked *baklava,* and the Italians cookies—*biscottini, scalidi,* and *tordidi*. The people toasted one another and feasted together on the international fare. There were no signs of the strike in this room tonight.

Stephen made his way through the crowd to Vini. "Veronika showed me her Christmas bonus. It's a fortune!"

"The ladies deserve it. They work hard. Besides, times are difficult, and families need the money."

"You know that every woman who received a bonus will share it with all the other families."

"I never doubted it, Stephen."

After dinner Father Mike disappeared and Santa Claus appeared. Huge bags of gifts for the children were carried in by Santa's helper—Father Martin Boyd, a jovial young priest. Rag dolls and carved wooden toys abounded. Blocks and boats, animals and wagons, even replicas of the Winton—modeled from a newspaper ad since nobody in Crested Butte had ever seen a motor car. Santa enjoyed himself immensely, and some of the children noticed that Santa Claus laughed just like the priest. He hugged each child as he called the name and gave the very gift desired, delighting the little ones and surprising their parents. Finally, Santa Claus departed, for all the presents were opened and every child was wide-eyed with the magic of Christmas.

Then came the mystery of Christmas. Vini felt the mood change as everyone circled the hall in a large human wreath, each with a candle. Father Mike reappeared and found a place beside her in the circle. He leaned down and whispered, "God's light shines in you in a beautiful way, Vini McGragor."

Reverend Lord started them in "Silent Night," and two hundred voices in many accents and native languages harmonized around the room, and the carol echoed down Elk Avenue. Vini looked at the beautiful faces behind the candles. People she had grown to love. Martha and Iber. Rose, standing with the miner's family who lived with her. Mr. Boyd, glowing proudly beside Father Martin. Even Henry had crossed the line and sided with the miners. And next to her was ever faithful Father Mike, and wonderful Ben. Two faces were missing. Joel's and Richard's. But they too were present in her heart.

CHAPTER 27

*M*ighty winter withered into spring, and in Crested Butte the miners greeted the new season with confidence. They had survived the worst and now looked forward to planting gardens and eating fresh food, fishing and being outdoors. Time had switched to their side.

But in Denver, Ben expected the worst. His articles had swayed public sentiment toward the Crested Butte miners and perhaps helped deter retaliation by M. Morgan Heffron Jr. Miners across Colorado had watched Machek's men refuse to give up, and that encouraged them to risk striking also. As spring brought warm weather, Ben expected strikes to spread like dandelions. He knew Heffron would expect the same thing, and he feared the use of severe retaliation to nip them in the bud.

The news on the telegraph confirmed Ben's prediction: Ludlow was on strike, and Dave Donegan was their leader. Anxiety clamped a vise around his chest and wouldn't let go.

It didn't help when unflappable Will Chaney called him into his office and closed the door. "I'm worried about the strikers, Ben."

"Me, too."

"One of our friends at the state capitol risked talking to me." Will stepped behind his desk and motioned Ben to the chair beside it. He lowered his voice. "It's highly confidential."

Everything was. For Will to remind him meant it came almost straight from the top.

"High dollars have rolled in from out-of-state. The militia is on standby."

"Oh God! No!"

"I've watched M. Morgan Heffron for many years. It's not unlike him to threaten to use force."

"Knowing the way King operates, a surprise attack would fit." Ben could taste the acid from his hatred of King.

"That won't happen. This is the Twentieth Century, and we're a civilized country."

"Whatever he plans will be severe enough to prevent strikes once and for all. He'll want to make the miners quake at the word 'strike'."

"I'm afraid I agree."

The telephone rang. Will seemed lost in thought so Ben answered. *"Rocky Mountain News."*

"I want to speak to Ben McGragor," said a hushed voice.

"I'm McGragor."

"I've read your articles. You don't go along with the financiers from the East. A lot of reporters do."

Ben wondered if he had a friend or foe on the line.

"I like that." The caller spoke even softer. "I can't reveal myself."

Ben put his hand over his free ear, straining to hear.

"But I work for the Colorado National Guard, and there's something strange going on around here."

"Tell me."

"They're being deployed."

"Where?"

"No one knows."

"When?"

"No one knows that either."

Ben held on to patience.

"This is the biggest secret ever kept around here. But I can tell you this. Some out-of-staters just arrived, and they're getting Colorado uniforms."

"You're sure?"

The voice came back in a whisper. "I issue them."

"Do you know more?"

"I heard a rumor that they're strikebreakers from West Virginia."

The vise tightened around Ben's chest. "They'll either be sent to Crested Butte or Ludlow. Can you find out which?"

"I'll try."

"It's important. Call back as soon as you know."

"Right."

"If I'm not here, talk to Will Chaney. No one else."

"Will Chaney," he repeated.

"And thanks." Ben looked at Will and summed up the tip.

Will flinched. "Have you ever heard of the Baldwin-Felts strikebreakers?"

"They're notorious."

"And from West Virginia."

"If they're involved, it'll be a bloody battle! Will, is there anyway we can prevent this?"

"Maybe. If we have enough time."

Calm resignation settled over Ben. "At least I can warn the miners. Maybe help them get organized."

"No, Ben. You're a reporter. Don't get in this fight. We both know it could be dangerous."

"We both also know that I'm the best reporter to follow this."

Will's eyes measured him. "Go home and pack." With a sigh of tension he added, "But remember, we report the news. We don't make it."

Ben pulled his satchel from under the bed and grabbed a couple of shirts.

"Mr. McGragor," called his landlady, knocking.

"Come in."

She handed him a letter. "This came in the mail today. The envelope sure has pretty handwriting."

He recognized the large fancy script immediately and felt the blood drain from his face. He hadn't forgotten, could never forget. Not really.

His landlady watched him. "You look pale, Mr. McGragor."

"I'm fine." He looked for a return address but found none.

"Do you need help packing?"

"No, thank you." His fingers trembled.

"How long are you going to be gone?"

"I'm not sure." He tore the letter open.

"I'll look after things while you're away."

"Thank you. If you'll excuse me, I have a train to catch."

"Are you sure—"

He took hold of the door and backed her out. "Goodbye," he said firmly, closing it behind her. As his shaking hands pulled out the letter, his mother's little gold cross fell with a ping to the floor.

Dear Ben,

I write you only to keep a promise to God I dare not break. But you must not respond to my letter in any way.

You have a son. When he was born, I almost died like my mother. I was afraid God was punishing me for running away and not telling you about our baby. I promised that if I could live, I would write you about him. I am better now, though I can never have any more children.

I remarried right away. My husband does not know about you or that the baby is not his. I am terrified of what he might do if he found out.

You told me about your father's dream of striking it rich. That dream has come true for your son—as long as you do not claim him. If you do, he will have nothing and neither will I.

I beg you not to make the mistake of trying to discover who I married or where I am. I would refuse to see you. Nothing would be gained, and everything would be lost.

> *I am afraid not to keep my promise to God. But even as I keep it,*
> *I am also afraid that you might try to find us. For your son's sake, Ben,*
> *if not for mine, you must burn this letter and erase it from your mind.*
>
>

As ever,

Crystal
>

A son! Joy soared. *Do not claim him.* Rage seethed. *Erase it from your mind.* Absurd!

He read the letter again. She had erased their past together, even with a baby as evidence! He saw her for the first time as she truly was, a beautiful but empty shell.

A *son.* He finished packing in a daze. The telephone rang as he closed his satchel. "Hello."

"It's Ludlow, Ben," said Will.

He thought of Stephen Machek. Thank God! He thought of Dave Donegan. Oh God!

"The train leaves in half an hour. Can you make it?"

"Sure."

"I'll see you at Union Station."

Ben immediately placed a call to Crested Butte, confident he would find his son, less confident about how to tend him. As soon as Vini answered, he said, "I'm in a hurry to catch a train to Ludlow. I don't have time to explain, but I want us to take a trip as soon as I return."

"I'd love that."

"There's a little matter I have to take care of, and I'll need your help on the way back home."

"What is it?"

"I can't go into it now. But I will tell you this. You have a grandson!" He hung up the receiver before she could respond, tucked the letter in his pocket, and hurried to Union Station.

Will met Ben at the depot. "I bought your ticket." They walked toward the train in silence. Before Ben boarded, they shook hands, lingering. Will's left hand clasped his shoulder. "Someday I want you to take my place: Benjamin Joel McGragor, editor of the *Rocky Mountain News.*"

"No one could ever take your place, Will." He looked into that no-nonsense face that he had always known. A face aging now, but it could still belt forth the best laugh he had ever heard. Merely to say thanks for all Will had done would be too small. But to tell him of the love he felt would be unmanly. He enfolded Will's plump hand in both of his. "I don't often show it, but I'm grateful to you."

"All aboard!" called the conductor.

"Ever since your father died, you've been like a son to me, Ben."

"And you've been like a father." A *son*. "When I get back, I'd like some time off. I need to take a trip."

"Just see that you get back."

Ben boarded the train and waved goodbye.

Ben arrived in Ludlow as the sun dipped behind the mountains. The sky bathed in changing colors and for a few moments serenity enfolded the earth. Ben headed immediately to the tent colony at the edge of town. The miners roamed between the rows of canvas shelters, visiting with each other. Dark-skinned and fair, bearded and clean-shaven, older and younger. Ben knew only Dave Donegan, but tonight he felt that they were all his friends.

Dave greeted him as always with their secret handshake from childhood days. "Come on, Ben," he grinned. "Don't be so serious. You've been an old man since you were ten years old."

"We need to talk."

Dave sobered and pointed toward some rocks a short distance away. "Let's take a walk."

Ben came straight to the point. "There's a confirmed rumor that the state militia is coming to Ludlow."

Dave halted. "The militia! When?"

"I don't know. But you need to prepare."

"Do you know how many?"

"No."

"Are they going to guard the mine? Or force us to go back to work?"

"I don't know that either. Will Chaney will telephone me if he gets more information."

"Surely they won't attack!"

"I hope not, Dave. But strikebreakers from West Virginia have been uniformed."

"Lord Jesus, have mercy!" Dave sank to a boulder and covered his head with his hands.

Ben felt a growing sense of urgency. He paced as Stephen would have, wishing he knew what Stephen would do. *Next time we have good plan.*

"If we stir up the miners, we'll have chaos."

"But we can't afford to dally." He stopped pacing. "We need a good plan for each possibility, including a surprise attack."

"I'll get the leaders together tonight and we'll work out a plan. We can meet with all the miners in the morning." He rose from the rock, slumped like a man who bore the weight of the whole tent colony on his back.

"I'm sorry, Dave." Ben put his arm across his friend's shoulders, trying to carry some of the weight.

"Don't tell Mary."

"Has the baby come?"

"I have a son!"

So do I. But he didn't tell his friend. It was too complicated to explain. "Congratulations! Next time I come, I'll bring a couple of Havanas." *And my son.*

When they entered the tent, Ben hugged Mary. "You are as pretty as ever."

Dave stooped over and looked at the baby. He slept in a box beside their pallets on the dirt floor of the tent. "David Iber Donegan," he said proudly. He took Mary's hand and smiled at her. "You and Ben can visit while I get some of the miners together for a meeting."

The pride in her eyes faded. "Is anything wrong?"

"You worry too much." Dave pecked her on the cheek as he left.

Ben moved closer to see the baby better and take Mary's mind off worrying. "How old is he?"

"Four weeks today."

About the age of my son. He stared at the tiny bit of humanity sleeping peacefully in his little box. A new kind of tenderness filled him.

The baby squeaked and began to wiggle. His little mouth sucked air with a smack and then puckered into a cry. Mary picked him up. "There, there." She ran her hand tenderly over his thin curly hair. The baby's eyes fluttered open, unfocused. His tiny hands clutched into wee fists thrashing the air. Mary swayed back and forth, rocking him in her arms.

Ben ached to provide a rocker for her. As he looked around the small tent with its leaky patches and cold dirt floor, he renewed his commitment to justice for the miners. He would write this story.

His thoughts returned to his own baby. How different his world is! Evidently a world of all that money can buy. Probably a world blind to the truth that a single human life is worth more than any fortune. No son of mine is going to grow up as shallow as Crystal, as cruel as King!

Mary began to hum to the baby, and he wondered if Crystal cared for his son herself or left him to a nursemaid.

"Would you like to hold him?" she asked.

He wanted to, was afraid to. "I've never held a baby before." She placed the infant carefully in his arms. Ben felt the warmth of the little body and looked in awe at the tiny face. He felt a powerful urge to run from the tent, escape from Ludlow, get on the train for King's home in Virginia and find his son. But as he held this fragile baby in his arms, he suppressed the urge. These people were his friends; he wanted to help them.

"How long are you going to be here, Ben?"

"A few days." He looked at the little bundle in his arms. "Then I have important business in the East." The most important of my life. To go to King and do whatever is necessary to find my son. And bring him home. With or without his mother.

Ben lay in bed in his rooming house in town unable to sleep. Mentally he reviewed last night's meeting with the leaders. Dave was a good man, but he lacked Stephen's knowledge and charisma. It had taken until midnight to develop a basic plan with variations depending on the situation. All the miners would meet right after breakfast to hear it. He stared at the ceiling. The rooming house was quiet, but his inner voice refused to be silent. Each heartbeat felt like a warning to leave Ludlow.

He watched the first rays of the sun shine through his window, proclaiming the arrival of April 20. It was too early for the meeting, but he rose anyway. He dressed, put Crystal's letter in his pocket, felt its sting through his shirt, and took a walk in the pines. Birds chirped the news of a trespasser, and chipmunks scurried out of his way. Thoughts twisted through his mind like the stream twisted through the trees. He thought about the miners and wished Stephen were here. He thought about his son and wondered when he would find him.

Suddenly he heard rhythmical footfalls, a soft double time without drum or bugle. He ran to the edge of the trees, ducking behind them. Far back he saw the militia. They marched toward the tent colony carrying machine guns and torches. A surprise attack at dawn! God forbid!

Ben raced through the pines. Defenseless miners. Women and children. Sleeping prey. Savage King!

Panting, he sped across the clearing to the tents. He yelled at the top of his lungs: "THE MILITIA!" He ran from tent to tent. "Wake up! The militia! Get the women and children to the rocks!"

Mary's head poked through her tent. Dave threw open the flap.

"The militia!"

"Lord Jesus, have mercy!"

A shot rang out.

Ben felt sick.

The militia advanced in a broad line. Their bullets blasted into the tents.

Children wailed as bullets tore through the canvas and struck their bedrolls. Mothers screamed. Fathers armed themselves. Picks. Shovels. A few guns. Some tried to get their families to the rocks. Others ran around the tents to face the army. One groaned as exploding bullets ripped his flesh.

Ben saw Dave run around his tent, rifle in hand. He fired at two guardsmen advancing with torches.

A battery of machine guns blasted.

Dave fell.

Ben ran to him.

"Save Mary," he wheezed. "Baby."

Ben grasped the hand of his dead friend. Then grabbed his rifle.

A guardsman hurled a torch into the Donegan tent. Ben darted to it in a swerving pattern. He slashed the inferno, clutched the baby and shoved Mary though the hole. He pulled her along to some boulders a safe distance away. "Hide! I'll find you."

He ran back to the massacre. More torches set tents ablaze. Screams of agony and smells of searing flesh rose from the colony. "Go to the rocks!" he shouted to the mothers.

Near the last tent a woman lay over her dead infant, sobbing. With a scream of anguish, she picked up a stone and ran toward the militia, her weapon raised. A volley of exploding bullets tore through her body.

A boy bolted from a tent and ran to the corpse of his father. He grabbed his pick and rushed a militiaman.

The guardsman aimed his machine gun at the boy.

Ben fired the rifle. The enemy fell. "Run!" he shouted to the boy. He tossed him the gun. "Run to the rocks!" Ben figure-eighted toward the dead militiaman and dived for his machine gun. Suddenly the boy jerked and toppled to the ground.

A small girl ran from a burning tent toward a boulder. Ben fired the machine gun into the guardsmen closest to her. Just before she reached the rocks, she screamed and stumbled. Blood spurted from her head and stained her little white nightgown.

A roar of red rage escaped from Ben. Rage against the militia's massacre. Rage against King who set it up. Rage against Heffron who paid for it. His soul cried out: Kill them! Kill them all!

He planted his feet firmly on the bloody ground and faced the militia. He fired the machine gun from side to side. Faceless uniforms fell. More advanced. He felt his flesh rip. Tasted blood in his mouth. Again he fired. Side to side. More uniforms fell. Bullets tore into him. The uniforms began to spin. He fired again and fell to the ground. The earth swirled. Light blurred. He fired again and again.

As pain burned Ben's body, his mind floated to the cave near the Red Lady. He smelled its musty dampness and saw the Indian painting on the wall. He heard the rippling stream and bent his knee on the hard rock floor to sip the cool water. Then he saw a reflection. He looked up, and his father stood on the other side of the stream, smiling at him. He reached for his hand to lead him home.

CHAPTER 28

*L*ate in the afternoon on Thursday, April 20, a shaken Father Mike hung up the receiver after Will's call. He fell to his knees in prayer:

O God, wake me from this nightmare! Let it not be true!

Why can't it be this worthless priest instead? This lonely man who kneels before you with his sin still in his heart. Who still knows a shameful longing for beautiful Vini who loves and gives and struggles for others.

How could you, You who have the power to create all that is, allow this worst of agonies to happen to her! You watched this morning's massacre! And you did not spare Ben! Just as you watched your Son go to the cross and did not spare him. My lips cannot say "Loving Holy One!" No! Not on this bloody day!

Yet, O God, my soul cries out to you. How can I tell this woman who brightens my heart that her only child is dead?

I know even in my anger and despair that you are with me. As you were with your Son when he died and also with hers. And with Dave Donegan. Strengthen me for this task. Wrap my words in your love. Shield her heart with your presence. And shield Martha and Iber.

He made the sign of the cross. *In the name of the Father and the Son and the Holy Spirit.*

Rising from his knees, he did one thing before going to Vini as the messenger of death. He cranked up the telephone and contacted Richard Sterling in Denver.

Father Mike knocked on Vini's door, trying not to hope she wouldn't be there. But the door opened, framing this woman he was about to devastate.

"Come in. I'll fix tea."

"Thank you." He didn't want tea, but she would need it. He followed her to the kitchen.

"You always seem to know when to come." There was no lilt in her voice, no bounce in her step. "I thought about coming to see you, but I decided it was silly."

"Oh?" He put off what he dreaded to do.

"I awoke at dawn this morning. With a start. Have you ever done that? Like something is wrong?" She didn't wait for an answer. "I had a terrible feeling about Ben. It was almost like I could hear his voice crying out. It has gripped me all day long." She handed him his tea, her hand lingering on the saucer. "It was so real, Father Mike."

"That's why I'm here, Vini." He set the tea down and heard the words he forced himself to speak. "Will telephoned. There was a surprise attack by the state militia at dawn this morning in Ludlow. The miners and their families were asleep in the tent colony. There were many casualties."

She stiffened and shook her head, her eyes pleading.

He would never forget Will's statistics about the Ludlow massacre: Thirteen women and children were burned to death. A mother and her three-month-old infant were killed by exploding bullets, along with a young boy, a little girl, and five miners. And Ben—facing the entire militia with a machine gun. Ben—firing into them even after he was down. Ben—shot fifty-one times. Father Mike did not repeat the statistics.

He put his arm around her shoulder and made himself continue, saying the words rapidly as though speed could belie their meaning. "Ben tried to save the miners and their families. He was . . ." Father Mike looked down at Vini and reached into his mind for words that would soften the blow. There were none.

Her eyes shadowed with the truth and gazed at him from a deep agony that wrenched the very core of his being. He took her in his arms. "I wish to God I could carry this burden for you, Vini." Beloved Vini.

He supposed her questions would come next. Questions about God, like after Joel's death and after the fire. But he had no nuggets of wisdom left for her. He had already spoken all the words that he knew.

The long silence throbbed with pain. She made no effort to move away, and he continued to hold her. He had been prepared for tears or hysteria. But not this interminable silence. Yet, he knew not to break it.

He felt her shudder. She hugged him close for a moment, as though drawing from his strength. He prayed for strength enough to comfort, as always, for this was a time when he too longed to be comforted. Then she drew apart and looked up at him, her face suddenly old and tired.

"After Joel died, you sat in a rocker at Company housing and talked to me about death. After the fire, you sat in the sanctuary at St. Patrick's and talked to me about loss. And now, you are the one sent to tell me about Ben." For an instant her small frame trembled. "Poor Father Mike, dearest of friends. How difficult for you!"

He was afraid that he would fall into her arms and weep.

She closed her eyes and set her jaw. Silent tears ran down her cheeks. "I will be all right." She swallowed hard, the sound loud in the hushed room. "It will take a long time. But I know that someday the sunrise will come again. It always has."

Father Mike knew then that Ben's death would not be the defining moment in Vini's life. He also knew that the strong faith witnessed by her response would always be a defining moment for his own life.

When she opened her lifeless eyes, she said in a hushed voice, "Once I carried Ben in my womb. Now, I will carry him tucked safely in my heart."

From dawn to dark over the weekend Vini greeted friends like a wind-up doll going through the motions. Martha and Iber came to call, telling her gratefully how Ben had saved Mary and little David's lives. They poured coffee they didn't drink, ate cookies they didn't taste.

Vini managed to function when friends came, a lifeless replica of the living, often staring into memory. She let friends hug her. But not reach her. She had gone inside herself. During moments alone, she closed the door of her bedroom, and the wind-up doll ran down. And the great knot of grief in the pit of her stomach erupted. She picked up the wash basin and sank to her bed, a pattern now. The knot stuck in her throat. She gagged and dry-heaved. Over and over. Then another knock would come, and she would wind herself up again.

On Monday morning Stephen, Veronika, and little Joseph knocked on Vini's door—the remnant of her family. They came early to be with her before the service. Ben would be buried in the Crested Butte Cemetery near the mass grave of his father.

Stephen loved him like a brother. In his mind he heard the Ludlow children scream and saw the blazing tents. And Ben, facing the entire militia, being shot again and again, giving his life when he could have hidden behind a rock and written the story.

Stephen quaked inside himself every time he faced the fact that the state militia could have come to Crested Butte instead. The miners had lived in a tent colony last summer and, with winter over, had planned to move into one again come Wednesday. For the first time in his life he knew true fear. Its tentacles clutched him, dug deep, and refused to let go.

"Come in." Vini greeted them with lifeless eyes, but a smile. She snuggled the toddler against her.

He bumped his lips against her cheek in a slobbery kiss. "Wuv Mama Gwaguh."

Stephen watched her pull the box of playthings from the shelf, habit taking over in the frailty of heart. Wooden spools and a piece of yarn to string them, two tin cups to bang, some spoons, and two dozen wooden blocks that Ben had played with years before. *Ben.*

Joseph played happily while his family sat quietly, joined in a sorrowful but comforting silence together.

A loud roar startled them. Stephen drew back the lace curtains and looked out the window. "A motor car! It looks like those little Wintons we carved for Christmas." It stopped in front of Vini's, and a man got out.

Stephen met him on the porch.

"Is this Vini McGragor's residence?"

"Yes, Sir," answered Stephen, protectively sizing him up. The man's dark hair was gray at the temples. He was lean of frame and immaculately dressed. His regal bearing struck Stephen most. He surveyed the lines in the man's face, reading the story they told of his life. He liked what he saw.

"I'm . . . an old friend."

His tone and something in his eyes brought to mind the conversation with Vini when he'd asked her if she'd ever thought about marrying again. *Once. He was a kind and gentle man.* Stephen smiled and extended his hand. "I'm Stephen Machek."

"Richard Sterling."

That afternoon Vini left the cemetery on Richard's arm. Ashes to ashes. Dust to dust. "I don't want to go back home right now." Exhaustion hit her. "I don't want to see any more people."

"I have a suite at the Elk Mountain House you may have. I can get another room."

"Do you know what I would like? Could we go to your big yellow house? I want to think again about Ben as a baby."

Richard drove her in his motor car and parked in front. He had barely opened the door to the house before the car had drawn a crowd.

Vini entered the hallway and stepped back from the stale musty odor. "Once it was so beautiful."

"It will be again." They walked through the rooms, sharing their memories of those months when she lived in the attic and Ben was a baby, and she pushed him from room to room in the pram Richard had given them.

"This is like turning back time, Vini. The two of us together in this house."

"We can't turn back time. Too much has happened."

"You and Ben brought me such happiness." His eyes still looked at her with special tenderness.

She wondered if hers did too. "I've never had a chance to thank you personally for the education funds you provided him. Your generosity meant —"

"Sh-h-h." He took her arm, and they started up the stairs. "He kept in touch with me in Denver. I cared deeply for Ben." His voice cracked as he said the name, and he turned away for a moment.

Vini wondered if he knew of Ben's marriage. Later she would ask him. But right now she couldn't deal with something that had hurt Ben so deeply.

When they came to the northeast bedroom, memory struck her cold. She saw again the knife in Roach's throat. She felt dizzy. The room closed in. Richard held her as her knees gave way.

"Dearest Vini."

Caressed by his soothing voice and wrapped in his arms, her tears broke the dam and flooded from the great knot of grief. Her heart heavy with the burial of Ben, there seemed to be nothing left but tears.

He continued to hold her. After some moments, he pulled his monogrammed handkerchief from his pocket and dabbed her cheeks. "No one's tears do I love more. Even after all these years."

She took a deep breath and looked closely at his face for the first time. "I like what age has done with you. You are still a handsome man, a kind and gentle man."

"You will always be a beautiful woman." He drew back a bit, getting a full view. "I don't think you've changed at all."

"You would probably be surprised how much I've changed," she said softly.

"I've thought about you nearly every day over these years. I want you to know, dearest Vini, that I'll be here as long as you need me."

"Are you planning to move back?" Oh, how she wished! "You and Alisa?"

"Not Alisa," he hinted. "But . . ." he waited for her eyes to meet his. "I am seriously considering it."

Richard brought her home late enough to spare her from having callers. She went right to bed. Will's editorial, "The Massacre of the Innocents," was still on the night table, unread. Poor Will. He had telephoned yesterday and apologized for not coming today, explaining in a voice that cracked that he just couldn't attend the service. *I'm to blame. I bought his ticket.*

But Heffron was to blame. With trembling fingers she reached for the *Rocky Mountain News* and began to read:

THE MASSACRE OF THE INNOCENTS

> . . . Where is the outlaw so far beyond the pale of humankind as to burn the tent over the heads of nursing mothers and helpless little babies?
>
> . . . It was private war, with the wealth of the richest man in the world behind the mine guards . . . .

The blood of women and children, burned and shot like rats, cries aloud from the ground. The great state of Colorado has failed them. It has betrayed them. Her militia, which should have been impartial protectors of the peace, have acted as murderous gunmen. The machine guns which played in the darkness upon the homes of humble men and women, whose only crime was an effort to earn an honest living, were bought and paid for by agents of the mine owners. Explosive bullets have been used on children. Does the bloodiest page in the French Revolution approach this in hideousness? . . .

Yes, Heffron was to blame. M. Morgan Heffron had always been the one to blame. Senior or Junior, one and the same. Hatred was rekindled in her heart. She sobbed into her pillow until she dropped off into a wakeful sleep.

Her nightmare returned from years before. Vividly she saw again the old wooden box containing severed limbs entangled. Still she couldn't find all of Joel's pieces to put him back together again. "I'm waiting," cried his voice from the box.

Then the wood became new, the hinges shiny. She started to open the coffin, but Stephen's words echoed in her dream: "Don't Vini. Remember Ben as he was when he was alive." Saturday's newspaper headline floated like a banner through her dream: HERO REPORTER SHOT 51 TIMES. The wooden box rested in a fresh grave. "I'm waiting," said Ben's voice. Slowly she reached for the lid.

Then the box transformed itself again. This time into a wooden cradle with a baby. "I'm waiting." The voice changed into an infant's wail. She reached down to pick up the baby and comfort him. He disappeared. She sank to her knees and wrapped her arms around the empty cradle. "I'll find you," she moaned in the darkness.

Her words woke her. Trembling she draped a green shawl around the shoulders of her white nightgown and stood at the window. The lips of the Red Lady smiled in the moonlight. "I don't know where your son is, Ben," she whispered into the universe. "But somehow I'll find him." She crossed herself, raised her hand to the heavens, and vowed aloud, "I swear it by the Holy Mother!"

First thing Tuesday morning, Vini asked Stephen to come to her office. She stood behind her chair, leaning her hands on the back of it. She gestured toward a seat but didn't take time to offer tea before getting to the point. "I want us to think about how to organize the miners in every Heffron Enterprise mine in this state."

He looked at her with eyes she'd never seen so black. "So we can have a hundred Ludlows?"

The sword struck and she gripped the chair. "So there can never be another Ludlow."

He buried his head in his hands. "It could have been Crested Butte, Vini. It could have been Veronika and little Joseph. It could still happen here."

"Fear is exactly what they want."

"If I thought there was any hope, I would enlist in your war."

"My war?" Yes, admitted the small voice deep within her. She stifled it.

"We're up against a system that can call in the state militia! We have to think of our families."

Vini put her hands on her hips. "Hello, Schwartz!"

Stephen's eyes sparked fire.

"Save your temper for the real enemy, Stephen."

"I will not risk the miners and their families in your personal vendetta against Heffron. He stood, towering over her. This morning I do not call you *mudre!*"

At the door, he turned around to face her. "I apologize for my temper, but not for my decision. We have already voted to end the strike. We go back to work tomorrow."

Vini stared through the open door, refusing to consider whether she wanted the war for herself. She should have offered him tea instead of behaving like a general at Vicksburg. The battle against Heffron would have to wait. She would take it up again in good time.

But finding the baby could not wait.

She telephoned Will and complimented his editorial before asking the important question. "Do you know anything about Ben's marriage?"

"Marriage!" His surprise answered for her. "Where did you get that idea?"

She felt uncomfortable. "Never mind." Why had Ben kept it so secret?

After a brief silence, Will said very gently, "This has been a terrible shock for you."

"And for you, dear friend."

"I knew it might be dangerous. I almost stopped him." His voice broke.

She tried to comfort him. "You were wonderful to Ben, Will. Like a father."

A father. She hung up the receiver, wondering where to turn for a clue about Ben's son.

Richard stood at the door, hat in hand, right on time. "Your office is beautiful, Vini."

"Thank you."

"Just like the house will be. I need your help to decorate it."

She was much more interested in finding a baby than playing house, but she agreed. "Would you like some tea?"

"You have Wedgewood," he said, admiring the teapot.

She chatted idly before getting to the point. "You mentioned that Ben kept in touch with you in Denver. Did he happen to mention that he was married?" She was almost afraid to hear his answer. Where would she turn if he too knew nothing?

"Married!"

Déjà vu.

"Who is she?"

"He didn't tell me. But—"

"You've never met her?"

"He called me last June and told me about the wedding. But—"

"You didn't go?"

"They were already married. But when Ben came home in July, he was alone and didn't want to talk about it."

Richard frowned. "I see."

"I honored that. Then he called me the day before he . . ." The word refused to come. "He told me, 'You have a grandson.'" She spoke barely above a whisper. "Those were his last words to me."

Richard's frown deepened. "Where is the baby?"

"I don't know."

His eyes measured her for a moment. "You've been under a great deal of strain, Vini." His tone sounded like Will's.

"Ben didn't have time to explain. He was in a hurry to catch the train." She closed her eyes against the wave of grief. "To Ludlow."

Tenderly he took her hand.

"I have to find that baby, Richard."

He sighed. "Do you know where they were married?"

"I assume in Denver." She thought for a moment. "I'm sure. When he telephoned that day in June he said he hadn't been out of Denver since Easter."

"I'll ask my attorney to check the marriage records. They'll give her name."

"I don't want anyone to know about this. Not until we have all the information. I couldn't stand gossip about Ben."

"My attorney will be discreet." He drew her to him. "Don't worry, dearest Vini. If that baby exists, we'll find him."

If that baby exists. If he had thrown lye in her face, it could have stung no more.

CHAPTER 29

*A*t seven o'clock on Wednesday morning, April 26, Vini heard the mine whistle shriek, and the miners went back to work. Courageous for a year. Now fearful. Nothing gained. *David and Goliath,* Stephen had said when it all began. But Goliath had a militia, and David didn't even have a slingshot. So where was hope? She was sure Father Mike could find it, but she couldn't.

On that day the letters began to arrive. "You have a bundle of mail," said the postmaster. "From all over Colorado."

Puzzled, she set the letters down on the wooden counter and opened one. "It's about Ben!" she exclaimed joyfully. It was a wonderful note from a miner who'd met him last fall. He expressed his appreciation and sympathy. She bundled the dozens of letters together again, deciding to read them gradually and savor each one.

Everyday new letters arrived, some from miners and some from readers of his series. And every night when Vini went to bed, she lost herself in their wonderful comments about her son, their respect for him, their stories about what he'd done for them. The pleasure of the notes melted the ice around her heart.

After a week of mine whistles, Vini was used to them again and seldom noticed. She saw Richard every day. He supervised the renovation of his house, and she chose colors, patterns, and furnishings. It was becoming a grand house again. If Alisa saw it, she might change her mind about returning to Crested Butte. That would all unfold in good time.

"We haven't looked at the attic yet," said Richard.

The steep narrow stairs creaked as they climbed. The sun beamed through the attic window, shining on cobwebs and broken furniture. How many evenings she had spent rocking Ben in this room! The agony of his absence stabbed her anew. She was learning to live with this pain, knowing that she would never get over it, but still believing that she would somehow get through it.

"Do you remember that this is where I first told you I love you?"

She nodded.

"I still do, dearest Vini."

"You haven't seen me in a decade. Time has changed both of us."

He found an old deacon's bench and brushed it off with his handkerchief. He took her hand as they sat down. "One of the things that makes you so special to me is that you have . . . Let me call it class."

"Class?" She didn't know what she'd expected him to say, but she felt disappointed. That was a word used to categorize people hierarchically. To her, each person had a special place in a colorful, dynamic kaleidoscope.

"No . . . You're a woman beyond class," he corrected. "You fit into any situation with any group of people. Authentically. You're the only woman I know who could be equally comfortable at a dinner party as the maid or as President Roosevelt's guest of honor!"

She traced the fingers of his hand and considered the compliment. "Oh, Richard," she sighed, "life was so much simpler when I saw everything as either black or white. Now I see a great deal of gray between the two."

"Like?"

"Like if we find we do love each other now, it still wouldn't be right."

He stiffened. "I can't believe this, Vini! Have we walked through another whole decade of our lives, and you are frozen in the sleigh?"

She nestled against his shoulder. "I'm not sure anymore, though, that it would be wrong. That's what frightens me."

He lifted her face toward his. "I might get you to marry me yet."

That's a possibility, she thought, looking into his love-filled eyes.

He lowered his lips to hers and kissed her. He kissed her as he had kissed her in the sleigh. But this time, she didn't pull away. They sat on the old deacon's bench in the attic, and the cobwebs danced with the sunbeams.

Late Friday afternoon as Vini was locking the door to *Marie-Vincente,* Richard pulled up in his motor car and opened the door for her. "I'll take you home," he said, adding with a masked face, "My attorney telephoned."

Obviously he was not the bearer of good news. She steeled herself, and they rode to her house in silence.

Richard ran his hand tenderly over the collection of Ben's stories that she kept on the coffee table. He commented on her new book, *Nostromo* by Joseph Conrad. He hinted for tea.

She knew he was stalling and grew more and more anxious. She was beginning to wonder if Ben had married a whisper woman! If so, she hoped it was one like Tillie. "Please tell me, Richard."

He sat down on the love seat and put his arm around her. "Vini, there's no record of a marriage."

"That can't be!"

"I'm sorry," he said gently. "No marriage. No divorce. No annulment."

Never in her life had she been so stunned.

"My attorney says he guarantees it."

"And what do you say, Richard?"

He hesitated. "I don't want to hurt you, but records don't vanish." Ever so gently, as a loving father to his child, he added, "I think we need to face reality."

"You're saying Ben just made it up?" The silence between them thundered. "Or I did!"

"Please don't look at me like that." He wiped his brow with his handkerchief. "I would give anything to be able to put a baby in your arms and pronounce him your grandson. But I can't do that." Concern filled his brown eyes. "I'm afraid no one can."

"I have a picture!" she argued, almost beginning to wonder herself if she were losing her mind.

"A wedding picture?"

"No. But—"

"People don't have to be married to have their picture taken together. It won't prove anything."

"Prove anything!"

He drew her closer. "Dearest Vini, you've had so much to endure in your life." His deep voice showered her with tenderness. "And now, losing your only child, has to be nearly unbearable."

This man, this voice, helped make it bearable. She sank against his shoulder.

"You must have dreamt of a grandson. A dream so real that you believe it now."

She gasped and jerked back in an inner leap away from him. "You offered to help me find my grandson. And now you expect me to deny that Ben was even married!" she shouted, near hysteria.

She had seen tenderness in his eyes many times, and sometimes pain, and even passion—but never until now had she seen raw anger. He used his voice to strike her. "For years I competed with your dead husband. Now I'm blocked by a fantasy baby!"

Vini lay in bed reading some of the kind letters about Ben, hoping the dreadful scene with Richard would recede from her mind. She jumped when her telephone rang. "Hello."

"Listen to me." She recognized Will's voice, but his tone alarmed her. "I'm calling from the hospital."

"Hospital!"

"You must stop asking questions about B— About that marriage."

She noticed he didn't say Ben's name and realized he hadn't said hers either. Did he have a reason? Fear trickled down her spine.

"It's imperative!"

"Why?"

"Even if anyone asks you, don't let on like you know anything about it!"

"I don't understand."

"You can't understand. Just remember. First, never mention it to anyone again. Second, deny knowledge if asked."

He was ranting, repeating himself. What was going on?

"Your life depends on it. Mine too." The phone clicked. The connection broke.

Vini stared at the receiver. Nothing frightened Will Chaney. His whole career demonstrated courage. But the voice of fear had spoken to her.

On Saturday morning Richard sent flowers and telephoned her to apologize. He invited her to have dinner with him at The Rose Petal tonight. She agreed. Yesterday had sent her reeling away from their relationship. But she needed more time.

If she took Will's telephone call seriously, she should protect Richard from further involvement regarding Ben's marriage and his son. And she should do so tonight. She could leave the impression that he had been correct. She could tell him that she hadn't been herself since Ben's death—true. And that she had dreamed about the baby—also true. But she felt uncomfortable. They were two truths that led to a lie. Besides, her pride was at stake. It came down to whether she took Will seriously.

She pondered the matter most of the day and while she dressed for the evening. She was in her bedroom, ready to go except for her hair, when she heard a knock on the screen door. She glanced at the clock. It wasn't like him to be thirty minutes early. But after yesterday, they were both unsure about what to except tonight. "Come in, Richard," she called out from the bedroom as she straightened her hair.

She walked into the parlor, startled to find a broad-shouldered stranger with the curliest auburn hair she'd ever seen.

"Mrs. McGragor?"

"Yes."

"I'm Jerry Jones, a reporter." The hard lines in his face drew into a smile. "Ben and I were close friends in Denver."

She offered him a seat. "It is always good to see one of Ben's friends. Would you like tea or coffee?"

"No thank you. I was in town and just wanted to drop by."

She started to invite him to spend the night. Her inner voice cautioned against it. *Not yet.*

His eyes scanned the room, like taking mental pictures. "I'm going to miss him. There was nothing either of us did without the other knowing it."

He might know about the marriage! She started to ask. Thought of getting the picture. Remembered Will's call. If this young man was so close to Ben, why hadn't she heard his name? Suspicion crept into her mind. But desperate for information, she considered taking the risk.

"Are you all right, Mrs. McGragor?"

"I'm sorry. This is a difficult time for me." The unknown name, the hardness in his eyes, the hands that looked more like they belonged to champion boxer James Jeffries than to a newspaperman. *Don't risk it.*

He sobered. "I know it must be hard. It is for me too. Ben was a good reporter." His pasted smile returned. "And quite a ladies' man."

"He didn't share that part of his life with me." She wondered if her smile looked as false as it felt.

"One girl seemed to capture him there for a bit."

"Really? Who?" she asked carefully casual, but hoping desperately for a clue.

"I thought he might get married."

Who seemed to be the unanswerable question. She gathered her courage to test this Jerry Jones. "He was married, you know."

His eyes penetrated her, his mask set, not a muscle of his face twitched. But ever so slightly his body edged forward. "Married." His tone was a perfect balance of noncommitment.

A friend would have expressed delight, whether or not the news came as a surprise. "Ben sat right there in that chair where you are, and said many times that he was married to the *News*," she lied.

Again, ever so slightly his body moved back, his eyes grew less intense. "Yes. He often said that to me, too."

Liar! Fear trickled down her spine as it had last night when Will telephoned. She was glad she had called out Richard's name and this stranger knew she was expecting someone. "Are you married?" she asked, trying to pretend this was a normal conversation.

"I consider it every time I take a girl out." His laugh sounded hollow.

"Well, choose one quickly, and give your mother some grandchildren."

"Do you have any grandchildren?"

"Ben was my only child."

He looked at his watch and stood. "It's been nice talking to you, Mrs. McGragor. I'm sure sorry about Ben."

"Thank you for stopping by." She walked him to the door and watched him down the street. Then, for the first time in two decades, she locked the door.

CHAPTER 30

*R*ichard sat across from Vini at The Rose Petal, puzzled. He had expected an edge of ice. Instead, he heard what he wanted to hear. She was agreeing totally with what he had tried to persuade her yesterday. No marriage. No baby. But why her obvious sense of urgency to convince him to forget about it? Something didn't ring true.

He was also uncomfortable with his reception in the restaurant—or lack of it. He took deference for granted in Denver and was used to people speaking to him when he walked into a room. Except for kind-hearted Rose, no one here seemed to notice him. But everyone spoke to Vini. He had been away too long, and only a few people were aware that this stranger with the motor car was still the president of The Bank of Crested Butte. He had helped build the foundation of this town, yet he felt like a stranger. Instead of being Vini's mentor, now she was his. He found the switch unsettling.

As the evening progressed, his discomfort grew, and he felt himself backing away from their relationship. But he needed more time.

"I suppose it isn't appropriate for a lady to invite a gentleman someplace."

"It would be in this case," he encouraged.

"You wouldn't invite me so soon after Ben's death."

"Invite you to what?"

"Next Saturday night there's a dance at the City Hall."

"Dance!" He was shocked, but pleased. "If you're sure . . ."

"Ecclesiastes tells us there is 'a time to mourn, and a time to dance.' I will always mourn Ben's death, but I must also learn to dance again."

How he would love to polka with her! "Nothing would please me more, dearest Vini."

For an instant the old sparkle returned to her eyes.

As Richard walked into the City Hall with Vini on his arm, he experienced a repeat of his entry into The Rose Petal. He didn't know how to be number two, and tonight also his discomfort grew. She danced with him a few times, but most of the evening, he sat on the sidelines watching her. It seemed to him that every man there invited her to dance, from the youngest to the oldest. She was alive, and compared to her he felt worn and weary.

As he watched her polka, he forced himself to look beyond his nostalgic fantasy from the past and see her in reality. She was right; she had changed. She was no longer the young girl with a tiny baby or the single mother with the growing boy, that lovely creature who had needed his protection years ago. She was a mature and beautiful woman who had grown in wisdom. A woman with indestructible vitality like Crested Butte itself. A woman with so much more to give than anyone he'd ever known. More to give, he feared, than he had. He had come to offer her strength, and he realized that perhaps she had grown stronger than he. This was the very thing that made it impossible for him, for his greatest need was to meet her needs. And he couldn't find them.

How different were the two women in his life! Vini—still slim and beautiful, and yet grown so independent and strong. Alisa—now plump and matronly, grown dependent and afraid. He remembered his wife's fearful eyes when he left Denver, sitting in her chair at the table, her coffee cup shaking. She had come to a stage in life when she needed him, and he was putting her through hell. But he had to resolve this unfinished business in his life.

He had come to save Vini. But as he watched her confidently dance the polka with her many friends, he wasn't sure that she needed, or even wanted, a savior. He felt inadequate, for he wasn't sure he knew how to be anything else. He wasn't even sure he wanted to learn. He sat on the sidelines, the image of Alisa's dependence drawing him to her.

On Monday morning Vini started packing her clothes to go to Denver and search for a clue about her grandson. She had protected Richard, and she would protect Will. But search, she must. Nothing was more important to her than finding that baby, not even her own life.

As soon as she returned, she would settle her relationship with Richard. She folded a clean white nightgown. Kind and gentle Richard whom she would always love. She smoothed the gown into the suitcase, looked in her armoir and chose two dresses. But marriage just wouldn't work. She had changed too much—while he seemed not to have changed at all. She folded each dress neatly, wondering what she would learn in Denver and when she would get back to Crested Butte.

When Vini reached Denver, she took a cab from Union Station to the hospital. Nurses hurried down the hall. Visitors whispered and wrung their hands. Patients groaned.

Will's head was bandaged, his left arm in a cast. It was hard to believe that those eyes had ever twinkled into a smile or that unhappy mouth had produced a robust laugh. "My dear friend." She dared not hug this battered man.

"Oh Vini, I can't get it out of my mind that I bought Ben's train ticket." Tears ran down his cheeks, in and out of the character lines that etched a strong man.

"Stop blaming yourself, Will. He would have gone anyway."

They sat in silence with their memories of Ben, the only way to be with him now. After a while she raised her eyes to the present. "What happened to you?"

"Please close the door." Once done, he motioned her closer and spoke barely above a whisper. "I was so sure I would know if Ben married that I didn't think anymore about your question. But evidently someone searched the records."

"Richard Sterling's attorney," she said. "He found nothing."

"They thought I was behind it."

"Who?"

"Probably the same people behind Peter Aubrey's death. He was a justice of the peace—which, of course, gave him the right to marry—and he was a friend of Ben's. He was killed last summer in a supposed accident exactly like mine."

The world suddenly seemed sinister.

"I was going around the same curve he was when I was forced off the cliff. It would have looked like an accident. Unlike Peter, I was lucky."

Not very lucky, she thought, looking at his bandages.

"Someone found me and brought me to the hospital. A couple of days later this note arrived." He reached under a flower vase and handed it to her.

She read it silently: *Don't dig up the past. Next time you and his mother both die.*

"You're in danger too, Vini. That's why I telephoned."

The image of the empty cradle still dominated her mind. "Do you have any idea who Ben might have married?"

Will did not respond.

"I have a picture."

Fear flashed in his ink-black eyes. "Destroy it!"

"You know!"

He stared at the hospital wall.

She could hardly restrain herself. "Tell me the identity of my son's wife!"

He shook his bandaged head. "I won't jeopardize you."

"I don't care if I'm in jeopardy! There's a baby."

"That's the reason! I wondered why they are taking risks like this."

"Ben intended to find him right after . . ."

"He told me he wanted some time off."

"I have to find that baby, Will!"

"You would have a fatal 'accident' before you even got close. You'd be committing suicide and also murder. Definitely mine. Perhaps the mother's. And even the baby's life might be endangered."

"Surely not . . ." Such evil surpassed her imagination.

With pleading eyes and plaintive voice he said, "Let it be, Vini. Maybe someday your grandson will find out the truth and come looking for you. Cling to that hope."

"And spend the rest of my life pulling back the curtains each morning to see if he's coming up the path? And then twiddle my thumbs passively until the next day?"

"Yes. That is far better than dying unnecessarily and not being there if he needs you someday."

The tragic irony hit her full force. "They have trapped us! I would risk my life, Will. But I won't risk yours."

"And I mine, but not yours. More important, both of us must be careful not to put that baby at risk."

Vini was greeted at the boarding house that night by Ben's landlady. She wore a strikingly beautiful and expensive dress of bright green satin with tiny pearl buttons and white Belgian lace at the neck and sleeves. An elegant dress, too tight and too young for its wearer. "He was a fine young man, he was, Mrs. McGragor." She led Vini up the stairs to the fourth floor and opened the door to Ben's room. "I packed everything up." The landlady pointed to the trunk. "It's all in there."

Vini felt her blood drain from her face. Her heart had no reason to beat. The trunk blurred into the wooden box of her nightmare. She forced herself to focus clearly.

"Last time I saw him he was in a hurry to catch a train. He hardly had time to read the letter—large fancy writing on the envelope. He turned white as new snow when I handed it to him."

"Where is the letter?" asked Vini, remembering the distinctive calligraphy of the photograph inscription.

"I couldn't find it. He must have taken it with him." She blushed. "I wasn't snooping, I wasn't. I just wanted to make sure I got everything packed up."

Vini realized how weary she felt. Weary of the landlady, the trip, the irony. She opened the trunk, gripped by Ben's absent presence as she gazed at his clothes and trinkets.

"His friend from the *Rocky Mountain News* came after you told him he could go through these things. Broadest shoulders and kinkiest hair I ever did see."

Jerry Jones.

"He searched real good for the notes to that story they were working on together. Went through everything. But he couldn't find them."

"He didn't take anything?"

"Oh no, Ma'am. I stood right here and watched him."

Vini picked up the box at the top of the trunk and opened it. The deed was there that she had given Ben for his birthday, his last birthday. And the little gold cross outlined in silver. She clutched it in her hand.

Vini returned to Crested Butte the next day, dreading to talk to Richard but knowing what she must do. As she unpacked, she tried to prepare what she would say. Through the window she saw a young man in an Elk Mountain House uniform turn into her yard. She went to the door before he knocked.

"Mr. Sterling sent this message for you," he said, handing her an envelope.

"Thank you." She took coins from her purse to tip him.

"No need for that, Ma'am. Mr. Sterling took care of it before he checked out. His motor car was really something!"

Vini closed her mouth on meaningless questions. Hasty exits seemed to be his pattern. At least this time he'd left her a note. The messenger boy departed, and she sat down on the love seat and opened the envelope which held a letter and a set of keys.

My dearest Vini,

I came here with the hope that the yellow house could be our home together. I have found, however, that I cannot leave a woman who is dependent upon me for one who in reality does not need me. So I am leaving Crested Butte for the final time.

Yet even as I go, I know that I would be happier with you. The most joyful moments of my life have been the ones we shared together. I will always be grateful that our lives entwined.

Though the house will not be a wedding gift as I had originally hoped, it is still a gift. I arranged for that before I left Denver. You will present to yourself innumerable arguments against accepting it. They are pointless. It is a fait accompli, *one that brings me a great deal of pleasure.*

I make it a gift to you for many reasons. First, it is to make up for allowing Alisa to put you and Ben in the attic long ago. Also, it is for that memorable evening when we celebrated the final payment of your mortgage, a memory that has been a light in my life all these years. Finally, it is for being who you are: one so alive, sensitive and gentle, and yet one with that rare quality of indestructible vitality. You are, indeed, a woman beyond class.

Love always,
Richard

Sorrow that their relationship was finally over collided with relief, and with joy that the conclusion was wrapped in beauty. She would always feel a special tenderness for him and hold him in her heart. His gift of the big yellow house on Elk surprised her immensely. The grandfather clock began to chime, bonging the passing not only of time but also of her relationship with Richard. *Fait accompli.* A finished finish.

Vini unlocked the door to the big yellow house on Elk Avenue. She walked through every room with a new awareness of its beauty. Upstairs she looked in each bedroom, ending in the northeast one. Sunlight flickered from the delicate new curtains and cast lacy shadows on the carpet.

She opened the door to the attic. The stairs creaked with each step, but it seemed more a welcome than a groan. She stood in the center and looked around. The attic was neat now, and light shined though clean windows at each end of the room. She supposed it was a bit crazy to turn this space into a secret nursery, but she wanted to keep up with her grandson's development and equip the nursery appropriately for each stage all along the way. Here in this space, she could be alone with her memories and hopes and imagine watching him grow. Sardonically she decided to celebrate his birthday on April 1. Maybe or maybe not the real date, but fitting for the cruel joke of having a grandson she couldn't know. She scooted the deacon's bench to the window and tenderly opened the baby book she'd bought in Denver. By fall her grandson should be able to roll over on his stomach, sit up if propped, and know that he is cute. She smiled.

She put the baby book down on the deacon's bench and stood by the window, looking out over the panoramic view of springtime's budding new life. *For everything there is a season, a time for every matter under heaven.* This was not the time to search for her grandson. But neither was it a time for sitting back and doing nothing. She glanced up at the ancient monolith called Crested Butte Mountain. She too stood alone. Alone in a battle against M. Morgan Heffron. But she would avenge Ben's death and the Ludlow Massacre and the theft of pride from the miners of Crested Butte who went back to work, fearful and cowed. She would do it with a good plan. And she would do it in good time. With the mettle born of suffering, she made two promises to herself: "Today I start preparing for battle. And I will never back off."

FIVE

RESURRECTION
1910

Primero, Col., February 2.—Monday's
explosion in the main mine of the
Colorado Fuel and Iron Company
claimed a total of 75 victims and left 35
widows and 65 father-less children.
          . . . All expectation has been
given up of recovering any more bodies
until the entrees have been cleared of
debris. This will require weeks and perhaps months . . . .
          No opinion was expressed as to
the cause of the disaster . . . .

New York Times
Feb. 3, 1910

CHAPTER 31

*A*lone on this Friday afternoon, April 1, Vini put the birthday cake with five candles down on the child-sized table in the attic of the big yellow house on Elk. She sat on a small chair beside it and glanced around the secret playroom, feeling close to her unknown grandson. A painted linoleum covered the floor, its brown path winding through all the colorful castles and huts of storybook land, with dwarfs and witches, Billy goats and pigs along the way. The curtains on the two windows matched the checked wallpaper border that decorated the top of the yellow walls, and a rainbow mural arched across the south wall, ending in a large pot-of-gold that stood on the floor. It contained the toys that changed from year to year as her grandson grew older. Now it held a baseball, a red toy Winton, a small hammer, and wooden blocks. Shelves under the west window displayed books, paints, scissors, paper, a tambourine, and a toy drum. Puppets smiled down at her from pegs along the north wall. A Teddy bear sat in the little chair opposite her. A small rocker, a bed with a one-drawer night stand beside it, and the old deacon's bench completed the furnishings. On the night stand beside a lamp was the picture of Ben and his wife right after their marriage, inscribed in distinctive calligraphy.

Above the night stand hung the saddlebag with its fancy *M* on the flap. She thought about its contents: the old picture of Joel when he was little, the white bone-handled knife, Papa's money purse she'd clutched on her journey from New Orleans, the collar of the dress worn at her wedding and tatted by Mama, the newspaper list of the Jokerville deaths with Joel's name added in pen, the seventeen cents, Nick's lucky silver dollar, the deed to the land up by the Red Lady, the "Massacre of the Innocents" editorial, and the bundle of letters about Ben. For a few moments she pondered life's maze.

With a sigh, Vini struck a match and lit the first candle on the birthday cake. That first year was her most difficult. Her nightmare continued, and there were times when the fact of Ben's death hit her with such force it took her breath away. She worked feverishly to free the miners from total dependence on the Company Store, the first stage in her war against M. Morgan Heffron Jr. She finally persuaded several community merchants to accept scrip, based on her personal guarantee to exchange it for cash. Whispers attributed her ability to do this through an arrangement with Richard Sterling's banks in Crested Butte and Denver, which was an amusing decoy for the simple truth—she paid the first part of her tithe in scrip. Father Mike had always taken the miners' church offerings to the Company to exchange the scrip for money. The Company grumbled about the sudden large increase but complied, fearing refusal would make an ugly story in bold headlines on the front page of the *Rocky Mountain News,* where Will Chaney was still at the helm. From there the story would likely be picked up and appear nationally. Ludlow had stained the reputation of M. Morgan Heffron Jr., and he did not want any more bad publicity.

Vini lit the second candle. Time had eased the frequency of her nightmare, and she began the long slow process of reconstructing her life without her son. She felt his presence as a silent partner when she followed his suggestion about expanding her business to other mining towns, the second stage of her battle against Heffron. Miners across Colorado knew of Ben. Some of them remembered his stay in their town when he wrote his series of miners' stories for the *News;* all of them knew of his heroism at Ludlow. As his mother, she was welcomed and trusted immediately. She began first in the town of his death. Now, she'd added a dozen others. The wages earned by miners' wives helped ease their families' financial struggles and lessened their dependence on scrip and the Company, and the education funds gave their children options. In the mining towns scattered across the state, wherever there was *Marie-Vincente,* there was also a growing sense of independence and pride.

She lit the next candle. Her grass roots influence increased as *Marie-Vincente* expanded. She entered the third stage of battle by persuading Will and Richard to convince the governor, first, to form an Advisory Committee on Mining Relations and, secondly, to appoint the mother of the heroic reporter to serve on it. It was a token appointment in the beginning, primarily to win the governor good publicity. But she did not serve in a token way. Gradually she won the respect of the male members and was now a frequent guest at parties given by Governor Shafroth, Senator Cain, and other state leaders. The appointment gave her personal contact with numerous government officials, access to mining information and, most important to her, an excuse to visit every Heffron Enterprise mine in the state. According to Will, she was viewed as a delightful friend and a fascinating foe.

She lit the fourth candle in full awareness of the power she wielded. Once Will had teased, "If it were legal, you could become the first woman governor of Colorado." In turn, she'd suggested, "Perhaps the law needs to be changed." She could almost guarantee that the next strike, through her own personal influence, would be statewide and result in bringing the Colorado steel industry to a standstill. She held enough political power to prevent the militia's intervention except as a peace-keeping force. Now she was biding her time, for the next strike must involve not only Heffron Enterprise underlings but also draw M. Morgan Heffron Jr. himself to the front line of battle.

Her plan had been put together in good time, one stage following another—slowly, carefully, thoroughly. She lit the fifth candle.

King caressed the diamond ring on his little finger and controlled his temper as Heffron lashed out. He didn't like being on the wrong side of the desk, especially when Heffron was in his bottled-nitrate mood.

"Trouble in Colorado! There is always trouble in Colorado!" Heffron paced when he stood, drummed his fingers on the desk when he sat, and even when his body stilled, the pupils of his eyes darted rapidly back and forth, thoughts racing.

"What works in the East doesn't work there."

"Of course not. We're dealing with a different breed of men."

King realized that was true. "Many of the older miners went west dreaming of owning a mine, not working in one."

"And the sons know of their fathers' dreams."

"Their restlessness contaminates others. We need to break them."

All of Heffron's energy focused in his brown eyes. "Like Ludlow?"

King wished he could divert the conversation. That incident had very nearly cost him his job. Only the insurance he had managed to obtain saved him. He felt sure that the next time it wouldn't. There couldn't be a next time. "Ludlow was unfortunate—"

"A disaster that tarnished my reputation." Heffron's cold dignified tone was deadlier than a shout. "I still can't believe women and children were victims."

"Again, it was unfortunate. But hard tactics were necessary to prevent other strikes. They were about to pop up all over the state."

"There hasn't been one since. I'll give you that. But I still sizzle when I think of how Will Chaney took a six-inch ink pen and pricked at me until I bled. Me—M. Morgan Heffron Jr.!" Heffron's eyes snapped. "'The Massacre of the Innocents.' Reprinted all over the country!"

"His 'sword of justice' it's called in Colorado. That editorial was something I couldn't predict."

"You are well paid to predict problems and prevent them."

King reflected for a moment. "You want a prediction? I'll give you one. I predict that the subtle change in attitude occurring in some of the mining towns—"

"Rebellion?" interrupted Heffron impatiently.

"They wouldn't dare. It's a kind of growing confidence among the miners, a lengthening shadow of self-pride. I predict it will lead to a move toward independence, toward a strong, statewide union."

"Ignoring it would be a mistake."

"Another prediction: Sentiment will not be on our side."

"Unless we can sway it." Heffron's pupils darted back and forth. Suddenly he smiled. "The poor and middle class tend to dislike the rich as a whole. It's much more difficult to rally against a wealthy man they've looked in the eye and heard ask about their family, especially a benefactor." He stood. "We'll go to Colorado."

"We? You too?"

Heffron nodded. "A good will tour. I'll do some hand shaking and baby kissing, maybe donate some things they would like to have in their communities."

King wasn't sure he wanted Heffron in Colorado. He preferred doing things his own way. "It would be a rough and exhausting trip from Washington." He received a cold stare that saw right through him. No one argued with Heffron.

"Do some checking in Denver. See if you can buy that private railroad coach that belonged to General Palmer before he died."

"The *Gypsy*." King made a note.

"I'll finally travel each mile of that narrow gauge track my money helped build." He looked at the letter boxes along the third row of his floor-to-ceiling, wall-to-wall bookshelves and removed the one marked COLORADO INVESTMENTS—COAL MINING.

King respected Heffron's organizational ability. Every piece of information he received was properly filed in the letter boxes. Heffron had developed the system for his father, and now it served him well. He was the only man King knew whose thoroughness regarding details matched—perhaps suprassed—his own.

Heffron thumbed through the letter box. "We'll study each mine's records as we travel." Without looking up, he said, "Notify the *Rocky Mountain News* of our tour. Will Chaney will have to publicize it."

"I'll make the arrangements. You, myself, a valet and secretary?"

"And Morgan third. It's time he experiences the Colorado aspect of the family business."

Heffron's proposed trip made headlines in the *Rocky Mountain News*, and the itinerary was reprinted in the Crested Butte *Pilot*. Vini read the article and immediately went to see Father Mike. "M. Morgan Heffron Jr. is coming to Crested Butte!"

"I saw the article." Father Mike's extraordinary eyes looked into her soul. "At last you come face-to-face with the devil and have an opportunity for revenge. Is that what you are thinking?"

She lowered her eyes from the priest who knew her too well. Yet, she felt his compassion, not his judgment. She admired and respected him more than any person she'd ever known, even the good bishop of St. Louis Cathedral in New Orleans. She'd never heard Father Mike talk about the reward of heaven, but she'd watched him walk through hell over and over again with members of his flock, including her. She could never lie to him, so she didn't answer.

"Tell me, Vini," he said, his tone now light, "do you plan to greet the *Gypsy* with a GET OUT OF TOWN placard?"

She put her hands together in her lap, intertwined her fingers, and met his gaze. "Actually, I'm thinking about inviting him to dinner."

A hush fell. Not even the air stirred. Then Father Mike blinked away surprise. "Why? To poison him?"

"One reason is because the rich tend to dislike the poor as a group. Heffron looks down on miners—even though they make him millions. He uses them like shoes—wear them out and discard them. I want to put faces on miners so he will see them as persons. I want us to sit around the table together as equals."

"You would invite some miners?"

"And their wives. Stephen and Veronika, for example."

"I'm not sure Stephen would attend. His feelings toward Heffron match yours, Vini."

"He is smart enough to welcome this opportunity."

"It is not easy to sit at the table with people we hate. It also becomes more difficult to hate someone who has sat at our table."

She ignored his remark. "There's another reason also. I've had many fantasy conversations with Heffron over the decades, and I don't want to miss this chance at a real one."

"You want to see the enemy close-up." Father Mike placed the palms of his hands together as though in prayer and pressed them to his lips. "That's risky, you know."

"I'm not afraid."

"What if close-up he doesn't look like the monster you've created in your mind?"

"I didn't create him. He became a monster all by himself."

"Do you suppose he had a little help from his own father?"

Over the years she had picked up enough bits and pieces about Father Mike's childhood to know that his father had been far less than ideal. "He could have counteracted that . . . like some people I know."

She realized that the priest's eyes no longer clouded at the mention of his father. He had reached the grace to forgive him, and in the process Father Mike himself had been healed.

"The last reason is that I want the satisfaction of knowing that at least once in M. Morgan Heffron's life, somebody stood up to him."

"You?" His eyes began to twinkle. "Maybe I'd better warn the invincible Mr. Heffron that he's about to be attacked by Vini McGragor and her lethal sewing needle!"

She didn't laugh.

"I'm sorry." The twinkle left his eyes as suddenly as it had come. "Watch your motives, Vini. Don't let his visit snarl your soul."

"I'm clear about my motive." *Vengeance is mine, saith Vini McGragor.* But some things were best left unspoken. "I'm going to have the most elegant dinner party the Gunnison Country has ever known!"

M. Morgan Heffron pulled back the lined scarlet drapes with gold fringe and gazed out the window of the *Gypsy*. The train rocked along on the narrow gauge track that wound its way by the river. "It won't be long now until we reach Crested Butte." He sat down in a plush chair and glanced at King who stared at a painting on the wall and caressed his diamond ring, apparently deep in thought; a thin smile appeared. "What are you hiding behind that smug smile?"

King, awakened from his memories, looked down at the carpet and shrugged. "I've played a lot of poker, and never lost a hand."

Heffron scrutinized his face. "Your luck won't change until you play *against* me instead of *for* me."

"Surely you know by now that you can rely on me."

Heffron opened the letter box, flipped to the section on Crested Butte, and reviewed the information. Like a political candidate, he mastered names and events on his way into a town. They rolled glibly off his tongue during the visit, impressing people with his knowledge and personal care. Then, like rote facts memorized for a final exam, he erased them as he pulled out of town, replacing them with the next set of facts. "Here's a telegram about the old Jokerville Disaster in '84. I'd forgotten about that."

"You're very good at this kind of thing. You are changing attitudes."

Heffron closed the letter box. "Frankly, I'll be glad when it's over. When you've seen one mining town, you've seen them all."

"Crested Butte will be the same. Coal dust. Coke oven odor. Crude and ignorant people."

"My father used to say that miners are just cogs in the money wheel." Heffron sighed. "They're a nuisance. But we need them."

"Unfortunately," said King.

"Do you realize we haven't had an interesting conversation, eaten excellent food, or seen a charming woman this whole time?"

"Mountain women have a hard life. They lose their beauty early. Far better for a woman to live in the comfort of the East or the South."

Heffron took the letter box with him and passed through the back doorway to the bedroom. To the left of the brass bed was a mirror and below it a basin with two faucets. He turned on the hot water and washed his face and hands. As he dried them on the monogrammed towel, the train came to a stop. He and his entourage had arrived in Crested Butte, Colorado.

As King followed Heffron down the train steps, a large stocky man greeted them. "Mr. Heffron? Mr. King? Welcome to Crested Butte," he said nervously. "I'm Ron Shun, Big Mine superintendent. I'm sure proud to be at your service, Mr. Heffron."

King knew Heffron's next line. True to form, he complimented Shun's fine performance in his job.

"Thank you, Mr. Heffron," said Shun, standing a little taller. He pulled a piece of paper from his pocket. "With your permission this is your schedule while you're here. If it's not all right, I'll sure be glad to change it."

King took the schedule. "Thank you, Ron. Give us a few minutes to look it over."

"Yes, Sir." He walked away to allow them to discuss it.

"The same old thing," said King. "This afternoon we look at the mine, Company housing, and the Company Store. Then we go to dinner."

"At the mine superintendent's house again, I suppose. I'm not sure I can endure another piece of fried chicken."

"It just says dinner." King turned the schedule over and back again. "The place isn't listed."

"Let me guess what follows. We're to be entertained."

King nodded. "There's a play tonight in your honor at the Princess Theatre. Mid-morning tomorrow we meet briefly with the superintendent and a few miners."

"His carefully picked supporters."

Shun rushed back to them. "I forgot to give you these. I sure am sorry." He handed each of them a small envelope.

Noting the high grade of paper, King pulled out an engraved invitation.

Marie-Vincente Prejean McGragor
requests the honor of your presence
for dinner
Six o'clock in the evening
July third
Nineteen hundred ten
414 Elk Avenue
Crested Butte, Colorado

King stared at the name. He had not predicted dining with the paternal grandmother of his grandson.

"This is different," said Heffron.

"Yes," responded King from a face of stone, "it is quite unexpected."

CHAPTER 32

V ini stood back and admired the table in the dining room of the big yellow house. Multi-colored wildflowers served as the center piece, with yellow columbines prominent among them. White candles in silver candlesticks stood beside them. The corners of the table and napkins were embroidered in a delicate blue leaf design that matched the Mistral pattern of her Theodore Haviland china. The silver gleamed. The crystal sparkled. *Parfait.* She stared at the place card remaining in her hand, then put it to her right. *M. Morgan Heffron Jr.* Guest of honor. "Tonight," she mumbled with a shiver, "I break bread with the anti-Christ!"

She stepped into the kitchen for one last check on the five-course dinner. "How is everything, Rose?"

"This will be the best dinner I have ever prepared."

"Thank you so much for doing it."

"If you weren't such a good friend, I wouldn't."

"I know you're worried about not being at The Rose Petal tonight."

"That doesn't bother me. What does, is cooking for Heffron." She sneered the name. "Sometimes I don't understand you, Vini."

"It's important to me."

"Frankly, it was hard not to bring a bit of strychnine!"

Tony and Arvo knocked, two young miners who had lived with her when they first arrived. She had arranged with Shun to let them off early. They had spent three Sunday afternoons in careful training for tonight. Vini had prepared the same meal last Sunday for practice, to show them exactly what to do and when to do it.

"Don't worry about the dinner," said Tony, handsome in a crisp white shirt and black waiter's garb. "We'll do a good job."

"I know." Satisfied with everything, she went upstairs to her northeast bedroom to dress. Her new blue-green satin gown lay carefully across her bed. She slipped her hand under the bodice and examined the intricate embroidery of gold thread. "Mama would be proud," she said aloud. She bathed and dressed, combed her hair, and gave herself a thorough inspection in the mirror. The dress perfectly matched her eyes, and the rich gold embroidery gave it an elegance that even jewels could not improve. She smiled at the forty-six year old widow, pleased with what she saw.

The clock chimed six, and she heard someone arrive. She started toward the bedroom door. On impulse, she went instead to the attic. Tony knew how to greet the guests and show them to the parlor. She looked around the secret playroom, glanced at the saddlebag hanging on the wall, hugged Ben's picture to her, and touched the cross beneath her dress. She closed her eyes against the pain of emptiness that even now nearly destroyed her at times. Tenderly she put the picture back on the night stand. "Tonight I avenge us all!"

"May I take your hat, Sir?"

From the top of the stairs Vini saw Tony accept the hat of an unknown man. An M. Morgan Heffron stood in her house! Junior, Senior—one and the same. Responsible for Ben's death. Responsible for Joel's death. A sense of foreboding caught her, and she felt sick. Had she made a terrible mistake? She closed her eyes and whispered, "Holy Mother, please be with me tonight." She took a deep breath and descended the stairs.

Heffron glanced upward. His thick white hair formed a shallow *V* above the hard lines of his forehead. Black brows streaked with white angled upward at the inner corners of his brown eyes. A close-clipped moustache topped his thin-lipped smile, and a cleft dented his chin. The chilling brown eyes focused on her face, slowly lowered to the gold-embroidered bodice of her gown, slowly, slowly, to her matching shoes. Two steps from the bottom she stopped, eye level with him.

"Mrs. McGragor, I presume. I am M. Morgan Heffron Jr." Not only the name but the voice commanded authority.

"How do you do?"

He took her hand as she came down the last two steps, bowed, and kissed it.

Spontaneously she recoiled and saw the flicker of surprise in his eyes. Controlling herself, she curtsied. "Welcome, Mr. Heffron." She did not plan to confront him about his treatment of miners and their families until after dinner, before he went to the play. In the meantime, she wanted to help the miners change his image of them.

"If I may be so bold, your gown is exquisite, meriting jewels but needing none."

"Thank you," she said, uncharmed. She felt King's eyes upon her and turned. "Mr. King," she said without smiling.

"It has been a long time, Mrs. McGragor."

The strange ways their lives had interlaced flashed through her mind and she remembered his visits to Alisa up these same stairs so long ago. "As I recall, you are quite familiar with this house. Please make yourself at home."

She led Heffron into the parlor. "Let me introduce you. I think you know Mr. Shun."

Heffron nodded.

"We sure do know each other," said Ron. "And this is the Mrs."

Vini smiled and moved on to Stephen. "Mr. and Mrs. Stephen Machek."

Stephen shook hands, his self-assurance a notable contrast to Shun's nervous awkwardness.

"Mr. Machek," said Heffron with surprise. "Ron spoke of you and your influence this afternoon. But I misunderstood him. I thought you were a miner."

Stephen flashed his charismatic smile. "I am."

Recovering, Heffron forced a smile. "I could use a man like you on my side, especially with your influence over the miners."

"And I could use a man like you on my side, especially with your influence over the coal barons," replied Stephen.

Vini realized that they were in a blinking contest. There was no way on God's good earth that Stephen would blink first. "*Touché,* gentlemen." She moved on. "State Senator and Mrs. Vernest Cain. Vernest is chairman of the Colorado Advisory Committee on Mining Relations."

She introduced the three remaining miners, who had also lived with her, and their spouses.

Tony and Arvo entered with wine and *hors d'oeuvres.*

Heffron tasted the wine and smiled, surprised. "Excellent! Dom Perignon. A good year." He scanned the room, missing nothing.

"This is quite different from Company housing, isn't it, Mr. Heffron?" said Vini.

He chuckled. "Now, how would a charming and lovely lady like yourself know anything about Company housing?"

"Personal experience." He almost choked on his wine, and she knew, as planned, that she had just added to the memorable moments of his life.

King entered their conversation. "Miners complain about being trapped—to be exact." His eyes swept the surroundings. "You obviously didn't suffer from entrapment. From Company housing to here must have been an . . . interesting journey."

She disregarded the innuendo. "It was not difficult for me to get out of Company housing. My new baby and I were evicted."

"Evicted?" asked Heffron.

"My husband was killed in the Jokerville Disaster."

"I remember the Jokerville well. Not a single day goes by that I don't rue that disaster, Mrs. McGragor. A terrible tragedy."

"The explosion of your mine in Primero, Colorado earlier this year was even worse." A knock saved her from erupting into a volcanic scene and spoiling her plan. Bad strategy! "Excuse me please."

"Jack!" she said, greeting the couple Tony had admitted. "How good to see you both!" Arm-in-arm between husband and wife, she went back into the parlor and stopped in front of Heffron. "May I present the Honorable and Mrs. John Shafroth, Governor of Colorado?" The astonishment in Heffron's eyes made the whole dinner worthwhile. "This is M. Morgan Heffron Jr. You may already know Fred King."

Again she heard a knock. "Ah, that will be Father Mike. Always the last to arrive."

The priest shook Heffron's hand. "I knew your mother. I served in her parish as a student. A kind and generous woman." As ever, his presence brought a sense of peace into the potential storm of this gathering.

Dinner began after Father Mike offered grace. Lively conversation rose and fell. Vini scanned the table. Heffron sat to her right and the governor to her left, Father Mike at the foot between King and the senator, Stephen and Veronika toward the middle, and the others filled in. They all broke bread together as equals.

Heffron complimented the meal and the service and tried to be charming. "What is her secret?" he asked the governor, nodding toward Vini. "Mrs. McGragor is as gracious and charming as a woman from east of the Mississippi, but there is something different about her."

She listened for Jack's response, curious.

He smiled at her. "She reflects the vitality of the West, but wraps it in a dainty package." He lowered his voice, as though pretending she couldn't hear. "A woman who is an ornament tarnishes with age, but Vini is like a diamond. She'll never lose her sparkle."

"All right, Governor," she laughed. "You have my vote."

"And maybe a campaign contribution next time round?"

"Are you interested in politics, Mrs. McGragor?" asked Heffron.

"I've become so since serving on the Advisory Committee for Mining Relations."

"You serve?"

"She is very active," said Jack.

"What do you think the miners need?" asked the coal baron.

"Better working conditions, higher wages, and union recognition."

"You know their words, don't you?"

"Those are my words, Mr. Heffron."

He leaned back in his chair. "You bring up something very difficult for me, Mrs. McGragor. You see, my father died while making a speech against unions."

❊

As the clock chimed the half-hour and dessert was being served, a knock at the door surprised Vini. Tony answered it.

"That is my valet," Heffron explained. "I told him to bring my son here at seven-thirty so he could go to the play. I want him to meet as many people as possible."

"I'm sorry," Vini apologized. "Had I known your son was traveling with you, I would have invited him to dinner also."

The boy entered, much younger than she expected. He looked around the table, saw his father, and smiled.

She scooted her chair so that he could sit between them. "Come," she said gently. "You are just in time for dessert."

Without moving he glanced toward his father, waiting for approval.

Heffron smiled at him. "You may join us."

"Arvo," she said, "please bring a chair and another dessert."

Heffron stood and tenderly took the boy's hand. The lad looked up at his father with eyes of devotion.

Stunned, Vini realized that the man she perceived as a monster was not only loved, but capable of loving. She saw Father Mike's eyes upon her.

"Mrs. McGragor," said Heffron with pride in his voice, "this is my son, Matthew Morgan Heffron, III."

Holy Mother, is the world never going to run out of M. Morgan Heffrons?"

He turned to his son. "Mrs. McGragor is the most delightful hostess west of the Mississippi River."

The boy bowed and responded like an adult. "How do you do, Mrs. McGragor?"

Heffron introduced him around the table, remembering every name and adding a complimentary detail about each person.

The boy seemed quite comfortable at the table with adults, a miniature adult himself. Only his Eton suit and his size gave him away.

"There you go, Matthew," she said as Arvo brought him dessert.

"I am called Morgan third."

"Is that what you want to be called?" she asked softly.

"Actually, Mrs. McGragor—"

She smiled inside herself. The phrase and its inflection could have come from a young man.

"—I like the way you said 'Matthew.'" He smiled at her. "You may call me Matthew." He leaned toward his father. "You don't mind, do you, Sir? This one time?"

Heffron beamed at him. "No, Son. Mrs. McGragor says Matthew in a lovely way. Her voice is like a song. But, of course, mine is not, so I shall continue to call you Morgan third."

Veronika said, "My son is about your size. He likes to play games. Do you?"

"Yes, Ma'am. I like to play checkers." He turned to Vini. "Do you, Mrs. McGragor?"

"Yes," she decided at that moment.

"I am good at checkers," he said. "Twice I even beat Father."

With dessert finished, Vini invited the guests to have coffee in the parlor. She leaned toward Matthew. "I'll get some checkers, and you can show me how well you play."

As the others moved from the dining room, Vini went upstairs.

"Morgan third!" called Heffron.

She turned at his voice. The boy had started to follow her. "It's all right," she said. She held her hand out to him and waited.

At the top of the stairs they went down the hall to her bedroom. "Wait here," she said, opening the door to the attic. Suddenly, she wondered if a real little boy would like the secret playroom. It was tempting. She debated. Why not—he'd be gone tomorrow anyway. "I have a playroom. Would you like to see it?"

He followed her, counting the attic steps. "One, two, three, four, five."

Vini thought about her grandson, wondered if he was about Matthew's size, if he was this precocious.

Matthew looked around the room, and his whole face smiled.

For an instant something about his eyes startled her. She sighed inwardly. Already they were cautious. Someday they, too, would be cold and hard. She watched the grown-up expectations of his father fall away as he ran around the playroom from one thing to another.

"I have some of these same toys at home!" he exclaimed. He saw the rainbow on the wall, and raced to the pot-of-gold. With his bare knees on the wool braided rug in front of it, he pulled out the toys one at a time. His eyes roamed curiously toward the books and then the puppets. He sat in the rocker just his size and rocked for a moment. Then he pointed to the saddlebag hanging on the wall. "What is that?"

"A saddlebag," she said.

"My saddle at home doesn't have a bag." He jumped up to see it better.

"It's very old," she said.

"It has my . . . my . . . the first letter of my name on it."

"Your initial," she helped. "Mine, too." She took the saddlebag down. "It's an 'M' for McGragor." She smiled at him. "Or Matthew."

With his finger he traced the letter on the flap. "Or Morgan," he added.

Wincing, she hung the saddlebag back up. "Do you know all the letters?"

"Yes, Ma'am. I can read, too." Adulthood squeezed back into his small body. "Father says I must take education very seriously because I will have a lot of responsibility when I grow up."

"That will be a while yet," she reminded.

"I will go to Groton and then to Harvard. Then I will be President."

She felt sad. "President of Heffron Enterprises," she said with a sigh.

"No, Ma'am. President of the United States." He made the statement with flat indifference, like stating a preconceived fact.

She hid her amusement. "Maybe you will be President, Matthew!" She decided to share a silly fantasy for a woman. "And maybe I'll be governor of Colorado. Or at least his chief advisor on mining relations."

"I think you would be a good governor." He smiled at her. "I plan to be a good President, too."

"We need to go back downstairs now. I'll get the checkers." She walked to the end of the room and bent to the stack of games on the bottom shelf beneath the window.

"Mrs. McGragor," he called.

She turned her face toward him. "What, Matthew?"

He sat on the bed, his feet dangling. His elbow leaned on the night table below the saddlebag, and his chin rested on his hand. He stared at the picture. "Who is that man with my mother?"

CHAPTER 33

$\mathscr{F}$or Vini, all life stopped. Impossible! She crossed the room to the boy.

He frowned. "I always have trouble reading Mother's writing. It's very fancy, you know." Joel's intense dark eyes looked into hers from the five-year-old face before her.

Lightning bolted through the clashing images of her mind and struck them into silent oblivion. Only the thunder of recognition remained.

"I've never seen that picture before," he said. "But there's one of Mother at home in the same dress."

Vini's feelings burst into colorful confetti that rose to the heavens and formed a rainbow that moved across the universe until it arched protectively over her grandson. Grandson.

He looked closely at the picture. "But in the other picture she has pearls around her neck instead of that cross. I've never seen it before."

Vini touched the cross beneath her dress.

"Father would be proud of me. He has taught me to remember details," the small adult explained. "One never knows which detail might be important later."

Vini's thoughts began to spin. How much should she tell him? Would he tell Heffron about the picture? Should she tell him he was confused? What would the truth do to him? What was best for him? She leaned against the wall to steady herself against the vertigo consuming her. She looked at her grandson. Again, Joel's eyes stared back at her.

"I'll carry the checkers," he offered. "Gentlemen carry things for ladies."

She wondered how much time had passed. As they came downstairs, King met them in the hall.

"Grandfather, guess what I saw!"

Grandfather! Vini reeled with the shock. She took hold of the banister. "He saw an old saddlebag," she interrupted, desperate to turn the conversation. Her knees trembled. She willed her voice to sound calm. "Matthew, you didn't tell me about your horse."

He began to chatter about the pony.

She withdrew into the carousel of her mind. In front of her was her grandson. With the blood not only of Prejean-McGragor, but also of King flowing in his veins. With the name of Heffron shaping his identity.

"Only one game, Morgan third," said Heffron, putting an affectionate hand on the boy's shoulder. "It's almost time to go to the theatre."

The look of concern on Father Mike's face told her that he knew something was wrong with her. She must control herself. "Why don't you play with him?" she suggested lightly to King. "I wouldn't be any competition for a checker champion like Matthew."

King's reluctance became acceptance when Heffron said, "Good. Be careful, Morgan third. If your grandfather is not on our side, he is our chief adversary." He addressed the boy like an employee in training.

Vini felt King's dislike of his grandson and wondered if Matthew could feel it, too.

He looked up at King and shrank a bit. Then he brushed his dark hair back from his face and made his first move.

One man dotes on him, she thought, and the other hates him. How confusing for the child! She watched King thrust his checkers across the board without mercy for the boy. Just as he had arranged for Will Chaney's accident and Peter Aubrey's death and Jake Neath's long before that. Somehow he had fooled Heffron. He would protect himself and his daughter at any cost. No wonder Will refused to tell her who Ben married!

Before Matthew saw it coming, five of his checkers fell victim to King in one sweep. So would she if he suspected she knew his secret.

She pondered what move to make herself.

Matthew jumped King's checker.

"Good, Son," Heffron congratulated.

She wondered if this doting father would turn against his heir if he knew the boy was not his. Would Heffron hurt him? His mother? She noted again the adoration in the coal baron's eyes. However small his heart, the boy had found his way securely into it.

King took the last of Matthew's checkers to win the game in record time. She felt her own disgust of him equaled by the others in the room. King had won, but lost.

Matthew squared his small shoulders.

"Do you recognize your mistakes?" asked Heffron.

"Yes, Father."

"Will you remember them?"

"Yes, Sir."

Vini's heart went out to her grandson. The pressure for perfection blocked a carefree childhood.

"To make a mistake once is costly," lectured Heffron, "but understandable. To make the same mistake twice is unacceptable. That is true in every aspect of life."

"Yes, Sir." The little face so relaxed in the playroom was drawn once again into the miniature lines of adulthood.

Whatever the risks, she would claim her grandson. "Five minutes until curtain time," she reminded everyone.

"But it's only a block," Stephen added, "and they never start on time."

Veronika laughed. "They always have to wait for Father Barrett."

Vini intercepted the priest. "It's too bad you and I can't go tonight," she said casually.

Immediately, his mask appeared as she'd hoped, and he didn't reveal surprise. "Yes, it is."

Thank you, Holy Mother, for good Father Mike. She would share this astonishing news with him, and he would help her devise a plan.

"Why?" asked Shun.

Vini told the truth. "We have to do some work for one of the contests tomorrow." She did not add that the boy would be the prize.

The governor assisted his wife with her shawl. "I've heard that Crested Butte really knows how to celebrate the Fourth of July. I'm looking forward to it."

"Tomorrow is an important day here," said Vini. *The most important since I arrived.*

Heffron took her hand and bowed. "Thank you for a delightful evening. And also for being so kind to my son."

She smiled at him. "I cannot tell you what a pleasure it has been for me, Mr. Heffron." The words rang with the sweet sincerity of truth.

"My friends call me Gan. I'd be honored for you to take that privilege." His thin laugh followed. "Unless we should ever face one another at the bargaining table!"

She said with a calm she did not feel, "That may be sooner than you expect." *There would be no confrontation tonight about mining after all. But tomorrow a war would begin.*

That night King paid little attention to the play at the Princess Theatre. He mentally replayed a more suspenseful drama that had occurred six years ago in his own life. He recalled the dangerous role he'd played to save Crystal—and played it perfectly, he thought smugly.

He had decided to tamper with the marriage registry rather than have the marriage annulled, getting rid of the existing record rather than adding another one. It had been risky but not impossible.

With Peter Aubrey's "accident," every loose end was neatly tied. Ben's death was an added bonus, but no one would have believed him anyway. Silently he congratulated himself on his thoroughness regarding details. Without evidence of the marriage, he and Crystal were both secure.

Crystal had played a dangerous role too. He had not realized just how dangerous until her immediate remarriage resulted in the "premature" birth of a son. She was surprisingly like him when the need arose. The secret was safe. Gan would never know. Life is a Jokerville, he thought, an interesting game of deceit.

Early the next morning Vini waited alone in her office for the clock to tick off the seconds until time to implement the plan Father Mike had helped devise. Restlessly she paced to the window and watched the helter-skelter preparations for the contests on Elk.

By now Heffron would have the message to meet her here. She reviewed the plan. Father Mike had warned that the plan would be a death-trap and begged her to keep the secret to herself. Yet, he understood that she simply could not. Her only advantage was the element of surprise; her only protection was being in her own territory. No one would dare harm her in Crested Butte. She withdrew from the window and glanced at the clock. Ten more minutes.

Her skin tingled. Her stomach pitched. She unlocked the desk drawer and took out the picture. How had Ben gotten mixed up with Fred King's daughter! Yet, he looked so happy in the picture. Vini felt the familiar stab of pain. Memory and a picture were scanty substitutes for presence.

The bell on the front door tinkled. Quickly she shut the drawer and turned the key. Through her open office door she saw Father Mike and felt relieved to have a few more moments reprieve before her confrontation with Heffron. "What are you doing here?"

"Protecting one of my flock."

"Please don't stay." He looked extremely weary. "Your involvement could endanger you."

"I've arranged for some protection."

"We may need more than angels."

"I'm not leaving."

Her hands were cold, her chest was tight, her heart raced. "I'm glad you're here," she admitted. "Were you able to relay the information?"

"A priest from Gunnison and I met halfway on horseback. He is delivering what I gave him."

She sighed, weary herself. "Thank you."

"We need to pray, Vini."

She nodded.

"For Heffron."

"No!"

"Don't argue. This is too important for grudges. If you are going to achieve what is best for Matthew, what God wants for his life, then you must clear your heart so that God's love and strength and presence can work through you. Hatred blocks the heart and will ultimately block your capacity to help that child." He took her hand and admonished, "Pray with me."

Loving Holy One, we pray for Matthew, that the outcome will help bring about what you want for his life.

We pray for M. Morgan Heffron Jr., as he learns that his son is not truly his. We pray that he will be able to see beyond his disappointment and his own desires and have a vision of what you want for that child.

We pray for his wife as he learns the truth, that she may not be hurt as she has hurt both him and Ben.

I pray for Vini, that you will protect her and sustain her and guide her words and actions during this formidable encounter. May she feel your presence and be strengthened by your love.

And we pray for faithfulness, O Holy One, whether or not your will for Matthew includes us.

They made the sign of the cross. *In the name of the Father and the Son and the Holy Spirit.*

Promptly at eight o'clock the bell above the door tinkled again. This time there was no reprieve. Father Mike glanced at Vini. "The faith strengthens the faithful," he said softly.

Heffron's frame filled her office door, his eyes missing nothing in the room. "Good morning, Mrs. McGragor. I can give you half an hour."

Already he had assumed control. She was no match for him. "Please sit down." She gestured toward the chair beside Father Mike and concentrated on centering herself. She placed both feet firmly on the floor, sat up straight, and breathed deeply. Noting Heffron's discomposure in the scaled down chair on the wrong side of the desk, she began the battle. "My son Ben was married for a brief time. Afterward, he never spoke of it again. I didn't even know the woman's name."

Heffron sat still, listening intently.

"The next summer, the day before he was killed at Ludlow, he learned about his newborn son and intended to find him. For five years I have wondered about my grandson. At first I tried to search for him, but their marriage record had disappeared, and the justice of the peace who performed the ceremony had a fatal accident."

"So there's no proof that your son was married?"

She shook her head.

"How very sad for you, Mrs. McGragor, but I don't see how I can help."

"Last night I learned who my grandson is."

Heffron waited, expressionless.

Vini looked forward to the sweet taste of vengeance. "You took from me the one who meant most to me. Twice. My husband in the Jokerville Disaster. My son in the Ludlow Massacre. Now, I tell you that the one who means most to you is another man's child. Ben's child. You have no son."

Heffron pulled a gold monogrammed cigarette case from his pocket. Nonchalantly he opened it and carefully selected a cigarette.

She waited impatiently.

"May I smoke, Mrs. McGragor?" It was a formality, not a question. He lit it and inhaled deeply. His eyes studied her face.

She had prepared herself for denial, a word fight, even violence. But this long intense waiting unnerved her. Her insides twisted into knots.

Slowly, he exhaled. "Is that all you wanted to see me about?"

"Matthew is my grandson!"

He stood. "Good day, Mrs. McGragor. Father Barrett."

Vini stood also. "The story that your heir is not your son has been delivered sealed to my liaison and will make national headlines in the newspapers unless I stop it."

He paused. "You erred in judgment, Mrs. McGragor. I do not respond to threats, including blackmail."

"Blackmail?"

"You have made up this story either for blackmail or revenge." He clicked open his gold watch on the chain across his vest, then snapped it closed. "I must go. This has been an interesting performance."

"Wait!" She unlocked the desk drawer. "I have proof—a picture."

Doubt flickered in his eyes.

Silent until now, Father Mike faced Heffron. "A picture can disappear just like a record can. And—"

"I don't like your insinuation."

"And your enemies suffer from a high accident rate."

"My hands are clean."

"But they count the pieces of silver into others' hands. I've arranged for some protection for Mrs. McGragor and myself. One of my brothers in the faith has the story and a copy of the picture, which he will hold indefinitely. Should either of us suddenly disappear or be killed in an accident, he will take them to the *New York Times*."

Vini stared at the priest. He had to be bluffing about another picture. But God Almighty would believe him.

Heffron looked up at Father Mike and stepped back, clearly a believer.

She pulled the picture from her drawer and laid it on the desk before Heffron. She watched him identify the woman and the fancy script. The hard eyes of the money-bitten financier rose from the picture to the unique cross at Vini's throat and lowered again. His silent lips moved: "To Mama with love. June 18, 1904."

"Matthew happened to see this picture last night and recognized his mother."

The mighty M. Morgan Heffron Jr. sank into the chair, defeated, toppling before her like Shah Mohammed Ali, deposed. The cigarette quivered in his hand. "Matthew may not be my son . . . But God knows, he *is* my son!"

The roaring silence was interrupted by King's entry. "We're going to be late for the miners' meeting." His eyes fell to Heffron, shrunken in the chair. "What is wrong?"

The blood crept back into Heffron's face in a slow-burning rage.

Fear flashed in King's eyes.

"You overlooked a most important detail!"

"What do you mean?"

Heffron gestured toward the desk.

King saw the picture and reeled. "Crystal!"

"I relied on you, Fred. On your thoroughness. On your fear that your life would depend on a perfect deception."

"You *knew*?" asked King, astonished.

"The moment the baby was born 'premature' but healthy."

"You went along with it!"

"Crystal was near death. The baby was helpless." The hard lines in Heffron's face softened as he shared the memory. "That first night I picked him up and held him . . ."

Francine's entrapment, the Jokerville, and Ludlow passed in review across Vini's mind. Yet, she saw love shine in the coal baron's eyes as he recalled the baby cradled in his arms. Compassion stirred for him. The taste of vengeance was no longer sweet. Her hatred took a small step toward healing.

"I decided that as long as no one knew, it didn't really matter." Heffron's voice hardened. "It was my moment of weakness."

No, thought Vini, it was your one moment of strength.

"But you didn't ensure the secret, Fred."

King's eyes burned into the picture. "I thought I did."

"*Thought!*" Heffron stood, and King cowered. "Your first mistake was deceiving me. Your second was not being thorough about the deception."

Heffron gestured toward the door. "You threw your daughter at me for job insurance. The policy is cancelled!"

Vini watched all of King's checkers fall in one sweep.

"Crystal is Matthew's mother and my wife, and I will continue to be her husband, King. But you are never again to be within my view!"

As the bell tinkled King's departure, Heffron turned to Vini, his authority intact once more. "You are a disturbing foe, Mrs. McGragor. Now, what is your price?"

"I want my grandson."

"That's nonnegotiable!"

"I want time with him. To get to know him. To care for him."

"I don't know what to do with you, Mrs. McGragor."

"I have decided what to do with you, Mr. Heffron. You adore Matthew. I could see it in your eyes last night and as you talked about him this morning. It is fair for you and his mother to have him during the school months, and I will have him in the summers."

"Absurd!"

"It is evident that Matthew loves you as much as you love him. I would do nothing to scar that love. I'll make the sacrifice . . ." Tears threatened. She willed them back. Her throat tightened. "The sacrifice of not telling Matthew about his birth father and that he is my grandson."

Heffron softened. "Suppose I agree. How do I know you won't tell him?"

"Because you have my word, and I have never broken it."

He stared at her with piercing eyes that looked beyond the surface into the depths of her heart. Then he nodded ever so slightly, almost imperceptibly.

"If Matthew ever asks, I will not lie to him. Not ever. But if you love him and treat him like a son, why would he ever question whether you are his father?"

"You drive a hard bargain."

"I do not bargain. You have until 8:15 this evening to bring Matthew to me, prepared to spend the rest of the summer, and every summer thereafter. I will be at the contests and later at the dance at the City Hall."

He studied her again. "Suppose I refuse? Suppose I simply take Morgan third and leave?"

"Unless I call my liaison before 8:30 tonight, the story will be unsealed and delivered to the newspapers."

"Tears stand in your eyes. They tell me of tenderness."

"Tenderness, yes. Weakness, no."

"I do not believe you could go through with something that would devastate your grandson."

Vini remembered stepping up to the cannon in the plaza on another Fourth of July. "Don't make the mistake of underestimating me! I've been put through the hell of Heffron Enterprises and have a backbone tempered to steel. Hear me, M. Morgan Heffron Jr." She fired the cannon. "*On this matter, I will not bend!*"

CHAPTER 34

*T*hat evening the people of Crested Butte danced, and the second floor of the City Hall vibrated to the rhythm. Vini saw Father Mike come in and waved at him. "Do you think he'll come?"

"I don't know, Vini."

"Did the story get delivered?"

"The nun will do as you asked. Burn it unread if I telephone her by 8:30 tonight. Or deliver it to the *Rocky Mountain News* and the *Denver Post* if I do not." He looked at the clock. "It's eight now."

She watched the door.

"Will you go through with it?" he asked.

She nearly panicked. "I wasn't convincing this morning?"

"Mightily! But I've known you a long, long time. Will you do it?"

"Heffron will come—and you'll never know."

"Why would he agree, Vini?"

"To keep the world from knowing King duped him when he married? Would that be reason enough?"

"I'm doubtful."

"To keep from putting Matthew through the gossip caused by the newspaper stories? Would that be reason enough?"

"Perhaps. I hope so."

"He has to come!"

"By the way, do you remember my mentioning to Heffron this morning the information for our protection? It sent it to young Father Martin Boyd who will keep it in a vault as continued insurance."

"You spoke of a copy of the picture."

"When you showed it to me last night, I recognized the background as Dan's Picture Parlor. His brother is a priest. A friend of mine. Dan keeps a duplicate of every sitting, filed by date. I telephoned him last night."

"So there really is another picture!"

"It's on it's way to Father Martin and will also be placed in the vault." He frowned at her. "Did you think I lied?"

"Bluffed." She smiled. "We could be detectives."

"Too dangerous. I prefer the safety of the sanctuary."

"Thank you for this morning."

"I wouldn't have missed it!"

"And for last night." She touched his arm, aware of God's love shining in his extraordinary blue eyes, that love she'd seen so often before. "And for so many things you've done for me for so many years."

He said nothing for a moment. Then he cleared his throat and looked at the clock. "It's 8:05."

Vini glanced again toward the door. "I can't stand it. I'm going to dance."

The Company smile, with Ron Shun behind it, interrupted them. "Excuse me, Vini. Father Barrett. Last night sure was good. Even the governor came! Mr. Heffron sure was impressed. The Mrs. and I sure do thank you."

"Dance with me, Ron."

"Sure!"

She tried to keep her toes out from under his boots. Not an easy task. Stephen Machek cut in.

"Thank you. My poor feet!"

He grinned. "I noticed. I've never seen you dance with the super before. Heffron didn't persuade you to change sides, did he?"

"Never! Just tell me when you think the time is right, Stephen. The next strike will be statewide. At least! And no militia—I personally guarantee it."

Abruptly the band quit in the middle of a measure, and the people stopped dancing. M. Morgan Heffron Jr. stood in the doorway.

Thank you, Holy Mother.

Heffron glanced around the room until he saw her.

Vini gestured to the man with the bandolin. He nodded, and the music began again. But no one danced. No one spoke. No one moved.

Except Heffron. He came toward her. Alone.

Every eye watched the coal baron approach Vini. He leaned down and whispered, "We can't talk in here. The music's too loud and there are too many ears." He took her arm. "Let's go for a walk."

Her inner voice warned her against the danger. But she ignored it and preceded him through the crowd, down the stairs, and into the twilight.

Once outside, he spoke with his customary authority. "I have made a decision, and I have spoken to Matthew. I've decided to agree to your proposition."

Her heart sang with the rushing waters of Coal Creek.

"But not because of your threat. There are three reasons." He looked at his watch and hurried on. "First, I think you will keep secret that I am not Morgan third's blood father. In other words, I believe I can trust you. That may not mean anything to you, but I have not trusted anyone in a good many years."

"I'm trustworthy."

"My attorneys are drawing up the contract."

"Why?" She stopped in front of The Rose Petal. "You just said you trust me. Besides, legal documents appear and disappear at your whim."

"Peace between us, Mrs. McGragor, please. I am contracting you to serve as the boy's summer governess. There has to be a public reason for this sudden and unusual arrangement."

She nodded, swallowing back her hurt at the distance between being called a "governess" and a "grandmother." But Matthew would always be her grandson. They crossed to the other side of Elk, turning back toward the City Hall.

"Secondly, I want him to be President and there are things you can teach him. I can give him Groton and Harvard. You can give him the frontier. I can give him a sense of power. You can give him sensitivity to different kinds of people. He can appeal to all the voters."

They passed the Forest Queen, and Heffron continued hurriedly. "I can teach him of the East, of finances and factories and traditional formalities."

Vini looked up at Crested Butte Mountain guarding the valley. "And I can teach him of the West. Where people climb to the peak of a mountain and stand above the clouds. Where they learn that their vision, like the land, has no bounds. Where even in the darkness of night, their dreams still shine in the starlit sky."

"Together we can provide him with a uniquely well-rounded education."

"And childhood," she added.

He stopped and looked down at her. "Finally, I'm agreeing because you are the only person who ever dared stand up to me and refused to back down."

She inspected the white-haired man with his hurried efficiency, his planned speech. "And you stood up to me, Gan."

He laughed, a thin sound that lingered in the mountain air like something seldom practiced. "I compliment you, Vini McGragor. You're a woman with both charm and courage."

Suddenly she saw Matthew and the valet walking toward them down Elk Avenue. In silence, she and Heffron watched the little boy they both loved, a love that placed them on a common foundation that nothing could crack. She said softly, almost like a prayer, "Perhaps the day will come when you trust Matthew's love so much that you will tell him the truth."

Unable to contain herself longer, Vini hurried toward her grandson, holding out her hands. He ran to her, and she enfolded him in her arms.

"May we play checkers?"

"Often, Matthew!" Tears filled her eyes.

Heffron cleared his throat, and Matthew came to attention. The man's hard eyes grew soft with love. "I will miss you, Morgan third. But being in the mountains will be better for you than the summer camps your mother discussed with me."

"Yes, Sir."

Heffron extended his hand. "Goodbye, Son."

The miniature adult shook hands. "Goodbye, Father."

Abruptly M. Morgan Heffron Jr. turned and walked down Elk Avenue without looking back.

Vini held Matthew's hand as they climbed the stairs to the second floor of the City Hall. Unconsciously she began to hum Joel's tune. Matthew joined in, and she turned in surprise. "How do you know that tune?"

"My mother taught me. She said it isn't written down anywhere and that I should remember it."

"Indeed you should." They hummed together until they reached the top of the stairs.

Father Mike smiled at Vini and winked at the boy. Then he looked at the clock. "It's 8:26."

"Make the telephone call," she said softly. She knew down deep in her heart that she would never have carried through with a threat that hurt Matthew. And she sensed that Heffron knew that, too.

She put her arm around the boy's shoulders, and the crowd made way for them to pass. The bandolin struck a chord. Vini curtsied to her grandson, and he bowed in return. She took his small hand in hers. "Come Matthew, let me teach you to polka."

EPILOGUE

"So . . . that's the story." Feeling stiff and weary from telling the long story, I glance at the President sitting across from me in the Oval Office. "I decided to wait until after your inauguration to tell you the truth."

The oversized black attaché stands empty. The initialed saddlebag and its contents are scattered on the table between us—the old picture of Joel as a little boy sitting with his relational father and Chief Ouray, the small gold cross first worn by his mother, and the white bone-handled knife that had belonged to his birth father, a Chiricahua Apache chief; the small leather money purse that had been Vini's father's and the elegant white collar tatted by her mother; the clipping from the *Gunnison Review Press* listing the Jokerville dead, with Joel's name added in pen; the four coins totaling seventeen cents, Nick's silver dollar, the inscribed picture of Ben and Crystal, and the deed to the land by the Red Lady; Will Chaney's "Massacre of the Innocents" editorial and the bundle of letters about Ben's heroism at Ludlow; and in the center stands a small oval-framed photograph of Vini.

The President sits quietly, eyes focused on the table, touching the mementos, each in its turn.

"When I visit the White House, I am always reminded that my grandmother Vini and the only father I knew both hoped that I would become President. But Senator was as close as I could get."

The President smiles and glances at me with blue-green eyes, then studies the photo of Vini wearing the cross. "Marie-Vincente Prejean McGragor. My great-grandmother."

"I've taught you everything I learned from her—including the polka."

"You and I have the Heffron name but not an ounce of Heffron blood."

"That is true."

The President touches the bone-handled knife, then picks up the picture of Ben and Crystal in one hand and, in the other hand, the picture of Joel when he was a little boy. "So . . . the people have elected a President whose grandfather was a reporter who died a hero and whose great-grandfather became a coal miner to save another's life."

I nod.

"And whose great-great-grandfather was a Chiricahua Apache chief who rode with Geronimo!"

I smile, proud of my daughter who reminds me so much of Vini. "Indeed so, Madam President."

HISTORICAL NOTES

*C*rested Butte is a work of fiction, and the major characters are not based on real persons, living or dead.

However, it is about a real place. Crested Butte, Colorado, was an old mining town that has become a bustling resort, especially in winter when it boasts of 5,000 skiers a day.

The story also includes some historical people by reference or in minor roles: Mayor Howard F. Smith and Marshal Charles B. Hays, who played an important part in Crested Butte's early days; General William Jackson Palmer, railroad baron who brought the D&RG to Crested Butte; Otto Mears, remembered as "The Pathfinder of the San Juans"; Ute Chief Ouray and Chipeta; Indian Commissioner George W. Manypenny; Interior Secretary Samuel J. Kirkwood; John Lewis Dyer, Methodist pastor fondly called "Father Dyer," who became known as the "Snow-Shoe Itinerant"; cannibal Alferd Packer; "Doc" Cyrus Wells Shores, Gunnison County Sheriff, who broke a Crested Butte strike (1891); Colorado Governors Davis H. Waite and John F. Shafroth; and Senator Vernest Cain.

The novel is built around historical events. The first train arrived on November 21, 1881. The Elk Mountain House opened December 7 (though its grand opening was not held until February 28, 1882). A Jokerville Mine accident killed one man (November, 1883), followed by an explosion on January 24, 1884, that resulted in the worst mine disaster in Colorado history to that time. Fire destroyed the block between Second and Third Streets on Elk Avenue (the north side of the street burned on January 15, 1890; the south side on January 6, 1893). Nine children and two infants were killed by Ludlow strikebreakers (April 20, 1914). *The Rocky Mountain News* editorial cited in the novel, "Massacre of the Innocents," was written by William L. Chenery following the Ludlow tragedy.

The miners killed in the Jokerville Disaster (as printed in the *Gunnison Review Press,* January 24, 1884) were:

Henry Anderson	John Williams	J. J. Stewart
John Martin	James O'Neil	Thomas Rogers
Jacob Laux	Thomas Roberts	James McCourt
Fred Brecht	Iber King	Joseph Weisenberg
H. Donegan	Joseph Kranst	James F. Stewart Jr.
William Neath	Richard James	David Hughes

P. McHanus	John Anderson	James Walsh
Peter Baker	William Davidson	John Price
James Driscoll	James Coughlin	W. T. King
John Creelman	John Hular	Thomas Williams
John Shun	Pat Barrett	John McGragor
John Myers	F. W. Smith	G. B. Nicholson
William Maroney	Nick Probst	Henry Stewart
B. Heffron	L. P. Heffron	W. L. Jones
John Donnelly	Carl Rodewald	Charles Sterling
Thomas Laffey	Dave Thomas	John Thomas
Miles Roach	Morgan Neath	Thomas Glancey
John Rutherford	A. W. Godfrey	Dan McDonal
William Aubrey	Ben Jeffries	Thomas Stewart

Many names for the characters in the novel were selected by mixing these first and last names, as a way of honoring the miners. The mass grave marker for the dead miners in the Crested Butte Cemetery did exist and contained the words cited in the novel; however, the marker is no longer there.

CPSIA information can be obtained
at www.ICGtesting.com
Printed in the USA
BVHW041400040320
574023BV00008B/69